CW01640592

# *Summer at Lucerne Lodge*

**Morton S. Gray**

***Other books by Morton S Gray:***

*The Girl on the Beach*
*The Truth Lies Buried*
*Christmas at Borteen Bay*
*Sunny Days at the Beach*
*Christmas at the Little Beach Café*

Choc Lit

*Where heroes are like chocolate – irresistible!*

Published 2021 by Choc Lit Limited
Penrose House, Crawley Drive, Camberley, Surrey GU15 2AB, UK
www.choc-lit.com



PRINT ISBN: 978-1-78189-487-3

*To Margaret Reuss-Newland who began this writing journey with me and continues to be a great support and valued friend.*

# Acknowledgements

*Summer at Lucerne Lodge* has been a long time in the making. Rosie and Tanner were in fact some of the first characters I wrote about when I made the decision to write romantic fiction. I have to thank Sue Johnson, the tutor on my first ever writing course, for encouraging me to continue writing, and here I am writing the acknowledgements and thanks for book six!

This book is dedicated to Margaret Reuss-Newland. We've only met in person once as she lives in Scotland and I live in Worcestershire, but we have held a firm friendship and companionship for many years now. We have read and critiqued each other's writing and helped each other along the way. At the moment, Maggie is concentrating on things other than writing, such as her wonderful patchwork, quilting and photography, but I hold a fond hope that one day her writing will be published too.

Karen Lord, friend and crystal therapist, was kind enough to check over the crystal therapy scenes and mentions of crystals in the book.

Michael Bryant's dog, Trixie, was given her name by Jodie Robbins-McGregor after winning a competition on the Apricot Plots writers' group on Facebook.

My support systems are invaluable in keeping me going: my mom, my sister, my husband, sons and almost daughter-in-law, together with my rich contingent of friends both physical and online. During this extraordinary time of the coronavirus pandemic, my Apricot Plots and Coffee Group Writers have kept me sane, along with Victoria Cornwall, Karen Lord and Sue Wood – thank you all. Sue, you might also recognise some memories from those blissful holidays at your caravan in Llandanawg.

Last and definitely not least, thanks to my editor for helping to improve this book, the Choc Lit team and the members of their Tasting Panel without whom this book would not have been published: Carol Orpwood, Lucie Wheatcroft, Gillian Cox, Honor Gilbert, Sally Pardey and Gillian Hill.

# Chapter One

Tanner Bryant looked closely at the photograph of Rosie Phillips. *Who exactly was she?* The mystery was quickly becoming an obsession.

Looking at Rosie's face had provoked that little tingle in his throat, the one he got if he found something – *or someone* – exciting and attractive. *No, Tanner, don't get carried away. You need to be sure of her link to your father first.* But the attraction was there, no matter how he fought it. People talked about love at first sight, but love at first sight of a photograph?

He placed the picture back on his father's desk and went to check his bow-tie in the mottled mirror. As he stared into the antique glass with the heavily decorated gilt frame, he wondered vaguely why he didn't just use a bow-tie on elastic – but it had become a matter of pride and determination that he remembered the sequence of juggling the black silk and moulding it into a decent knot and bow. He smoothed the fine black wool of his dinner jacket and tugged at the cuffs of his dress shirt so that the cube-shaped jet cufflinks showed beneath the sleeves of the coat.

Moving back to the desk and like a moth to a flame, he flipped open the bulging blue folder yet again. He sorted through the photographs and papers, and pulled out his favourite picture of Rosie. In this candid shot, she was getting out of a small red car, her long legs clad in jeans and her blonde hair, caught by a sudden gust of wind, swirling around her face.

He spoke aloud to her image. 'Who are you, Rosie Phillips, and why has my father shown such an interest in you? Does he find you attractive, too?'

The question had plagued his thoughts ever since he'd found the file about the girl on his father's desk. Tanner had wanted to ask his father about it, but anything more than the briefest of conversations was now impossible, and even those made his father gasp behind the oxygen mask as he struggled to breathe … to stay alive.

Earlier that day, Tanner had again decided to try to broach the subject of the big blue file about Rosie, but his father was so very weak that the nurses at the private clinic, where Michael Bryant looked likely to end his days, had asked Tanner to leave him to rest. He'd been forced to restrain his curiosity once again.

Michael Bryant had appeared much weaker today. He seemed to have deteriorated much more rapidly since a visit from his ex-wife, Tanner's mother, two weeks before. Tanner wondered what on earth Georgia had said to the sick man to make him request a consultation with his solicitor, Justin Sadler, the day afterwards. The effort that visit had taken, and the time with his solicitor, seemed to have severely depleted his father's limited energy reserves.

The first time he'd mentioned the file, his father had become extremely agitated, so Tanner was convinced there was a story to uncover. But it was looking less likely that he would find out the truth about it before his father died.

Tanner sighed, replacing the photograph of Rosie in the folder. Time to go outside and do his duty.

As he stepped out into the late afternoon sunshine, the first thing he noticed was the flapping white canvas of the marquee on the vast lawn of Lucerne Lodge, his father's home and where Tanner has spent his childhood when he wasn't away at school.

Beyond the marquee, the lake glittered in the sunlight and the drive snaked away up the hillside to the huge wrought-iron gate, hidden from his view by the tall pine trees flanking the drive. The honey-coloured stone walls of the house rose behind him, casting a vast shadow over the grass that didn't reach as far as the marquee. Part of the lawn had been cordoned off and was being used as a car park. The sun glinted on the shiny paintwork of the cars.

No one took much notice of Tanner as he walked into the marquee. The tented space was divided into two distinct areas. The end where he stood had a raised platform and rows and rows of green plastic chairs, many of which were already occupied. Beyond the chairs, a sea of people moved like a swarm of honey bees around the bar and food tables. The smell of onion bhajis and chicken satay sticks competed with the myriad scents and aftershaves of some two hundred people in the marquee. It was a little overwhelming.

'Tanner, at last.' A woman, whose hair had clearly *once* been neatly caught up in a pile on her head, took him by the arm and led him to the back of the tent. Even with her dishevelled hair, Elisa managed to look cool, calm and stylish. Tanner ignored her too obvious efforts to flirt with him and instead looked at the varied selection of items, each with a numbered tag, arranged on sheets behind the platform. He caught sight of some oil paintings, a decorative lamp and lots of boxes and bags.

‘We’ve done really well. Forty-two lots donated so far,’ said Elisa, excitement in her voice.

‘That’s wonderful. What overwhelming support.’

‘To be honest, it seems to have become an annual competition to donate the most.’

‘I’m pleased for this year’s charity in any case.’

‘I’ve written a short description for each auction lot. I’ll hand it to you with the item when it’s time to sell that number.’

‘Great. What time do we start?’ Tanner hoped that his voice suggested more enthusiasm than he was feeling.

Elisa glanced at the ornate watch encircling her wrist. ‘Fifteen minutes, okay?’

Tanner nodded and went to see if everything was running smoothly at the other end of the tent. He realised too late that this was a mistake. Some of his father’s friends and business associates recognised him.

‘Tanner, how’s your father? Such a pity he’s not here in his usual role.’

A small crowd massed around him, and Tanner found himself with a dilemma – should he be totally honest about his dad or tell a few white lies? He decided that the brutal truth, that his father would be unlikely to last until his birthday in October, would definitely dampen the mood of the party.

‘Thank you for asking. Dad’s bearing up. He’s in a comfortable clinic.’

‘You must let me have the address, I’d like to visit him,’ piped up another man.

‘Maybe in a couple of weeks. The doctors have ordered complete rest for him at the moment.’

A woman, who Tanner vaguely recognised but whose name he couldn’t recall, put her hand on his shoulder.

‘Please give him our love. I’ll organise some signatures on one of today’s programmes and you can take it to dear Michael to show he’s in our thoughts.’

‘That sounds like a lovely idea. Now, if you’ll excuse me, I have an auction to run.’

Tanner smiled at the fact he’d almost bowed to these people as if they were royalty. *Come to think of it, some of them probably were!* He made a break for freedom and walked back along the tented space to the stage.

The annual party had been held in the grounds of Lucerne Lodge on the last Saturday in June for many years. The invited companies and many individuals donated items for an auction to raise money for a designated charity. A different charity was chosen each year, this time the Multiple Sclerosis Society would benefit, last year it had been Cystic Fibrosis. Tanner had a thank you letter in his pocket for the previous year's donation from the president of the Cystic Fibrosis charity that he intended to read out at some point in the proceedings.

His father had always enjoyed acting as auctioneer, but this year, as he lay gravely ill in his private clinic, his son was reluctantly but dutifully taking his place. Tanner had watched his father perform on a stage like this many times. A brilliant actor in front of the crowd, no one watching Michael Bryant in action with his auctioneer's gavel would dream that he was a surly loner.

It seemed a hard act to follow, but after making sure everything else was running smoothly, Tanner took a deep breath and walked up to the lectern. He banged the wooden gavel to hush the crowd and attract the attention of those not yet seated.

Like father, like son, he was a loner too, but capable of looking the extrovert if a situation required it, as it did right now. He remembered a trick he'd been taught at university for occasions when you were daunted by large numbers of people. His favourite lecturer had advised him to imagine the heads of those in front of him as cabbages. At least it meant he smiled as he faced the audience, because in his mind he stood before a field of green vegetables.

Tanner had battled with himself in the days leading up to this event about why he was willing to play the role he knew his father would expect when he'd spent a lifetime rebelling against Michael Bryant's world and its expectations. He supposed it was because the latest meeting with his father's doctors had made Tanner realise that the time for rebellion was well and truly over.

'Hello, ladies and gentlemen. I'm Tanner, your auctioneer for today.' Spontaneous applause broke out, and Tanner had to wait until it had died down. 'I would remind you all that proceeds from this auction will be donated to charity, so please bid generously. This year's charity, chosen from suggestions made by those who came to last year's event, is … The Multiple Sclerosis Society.'

There was a cheer and another round of applause. Tanner waited until it had faded away. He turned to Elisa, and she handed him a box with a hand-written note on top.

'Item number one, donated by Borden Glass Plc: a man's gold watch and cufflinks.' His voice booming through the microphone sounded so unlike his own that it almost scared him. He held the open box up in the air so that the audience could see a glint of gold. Bids were soon raining in as the wealthy patrons vied to show how much they could afford to donate for a charitable cause.

Everything was going to plan, indeed a lot better than Tanner had expected, and he began to relax, even to enjoy himself, but then he recognised the face of Rosie Phillips in the sea of people before him. He'd seen many photographs of her in the file on his father's desk – Rosie getting out of her car, Rosie laughing with friends at a café, Rosie emerging from her local corner shop with a loaf of bread – but now, for the first time, he was seeing her face-to-face.

He'd known that she would be here of course – he'd engineered her invitation, for goodness sake – but the actual first sight of her in the flesh still shook him. To his annoyance, he momentarily lost his train of thought. It was only a few seconds, but it took all of his determination to recover and get back on track with the sale. From that point, he tried to avoid looking at Rosie, but like the proverbial moth to the flame, his eyes were drawn back to her time and time again.

# *Chapter Two*

Rosie, who was sitting amongst the crowd on an uncomfortable green plastic chair, wondered if she imagined that the rather dishy auctioneer appeared to keep staring at her. He would take an item from his glamorous assistant, glance at the note, describe the item for sale and then look straight back at Rosie. His eyes locked onto hers, he would look away as he scanned the faces for bids and as soon as his gavel had fallen to seal the sale of an item, he glanced at her again. She looked over her shoulder, but there was no one behind her, nobody else who he could be looking at but her. She ran her hands over her face and down her white linen dress. Everything seemed normal. Why would this man's eyes be magnetised to hers? He was a very attractive man, but even so …

After trying to ignore his scrutiny while several lots were sold in the auction, Rosie began to wonder if she'd met the man before. Surely she would have remembered his face, with its distinctive nose and long, curly blond hair? Maybe she was mistaken and he hadn't been watching her at all.

Gulping her wine in growing embarrassment, she misjudged the amount and choked. The expression passing across the auctioneer's face told her that he'd noticed and confirmed that he was indeed watching her, not someone near to her. Rosie grew hot and knew that she was blushing. She debated whether to get up and walk away. She hadn't been bidding – most of the items had starting prices way beyond her means – but it didn't seem polite to walk out of an auction where everything was being sold to raise money for charity.

As she wondered what to do, the auctioneer paused as he fixed his eyes on her yet again. She'd agonised over her appearance, but she didn't think that even the expensive dress could magic her into a sylph-like beauty. Her mother had always said that her looks were quirky and interesting; comments that had not helped Rosie feel at all confident in her appearance over the years.

The auctioneer held each item up towards the crowd before inviting bids. Lot forty-two happened to be three hours of cleaning services from Lulabelle Martin, a vivacious lady brandishing a feather duster and wearing an incredibly short skirt. She insisted that the auctioneer hold her up to the audience too. He showed willing by lifting her an inch off the ground. The crowd found this hilarious and applauded loudly. Lulabelle gave him a smacking kiss with her scarlet lips as bid after bid came in for her cleaning services.

Rosie laughed along with everyone else. She couldn't help feeling disappointed that the auctioneer scurried off as fast as he could once the sale had finished, leaving his assistant to tell the crowd how much money had been raised. By now, Rosie had managed to convince herself that the man hadn't been interested in her at all.

She wandered outside of the marquee into the well-groomed grounds. *It must take an army of gardeners to even keep the hedges trimmed*, she decided. She'd been excited about her invitation to this renowned event at Lucerne Lodge, an estate set in the countryside between the small seaside town of Borteen and the larger town of Sowden. She'd travelled with her new work colleague, Becky, and had been enjoying the opportunity to chat on a personal level with her – that was, until Becky had abandoned her within five minutes of arriving. Rosie had last seen her heading into the shrubbery with a ginger-haired young man, reputedly, according to Becky's hurried whisper, an up-and-coming rock star.

Rosie had been surprised, but pleased, when Becky had asked her to go to the party, as they'd previously only smiled at each other in the office corridor. She supposed that someone had suggested that Becky invite her because Rosie had just moved to the decorative glass side of the company, having previously worked in London at their industrial glass site. As she had not long relocated, she knew nobody else at the event, although she recognised some of the directors of Borden Glass where she worked.

She began to relax, but then the DJ played the song that she and Ollie had claimed as their own. It blared out from the tent, each beat a stabbing reminder of how just over a year ago, he'd ended their relationship to date the waitress at his favourite restaurant. Thank goodness she'd never moved in with him. Annoyed that she couldn't help but sing along to the lyrics, she vowed once more to concentrate on her career and to avoid any romantic entanglements.

The song finished and she walked across the grass, troubled by a tinge of guilt that she actually didn't miss Ollie at all. She did miss the comfortable security of being part of a couple however, and hated the fact that her confidence in herself and her appearance had nose-dived after being dumped.

The auction had taken well over an hour. It was nice to be out of the marquee and enjoying the pleasantly warm late afternoon sunshine. Rosie perched on a stone balustrade with her glass of wine, indulging in her favourite pastime of people watching. Surveying the fashionably dressed women and dark-suited men, she observed their body language, trying to guess details about their lives and what made them tick.

Everyone was taking advantage of the fine weather, giving Rosie plenty of people to observe. Waiters circulated with large trays of food and drinks. She was just trying to make out the relationship between a portly elderly man and his companion, who in her heels stood at least two feet taller than he did, when a commotion broke out behind her.

Something fell against her, making her jump. There was a clanging noise as an object hit the stonework where she sat. She jumped up, put her hand to her back and to her disbelief found it coated in what appeared to be … prawn cocktail. She twisted her head to try to see the back of her dress. It *was* prawn cocktail! The fine white linen now had a thick coating of pink-tinged mayonnaise. The waiter, who must have been carrying the tray of food, apologised profusely and began swatting prawns back onto the tray. The auctioneer stood next to him with a very sheepish look on his face.

'I'm so *so* sorry, I'm afraid it was all my fault. I bumped into the tray,' he stammered.

Rosie became extra angry because of her embarrassment. 'Do you realise how much this dress cost?'

'I'm really am sorry.' He had his hands raised in front of him as if to shield himself from her annoyance.

'Sorry isn't really good enough. Now what am I supposed to do?' She dabbed at the horrible mess on the back of her dress with her napkin, whilst juggling her empty wine glass and handbag. She glared at the auctioneer, waved the waiter away and tried not to burst into tears.

The dabbing was having little effect. The saying "if looks could kill" came to her mind. If she hadn't been miles away, musing about the relationship of that couple at the other side of the lawn, she might have noticed what was happening right behind her and the accident would never have happened. She recalled the countless hours of trudging around the Sowden shops it had taken to find her outfit for today and glared even harder.

'I'm Tanner.'

Rosie reddened under the auctioneer's scrutiny and ignored his extended hand. He took a step back as if he feared she might hit him.

'Rosie. Tanner, did you say? I've not heard that name before ...' She couldn't believe she could even think to question his name when she was in this prawn cocktail predicament.

'My mother's American. Tanner was her maiden surname.'

His imposing build, dressed in a black dinner jacket, made even five-foot-eight Rosie feel short. His bow-tie had twisted to one side and she had an urge to straighten it for him, that or strangle him with it. She couldn't decide which.

'Look, I can't claim to have any experience, but I think you'll have to act fast to stop that sauce from staining your dress.'

'I think my poor dress is beyond saving,' muttered Rosie, twisting again to try to examine her back. The slimy pink mess stood out like a birth mark on the snowy surface, and Rosie was mortified to realise that she now smelt fishy on top of everything else. The guests nearby had moved away slightly, but several stood watching and listening to what was going on.

'I'm sure I remember something about cold water, vinegar and salt,' said Tanner.

'I think that's for red wine stains.' She still felt annoyed, but with the maxim "no point crying over spilt milk" echoing in her mind, she made a real effort to calm down. *What to do?*

Rosie glanced past Tanner at the huge marquee, which housed the party food and drinks. People were beginning to get rosy cheeks as they overindulged at the bar. Couples with loaded food plates were migrating across the lawns to sit by the lake. Beyond, the large country house nestled comfortably in the wooded valley.

She focused back on Tanner to find that he was smiling at her. 'Come on, we have to at least try to clean you up. I feel so awful that this has happened.'

He held out his hand. She ignored it, but, as she really didn't have any other options, she followed him across the lawn towards the house. He went around the side of the imposing building to a back door with peeling white paint and led her into an ultra-modern kitchen. Acres of polished amber marble stretched around the room. Tanner began opening and closing cupboard doors, and emerged from one with a bottle of vinegar and a salt pot. Rosie glanced about uneasily, hoping that no one found them trespassing in the house. Tanner appeared perfectly at home.

'I'll go and find you something else to wear.'

‘What?’

‘We can’t try to save your dress while you’re in it, can we?’

He put down the bottle of vinegar and salt and disappeared through another door.

Returning a few moments later, he handed Rosie some men’s football shorts and a vest. ‘Here, try these.’

Uncomfortable with the situation, but desperate for a miracle, she began to unzip her dress.

‘Turn your back, please.’

She really didn’t want Tanner to see what she was wearing underneath her dress. The television programme advertising the garment had been right about it giving her a better shape, but without the dress the Lycra “scaffolding” was hardly flattering – and definitely *not* to be viewed by a man as attractive as Tanner.

He turned around and she changed quickly. The shorts, thankfully, had a draw string, so she could make them fit her waist, and the vest top, although much too large, at least showed that she had a decent cleavage. She wished that the kit wasn’t bright yellow, as it was most definitely not her colour. She also worried that Tanner might be watching her in the reflection of the gleaming hoods of the Aga.

Before she had chance to do or say anything, Tanner bent to pick up the dress from the floor and threw it into the Belfast sink.

‘Surely you’re only going to sponge it!’ Her exclamation ended in a yelp, as he poured salt onto the pink mark, doused it in the whole bottle of vinegar and covered the lot in water. She had a feeling that the label had said dry clean only and had visions of a Barbie-sized garment emerging from the bowl. It seemed too late at this point to ask how they were going to dry it.

‘It’s working. Look.’ Tanner peered into the water. The acrid smell of vinegar filled the air. She edged closer. Her bare arm brushed against the silkiness of his jacket and an electric shock spiked through her. She caught traces of his subtle aftershave, and the scent did strange things to her insides. *Rosie Phillips. No men, remember?*

Tanner swirled the water with his fingertips, being careful not to wet his jacket or shirt sleeves. The liquid in the bowl had taken on a distinct pink tinge.

‘It’ll probably be ruined anyway. I don’t think it’s washable.’

‘Pessimist.’

The door opened noisily. They sprang apart. A dinner-jacketed young man stood in the doorway, his face covered with acne.

'I've been sent to fetch you, Tanner. You're needed in the marquee.'

'Coming.' Tanner shrugged his shoulders at Rosie and disappeared out of the room. She felt somehow disappointed.

After a few moments analysing the effect Tanner had on her senses, reality struck Rosie hard. She was at an exclusive party, clad in a borrowed football kit. All of the other guests were in smart dresses and dinner jackets. The garments she wore barely covered her body-sculpting underwear and the vest smelled as if someone had been playing football in it very recently. The most expensive dress she had ever owned lay stained and sopping wet in the sink, and she doubted that the label would say 'tumble dry' even if she could discover a machine. She couldn't decide whether to laugh or cry.

Peering into the water again, she squealed in horror. All of the fabric now looked pink and the seams showed definite signs of shrinkage. It was ruined. *Why ever did I listen to that man?*

Suddenly worried that she might be suspected of being a burglar, she frantically opened a door leading off from the kitchen. She pounced gratefully on a man's long green coat she found hanging on a hook. Putting up the collar, in a vain attempt to make it look more stylish, she tied the belt rather than fastening it. At least she was decently covered when she emerged self-consciously into the sunshine. Thankfully, the guests were all inside the marquee. She could hear a voice booming out over the loudspeaker. It sounded like Tanner.

She was disappointed to be leaving, but what choice did she have? Her self-confidence was not robust enough to brave the party in her borrowed inappropriate clothing. She had *so* been looking forward to spotting celebrities on the dance floor later in the evening.

Thankful she had a mobile signal, she ordered a taxi. Plunging her hands into the coat pockets and making an effort to appear as relaxed as she could, she trudged towards the main gate.

It was probably a good job she didn't run into Tanner, as by this time she'd rehearsed several versions of what she would say to him, most of which would guarantee he would never want to set eyes on her again. *Hang on, do I want to see him again?*

Putting her hands even deeper into the coat pockets, still making an effort to appear relaxed, she walked to the main gate as fast as she could.

Her fingers closed on a piece of paper in the coat pocket. She pulled it out. The message written on it stopped her in her tracks. It read *Party Saturday – Rosie Phillips will be there.*

# *Chapter Three*

Tanner hurried back to the kitchen after drawing the winning raffle tickets to find Rosie had gone. *Damn it.* He now felt even more resentful that he'd had to stand in for his father as master of ceremonies.

The garden party and auction had been planned since last year's event, and it had seemed mean to cancel it because his father had become ill. He'd deliberately made no mention of an event for next year, because who knew what could have happened by then? He'd found it exhausting making light of Michael Bryant's health condition to yet more guests who took the time to ask about his father.

He looked into the Belfast sink and realised Rosie's dress still lay there. He wrinkled his nose at the fishy, vinegary smell. What an idiot he'd been to think he could successfully remove the stain and send her happily on her way. He owed her a dress – that was if he could ever get her to speak to him again.

Her attendance at the party had cost him a fifty-pound bribe to a girl at Rosie's office. Despite all of this effort, he was still no closer to solving the mystery of her connection to his father, apart from her working at Borden Glass, but at least he'd actually met her. It was very different meeting the real-life Rosie to looking at photographs of her. She was taller than he'd imagined and, to his annoyance, even more appealing than her photographs. He was a little wary about being attracted to anyone these days, as he'd had so many bad experiences with relationships in the past.

Where on earth had she gone wearing his football kit? She could hardly re-join the party ... *or could she?*

He strode up the wide, sweeping staircase and into a small room overlooking the driveway. Monitors hummed with revolving camera views of the grounds, gates and doors. The security guard sat up straighter as Tanner entered the room.

'Hi, Demetri. Strange request, but you haven't seen a girl in my yellow football kit, have you?'

'No, but I did notice one in your big green coat. She skirted the marquee and made for the main gate.'

'She walked?'

'Must have called a taxi. It arrived about five minutes ago.' Demetri's look was inquisitive.

Tanner decided that he didn't want to explain.

'Thanks. You win some, you lose some.' He sighed deeply, turned and went back down the staircase. He would need to arrange to see Rosie Phillips again …

He strode outside, but not towards the marquee – he'd had all he could take of polite small talk. His father's aged spaniel, Trixie, lived in a large run with a kennel at the back of the house. Tanner fussed the dog's silky ears and threw a soft ball for her to fetch. Staff at the house ensured the dog got regular short walks, but Tanner hated the fact he couldn't explain to Trixie why her master had stopped coming to see her.

He could hear the party music from here. He didn't want to re-join the crowds, but knew that he would have to sooner rather than later.

'So, Trixie, I met the mysterious Rosie Phillips. Who is she, girl? I ruined her dress, so I don't think she'll ever want to speak to me again. I'm an idiot, aren't I?'

The dog nuzzled closer, responding to Tanner's deliberately soft tones. He made a mental note to return to the house and brush off the long dog hairs before he went back to the marquee. His stomach rumbled. Despite the copious amount of food circulating during the afternoon, he'd eaten nothing since breakfast.

'Have you got plenty to eat and drink, Trixie?'

He stood and went to check the dog's food and water bowls. She had all she needed, but he did wonder if she was eating properly when she so obviously missed his father.

'Your master still cares about you, Trixie. I'm sorry he's had to go away.'

The dog followed close on Tanner's heels and whined as he reached for the latch of the gate.

'I'm sorry, girl, I'll come back tomorrow and take you for a run on the lawn. I'll need plenty of fresh air to get over this gathering. Maybe I'll speak to the clinic about taking you for a short visit. I'm sure dad would love to see you too.'

Tanner disliked the idea of anyone, even Trixie, feeling let down and lonely, probably because that's how he'd felt for most of his childhood. The dog's whines tore at his heart strings as he turned back towards the house. If, or rather when his father died, he'd need to arrange a loving home for Trixie. The dog deserved to be in a family with lots of attention. It seemed mean to leave her in the pen when she so clearly needed human contact.

Rosie had felt unsettled since she'd escaped from Lucerne Lodge. Thank goodness for mobile phones. She'd ordered a taxi, sent a text to Becky saying she was leaving and made her getaway as quickly as possible.

She'd photographed the strange note she'd found in the pocket of the borrowed coat. She didn't know how she could find who the owner of the coat was, or why the note had been written, but she had a feeling the photo might come in useful at some point in the future.

Maybe she would never have any answers, but finding the note had made her feel uneasy. Who would be interested in her attendance at the party? Tanner? The owner of Lucerne Lodge? She replayed her encounter with Tanner many times and still couldn't make sense of it.

She'd washed the football kit – it smelled much sweeter than when she'd been wearing it – and parcelled up the vest, shorts and coat. It was the Friday after the party, and she'd finished work early, so she'd decided to take a trip out to Lucerne Lodge to return them on her way to meet her friends for the evening.

As she negotiated the narrow twisting lanes in her red Fiesta, she imagined various scenes in which she confronted the owner of the lodge and demanded to know why he or she was interested in her attendance at the party.

However, as she stood outside of the huge wrought iron gate, she felt unsure. There was a security intercom built into the brick pillar at the side of the locked gate, but she didn't want to press the bell and alert anyone to her presence. If someone were interested in her, would she be putting herself in danger if she confronted them?

*Rosie Phillips, you are not a character in a novel. The things you are imagining don't happen to normal everyday people. Get a grip.*

The house wasn't visible from the gate, just the rolling parkland. She could glimpse the lake but, as it was a cloudy day, the whole scene didn't look as inviting as it had on Saturday.

The railing seemed cold and hard beneath her hand as she stared for a long time at the landscape, trying to decide what to do. Did Tanner live here? Now that she thought about it, he'd appeared very comfortable in that kitchen ...

Rosie would have been even more uneasy if she could have seen into the security room at Lucerne Lodge, where the cameras scanning the grounds were monitored around the clock. Tanner Bryant, summoned by the security guard when he'd noticed the woman hanging around outside the gate, stood watching Rosie on the monitors. He wondered what thoughts were going through her head.

Fresh from the shower and clean shaven, the cuffs of his shirt hung down past his wrists as he had not yet attached his cufflinks. His bow-tie draped limply at either side of the collar, awaiting a perfect knot. He'd been in the process of dressing for a dinner he was attending that evening.

What would he do if Rosie pushed the intercom button and spoke? He presumed she must be returning the clothing that she'd borrowed on the day of the party. Did he go out to her himself? His brow furrowed. He had so many unanswered questions, and he guessed she would have a few of her own. He also owed her a big apology for ruining her dress.

'Do you want me to go out to her, Tanner? It's the girl from the party, isn't it? The one who left early.'

'Yes, it's her. Don't go out yet, Demetri, let's watch for a moment. I'm curious to see what she'll do.'

Eventually, Rosie left the parcel below the Lodge's oversized letterbox in the opposite pillar to the intercom. She turned away. Tanner felt a little disappointed as he watched her walk to her car and drive off. But at least he had plans in place to meet her again.

# *Chapter Four*

Rosie sat at her desk in the large open-plan office at Borden Glass. Everyone else had, one by one, called "goodnight" and left her slaving over her computer keyboard. The presentation tomorrow morning was crucial. Or rather, Rosie sensed it was. The company directors would soon appoint a marketing manager to replace the one who had left last month, and there were, in her reckoning, three internal candidates, including Rosie herself. Her report was to be presented in front of three of the directors and she knew that, although it wasn't overtly part of a selection process, it would make up their minds about her prospects for promotion. She'd only been working at this branch of the company for a few months, but she knew that her experience and qualifications made her a strong contender for the next level.

She checked and rechecked her slides, combing them for bad grammar and spelling errors. She asked herself countless hypothetical questions whilst trying to anticipate her audience's reactions. Rosie rubbed her aching eyes and tried to ease the niggling pain in her back. She fiddled ineffectually with the settings of her chair but only succeeded in making herself less comfortable than before. It had been a hot day and the air in the office smelled stale, despite the irritating drone of the air conditioning.

'Working late?' The disembodied voice came from further down the office.

'Yes, unfortunately.' Rosie tried to place the male voice which she knew she'd heard somewhere before.

'I've only just started my working day.' The man emerged from behind a bank of filing cabinets. He wore shapeless green trousers and T-shirt, safety boots and purple rubber gloves. But ... *his face*. Rosie almost fell off her chair.

'You!' was all she managed to utter.

'Me.' He grinned and ran a vivid purple hand through his blond curls.

Rosie's mind clamoured with questions, none of which came out of her mouth. Tanner, charity auctioneer, dress destroyer and, after their encounter at the charity party, subject of many thoughts and questions, was a cleaner at Borden Glass? Really? She shook herself in a bid to return to reality. Surely he was a mirage caused by her over-tired brain?

Tanner stood by her desk and, despite his strange apparel, still managed to look like a girl's dream hero from a film with his tousled blond curls and clean-shaven chin.

'You owe me a dress.' She deliberately tried to sound stern but knew her expression didn't match her words.

'I do indeed. We'll have to arrange a shopping trip sometime soon.'

Rosie ignored his comment. She decided to be direct. 'Tanner, do you live at Lucerne Lodge?'

'No, I have a two-bed flat.' Did she imagine his uncomfortable expression? *Was he telling the truth?*

'You seemed to be really comfortable in that kitchen.'

'I've visited there so often, it sometimes feels like my home. I couldn't find you when I returned from the marquee.'

'That's because I left. You didn't expect me to re-join the party in a borrowed football kit, did you?'

'I suppose not.'

She was still suspicious. 'Who owns Lucerne Lodge then?'

'The owner of Borden Glass.'

'Ah, so that's why you're working here too?'

This time, Tanner ignored her question. *Or, was he deliberately changing the subject?*

'Why are you working so late?'

Rosie paused before answering. 'Important presentation to finish for tomorrow.'

'Must be very important to make you look so stressed.'

'Do I?' Rosie tried to look at herself in the reflection of her computer screen.

'Dark rings under eyes, tense posture.'

Rosie sighed and ran her hands over her face. 'Feels right now as if my whole life depends on it, or the future of my career anyway.'

'Serious stuff,' said Tanner, waving a disconcertingly purple hand.

'I'm probably making too big a deal out of it. I bet they've already decided who they're going to promote.'

'That serious, eh?'

Rosie nodded, annoyed with herself for pouring out her inner thoughts and anxieties to this man of all people.

'I could put in a good word for you, if you like.'

'What?' Rosie knew her eyes had widened with alarm.

‘I’m cleaning the Managing Director’s suite later. He might still be there.’

‘No, please!’ Rosie’s mind conjured up a horrific caricature of the cleaner recommending her for promotion. The image came complete with speech bubbles and inner thought clouds.

‘Suit yourself. I’d better get back to work.’ He began dusting the windowsill and desk surfaces near to Rosie with a pink feather duster.

She resumed scanning her slides but found it difficult to focus with Tanner so close by. She had many, many questions, which she couldn’t find the right words or the courage to ask him.

Just as she managed to achieve a modicum of concentration, Tanner popped up from behind a desk, making her jump.

‘I have an idea.’ He smiled. ‘I’ll be here for at least twenty minutes. Why don’t you try your presentation out on me?’

‘Oh, no, don’t worry. It probably wouldn’t mean anything to you.’

The words were out of her mouth before she’d had time to think, and she wondered if she might have offended him with her obvious implication that he would know nothing about marketing strategy.

‘Go on. It will make my cleaning more interesting and it will be practice for you,’ he persisted. ‘Even if I don’t pretend to understand it.’ He emphasised the word “pretend”.

Rosie looked up quickly as he spoke, but his words, thankfully, appeared to have been made in jest, not irritation or offence. He winked at her.

Not convinced that it was the best idea, she turned to her first slide and launched into the introduction. Tanner moved around emptying bins, dusting desks, windowsills and skirting. He occasionally interrupted to make suggestions about Rosie’s script. She found herself taking rapid notes on the comments he threw out. They were helpful and intelligent. *Why was she surprised?* She did begin to wonder how he came to be working as a cleaner when he clearly had such a good grasp of business, and marketing in particular.

She came to her closing remarks and peered up into Tanner’s eyes as he perched on the desk next to hers. Feeling in danger of falling off her chair, she asked, ‘Can I have the job?’

‘Most definitely.’

He moved closer and under his unnerving gaze, it suddenly seemed too quiet in the cavernous office. For some reason, her thoughts kept straying to what it would feel like to be kissed by him. Desperate to fill the silence, Rosie blurted out, 'I wish I didn't go to pieces in front of an audience.'

'Turn them into cabbages.'

'Excuse me?'

'Imagine their heads are cabbages – you won't be scared of them then.'

Rosie giggled, 'Okay, I'll try that. Is that what you did at the auction?'

'Maybe. Anyway, I must get on. Managing Director's suite next.' He winked again and disappeared through the double doors before she had time to say anything more. She fervently hoped that he wouldn't mention anything about her or her presentation to the MD.

Tanner felt a complete fraud. He'd enjoyed helping Rosie with her presentation. He could tell she was confused about his cleaning role, but too polite to say anything. He couldn't believe his luck that she'd been working late.

When her computer screen-saver flashed onto her screen, he'd nearly given himself away. He recognised the photograph, or rather the setting of the photograph. Its twin was on the wall at Lucerne Lodge in his father's study. He hoped that he'd disguised his surprise and diverted her attention. But now he was even more intrigued about his father's past and the file about Rosie ...

'Damn rubber gloves,' he swore, trying to get them off his hands, but they seemed welded to his fingers. He threw the purple offenders in a nearby bin in frustration.

# *Chapter Five*

Rosie was pleased with her performance at her marketing presentation. She'd smiled throughout, and the smile had taken away her usual nerves. Tanner had been the cause of the smile, as his suggestion to turn the audience's heads into cabbages had worked. She even managed to get through the question and answer session without being floored by a question. Thanks to her thorough research and planning, she could handle anything they threw at her. The sight of the directors nodding to each other as she left the room was so satisfying. She had to resist the urge to do a high kick and a squeal on the way down the corridor.

She floated on such a high after the presentation was finished that she found it difficult to concentrate on anything else. She left the office early, intending to have a relaxed evening, but then she remembered that her mother's WI branch had an art sale, which she'd faithfully promised to attend. She knew she couldn't let her mother down, so she settled for tea at her favourite café and a little retail therapy before heading to the event.

The sale turned out to be a much larger affair than Rosie had imagined. It was held in Sowden library foyer and was opened by the mayor. There were a lot of exhibitors displaying all kinds of artistic work.

Frances Phillips had been painting in watercolour for years, and Rosie already had several of her paintings on her own walls. Each lady from the WI painting group had been given their own wall space and a table to display their work.

Rosie went straight over to her mother's table. Frances Phillips, as always, looked neat and demure in a pastel skirt and patterned top. Rosie, not for the first time, wished that she had inherited her mother's seemingly effortless style.

'Rosie, you came! Thank you, darling.'

'I'll go for a look round first, Mum.'

'Off you go. You can report back to me with your thoughts.' Her mother winked and Rosie wondered what that meant.

She walked around the tables, noting how the standard and type of painting varied greatly. There were one or two landscapes which she admired, but she wondered how her mother would react if she bought someone else's work. She spotted the stall her mother must have been winking about. Rosie wasn't surprised.

She made her way back to her mother.

‘Yours are the best,’ she said.

‘Maybe slightly biased, given that I’m your mother?’ Frances smiled wryly.

‘No, Mum, yours are definitely more to my taste than most of them.’

Frances fussed over her table display and whispered to her daughter. ‘What did you think of Mira Green’s?’

Rosie leaned closer, wary of her words being overheard. ‘Do you mean the lady who has done the nudes in acrylic?’

Frances nodded vigorously.

‘You know I’m not a prude, but even I’m a little shocked. Am I right that some of the images are of people in this room?’

‘Yes, she asked for volunteers from our group. I’m so glad I refused. I would have had to buy any painting of me just to get it off the wall.’

Rosie noticed that she wasn’t the only one to dodge quickly past Mira’s display table, although one man seemed transfixed by her work and stared at each painting carefully before glancing around the room. Rosie decided he was matching paintings to their subjects, which seemed a little creepy.

Potential buyers approached Frances, so Rosie drifted around the room again. It had become a game to spot the ladies who had said yes to sitting for the nude paintings.

When her mum had parcelled up a couple’s purchases, Rosie went back to her.

‘Are you okay to pack up at the end of the evening, or do you want me to hang around?’

‘I’ll be fine, darling. There are loads of others to help. You go home and relax.’

Rosie had lived on the outskirts of Sowden until she’d left for university, and her mother still lived in the same house. When Rosie had lived in London, she had been excited to connect with Jenny Simpson who came from Borteen. They’d met at a social activity group event and, once they’d established they came from the same part of the country, had become firm friends, until Jenny had had to return to Borteen suddenly to nurse her sick mother.

They’d kept in touch, and Jenny had even visited Rosie in London. Rosie had really imagined the pair would slip back into their close friendship when her job was transferred to the Sowden branch of Borden

Glass, but it hadn't quite worked out like that as Jenny was now married with a small child, and the circles the women moved in were very different.

She still liked to visit Jenny, adored her little boy, Jack, but it didn't seem quite the same. Somehow, Jenny's successes with husband and child seemed to highlight Rosie's failed relationship with Ollie. Thankfully, after going to an evening class to learn meditation, Rosie had met and clicked with two new friends, Lucy and Connie. Both were divorced and working full time. They hadn't known each other very long, but it was an easy friendship and few topics were off limits.

The Sunshine Restaurant on Borteen high street was one of Rosie's favourite haunts. It served tasty food at reasonable prices and was a small, comfortable place where you could share a meal with friends, or go on your own to have lunch or a coffee. It was perfect for Saturday brunch with her friends and had the advantage of being close to the shops.

The walls were covered in pictures of sunrises and sunsets. Even the salt and pepper pots had little sun faces on them. To some it might have appeared garish, but Rosie felt that the whole atmosphere was optimistic and uplifting.

Lucy was in full flow describing her latest dating escapade. The decibels in their corner of the restaurant had increased considerably as the girls laughed at Lucy's experiences speed dating the previous evening. Lucy was small and dainty, but with a voice deepened by heavy smoking in her late teens. She worked at an accountants in Sowden as an administrator. As she spoke, she brandished a teaspoon, as if it were a longed-for cigarette. Since her divorce, she'd tried lots of different ways to meet the perfect man and delighted in sharing the details of her adventures with her friends.

'He asked you what?' asked Connie. She always had a permanent tan, thanks to her naturally olive skin. Her hair ended up in corkscrew curls no matter how many times she straightened it. Connie worked as a secretary, but longed to find a new career.

Rosie loved being out with the girls, but she feared today they were being too loud.

In a mock Liverpudlian accent Lucy continued. 'He asked me, "If I were a jelly, what colour and flavour would I be?" and he had a straight face, as if he'd asked a normal question!'

'What did you say?' asked Rosie.

'Red, of course, tasting of raspberries and promise.' Lucy pouted and adopted a flirtatious pose as she spoke.

'Did you put him as one of your choices at the end of the night?' asked Connie.

'Are you kidding? He was a total fruitcake – he was wearing a turquoise waistcoat and a tusk earring.'

The girls swallowed down their laughter as the waitress approached their table with her pencil poised over her order pad. Rosie was secretly glad that the interruption quietened them down.

'Come on then, Connie, what outrageous question would you ask at speed dating?' Lucy challenged, as soon as the waitress had left them.

'Oooh. I think I'd ask if he could make love to the rhythm of the William Tell Overture. I've always fancied finding someone who could.'

Lucy shrieked with laughter. 'Rosie?'

'You wouldn't catch me speed dating in the first place.'

'Aw, spoil sport.'

'I don't know why you're so keen to find another man anyway. It always ends in heartache or frustration.'

'Well, I'm not going to listen to you. I have a date tonight with a guy I ticked on the speed dating sheet, and he'd ticked me too. Wish me luck'

'Good luck,' chorused Rosie and Connie.

Rosie took a sip of her cappuccino and noticed the waiter standing by the entrance to the kitchen. She closed her eyes and told herself it was just her overactive imagination. She looked again and choked on the next mouthful of her drink. Tears streamed down her face, but when they cleared and she'd mopped her face with a napkin, the waiter was still the same – Tanner!

Tanner, wearing a white shirt and black trousers, his wayward hair smoothed back, approached the table. He had a look of concern on his face.

'Are you all right, Rosie? Can I get you some water?'

She looked up at Tanner, still not believing what her eyes were seeing. 'Yes, could I have a glass of water, please?'

Three pairs of eyes watched Tanner walk to the kitchen. As he disappeared through the door, Lucy and Connie pounced on Rosie, their faces brimming with curiosity.

'Who is the drop-dead gorgeous guy?' sighed Lucy.

'You know him?' Connie said at the same time.

Rosie took another cautious sip of coffee. 'He's called Tanner. But I have no idea what he's doing here.'

'Hang on a minute, isn't that the guy from the party? The one who ruined your dress?' Connie had already put two and two together. Rosie tried to remember what she had told the girls about her first encounter with Tanner.

'*Shh.* He's coming back. Not a word, you two. Please. Pretty please.' She crossed her fingers under the table, praying that the girls wouldn't embarrass her further.

He put a glass in front of Rosie with a smile and retreated. Lucy and Connie giggled behind their hands, much to Rosie's embarrassment. She sipped her water and studied her napkin as if it had the secret of life written on it.

Lucy and Connie were soon locked in a discussion about a guy at their gym, but Rosie found her thoughts straying away to Tanner. She wondered about him having to work at two jobs to make ends meet – lunches at the restaurant and evenings cleaning at Borden Glass. She resolved to give him a decent tip at the end of their meal.

Her eyes followed him whenever he came into the restaurant from the kitchen. She noted that he appeared rather clumsy for a waiter, forever apologising about spilling coffee into saucers and missing plates as he served vegetables. He couldn't pile up the crockery as he cleared a table and seemed prone to dropping cutlery on the floor. Maybe he hadn't been in the job very long.

She came out of her reverie to find Connie and Lucy staring at her.

'You're miles away,' observed Connie.

'Got the hots for someone.' Lucy laughed.

'Oh no. No!' exclaimed Rosie.

Connie and Lucy exchanged knowing glances.

'Anyway, Rosie, are you still up for those courses next Saturday?' asked Connie.

'Of course, if you want me to come with you. What were they again?'

'An introduction to reflexology on Saturday morning, and Indian head massage in the afternoon.'

'Not sure they're my thing, but I'll keep an open mind. I did enjoy meditation, yoga and an acupressure massage when I stayed for a week at a retreat in Somerset after Ollie and I split.'

'I want to learn all about therapies. It could be my new career.'

Rosie smiled. She had one friend anxious to meet the man of her dreams and another desperate to find the right career path. In a way, Rosie wished she was as clear about what she wanted for her own future. She only knew that she didn't want to spend the rest of her days working for someone else and feeling that she'd somehow failed in her personal life.

She picked up the saucer they'd piled their money on to pay the bill, and walked over to Tanner. He smiled and took it from her. His face was a picture as Rosie handed him a twenty pound note. 'Your tip.'

'That's very kind, but I'd prefer it if you put the money towards a new dress. I do owe you one after all.' He handed back the note and Rosie reluctantly took it.

'I need to thank you for your help with my presentation by the way, especially for the suggestion about turning scary people's heads into cabbages.'

Tanner laughed. 'I'm glad it helped. Did you get your promotion?'

'They're deciding soon. Let's put it this way, I didn't do myself any harm. Thank you again.'

'I'll fetch your coats.' He seemed reluctant to prolong the conversation, and Rosie guessed it was because he was working.

Tanner watched the friends walk away down the street. He knew that he was playing games with the information he had about Rosie, but at least he was killing two birds with one stone. He worried that he would alienate her rather than get to know her, but somehow he couldn't stop himself now he'd decided on his course of action.

# *Chapter Six*

Rosie felt unaccountably nervous. She knew nothing about reflexology and even though it was a beginner's course, she thought it would be obvious to everyone that she was only there because Connie lacked the confidence to attend on her own.

She needn't have worried. It was truly a course for those curious about the therapy, and the group of eight women were all friendly.

'Sorry I dragged you along. I think I would have been fine on my own,' whispered Connie.

'No problem. Anyway, I'm intrigued.'

The tutor explained the basics of reflexology. Parts of the body were supposed to be linked to different areas of the feet. If those points on the feet were massaged, the corresponding area of the body would be healthier. She showed the group colourful maps of feet detailing the connections.

Before Rosie had chance to be sceptical, they were working in pairs. First they were asked to clean their "patient's" feet with scented wipes and to gently press the soles. They were instructed to see if they could find any sign of the links on the chart. Rosie was amazed when Connie pressed the part of her foot that was supposed to relate to her ear and she sensed a corresponding tingle in her earlobe. They swapped over. Rosie felt immediately squeamish. It was one thing to be close to your friends, even to hug them, but it was a totally different matter to touch their feet in this way.

'This feels weird, Connie. I don't normally get this close to you.'

'Thank your lucky stars you're only touching my feet! I know what you mean though, it *is* a bit strange.'

'I don't think I could do this for a living. You have lovely little feet, but I couldn't cope with hairy, smelly feet.'

'Maybe reflexology isn't the career for you.' Connie laughed.

The two hours went by in no time. They had learned how to do a relaxing foot massage using a softening cream.

'I feel so chilled, Connie. I don't think I'm fit to walk anywhere for lunch. If I get stressed at work, I'll have to give you a ring and you can come and sort out my feet like this.'

'Maybe we'd better head to the nearest café for a strong coffee. I can't remember my feet ever feeling like this either – it's as if they're floating above the ground rather than connected to it.'

'I know exactly what you mean, a bit like a personal hovercraft. Was the course what you thought it would be?'

Connie turned shining eyes to her. 'Much more. I'm hooked! I'll definitely be signing up for the diploma course.'

'I'll be your practise patient anytime.'

'I might hold you to that, and rope Lucy in too.'

'So, we've got the Indian head massage taster this afternoon. If that's any way near as relaxing, I'm going to be comatose by this evening!'

Rosie was right. Following an afternoon of head and shoulder massage, she was so relaxed that she could hardly move. The dreamy feeling was so alien that she realised she must normally be quite tense.

Connie signed up for the full courses in both reflexology and Indian head massage. She was convinced that she had found her vocation and Rosie hoped that she was right. Her friend deserved to find her dream career.

Rosie was looking forward to an early night, but it was not to be. Lucy turned up in a tearful state with a bottle of wine and a tub of ice cream. Her latest boyfriend from the speed dating had told her he didn't want to see her again. They'd only met up a couple of times, but it seemed that Lucy had convinced herself that he was "the one".

Once she'd sobbed on Rosie's shoulder, and the ice cream was in danger of melting before they had eaten it, Rosie sent her off to wash her face. She spooned out two large bowlfuls of ice cream and poured the wine.

'I'm never going to meet that special person, Rosie.'

'I'm probably not the best person to talk to about that. My track record is hardly the best.'

'No, but at least you had eight years with Ollie. My marriage lasted a year and my current record seems to be three dates.'

'Do you think you're looking in the right places?' Rosie was wary of what she was saying but couldn't help feeling that Lucy's relentless searching was attracting similarly desperate males.

'Where's the best place to find a man, do you think?'

Rosie thoughtfully sucked the ice cream off her spoon before replying. 'As I said before, I'm no expert ... but I would have thought you'd be more likely to meet someone by following your interests.'

'I haven't really got any hobbies, apart from trying to find a man.' Lucy giggled and wiped a blob of ice cream off her lip.

'Well, maybe you should find some hobbies first.'

Lucy's eyes acquired a faraway look as she picked up her glass and sipped her wine. 'Scuba diving?'

'I didn't think you were a confident swimmer!'

'Okay, archery?'

'That sounds more like it, but I didn't really mean that you should go for hobbies where you're most likely to meet men – more that you should spend time doing things because you're interested in them.'

'I wonder what that lovely man Tanner is doing this evening ...' Lucy looked thoughtful.

Rosie felt an involuntary tightening of her tummy muscles. 'No idea, but he seems to have several jobs, so my guess would be working.'

'Are you interested in him, Rosie? As in "interested" in him?'

'No, I'm off men completely, remember?' Rosie had a strange reaction inside as she said the words.

'So, you wouldn't mind if I went back to The Sunshine Restaurant and did some serious flirting?'

'That's up to you. I don't have any claim on him.'

'Oooh, something to look forward to then.' Lucy appeared immediately more cheerful.

Rosie continued to sip at her wine, mulling over why the idea of Lucy and Tanner together made her feel uncomfortable.

All too soon, another weekend had gone. Rosie was late for work. She had slept fitfully. A typical Monday – it was one of those days where she felt as if she was wading through treacle trying to get dressed. Her hair, which normally behaved and hung in a sleek curtain around her face, was full of static and stuck out at strange angles on her head. The blouse she'd intended to wear had a stain on it, which she must have missed due to ironing it inside out. She thought she was ready, but then her keys had done a disappearing act and it had taken a frantic five minutes to find them behind a cushion on a chair.

Feeling flustered because she'd been rushing, she cursed the heavy traffic on the Sowden ring road. Each car in front of her seemed like an enemy trying to stop her reaching her destination. It was amazing how a couple of minutes either side of her target departure time from Borteen altered the traffic flows, and she'd got stuck behind a slow driver on the twisty roads over Pink Moor.

Stopping at a set of traffic lights, she stalled her car. As she fumbled with the handbrake and ignition, she noticed a man on the pavement. He wore a huge cardboard pizza box.

Rosie had read in the local newspaper about the outrage caused by the use of these human advertisements. The article she'd read proclaimed it inhumane to expect workers to stand at the side of the road in such degrading outfits in all weathers, and often to be paid less than minimum wage. It was the first time she'd actually seen one of them featuring the local pizza parlour, but she would recognise the wearer anywhere. *Tanner*! How many jobs did this man have?

There was no mistaking that wild blond hair escaping from the chef's hat rammed over it. Tanner looked thoroughly dejected. He wasn't a very positive advertisement for the pizza company. Rosie found herself starting to giggle.

As she stared, someone behind her beeped their horn – the traffic lights had turned green and she hadn't noticed them changing. Tanner looked over and recognition sparked in his eyes.

Rosie finally got her brain and her car in gear and as she pulled away, Tanner gave her a smile and a half wave. She beeped her horn and drove off, grinning.

*Tanner packaged in a box. What a thought. More seriously though*, Rosie pondered, *could he be so terrible at his jobs that he kept being sacked, or was he working at all of these jobs on a part-time basis?* He was very articulate and intelligent, so why was he working in these low-paid jobs anyway? Had he a dark secret? She thought more about Tanner and his work habits right up until she parked her car at Borden Glass. The man was beginning to haunt her, or was that stalk her? Despite that thought, she couldn't help but smile.

# *Chapter Seven*

Tanner knew that Rosie had spotted him, as he worked behind the counter in the corner store. The chatter of the elderly lady at the front of the queue merged into nonsense with his distraction. He didn't know why he was surprised to see Rosie. After all, he was well aware that she regularly used this shop to get sandwiches for her lunch on a work day.

He loaded the customer's loaf of bread, pack of butter, sausages and tomato sauce into a carrier bag and counted change into her wrinkled hand. She smiled at him gratefully, oblivious that she'd lost his attention, and shuffled out of the shop.

The next customer had flowers and a newspaper. Tanner put the money into the till and looked up into furious blue eyes.

'I would like a word with you outside.'

Tanner motioned to his colleague, who had been stacking shelves nearby. Her eyebrows were raised in an unspoken question as she took over from him at the till.

He gestured to Rosie to follow him to the back of the shop. It was one of those old-fashioned corner stores, loaded with everything from mothballs to teabags. The stock spilled from the shelves into baskets on the floor, and the overriding smells were polish, bread and cabbage.

Rosie marched behind him through the cluttered and untidy storeroom and out of the back door. Here, there was a small grimy yard, piled high with bread crates and cardboard boxes. Pigeons cooed on the guttering overhead, regularly depositing droppings onto the ground below. A blocked drain smell filled the air.

As Tanner turned to face her, Rosie wasted no time in sharing what was bothering her.

'Are you stalking me?'

'Stalking you?' Tanner laughed.

'You keep appearing in my life. It's started to feel more than coincidental.'

He shrugged. 'I'm only trying to earn a living.'

'I appreciate that, but you've had far too many jobs this month – and all in places I go to.' Her hands were on her hips and her face full of accusation.

'Absolute coincidence, Rosie, but it is always lovely to see you.' He smiled in a way he'd used to good effect in the past to get what he wanted, but Rosie's expression remained suspicious and unforgiving.

'This is beyond coincidence. What is going on?'

'I really don't understand what you mean. It's probably Red Car Theory.'

'What?'

'Red Car Theory. You know, you buy a red car and suddenly you see red cars of the same make and model everywhere.' Tanner could tell Rosie had softened slightly. *Maybe he could get away with this after all.*

'Now you come to mention it, I have noticed that. I once had an unusual bronze-coloured car, or at least I thought it was different. Then everywhere I went, I saw its twin.' She looked thoughtful.

'Think of me as an unusual car. That's why you keep noticing me, because you're focusing on me.'

Rosie blushed at the implication, but Tanner sensed he had very nearly dug himself out of his deep, deep hole. His heart thumped, and he hoped that Rosie couldn't see the ripples its heavy beats were creating on the front of his corner-shop-logo-emblazoned T-shirt.

'Look, why don't we have a meal together this evening? We can talk about this.'

Her face closed down again. 'How can I be sure that I'm safe having dinner with a stalker? You could be an axe murderer for all I know.'

'Rosie—'

'You're going to say that of course you're not a stalker or an axe murderer, but how do I know that? You could say anything.'

'Would a stalker run a charity event? And I could hardly have planned to be in a pizza box on the side of a road you were driving down, could I? Now ... dinner?'

'With the condition that I get to choose where.'

They arranged to meet at the pizza restaurant in Sowden, opposite to the cathedral. Maybe it was time to come clean and explain to Rosie his motives for appearing so often in her life? He was going to have to be honest with her soon, or he feared she would get totally the wrong impression.

Rosie rang both Connie and Lucy to tell them about her meeting with Tanner.

‘It doesn’t sound safe, Rosie. I want to come along and lurk at the back of the restaurant with my pepper spray, just in case,’ said Connie with obvious concern in her voice.

‘He’s right, though. He *has* been turning up in my usual haunts, but he couldn’t have planned for me being on that exact road, at that exact time, to see his pizza box advert. I’m sure he’s probably harmless.’

‘I wish I was as convinced. Be careful leaving the restaurant. Park your car close and text me as soon as you’re in it with your doors locked.’

‘Yes, Mum,’ teased Rosie.

Lucy had a completely different take on the situation. ‘He fancies you. Maybe you’ve met your special someone. I just knew he wouldn’t be interested in me.’

‘Lucy, it isn’t a date. He wants to explain what’s been going on with all of his jobs.’

‘Yeah, right. You mark my words, he’s after you. And let’s face it, he’s gorgeous. I’m so jealous.’

*Why wasn’t that reassuring?* Rosie promised to text Lucy with an update too, and spent the rest of the day wondering whether she was playing with fire when she should have been concentrating on a work project.

Tanner visited his father after he had finished his shift at the corner shop. The private clinic room was comfortable with its expensive-looking patterned curtains, fresh flowers and leather visitors’ chairs, but the surroundings couldn’t disguise the fact that Michael Bryant had embarked on the last stage of his life.

‘Dad, I need to know what Rosie Phillips has to do with our family.’

Michael Bryant shrugged.

Tanner asked again.

Michael Bryant appeared to sigh. He lifted the corner of his life-sustaining oxygen mask with a shaking hand and gasped, ‘Owe a debt to her family.’

Tanner felt far from satisfied by the evasive answer, but he knew he would be unlikely to get much more information. He could not equate the shrunken skeleton of a man who wheezed through each day, as white as the sheets of the bed, with the tall, stern man who had ruled his life since birth. There was little affection between them, but the ties of duty and expectation hung heavily in the air.

He sat on the leather chair and gazed, unseeing, through the window. What should he say to Rosie tonight? How could he explain his recent behaviour to himself, let alone to her?

It had all begun as curiosity after he'd found the file about her on his father's desk.

Michael Bryant said he owed a debt to Rosie's family. That could mean so many things. Maybe her mother had given Michael Bryant a loan in the days before he made his fortune? Maybe her father had saved Michael's life? Maybe the families were very close friends?

Perhaps he could ask Rosie's opinion on their family link? He sighed. *Maybe not.* He couldn't imagine himself saying, "Why was my father having you followed?"

Running his fingers through his unruly hair, he reflected that she would hardly find him trustworthy when he'd effectively stalked her as she had suspected. Maybe the corner shop job had been a step too far. On the other hand, if he did explain, maybe Rosie would already know the story of their connection and solve the mystery?

Tanner glanced over to the bed. His father had fallen asleep. Michael Bryant no longer looked like a tyrannical, powerful man, but a shadow of his former self. Very unlike the man in the photograph of his parents on the wall in the study at Lucerne Lodge. He'd looked at that photograph carefully after seeing Rosie's screen saver picture on the day he'd posed as the cleaner in her office. It did indeed look as if another person, or perhaps more than one person, had been standing next to the couple before the photograph had been cropped. You could see another arm and shoulder at the side of the picture. Tanner was pretty sure that the image on Rosie's computer screen was the other half of that shot. And it didn't take a genius to work out that the screen saver showed Rosie's parents. He couldn't really understand why his father kept the picture in such a prominent place, as Georgia had been his ex-wife for so long. Another mystery he was unlikely to learn about now.

Tanner shook himself. He needed to get ready to meet Rosie. He was no closer to knowing how to play this evening, but he was sure that it wouldn't be wise to be late.

# *Chapter Eight*

Rosie walked into the pizza restaurant at ten to seven. She'd decided that she would prefer to be sitting at a table before Tanner arrived, rather than having to make a grand entrance. For once, she had been decisive about what to wear and felt confident in her blue chinos, red blouse and lacy cream cardigan. Her blue trainers exactly matched the shade of her trousers. She was determined to get some answers to the questions that had been burning in her mind for the last couple of weeks.

She'd parked her car right outside the door, as Connie had suggested, in case she wanted to make a quick getaway, thankful there had been a space free when she arrived. The restaurant was utilitarian in décor as it was mainly designed to survive the onslaught of toddlers and teenagers. Rosie had decided that the open-plan layout would make her feel safer than a restaurant with more intimate seating arrangements. It also amused her that this had been the pizza chain whose advertising board Tanner had been wearing when she spotted him by the traffic lights earlier in the week.

She asked for a table for two and the waiter took her to one by the window. There were many identical empty tables around her. Children's teas had finished and the evening rush had yet to begin. The piped background music was painfully modern and tuneless. There were sticky marks on the table's surface. She placed her mobile phone in a prominent position to await the text messages Lucy and Connie had promised to send to check on her wellbeing.

Ordering a bottle of her favourite Italian sparkling water, she looked out of the window. She indulged in people watching as usual, in an attempt to stop her uneasy thoughts about meeting Tanner. She sat bolt upright as she noticed a blond-haired man dodging between the cars on the road outside. Tanner's recklessness made her unaccountably angry. He could have easily been clipped by a car.

He recognised Rosie sitting in the window, waved and strode for the door. Arriving a little breathless at the table, he sat down in the opposite chair. She took in his faded denim jeans and open-necked black shirt as he shrugged off his jacket. A subtle cloud of delicious aftershave reached out to her across the table.

'Sorry I'm late.'

'You aren't. I'm early.'

He grinned. 'Have you ordered?'

'Just the water.' She gestured to the large bottle and was annoyed that she couldn't resist smiling back.

'May I?' Tanner gestured towards the water.

'Help yourself,' said Rosie, still trying to regain control of her grinning lips.

The waiter arrived with oversized menus. Rosie retreated behind hers to collect her thoughts, but found that she wasn't taking in any of the words on the sheet. It might as well have been written in Chinese. Tanner's voice broke into her confusion.

'Have you decided what to have?'

'There's so much choice. I'm still trying to make up my mind.' She peered around the large menu, but Tanner was hidden behind his.

'Have you tried this new very thin-based pizza with pureed peppers instead of tomato sauce?'

'No, but it sounds rather yummy.' She glanced over the top of the menu and realised that he was now staring back over his.

'How about half of one of those pizzas each with a salad?'

Rosie lowered the menu and smiled. 'Sounds great.'

After they'd ordered, Rosie made up her mind to be direct. 'So, back to the reason we came here in the first place. Can you please be honest – are you stalking me?'

'Whoa, straight to the point.' Tanner looked very uncomfortable. 'Pure coincidence, I promise you. I've been trying out lots of different jobs, and some of them happened to be in the places you must go to too.'

'It still sounds very fishy to me.' Rosie's mind battled to be rational as Tanner's aftershave continued to distract her.

'Maybe, and I can see why you would think that, but I promise, hand on heart, that I'm not a weirdo. I have no bad intentions towards you.'

Rosie fell quiet as she let his words sink in. She studied the pattern on her cutlery. Her instincts told her that there was more to this than he was admitting. She felt a distinct need to be on her guard.

'So, why did you ask me to meet you this evening?'

'I thought that if we could meet on neutral ground, maybe we'd be able to resolve your worries and perhaps become friends.'

'Friends?'

'You did say you'd recently returned to the area. Is it such a strange idea, to make a new friend?'

Despite Rosie's reservations and suspicions, their conversation became easier as the time passed, ranging through books, films, novels, plays, childhood holidays and favourite things, as they ate the delicious pizza with salad, followed by dessert and then coffee.

Rosie was able to send reassuring replies to both Connie and Lucy when their promised text messages to check up on her came through.

However, regardless of the friendly chat, Rosie kept waiting for Tanner to get to the real point of their meeting. The unspoken issue grew larger with each passing minute. He seemed on the verge of broaching a different subject on several occasions, but each time he appeared to back away from it again.

'Excuse me a minute.' She got up and started towards the ladies' toilets.

'There's something else I'd like to discuss with you when you come back.' Tanner's face had a strange expression that, even with her years of people watching, she couldn't read. Now he seemed ready to talk, she felt rather spooked, even though she wanted to know what was really going on here.

Ten minutes later, Tanner wondered if Rosie had decided to go home. He began to feel strangely uncomfortable and self-conscious. Given the anticipation and worry about how much to confess this evening, he couldn't believe she'd left when he'd finally felt ready to discuss the main issue.

The restaurant had filled up while they were eating, and to Tanner it seemed as if everyone was staring at him. It felt like they all knew Rosie had gone, probably sneaked out of a back door. He even caught the waiter's eye and imagined that he could see pity there. *Hang on a minute, though ...* he was sat facing the door marked "Toilets", and no one had gone in or out since Rosie had disappeared through the door.

He got up and walked across the space, dodging the tables. Beyond the heavy swing door, he hesitated in the tiled hallway. A door for ladies, a door for gents, a disabled cubicle, a baby cubicle and a thin wailing voice, '*Help.*'

Tanner Bryant had been in some scrapes in his time, but he could, hand on heart, say that he had never ventured into a ladies' toilet before. He pushed open the door cautiously.

'Help!' Rosie's voice became louder and more desperate in tone.

Holding onto the door, Tanner put his head as far around it as he could without moving his feet inside.

'Rosie?'

'Oh, no! Anyone but you.' Her tone changed, 'Tanner, thank goodness. I'm stuck. The door handle fell off.'

Tanner looked behind him to check that there was no one around and launched himself through the door. Beyond, there were three cubicles and three sinks. The middle door was shut. There was a safety opening catch on the outside of the door handle. He took a coin out of his pocket and used it to turn it.

Rosie came out of the cubicle like a cork from a champagne bottle. She launched herself into his arms and kissed him.

He pulled away. 'Rosie, don't!'

A look of confusion and embarrassment crossed her face.

'I'm sorry. I'm so relieved to be out of there, that's all. Shock reaction.' Her face matched her red blouse.

For once, Tanner didn't know what to say, so he bolted out of the door.

Rosie took a few moments to calm down. She carefully reapplied her lipstick. She kicked herself that she had kissed Tanner, but it truly was just a reaction to being shut up in the toilet cubicle and feeling trapped for what had felt like a long time. He obviously didn't like her kissing him – that much was clear. He must have been serious about them just being friends. This was uncharted territory, and Rosie was completely confused.

She emerged from the ladies' ready to apologise, but their table had already been cleared. Tanner was nowhere to be seen and when she asked their waiter, he said that Tanner had already paid the bill and left.

She couldn't see any sign of him in the street outside, so Rosie got into her car and drove home in a daze. *What was going on?*

# *Chapter Nine*

'Earth to Rosie.' Rosie's mum was looking at her quizzically. 'You know you have the same expression you used to get sometimes as a little girl.'

Rosie had arrived at her mother's cottage five minutes earlier to find Frances on the phone, so had sat staring at the garden through the window, petting the ears of her mother's springer spaniel, Dusty. She stayed over at her mother's house on the last Saturday of each month so that they could have a longer time to talk and relax together. Mum and daughter had always been very close, Rosie's father having died when she was a small child.

'Have I?' Rosie widened her eyes to feign innocence.

'Yes, you have, Rosie Phillips. Come on, tell me what you're mulling over in that head of yours.'

'Can I have a cup of tea first?' asked Rosie, moving to the tap to fill the kettle.

The square kitchen always seemed to Rosie the epitome of what a kitchen should be like. The cabinets were pale green-painted wood with cream handles, and the wooden work surfaces showed obvious signs of years of use. A big table stood in the middle of the room and was used as both work surface and eating area. The huge flower arrangement, with flowers from the garden, and overflowing fruit bowl, added to the feeling of a real kitchen. The smell of baking hung in the air, and Rosie knew that her healthy eating campaign would be under assault later from whatever delicious treat her mother had prepared.

'Serious problem, then?' her mother persisted.

'I'm a little mixed up at the moment. I met someone and, well, I'm just a little confused by his behaviour.'

Rosie's mum grasped her arm and smiled. 'Goodness, he must be special.'

Rosie's eyes filled with tears. 'It's not like that, Mum. In fact, I'm not sure what's going on at all.'

'Hey, darling, it's always scary if you risk your heart.'

'No, no, you've got totally the wrong idea. I don't think there's even a chance of him being a love interest and, anyway, since Ollie and I ended in disaster, it's made me wonder if I'm any good at relationships. I'm trying to avoid romantic stuff these days.'

'But this feels different?'

'Very different. I didn't even like him at first. Well, that's not quite true – physically, he's attractive, but I wasn't sure about his attitude or intentions.'

'They say hate and love are very close together, dear.'

Rosie clattered rose-patterned mugs out of the cupboard and added tea bags. She went to get the milk out of the fridge. 'Don't get your hopes up, Mum. I think it's over before it's even begun.'

Thankfully, her mum stopped asking questions. Rosie didn't know the answers anyway. There had been no contact with Tanner since "the kiss". It had gone from him appearing in her life seemingly all the time to no sightings whatsoever.

She spent the evening companionably with her mother. Even though she had not lived at home for many years, they fell back into well-established roles as they prepared an evening meal and cleared up afterwards.

Rosie felt satisfyingly full as they sat chatting. She admired her mother's latest painting, discussed news items and heard all about the escapades of Frances' friends, including the infamous nude painter, Mira.

Eventually, Rosie yawned and, bidding her mother goodnight, went to snuggle up under the faded Barbie quilt in her old room, trying not to think about Tanner. Somehow mentioning him to her mother had reawakened her thoughts about him.

The next morning, Rosie sipped her strong coffee and nibbled at an overdone piece of toast. She hadn't quite got up in time to share breakfast with her mother. Frances Phillips, in walking boots and hat, had left Rosie in her pyjamas to stride to the newsagents with Dusty.

Her mother was red-faced with exertion, clutching the dog lead, a fluorescent green poo bag and the Sunday newspapers, when she came back into the kitchen.

Rosie abandoned thoughts of getting dressed for now. She poured her mother a cup of coffee and refilled her own. They both settled down with a portion of the newspaper. It was warm in the room and Rosie began to feel her eyelids closing, despite having slept soundly in her old bedroom.

Her mother's voice roused her from drowsiness.

'Well, now, he's a bit of all right.'

'Sorry, who?'

'The young man, who's written this article. Now, if I was twenty years younger ...'

'Let's see,' said Rosie half-heartedly.

Her mother flapped the magazine down on the table and Rosie froze. Pinpricks of goose pimples stood up on her skin and her vision momentarily blurred. There was a quarter-page picture of a man holding purple rubber gloves in one hand and a tray of empty plates in the other. He was unmistakable. The blond curls, unruly despite being recently brushed, the smile – Tanner.

'Are you all right Rosie?' Her mother was looking alarmed. 'You've gone very pale.'

Rosie couldn't answer. She wasn't sure what to think as she tried to get her eyes to focus on the article next to Tanner's picture.

'Sorry, Mum. I'm just surprised. I've met him.'

'You know this dishy young man?' Her mother pulled the magazine back and put her reading glasses on. 'Tanner Bryant, freelance journalist. Have I met him too? He looks awfully familiar ... and with that name.'

'I don't think so, Mum, but you never know. Can I have a look when you've finished reading?'

Rosie amazed herself at how casually she'd asked the question, when really she wanted to wrench the magazine from her mother's grasp. Could this article explain Tanner's strange behaviour? Added to all of this, the owner of Borden Glass was called Michael Bryant. *His father?* Freelance journalist, indeed. Was there a biographical paragraph at the end of the article to explain the truth about her mystery man?

She willed her mother to read faster, but as she showed no sign of hurrying, Rosie forced herself to go upstairs to take a shower. Her turbulent thoughts meant that she performed her toilette on autopilot, nearly plastering hand cream on her face in her distraction.

She dressed in an ankle-length skirt and cream blouse, complemented by amber beads, earrings and a long, fluffy cardigan. It was a good job that she had only bought one set of clothes with her because in her current state she would have been incapable of choosing between outfits.

When she came back into the warmth of the kitchen, the unwashed breakfast things were piled by the sink. Rosie could see her mother and the dog in the garden. Frances was seemingly angrily sweeping garden cuttings into piles, but Dusty appeared to think that she was playing a game and was scattering them everywhere.

Rosie smiled at the scene. Turning, she took a sharp breath as she caught sight of Tanner's picture lying on the coffee table, where her mother had left the magazine open for her. Looking at his photograph, she couldn't help but remember the sparkle in those blue eyes. She wasn't sure she wanted to know the truth any more, but she picked up the magazine and settled into her favourite rocking chair to read. Her heart was thudding as she rocked back and forth a little too fast.

The article was informative and well written. It focused on the pros and cons of low-paid work. The jobs Tanner had had personal experience of, as he conducted research for the article, were listed in a box to one side of the text. They included his cleaning job at Borden Glass, his waiting job at The Sunshine Restaurant, human pizza advertisement and corner shop assistant. He'd also listed street cleaning and a telephone call centre operative. *Maybe he hadn't stalked her after all.* As Rosie reached the end of the piece, she realised that all of the way through the article she had heard Tanner's voice reading it to her as if he was the narrator of a radio story.

As she'd hoped, there was a box at the end of the article entitled "About the Writer". However, it was unsatisfactorily bland and short, apart from one intriguing line – "Tanner Bryant currently combines his work as a freelance journalist with standing in for his father in the family business."

Rosie was so absorbed in her thoughts and the hypnotic rocking of the chair that she didn't hear her mother come back indoors.

'I knew he looked familiar,' her mother said in a harsh tone Rosie hadn't heard for many years. 'He's the spawn of the man who killed your father.'

Rosie launched herself from the rocking chair, then wished she hadn't as her legs were so unsteady. 'What do you mean, Mum?'

'Tanner is the son of Michael Bryant. He used to be an investor in your father's business.'

Rosie had only been five when her father had died, so she didn't know much about the details surrounding his death. There never seemed to be a right moment to ask her mother about it, and on the few occasions she had broached the subject, Frances had closed down and refused to talk. Now the hatred in her mother's voice filled the normally tranquil kitchen.

'Mum, if it's not too painful, tell me more about what happened back then. I was too small to remember anything.'

Rosie sat back down in the rocking chair, but this time she kept it still, as far forward as the rockers would go. She almost didn't want to hear what her mother had to say. A tremble took up residence in her knees.

Frances had a faraway look. She shook herself and stared directly at Rosie. 'Why do I get the impression that there's more to this Tanner Bryant thing than you're telling me?'

Unbidden, a big tear escaped Rosie's eye. She wiped it away in an impatient gesture, but not before Frances had noticed.

'Oh love, please don't tell me that this is the man you've fallen for.'

Rosie shook her head, but in a way that confirmed Frances was right. 'There's more … Michael Bryant owns the company I work for too.'

'He owns Borden Glass? Oh, Rosie, I would have told you not to take that job if I'd known. He's always had businesses in Sowden.'

'I think you need to tell me more about what happened with Dad, so that I understand.'

'Let me make a fresh pot of tea. I suppose the time has come to tell you about what happened back in those days.'

Rosie smiled despite her agitation. Her mother always seemed to think a hot drink of tea or coffee would ease any situation or heartache.

'Rosie, darling, one thing I am very clear about – you must stop seeing Tanner Bryant, that's if you are. I would even go as far as saying it's crucial. Please trust your mother on this.' Frances clattered the cups in their saucers, alerting Rosie to the state of her nerves.

'What do you mean, Mum? I'm not sixteen. I don't need your approval.'

'Please tell me you haven't slept with him.'

Rosie reddened. 'It's not like that at all.'

'Rosie, I do have my reasons. You must *not* get involved with that man, preferably not on any level.' Sitting down on a kitchen stool, Frances looked at Rosie with a serious face. Her hands were twisting together over and over again, but she seemed unaware of this.

'Right, Mum, please explain. There's obviously something going on here that I don't understand.'

'There are things in the past that I hoped I would never have to explain to you, but this is one of those moments when I have to speak honestly.'

'In the past? You mean about you and Dad?'

'Yes. This is extremely painful for me, and I don't want you to comment, just listen. Okay?'

Despite its inappropriateness, given the subject matter, Rosie could hear the well-worn phrase, "are you sitting comfortably? Then I'll begin" in her head. 'This all sounds rather ominous, but I won't say a word.'

'In the good old days, when your father's business was doing well, we used to go around with another couple … Georgia and Michael Bryant.'

Rosie's sharp intake of breath echoed around the kitchen. She clutched at her throat to stop herself from speaking.

'Yes, Tanner Bryant's parents were our best friends.'

'But—'

'Let me finish – you promised.'

Rosie nodded, her stomach muscles tightening as she waited to hear what her mother was about to say.

'We did everything together: meals, tennis, holidays. I didn't even suspect that your father and Georgia were getting closer. Far too close.' A tear ran down Frances' cheek. 'Oh dear, I knew I'd cry. So silly really, it was so long ago.'

Rosie got up, searched around the kitchen and produced a wad of tissues for her mother.

'Anyway, Michael found them in bed together and our friendship ceased on the spot. It was such a shock as we had been like a family, a close family. Your father swore that it was a one-off and he was very contrite, but things were obviously never the same between the four of us again, or between me and John, of course.' She grimaced.

Rosie reached out and clasped her hand for a moment, but Frances shook her off after a moment.

'Let me finish, Rosie. I've started now, so I might as well tell you more. Well, either the affair didn't stop or else it started up again when you were about five. When your father's business failed, it was because Michael Bryant had deliberately bought up and foreclosed on loans your father had taken out for an expansion plan. John died shortly afterwards.'

Here Frances paused and Rosie could tell she was debating whether to say more. 'Go on, Mum …'

Frances took a deep shuddering breath. 'That's not the complete truth – brace yourself, Rosie, I think you deserve to know this. I've always shielded you from it before. Things got so bad that your father had a heart attack. I firmly believe it was caused by the stress and pressure Michael Bryant put him under.'

Rosie was crying now. Big, hot tears welled up and spilled down her cheeks and onto her shirt. She'd always felt that there was something more to know about her father's death. Frances had done a good job of keeping this truth from her daughter for all of these years. She couldn't help speaking. 'Wasn't there something about Dad being found in water?'

'Yes. At first, I was worried he'd drowned *himself* in the … in the lake at Lucerne Lodge. The post mortem said he'd had a fatal heart attack and must have fallen into the lake as a result of it.'

'Hang on a minute, you know that I went to a charity party at Lucerne Lodge? That's how I met Tanner. I had no idea …' In her mind, she was back on the lawn, admiring the view, particularly of the lake. It was a shock to think that her father had died there.

'You mentioned you'd been to the Lodge, but well ... it didn't feel right saying anything after you'd already been there. Michael Bryant owns it. Your father went over on the day he died to beg him to extend the loans. He never came home.'

Rosie was catching up. 'So Tanner does live there?'

'I'm not sure. But he didn't tell you that Lucerne Lodge is his family home?'

When she found her voice, her 'no' was forlorn and confused.

'So you see, Rosie, there are lots of reasons why you shouldn't even be "friends" with Tanner Bryant.'

'Oh, Mum,' sobbed Rosie. 'What a mess.'

'It was a mess way back then too ... I did hope I would never have to revisit it. Didn't you ever wonder why I never took you to Borteen beach as a child? It was because I couldn't bear to go past the road to Lucerne Lodge. Still find it hard, even though you live in Borteen now.'

The two women clung together until their tears dried. One miserable because of a memory and secrets kept for so long, the other in shock about the truth surrounding her father's death and Tanner Bryant's deception.

# *Chapter Ten*

Rosie was meeting the girls for brunch. The Sunshine Restaurant was somehow diminished without Tanner as a waiter, but she was also relieved he wasn't there. She hadn't heard from him since the evening at the pizza restaurant but, given what her mother had told her, it was probably for the best. Even so, she examined each of the restaurant staff carefully, just in case. *Don't be silly, Rosie, he's not a waiter. He's a journalist and he lied to you!*

Lucy and Connie arrived together. They had already been clothes shopping, judging by the number of carrier bags they were each holding. A couple of chaotic minutes followed, whilst they put their bags under the table and the three girls hugged each other in turn. Connie and Lucy must also have been to a perfume counter, as their combined scents threatened to drown out the smell of the coffee.

'Rosie, you looked miles away when we came in. Come on, we want to know more about your pizza date,' said Lucy, settling herself onto the bench seat next to her.

'Ancient history now. Don't ask. I think I'd rather forget all about that evening,' Rosie growled.

Lucy put down her menu, a shocked expression on her face. 'That bad, eh?'

Rosie made an effort to smile and sit up straight. She knew she must look like a puppet whose strings were being held taut, but somehow she had to put a brave face on all of this.

'You okay, Rosie? He wasn't mean or anything?' Connie's brow was furrowed with concern.

'I'm fine, and it depends how you define "mean".'

'Is that the "Fucked up, Insecure, Neurotic and Exhausted" kind of fine?' asked Lucy.

'*No*! I … oh, I guess so.' Rosie gave in. She slumped and put her hands over her face.

'I thought as much looking at your poor croissant.'

Rosie glanced down at the shredded mess on her plate. She couldn't remember pulling the pastry into flakes. She took a deep drink of her latte, while Connie and Lucy ordered food and drinks.

'Spill,' demanded Lucy, as soon as the waitress moved away.

Rosie was annoyed as tears started to blur her vision and fall onto her dead croissant. Could she really cry again? She'd already shed enough tears to fill Lucerne Lodge lake. Tanner's hurried exit without explanation had left her wondering what was wrong with her. It had knocked her confidence more than she would even admit to her friends. And then there was the newspaper article, Tanner not being honest about what he was doing and everything her mother had told her.

'Hey, hey, Rosie. Come on, what's up?' Lucy put her arm around her.

It took her a few moments to compose herself enough to speak. She mopped her face with the tissue Connie had thoughtfully put into her hand. Rosie raised her head to face the inquisition of two blue and two brown eyes. 'It's Tanner ...'

'I think we guessed that much.' Connie raised her eyebrows heavenwards.

'He ran away from me at the restaurant, and Mum has asked me not to see him again.'

'Excuse me?' Lucy's voice had acquired an even deeper tone than normal. 'What on earth has it got to do with your mother?'

'He ran away?' said Connie at the same time. 'Why on earth would he do that?'

'Tanner's not who he seems. My mum knew his parents when she was younger and ... oh, it's such a complicated mess.' She came to a halt, her voice sounding nearly hysterical to her own ears.

'He's not who he seems? You mean he doesn't clean for Borden Glass, wait on tables here, advertise pizza and serve at the corner shop?' Connie's expression was a mixture of concern and puzzlement. She glanced around for a moment, as if expecting Tanner to approach the table.

'No ...' Rosie paused, looking into the expectant eyes of her friends.

'But why did he run away?'

'I kissed him.' Rosie tried to swallow the lump in her throat.

'I never had you down for a terrible kisser.' Connie began to laugh and then seemed to realise what she'd said.

'That's not funny.' Rosie sniffed.

'Sorry.'

'He said that he wanted us to be friends, probably given what happened next, he really *did* mean just friends. He freaked out when I kissed him. It wasn't even a passionate kiss.' Rosie blushed. 'I got locked in the loo at the restaurant and Tanner rescued me. I kissed him in relief at being out of that horrible cubicle. He looked absolutely horrified and then did a runner.'

'I hope he at least paid the bill.'

'Oh yes, he did do that.' Rosie was disconcerted that Connie and Lucy were smirking. 'By the way, he's actually a journalist.' She was relieved to see their amusement turn to shock.

'What! So, he was stalking you? Was he after some sort of story?' exclaimed Lucy.

'I'm not absolutely sure about that bit. He was doing all of those different jobs because he was writing an article on low-paid work.' Rosie felt the stirrings of a new uneasiness.

Lucy put her arm around her friend's shoulders. 'Hey, Rosie, is there anything we can do to help you?'

'No, it's too complicated,' said Rosie. 'I think I'd rather forget about the whole sorry episode … put it behind me.'

The girls ate brunch, but Connie and Lucy kept looking at Rosie with worried expressions on their faces. She withdrew even more into herself as she mulled things over and she could see pity in her friends' eyes. They were probably imagining she was thinking of Tanner as a love interest. She managed to stay in the restaurant for an hour and then made an excuse so that she could leave. Her friends made her promise to get in touch with them later so that they knew she was okay.

When she reached home, Rosie considered how grateful she was that she'd opted to rent a tiny cottage on her own, rather than share a bigger one with someone else, or to move in with her mother. There was something satisfying about shutting your own front door, especially if you were feeling as awful as she did today.

She heated a mug of milk. She never drank milk, but there was an ingrained memory from the past of her mother making her hot milk when she was upset or under the weather.

She sat on her rocking chair, a carbon copy of the one at her mother's house, and took a sip of the warm drink. *Yuck*. It didn't taste as nice as she remembered. Maybe she should open a bottle of wine instead. She glanced at the clock. It was only midday – maybe a bit early for wine.

Thinking about her initial attraction to Tanner, she let her mind work on that for a moment. Why couldn't she be like other people? Why couldn't she find someone to love, who loved her back? Why couldn't she have a relationship without complications? Despite her protests to herself, her friends and her mother, deep down she wanted a home and a family of her own. Time seemed against her as she was thirty-one already. She was single again, and her imagined hope for the future had disintegrated.

Rosie began the inevitable self-analysis demanded on those days when you felt that you had made a complete mess of your life.

She was well aware that she had prolonged her relationship with Ollie far longer than was sensible. She should have guessed that it was going nowhere when he made no move to set up home with her. The cracks had begun to appear a full two years before she had finally admitted their relationship wasn't working. Rosie continued her self-assassination. *Why me? Why does everyone else have a normal relationship? Well, apart from Connie and Lucy ...*

Trying to find a life partner was like searching for a tiny diamond in a sack of rice. So many men in the world, but so many rogues, so many ulterior motives and agendas. Where were the honest, hardworking, thoughtful men? The ones you read about in romance novels, who would scoop you up, protect you and fulfil your wildest dreams financially and sexually? Rosie sighed as she all but resigned herself to a life of lonely celibacy as a singleton. *Oh dear, she was starting to sound like Lucy.*

She got up, deciding to open that bottle of wine despite the early hour, and stubbed her toe on the door frame. The resulting tears and feelings of woe were far out of proportion to the injury. She felt so alone. She knew she could phone her mother, or even just turn up at her door, she had fantastic friends, but somehow it wasn't the same.

The fallout from her mother's revelations about her father's death continued to circulate through her head. She dredged up her childhood recollections. Her father was now hazy in her mind. She'd been so young when he'd died, and her memories were more vague impressions of isolated events: being in a boat with her dad, rolling down grassy hills, and huge hugs before he hoisted her onto his shoulders. She supposed her mother must have protected her from the details of what happened when he died. She somehow knew that her father had been found in water, but had never imagined that it was at Lucerne Lodge and had no knowledge of the circumstances that appeared to have led to his death. She wanted to ask her mother more questions, but had no wish to upset her again.

But now it was another question that filled her mind. She'd been so focused on her embarrassment of Tanner doing a runner after she kissed him, his real career and the details of her own father's death, that she'd missed something …

She still didn't really know one hundred per cent that Tanner hadn't deliberately set out to meet her that day, or indeed stalked her as she'd suspected, despite the cover of writing that article. She flicked to the photographs on her phone screen and looked at the one of the note in the coat pocket about her attendance at the auction. It was intriguing and rather unsettling. Had that note been for Tanner?

Even if he had wanted to meet her, the big question was why? Had he found out something about her father's death, their parents' former friendship? But even if he had, what was his motivation for getting to know Rosie as a "friend"?

She concluded that she wasn't sure that she wanted to find out the truth. She was, however, determined to avoid Tanner Bryant in the future.

# *Chapter Eleven*

Bright lights crept into Rosie's awareness as she prised her eyelids open. She turned her head, so that the strip lights overhead didn't blind her and attempted to rearrange her mouth, sure that she'd been slack-jawed and dribbling. Her bones appeared to have melted during the therapy treatment.

The therapist, Anna, stood patiently by the side of the couch. She put a plastic cup of water into Rosie's hand when she finally sat up. Rosie dangled her legs over the edge of the couch as she sipped the cool liquid.

'What did you say this therapy was called?'

'Reiki. Did you enjoy your treatment?'

'I can't remember ever feeling so totally relaxed. I'm not sure I can walk.'

Anna laughed softly. 'You'll be back to normal in a minute or two. Make sure you drink plenty of water for the rest of the day.'

'I saw purple swirly lights behind my eyelids, and it felt like I was miles away. Is that normal?'

'Everyone experiences Reiki in a different way, but the purple lights are common. Purple is a colour associated closely with Reiki.' Anna slipped a business card into Rosie's hand.

'Have you any details of Reiki training, Anna? My friend is looking to set herself up as a therapist. She asked me to have this taster session with you to see what I thought about it.'

'And?'

'Amazingly relaxing. How lucky would I be if my friend was trained in this? In fact, *I* might train in this …' Rosie was astounded that what had started out as simply being a supportive friend was morphing into a genuine interest in therapies.

Anna smiled. 'I'm what's called a Reiki Master, so I do train people. Here's my training leaflet, but it might be best if your friend had a taster treatment too.'

'I'll tell her to come and book in ... as soon as I find her.'

Rosie slowly got off the couch, thanked Anna and went to find Connie.

The health fair was being held in Sowden Guild Hall. Lots of different therapies, clinics and health products were represented on the numerous stalls laid out around the cavernous space. The noise level was tremendous with so many people discussing therapies and treatments. A lot of the stalls were burning incense or perfumed candles, which made the air hazy and full of pungent scents.

Rosie picked up some of the products on an aloe vera stall. She read the descriptions and uses with interest. She promised the stallholder she would return to try a complimentary hand massage as soon as she had found her friend.

She recognised Connie by her bright blue blouse. She was lying on her side on a therapy couch and had a lit candle protruding from what looked like a paper plate in her ear. Connie's eyes were closed, and Rosie stood quietly waiting for her friend's treatment to finish. She wondered what on earth this therapy was and what it was designed to do. It looked like some form of medieval torture.

Connie noticed her as soon as she opened her eyes. The therapist made sure that she sat up carefully and gave her water to drink. Rosie heard her friend asking about training courses in the therapy and how many clients asked for candling. Then she left the therapist to his next client.

'Wow, that was amazing. So relaxing.'

'It looked horrendous. What therapy is it?'

'Hopi ear candles.' Connie yawned. 'It is supposed to remove ear wax and toxins from the body. I found it surprisingly soothing.'

'My Reiki treatment was pretty fantastic too. I'm so chilled. I think my bones have melted. Here, I've got details of training courses for you, but Anna, the Reiki therapist, suggested you try a session first. These taster sessions are such a brilliant idea and good value for five pounds each one.'

'Sounds fab. But I think right now I need a drink and some sugary food to help my light-headedness. Let's investigate the refreshments before we do anything else.'

'I imagine that at an event like this, the café will be low fat, low sugar, low everything.' Rosie pulled a face.

'I hope not,' said Connie. 'I feel the need for a full-strength coffee and a cake.'

'You're not intending to train in all of these therapies are you, Connie?'

'Eventually maybe, but I'll need to pick and choose to begin with.'

'Oooh, I'll be so lucky having a friend who can deliver complete relaxation and health. Make sure you add Reiki to your to-do list.'

‘Are you being cheeky about my new career?’

‘Not at all. I’m even tempted to train in Reiki myself.’ Rosie winked.

‘Goodness, I’d better have a Reiki taster treatment before we leave if you were that impressed.’

‘Where’s Lucy today? Didn’t you try to persuade her to come here too?’

‘She’s gone sailing with her latest man. Tony, is it?’

‘I can never keep up with the names of her boyfriends – she has so many. Sailing? Goodness, I wouldn’t have thought that was Lucy’s thing.’

‘I must admit to giggling when she told me where she was going. She wasn’t best pleased with me.’

Rosie was laughing too as they walked down the aisle between the stalls, but then she froze. *It couldn’t possibly be, could it?* A man lay flat on his back on a massage couch, with a therapist placing crystals on his face and body. It was his blond curly hair that Rosie had noticed. Thankfully, his eyes were closed, so he wasn’t aware of her stare.

Rosie pulled Connie to one side. ‘I’m sure that’s Tanner over there,’ she whispered.

Connie walked past the couch to have a better look at the man. The therapist applied a pink crystal disc to his forehead.

‘Could I sign up for a session later, please?’ asked Connie.

Rosie worried that the man would open his eyes, so she turned to the table behind her. She scuttled past to join Connie after her friend had put her name down for a treatment.

‘Connie! That could have been really embarrassing.’

Her friend linked her arm in Rosie’s, laughed and winked, as they walked towards the refreshment sign. ‘I couldn’t be sure if it was him or not. I only saw him that once as a waiter. Does it matter if it is Tanner anyway?’

‘No, I don’t suppose it does. I’m ninety per cent sure it was him. I’m still curious about why he ran off that night, but I’d be far too mortified to challenge him about it. I’d prefer to avoid him forever.’ Rosie decided she didn’t want to tell Connie any more than that until everything was clear in her own head.

‘We’d better stay out of sight for a while then. Oh, I spy cake.’

They queued at the food counter, and Connie got increasingly excited about the range of cupcakes in the glass cabinet.

Rosie's relaxed feeling had gone and tension pulled at her muscles, as all of the unsettling thoughts concerning Tanner's desertion in the restaurant and his motives in the first place flooded her mind yet again.

'Rosie ... Rosie?' Connie was waving a hand in front of her face. 'You're miles away. With a blond-headed man by any chance? Have you decided what you'd like to eat and drink?'

'Surprise me.' Her heart wasn't in choosing cake any more, as her mind stretched outside to the possible Tanner sighting. Why would he be at an alternative health fair? *He must be writing another article*, she supposed.

When they'd eaten, the girls went back to the main hall. Rosie scanned the crowd for Tanner, but he, or at least his lookalike at the crystal healing stand, appeared to have vanished.

Nevertheless, she couldn't stop herself gravitating to the crystal therapy stall. The couch was empty and the therapist had a vacant slot. Rosie tried her hardest to see the other names on the list, but the woman had a cloth obscuring the earlier entries. Rosie paid her five pounds and settled herself on the couch.

It was hard to believe the different types of sensation the various crystals the therapist used produced in her body. The amethyst placed on her forehead radiated heat, and the rose quartz over her heart seemed to soak up the residual tension. This treatment zonked her out just as much as the Reiki. She opened her eyes, feeling sleepy and relaxed again.

'Rosie, I wondered if you would mind giving your reactions to your treatment to this gentleman? He's writing an article on alternative therapies.'

Rosie's tension arrived back in her body with a thump. She turned with resignation towards a very surprised Tanner Bryant. 'Hello, Tanner. Fancy meeting you here.'

# *Chapter Twelve*

Tanner knew that his face must show complete surprise that his next interviewee was Rosie. The crystal therapist looked from one to the other as she realised something was going on. Tanner froze and couldn't speak.

'Do you two know each other?' she asked.

'Mmm, yes, sort of,' replied Rosie, staring at Tanner as if she were a rabbit in the headlights.

'Rosie, can we go for a coffee? I need to explain some things …' he began.

The other woman standing next to Rosie swept in between them. She looked vaguely familiar as she stood with her hands on her hips, as if she was ready to protect Rosie from attack. Tanner started to speak again, but the woman held up her hand to silence him.

'Come on, Rosie. Let's get out of here. You don't have to speak to *him.*'

The emphasis on the word "him" must have made the crystal therapist even more suspicious. Did he imagine her inching a bit further away?

Rosie's companion gave him a withering look and whisked Rosie away as if Tanner was some sort of pervert. Rosie began to protest, but eventually allowed herself to be led away.

'I'm not sure what just happened, Mr Bryant, but I think I'd prefer not to take any further part in setting up interviews for you,' said the crystal therapist coldly.

Her stare made Tanner feel like a criminal. He thanked her for what she'd done already and decided to abandon his interviews.

He drove back to Lucerne Lodge with a troubled mind, wishing yet again that he'd told Rosie exactly why he'd wanted to meet her when they'd been out for that pizza in Sowden.

Even taking Trixie for a walk failed to calm him. He sat at his father's desk and tried to write some emails, but his thoughts kept straying back to that expression on Rosie's face.

He suddenly wanted to escape this current reality and go back to his life in London. At least there he was his own man, not living forever in the shadow of his father and his strict standards and immovable expectations.

But who was he kidding? In London he'd still be Tanner Bryant the loner. He knew that his father was bitterly disappointed that he hadn't married "well" and produced the required heir to his business empire. Was that yet another rebellion on Tanner's part, or just bad luck? A couple of years ago he'd come close to proposing, only to discover, almost at the last minute, that the girl he'd imagined besotted with him had actually researched his family, knew exactly who his father was and how much he was worth. She'd targeted Tanner specifically for a cushy life.

Even just allowing these thoughts to cross his mind had Tanner reliving the pain of finding Mary's notes about him and his family in a notebook she'd dropped by accident in his flat. When he'd found it under the table, he'd innocently opened it because he hadn't seen it before and then he hadn't been able to stop reading the information written inside, his disbelief growing, his imagined happy future crumbling as the words became like daggers as he read.

He'd felt betrayed, disappointed in himself and in Mary, and that had had a lasting effect on him. Who could be that calculating, or such a good actress? Even if she might have had some real feelings for him, things could never have been the same between them as the trust had gone. It had all but destroyed Tanner and his belief in happy-ever-afters. Just thinking about that episode in his life made him so miserable.

He fervently wished that he knew the actual truth about the Rosie file. How wonderful would it be to speak to her completely openly with no barriers between them? But his doubts about his father's motivations for employing the private investigator and Tanner's own awful past experience were huge issues to make him hesitate. And now, with his curiosity and reticence, he'd completely destroyed any hope of trust or friendship with Rosie, and he still didn't have real answers to the questions he'd had in the first place.

He picked up the private investigator's file about Rosie and flung it in exasperation across the room. It hit the door and all of the papers and photographs flew out. Images of Rosie were now scattered all across the floor.

As he wondered what to do, how to find a way forward, a call came in from the clinic. Michael Bryant's condition had worsened, and they were asking him to come without delay to his father's bedside. The caller's tone was serious, and Tanner's heart began a rhythmic thumping.

Even if they didn't have a close relationship, his father had been such a vital man all of his life. Tanner found it difficult to contemplate that his last memories of him would be as a fragile shell, shrunken and diminished. His father was not a good patient and, consequently, had often been impatient and brusque whenever he visited, as if Tanner was somehow to blame for him being sick or confined to the clinic.

He grabbed his coat and car keys and rushed out of the door. There were several things he still needed to ask Michael Bryant before it was too late.

Tanner had learned over the years to be well prepared before he put any question to his father. If there was a hole in your argument, then Michael Bryant would find it and enlarge it, before making you feel like a complete and utter idiot.

His lack of affection for his father was sad, tragic even. Michael Bryant had always been so distant, formal and stern. It was his mother who Tanner had idolised, even though, she too had little time for him whilst running her own fashion business. As a small child, Tanner had relished her huge hugs, even if they were infrequent. She had moved back to New York when his parents divorced. There had never seemed to be any question of Tanner going with her. No one had recognised the pain this had caused him. As far as he could remember, neither of his parents had ever asked him how he felt about the situation. He'd hidden his raw wound under a plaster of academic achievement but had vowed that he would not bring a child into the world himself, unless he was completely sure of his partner and had sufficient time to devote to his son or daughter.

A short while later, after a journey he couldn't really remember making, he reversed his black sports car into a visitor's slot outside of the imposing white façade of Primrose Clinic on the outskirts of Sowden. A solemn-faced nurse was waiting for him in the reception hall.

'Mr Bryant. I'm so sorry …'

Tanner's heart lurched. He could tell by her face what had happened. 'He's dead?' He cut off her rehearsed speech. 'Dead?' He felt stunned, cheated.

'Yes, about fifteen minutes ago, just after we made the call to you, in fact.' She looked upset, the redness of her cheeks accentuated by the white of her uniform.

Tanner was tempted to walk straight back out of the door. *No, I'm going to ask my questions.* 'Can I see him?'

'Of course, follow me.'

The woman was probably imagining that Tanner was distressed, but he was actually seething with pent-up anger.

The nurses had tidied the room and put a vase of flowers and a cross on the bedside. The room smelled of air freshener spray. Michael Bryant appeared pale, but just as if he was asleep, with the white sheet neatly folded down beneath his chin. He actually looked better than he had for a long while, without the oxygen mask and bleeping machines around him.

'I'll leave you with your father. Take as long as you like.' The nurse smiled and put her hand on his arm for a few seconds in what she must have imagined was a comforting gesture.

Tanner closed the door. He knew that it was irrational to question his father now, but the tension that had been building in him during the journey to the clinic drove him on.

'Why were you always so strict and distant, Dad? I can't ever remember getting a hug or any praise from you. Why? For goodness sake, why? Am I so unlovable?'

He voiced aloud his well-rehearsed questions about his mother, about Rosie, about himself. He knew he would never get any answers, but he paused after each one just the same. By the end of his monologue question time, he'd reduced himself to frustrated tears, which he batted away with his hands in bewilderment. The shell of the man in the bed hadn't moved, of course, and, for once, had not made acerbic comments. Tanner could take the silence no longer and, flinging open the door, he rushed out and back down the corridor.

The nurse who had greeted him when he arrived tried to waylay him, but he ignored her and dashed to his car. The need to get away was overwhelming.

His mind numb, he selected the wrong gear and succeeded in reversing into the wall behind his car. Not even pausing to have a look at any damage, he slammed the gear stick into first and screeched out of the car park.

On autopilot, he turned his car onto the ring road and headed down the coast. He kept going, his foot hard on the accelerator. He flashed his lights at any driver who impeded his progress as he drove aggressively south. After a while, the torrent of feelings began to subside, and he became conscious that he was doing 40 mph in the slow lane of a dual carriageway. With the return to full awareness, his body was achingly weary and he knew that he had to pull over.

The next junction name surprised him – Trinam – he'd not been there for years. He'd driven quite a way. Turning off, his focus came back to the sunny day, the greenery and, in the distance, the sea. His father had chosen a lovely day to die.

He drove to a car park near to the beach, ignored the pay and display sign, and walked onto the sand. He would eventually have to go home and face the barrage of sympathy and paperwork, but, for now, he was a beachcomber. He kicked off his shoes, pulled off his socks and rolled his chinos up to his knees.

The sand felt cool and surprisingly hard beneath his feet as he walked towards the water's edge. On the way, he turned over a pebble and noticed a dead crab. The salty sea air invaded his nostrils. As the surf washed over his toes, the tears began to well up. This must be grief, but was it for the loss of his father or for himself? The pain of what ifs and maybes thundered around in his head, and he was thankful this part of the beach was deserted.

He would have to play dutiful son and executor to his outwardly successful father, but how different the reality – so full of unexpressed feelings and missed possibilities to have a proper relationship with his son.

# *Chapter Thirteen*

'Michael Bryant died,' Frances told Rosie as soon as she came through the door of her mother's house. She had obviously been waiting to tell her daughter the news because the announcement came out in a rush, before Rosie had time to say anything. She handed a bunch of flowers to her mother and shrugged out of her coat.

'How did you find out?'

'There was a death notice in the newspaper.'

Frances diligently read the local free newspaper, *The Sowden Gazette*, every week.

'I was just on my way to tell you. There was an announcement at work. I wonder if it was sudden?'

'Expected, I think. He died in a clinic. Rosie, will you come to the funeral with me?'

'What! I didn't expect you to ask me that. I'd actually prefer not to, Mum. Tanner will be there and other people from Borden Glass. Why on earth do you want to go anyway?'

The last time Michael Bryant had been mentioned by her mother, Frances had seemed terribly bitter about the past. Now she wanted to go to his funeral? It didn't make any sense.

'Seriously, Mum, why would you want to go to the funeral of the man you say was responsible for Dad's death?'

'I just feel I want to say goodbye to someone who was a dear friend before everything went wrong. We used to have such fun and often danced the night away. We'd talk for hours, actually mainly John, Georgia and myself. Michael was the quiet one.' Frances spoke with a wistful tone in her voice. She took the wrapping off the flowers and began to trim the stems of the roses.

'But, why do I have to come too?'

'Please, Rosie. I don't want to go on my own. How sad would that be?'

Frances was cutting the stems of the flowers shorter and shorter in her distracted state. Rosie had to put her hand out to stop her cutting again, or else the flowers would have been too short for the vase.

'Okay, I'll come with you. As long as we sit at the back and out of sight.'

Rosie didn't feel happy about the prospect of the funeral at all.

Rosie stayed over at her mother's house on the night before Michael Bryant's funeral. After a night of tossing and turning, with wild dreams about Tanner and coffins, she peered into the mirror and decided that she didn't look her best. She viciously applied under-eye concealer and prodded at a spot on her chin. Her hair refused to be tamed so she had no choice but to scoop it into a clip at the back of her neck. The result made her look quite studious and severe.

She pulled at the hem of her black dress. It suddenly felt too short for a funeral and she wished she'd packed a suit. The collar of the dress wouldn't drape properly, no matter how many times she rearranged it. She scolded her reflection in the mirror. *Why are you worrying so much about how you look? It's a funeral, for goodness sake. Tanner will be in no state to notice you anyway. And, while we're at it, why are you still thinking about that man at all?*

She stormed downstairs in a thoroughly bad mood.

Frances, on the other hand, was the picture of elegance. Her black suit was teamed with a cream blouse. Her handbag and shoes were matching black taffeta with silk detailing. The pearls at her throat and ears added an expensive air to the outfit. Her swinging grey hair was immaculately styled. Her mother checked the contents of her clutch bag, and Rosie watched as she folded a large pile of tissues and put them inside before snapping the catch shut. 'Ready.' She smiled. 'Or, at least as ready as I'll ever be.'

Rosie noticed a small gold locket beneath the pearls. She couldn't recall ever seeing it before. When she mentioned it, Frances claimed that she'd had it for a long time, but Rosie couldn't read the strange expression in her mother's eyes.

'You look beautiful, Mum.'

'Thank you, darling. You have lipstick on your teeth.'

Rosie rushed to the mirror to remove the red stain and, once again, asked her reflection why she didn't have her mother's apparently effortless style. The dull weather, with wall-to-wall grey skies, although thankfully no rain, seemed to echo Rosie's lack of enthusiasm for where they were going.

As they approached the church, its spire visible for miles, they could see that the funeral was very well attended. Parking a long way down the lane, as there were so many cars there already, they walked back to the church.

The mourners had gathered in the churchyard. Rosie thought the groups in black clothing resembled crows. Some were sneaking a last cigarette before the service. Rosie made a mental note to make it known that she wanted people to wear bright colours at her own funeral. Frances led her away from the church lych gate, and Rosie's heels sank into the soft ground.

She recognised staff and managers from Borden Glass in the groups of people waiting. She tried to avoid their eyes, as if this would prevent questions about why she was there. She nodded quickly to the few she couldn't avoid who appeared to recognise her.

The hearse arrived at eleven o'clock on the dot, followed by two black family cars. Tanner looked striking in his dark suit, but his face was gaunt and he had shadowed eyes. Rosie wished she'd worn a hat so she had something to hide beneath. She studied the blades of grass beneath her feet until she was sure Tanner had moved past where she was standing. Then it was her mother's turn to hide behind Rosie.

'What's the matter, Mum? Who are you trying to avoid?'

'Georgia, Michael's ex. I don't want her to see me yet, if at all,' hissed Frances. Rosie caught sight of an angular woman wearing black and white. 'She must be over from America.'

The coffin was wheeled up the path to the church door on a trolley. As it stopped, six men, including Tanner, hoisted it onto their shoulders and carried it into the church. Tanner's hair looked very blond against the polished mahogany of the casket.

'Come on, Rosie, they're going in. We'll sit at the back as you suggested.'

The unusually sharp tone made Rosie glance at her mother. Did she imagine the glint of tears in her eyes?

Georgia passed by them in a cloud of expensive perfume. She turned back and faced them.

'Well, well, Frances Phillips. Fancy seeing you here.' There was a frostiness in her tone. 'And this must be your daughter.'

'Still looking good, Georgia,' commented Frances.

Georgia moved on without another word or glance.

'So that's Tanner's mother and the woman who …?' Rosie trailed off not wanting to say *the woman who my dad had an affair with that ultimately led to his death.*

'Yes, she hasn't changed at all.'

They waited until most of the other mourners had gone ahead and then slipped into the church.

Inside, the scents of flowers and incense enveloped them. Not religious in the traditional sense, Rosie nevertheless loved ecclesiastical buildings. Her mother's head was bent, possibly in prayer, but Rosie was examining the jewelled colours of the stained glass and the intricate embroideries.

Judging by the lack of singing volume during the first hymn, it was obvious most of the congregation weren't regular churchgoers either. In contrast, Tanner's voice rang out loud and clear. Rosie was glad of the pillar in front of her. She could hide behind it, but peep out if she wanted to catch a glimpse of Tanner.

In dark suit, shirt and tie, his wayward hair brushed and tied tightly at the nape of his neck, it struck Rosie that he looked very contained, very alone, even if his mother did keep touching his arm and whispering in his ear.

Rosie was still bewildered about what she had done wrong that night at the restaurant. How had she have completely misread the situation and scared this attractive man off? But then she reminded herself that there was much more to her meeting with Tanner that she still didn't understand. It was far removed from a simple boy-meets-girl situation.

She was so wrapped up in her thoughts that she jumped when Frances grasped her hand. The minister was talking about Michael Bryant's early life and achievements, and Frances had channels of tears running down her cheeks. Rosie picked up her mother's bag and extracted some of the carefully folded tissues. Frances clasped them to her face.

Rosie was rather bewildered. Her mother had claimed to hate this man at one point in her life, so why so many tears over him in death? The tears continued to stream down Frances' face. Despite what she had said about her locket, she now turned it between her fingers as if she was holding some kind of talisman against evil.

Tanner made his way to the lectern. He turned to face the congregation and Rosie was once again struck by the pallor of his skin. The dark rings beneath his eyes suggested he was starved of sleep. His blond curls were beginning to spring rebelliously out of their fastening. Rosie peered around the pillar, and her heart reached out to lend him strength. His voice was strong and loud despite how unhappy he looked, and somehow that gave his words even more poignancy.

As she listened to his tribute to his father, tears began to gather in her own eyes in reaction to the memories Tanner related. When he halted for a few moments, overcome with emotion, Rosie had a large lump in her own throat and reached for Frances' bag to find the tissue stash had all gone. The service was having the same effect on many of those present, and Tanner's speech was punctuated with nose blowing and even at one point a loud sob from somewhere near the front.

Rosie had been too young to remember her own father's funeral. She must ask her mother about it and if she'd gone to it. It suddenly seemed very important to have details of some of the things she would never know unless her mother told her about them.

There was a tribute from the Managing Director of Borden Glass relating to Michael Bryant's professional life. Another hymn was followed by the closing prayer, and then the coffin was carried back down the nave, destined for a private family burial in the churchyard. The magnificent mahogany casket preceded everyone out of the church, and it wasn't until it had disappeared from view that it occurred to Rosie that Tanner would more than likely be standing outside of the church door to thank mourners for attending the funeral.

Frances tidied her face and hair using a little compact mirror from her bag. She did a good job, but couldn't disguise the puffiness around her eyes and the red tip of her nose.

'Do I look presentable?'

'Lovely as always,' said Rosie. Her fears of having to speak to Tanner were accumulating as tension in her chest. 'Is there a back way out, Mum?'

'Don't be ridiculous. You can't sneak out of a funeral.'

'I don't want to see Tanner today. He's got enough going on.'

'We haven't much choice, dear.' Her mother's hand brushed the back of hers for a few comforting seconds.

Rosie gathered her things and stood up, her uneasiness mounting.

# *Chapter Fourteen*

Tanner was mechanically grasping and shaking the hands offered to him, as people filed out of the church. The service had gone by in a blur. He was very clear of what his father would expect of him in this situation and, for once, he concentrated on trying to live up to his standards. His father's friends and business associates made up the majority of the mourners. Tanner could see standards and expectations in their eyes too, but very little actual grief at his father's passing.

It took him a few moments to register whose hand he had just grasped. A slender hand with a flower-shaped ring. He looked up, speaking much louder than he had intended. 'Rosie! What are you doing here?' The words were out of his mouth before he could stop them. 'Sorry, I mean, I didn't expect to see you here ... but thank you for coming.'

He was aware of the queue bunching up behind her and knew that he only had a few moments to speak to her. Once again, he was annoyed that he hadn't had the conversation with her before this about his past behaviour.

He wished for the millionth time that he didn't find her intriguing, that he didn't notice how her hair moved and her eyes flashed. If only Michael Bryant had been more forthcoming about his relationship to her family. *Too late now.*

'My mother wanted to pay her respects,' Rosie said, inclining her head towards the woman behind her.

'Mrs Phillips, I presume.' Tanner took Frances' hand. She was an elegant, shorter version of Rosie. Someone had told him once that if you wanted to know what a woman would look like at an older age, you needed to study her mother. The signs were that Rosie would age well. 'I hope you'll join us later for refreshments at Lucerne Lodge.' Maybe then he could take Rosie to one side and have that long overdue conversation.

'Oh no. We couldn't,' said Rosie and her mother together. They moved on and Tanner continued shaking the remaining few hands. He tried to watch the two women walk away from the church, but the minister spoke to him and he had to turn away.

'Your father was a pillar of this community and so generous to the church.'

Tanner smiled. 'I think you'll find he has been generous after his death too, Reverend.'

'Lovely man.' The minister shook his head. 'He will be much missed in the congregation.'

Not attending regular church services, from when he was old enough to refuse to go, had been another of Tanner's rebellions. His father had expected him to be a choir boy and then to study for his confirmation. Tanner had successfully resisted both. He wasn't sure how strong his father's faith was – perhaps the Sunday ritual had been just another part of his business networking practices, like the squash playing and rounds of golf – but maybe he was being unfair to think like that.

Tanner would have preferred to escape from all of the formalities and dutiful son pretence, but there was still the burial and formal buffet to be tackled. He was sure that he wouldn't be able to face anything to eat himself. He tried to remember the last time he'd eaten a proper meal ... no wonder the waistband of his trousers was so loose.

The marquee was flapping its white canvas on the lawn at Lucerne Lodge once again. Tanner wanted to give his father a good send off. The event felt as if someone was missing and, of course, it was Michael Bryant himself. Quiet, but charming at social events, particularly if he was host, Tanner kept expecting to see his father's tall figure striding through the crowd. Michael's friends were enjoying catching up with each other's news, and occasionally Tanner observed a look of horror and guilt pass over their faces when they spotted him and, he imagined, felt they were perhaps enjoying themselves a little too much for a funeral.

Rosie had said that her mother wanted to pay her respects to his father. Did that tally with Michael's assertion that he owed a debt to the family?

He took a drink from one of the loaded trays and went to slip outside. In need of some time alone to decant his feelings, about both his father's passing and Rosie's appearance at the funeral earlier, he was waylaid by several couples expressing concern about his loss. He never managed to make it out of the tent after all.

One man, whose name Tanner couldn't recall, questioned what was to become of his father's business interests. Another asked if Tanner was going to make Lucerne Lodge his permanent home. It was a question Tanner had not yet answered for himself. Could this large house ever be his home, or would the ghosts of the past prevent him from settling here?

He began to feel like a ball being batted around a tennis court as he spoke to so many people and was exhausted by the time the last guest went home in the early evening. He stood on the lawn, looking at the house silhouetted against the dusk. *What did his father's will say about the house?* he wondered. Would he want to live here if it now belonged to him, or would he be better off selling it?

Rosie was drained after the funeral. Her mother's reaction to Michael Bryant's death puzzled her immensely. Why would she be so upset about the passing of a man who had caused so much distress in her life? They had been friends when they were younger, true, but surely Frances' husband's infidelity and death would have taken away any feelings of affection? Rosie could only suppose it had reminded her mother of her own mortality. This thought set up another worry chain – could her mother be ill and keeping it to herself?

She went out for a drink with Lucy that evening, hoping to relax and maybe to talk over her thoughts with her friend. However, after an hour of Lucy relating the details of her latest failed relationship with Tony, the sailor, she knew that she would have been better off having a quiet evening at home.

She loved her friend, but she couldn't help secret amusement at how being dumped by Tony had made Lucy look at their dating history in a very different light. Sailing, which for the last couple of weeks had been the best thing she'd ever done, was now the worst experience of Lucy's life.

'The smell of fishy water, Rosie – awful. Constant wet feet, freezing cold, damp sandwiches. Yuck! Why couldn't he have had a yacht instead of a stupid dinghy?'

Love and hate were truly close together, and Lucy had learned to switch from one to the other depending on the current state of her love life.

Rosie purposely didn't drink alcohol and was determined not to stay out too late because she had a busy schedule at work for the next few days. She listened to Lucy's woes, but at the same time she was mentally compiling a check list of things she needed to accomplish.

'Lucy, I do wish you would relax about this meeting a man thing. I'm sure you would meet someone nicer if you did.'

'I wish I was like you, Rosie, not bothered at all about having a man in my life.'

Rosie smiled. Lucy didn't realise the true state of her feelings at all.

# *Chapter Fifteen*

'Surely you want to speak to Mrs Frances Phillips?' asked Rosie for a second time.

The voice on the other end of the telephone line was starting to sound impatient. 'The request is for Miss Rosie Phillips to attend the reading of the late Michael Bryant's will at Sadler's Solicitors' Borteen office on Wednesday at one in the afternoon. If you're Rosie Phillips, then the request is for you.'

'But, I don't ... *didn't* know Mr Bryant personally. It must be my mother's invitation, surely?'

'I don't wish to be rude, but I have passed on the message I was asked to give to you, and this telephone call will be followed by an official letter confirming all of the details. If you still have a problem when you've read the letter, perhaps you could contact us again.'

Rosie knew she detected frustration in the woman's voice, but she couldn't help her shock and curiosity at being asked to attend the reading of Michael Bryant's will.

She rang her mother straight away and asked if she'd been invited too – she had. There was a strange tone in Frances' voice when she spoke about it.

Her mother repeated what Rosie had just said to her in a voice that sounded as if it was a recording playback set to extra slow. 'So, *you've* been invited to attend?'

'Yes, and I don't really know why.'

'At least we can travel together.' Frances didn't sound too thrilled about the idea.

Rosie walked cautiously into the solicitor's large office on Wednesday afternoon. Her mother was trailing behind her like a lost dog. For once, Frances didn't look her elegant self. She appeared to have aged ten years since the funeral. Rosie was at a loss to explain this, and Frances refused to comment when Rosie had asked if anything was wrong.

A man in a sharply cut suit and designer dark-rimmed glasses shuffled papers on an old-fashioned oak desk. Chairs, arranged in two rows, were already half full. The blinds, virtually closed, shut out the sun. Rosie and her mother slipped into seats at the back.

Rosie studied the gold pattern on the red carpet as she composed herself and then allowed her eyes to scan the room with curiosity. Tanner sat, motionless, facing forward on one of the front seats. His mother was holding court in a corner with several men in suits. Her high-pitched American tones were unmistakable. The Managing Director of Borden Glass was talking to a man she'd seen at the funeral. She didn't recognise the other people present.

'Shall I begin, Mr Bryant?' The man behind the desk addressed Tanner.

'Yes, please, Justin.'

When he was sure he had everyone's attention, the solicitor, who introduced himself as Justin Sadler, stood up with a sheaf of papers in his hand. 'It isn't usual these days to have a will reading event such as this, but we are here to read the will of the late Michael Joseph Bryant … who left instructions that things should be done this way …'

Rosie found her concentration wandering as the legalese echoed around the room. The atmosphere was stuffy, and Justin Sadler's voice a low drone. She heard her name mentioned and was confused as she tried to take in what had just been said, and then Tanner began to shout …

'*Sister*? What sister?' Tanner swallowed down the swear words that were threatening to erupt from his mouth but didn't seem at all appropriate at the reading of his father's will. He didn't normally swear out loud, but every man had his limits, and this was ridiculous. Absolutely ludicrous, in fact.

'Mr Bryant … Tanner … I understand that this might all be an enormous shock, but I have a duty to read your father's wishes verbatim. There are conventions to be observed. You will, of course, have the opportunity to comment and ask me questions later.' Justin Sadler, pulled at the lapels of his dark suit jacket, his face showing obvious alarm.

'Shock, *shock*? I'll say it's a shock. I've lived for thirty-one years with no mention of any … sister.' Tanner was aware his voice was getting louder, but he didn't seem to be able to stop his uncharacteristic outburst. The fact that he was reacting like this was upsetting him almost as much as the cause for his eruption. He ran a finger around the collar of his crisp white shirt, which suddenly felt much too tight. His silk tie appeared intent on strangling him. 'Is she here?'

Tanner stood up and scanned the room. His eyes found Rosie Phillips sitting on the back row near to the door. He hadn't seen her arrive. Hadn't been aware she was there until their eyes met. He felt a familiar and, it now seemed, totally inappropriate jolt of interest dive down his spine, before his father's voice arrived in his head to warn about the perils of scandal to the Bryant family. He mentally slotted back the icy boards of protection around his heart; Lord knew he'd needed them enough over the years to guard against his mother, father, his professional world and now it appeared against this woman. He felt the light go out of his eyes as he purposely extinguished any open vulnerability and allowed the habitual ruthlessness to return as he straightened his spine. Tanner Bryant, the island, was back – suited, booted and ready to face the world.

When he'd found the private investigator's file about Rosie Phillips on his father's desk, he'd been curious. He'd set out to meet the girl Michael Bryant had shown such an active interest in. What had his darling nanny always said, "curiosity killed the cat"? Of all the roles he'd ever imagined Rosie had played in his father's life, daughter hadn't been the one he'd given more than a fleeting thought.

The whole room was frozen with an expectant silence. Rosie visibly drew back in her chair and blanched under Tanner's furious gaze, and indeed the looks of everyone else in the room. She looked like a rabbit caught in the proverbial headlights. The cornflower-blue eyes Tanner had found so fascinating, were wide with … what? Shock? Fear? It dawned on him that, until this moment, Rosie more than likely hadn't known the truth about her parentage either.

The older woman sitting next to her, who had been introduced as Rosie's mother at the funeral, began to cry. As tears streamed down her cheeks, the woman put her hands over her face and rocked in her chair.

'With respect, Mr Bryant, please allow me to continue.' Without waiting for a reply, the solicitor repositioned his glasses with a visibly shaking hand, lifted the document from his desk and began to read again, cutting off any more argument and causing everyone in the room to turn back to him. He repeated the paragraph that had caused Tanner to explode in a slow and deliberate voice, his cultured tones echoing around the silent room.

'I divide my estate equally between my son, Tanner Bryant, and my daughter, Rosie Phillips, with the request that they jointly work together to run the businesses, house and lands for a minimum period of twelve months before considering the sale or division of all, or any part of these assets.'

Tanner's intake of breath surprised even himself with its volume, as the implications of the last part of the earth-shattering paragraph became clear. He didn't dare glance behind him to where Rosie was sitting, no doubt as stunned as he was.

*Michael Bryant's daughter. That meant she really was his sister.*

How could that be?

How could Michael Bryant, no matter how tumultuous the relationship between father and son, have kept something so hugely significant from Tanner?

A surge of anger began to rise up through his body. How dare his father leave him in this mess, saddle him with this woman, not tell him face to face what was to happen after his death? After all, there had been ample time to talk to him, to explain why he changed his will not long before he died. What happened to his father's well-worn phrase – "honesty is our byword"?

The foundations on which Tanner had built his life were crashing down like a tower of cards, tumbling around him. What else was a lie? What else had been hidden, covered up, conveniently not mentioned? And why, after all he'd been through relationship-wise, had he had an inkling of attraction to Rosie Phillips, of all women? *Fool!*

He'd been intrigued about why his father had gone to such lengths to find out all about Rosie. She was born in the same year as Tanner; her birthday was in June, his in April. The fact that Michael Bryant had asked a private investigator to prepare the file made it possible that his father had suspected rather than known that Rosie Phillips shared his blood.

What had convinced him and satisfied him sufficiently for him to change his will to recognise Rosie publicly as his daughter and give her such a huge bequest? And why on earth had his father insisted on trying to tie the two of them together like this? Tanner's head was beginning to ache with all of the somersaulting questions.

He recalled the nurses at the clinic telling him about that row with Georgia, his mother. *Is this what it had been about?*

He schooled his face to a calm and impassive expression. This was a tremendous shock, but he had to regain his composure and move on. What had his father always said? *Put a mask over your real feelings, son, it helps you to maintain dignity and gives you choices over how to react to a situation, however dire it or the implications of it may be.* Dire didn't cover this one – life-changing, earth-shattering? *Calm*, Tanner, *calm ... and breathe ...*

He hadn't had a conventional upbringing. His nanny had taught him about love, sharing and consideration, but his father had passed on the belief system of the Bryants, mainly maxims about maintaining the reputation of the family and increasing their wealth and status.

What a fool he'd been, allowing himself to be interested in Rosie Phillips. *Idiot, complete prize idiot.*

The will reading continued. There were minor bequests for the gardener at Lucerne Lodge, as well as for the cook, his father's driver and Tanner's old nanny – the nanny who had been more constant in his life than either his mother or father had ever been.

Tanner could see that his mother, who had flown from her home in America for her ex-husband's funeral, was getting twitchy. She hadn't been mentioned yet, but then did she really expect to be when his parents hadn't been together as man and wife since Georgia had run back to her homeland and, in effect, ceased to be mother to five-year-old Tanner? He knew they'd always been in touch, but still …

Tanner wished now he'd been looking at his mother when he'd had his earlier outburst, to see if her face gave him any clues. He was intrigued to know if Georgia had known about Rosie Phillips all along, or recently, or not at all. He concluded that she must know, or at least suspect, as she wasn't showing any extreme reaction to the will now as far as he could tell. Could this truth be the reason she'd left all those years ago? He needed to speak to her to find out her side of this story, but they had such a formal, distant relationship these days, he wasn't confident she'd tell him what she knew in any case.

Right at the end of the will, almost as an afterthought – and Tanner was pretty sure his father had done this on purpose – Georgia's name was linked to a pocket watch and a pearl necklace. Tanner guessed his mother would be disappointed with just these. He'd got the impression she was always short of funds and must surely have been hoping for a deathbed pay-out from her ex.

Rosie sat at the back of the room and wanted the floor to open up and swallow her whole. Mortified, shocked and full of embarrassment, she'd squirmed in her chair under the gaze of a horrified-looking Tanner Bryant and the astonishment of everyone else in the room. Only her shock at what had been said by the solicitor and Tanner's outburst had kept her sitting there to listen to the rest of the will.

The words were still echoing in her head, especially the statement following the part where Tanner had erupted – "The said Tanner Bryant and Rosie Phillips shall share equally ownership of my estate Lucerne Lodge and my business interests, including Borden Glass plc." Rosie felt her mouth form an "o", as the shock took a greater hold on her. Why had Michael Bryant bequeathed her anything at all?

She'd naively thought she was only here to support her mother, as an old friend of Michael Bryant. What a joke that her mother had said she was *just* an old friend. If the will was to be believed, she was much more than that. Propriety demanded that Rosie sit still and listen to the requests of a dead man. A dead man, whose funeral she had attended with her mother, having no idea that they were actually related. The implications of him being her father were only just sinking in. Rosie couldn't even name the confusing emotions boiling around inside of her.

*Her father!*

How could that be?

And the enraged man at the front of the room was her brother?

How could *that* be?

The question went around and around in her head.

Why this man of all men? Tanner Bryant, the first man she'd been remotely interested in for years. Her stomach churned. They'd flirted a little over the last few weeks. She'd even kissed him – thankfully, not a lingering kiss. What if they'd taken it further? It would have been so easy to do so.

*My God, I could have slept with my brother!*

She'd thought about it, let herself dream about Tanner even. Dreamt about those strong, long fingers in her hair, caressing her naked skin. *What a mess*. No, more than that – this was a tragedy, like something out of a novel even.

Tanner had obviously been unaware about their close connection too. Although he had reacted very strangely when she'd kissed him, so maybe he'd had an inkling or a suspicion at least. Rosie had absolutely no wish to be shackled to him by the terms of this will for a year that would surely be some form of ultimate torture. She didn't want anything to do with this unexpected legacy. True, like most people, she'd dreamed of a big lottery win, but this win, if it could be called such a thing, had huge strings attached. It all felt wrong.

The implications could be life changing, but she didn't necessarily want her life to be changed in this way. All she wanted was to find that special man with whom to share her dreams – she'd mistakenly thought she might potentially have done that when she'd met Tanner Bryant.

Her mother was snivelling next to her, her face buried in a handful of tissues. Rosie needed an urgent conversation with Frances, but first she needed to regain control over her emotions, or else she might shatter their closely bonded relationship forever. Her crying was irritating Rosie as it was.

How could her mother have let her believe that her beloved Dada was her real father? She'd grieved all of these years, only to find she wasn't even related to the man. *Outrageous.*

And how had her mother kept such a huge secret for so long? Maybe it simply wasn't true and Michael Bryant had been deluded. Rosie crossed her fingers, but remembering the look on her mother's face during Tanner's outburst had her discounting that possibility. The expression on her mother's face right now, the tears pooling in her eyes, said that this enormous revelation was indeed the truth. Michael Bryant was Rosie's father, and all of those years of Frances drumming into her to always tell the truth were rubbish and a sham – her mother had done anything but tell Rosie the truth, and for her entire life.

Just this morning, Rosie had been confused about why she'd been invited to the reading of Michael Bryant's will. She could have understood it if her mother had been summoned, after all she'd been friends with Michael Bryant, but Rosie had never met the man properly, even though she worked in his company – she'd seen him at a couple of presentations and events, but that was all. She'd thought maybe he'd left her mother a small token but, thinking back, the solicitor's secretary had been insistent that Rosie herself be there.

Rosie had mistakenly thought she knew everything about her mother. They'd been so close since her father had died. She couldn't imagine how she'd kept such an enormous secret and allowed Rosie to continue living a complete lie.

When the solicitor finally folded the papers in his hand and sat down, Rosie gave in to her desperate urge, jumped up and headed for the door. She grabbed her mother's hand and dragged her along with her, even though her first instinct had been to leave her behind. She didn't even look back at Tanner. *How could she?*

The solicitor rushed after them down the echoing, high-ceilinged corridor and pressed a copy of the will into her hand.

'I can see that you're shocked, Miss Phillips. Please ring me with any questions you may have.'

Rosie stopped just long enough to nod at him, not trusting herself to speak out loud, and then she led a mute Frances out of the door and down the road to her car. She knew she had to get away, as far away as possible. Mentally, she'd already packed a suitcase, but first she needed to ask her mum some questions …

Rosie had to concentrate very carefully on starting the engine of her car and pulling away. Her mother sat in the passenger seat, white-faced, her lips forming a severe line. They drove in silence for a while.

'Rosie, stop somewhere so we can talk,' said Frances eventually.

'We'll talk when I get you home, Mum, or else I won't be able to drive.' She'd collected her mother after working that morning.

Rosie was still hoping that she would wake up from this nightmare.

Before long, they were pulling into Frances' driveway. The roses were heavy with petals and scent. Normally, Frances would get out of the car and admire the blooms, but today she ignored them and, Rosie noticed, even knocked clumsily into several flowers, scattering their red and pink petals onto the path.

Rosie marched behind her mother, clutching the sheaf of papers that the solicitor had handed to her. As soon as the front door closed, a tidal wave of emotion and questions burst through the fragile dam she had built during the reading of the will.

'Why?' It was a question directed at no one in particular. 'Why would Michael Bryant leave me half of his estate?' The tears flowed unchecked down her face.

Frances sat down in the rocking chair, pulling the crocheted blanket she kept draped over the back across her knees. She began to rock back and forth. Her face was ashen.

'Mum, what's this all about? Is it true?'

'Whatever do you mean?'

'Mum! Come on, please. I want to understand your strange behaviour and why Michael Bryant left me his money.'

'You don't really want to know. I hoped I'd never have to tell you.'

'Yes, I do want to know. Please, Mum, be honest with me.' Rosie had a prickling sensation all over her skin. Her mother's reply had the power to change the course of her life forever.

Frances looked up with a haunted expression in her eyes. 'You understand, Rosie, that I love you more than anything – *anything* in the world.'

Rosie nodded.

'Michael Bryant is indeed your father.'

Rosie dropped down onto a chair. 'What!'

'Michael Bryant was your biological father.'

'How? Are you sure?' Rosie's brain was on fire with emotion.

'Yes, I'm one hundred per cent sure.'

'But … but.' Rosie thought her head was about to explode. 'You've let me go to my own father's funeral without telling me I was related. I think I'm owed an explanation.'

'He was never your father really. He only ... supplied the sperm.'

Rosie got up and began pacing around the kitchen. 'Supplied the sperm! You make it sound so impersonal, like artificial insemination. I mean you must have gone to bed with him, had some sort of relationship with him?'

'Rosie, please. There are certain things you don't discuss with a daughter.'

'Things you don't discuss with a daughter? I'll say! Surely my parentage is my business? Did my dada know?' Rosie used her childhood name for John Phillips. She stopped pacing and ran her hands through her hair, oblivious of the hair clip dropping to the kitchen floor.

'I didn't ever confess the truth to him, and he never said anything to suggest he had any suspicions that you weren't his. He loved you so much, Rosie. I think you had the best deal anyway. Michael Bryant was a cold fish.'

'So, why did you go to bed with him?' Rosie was having difficulty controlling the rising volume of her voice.

'We all do strange things in life sometimes. It's difficult to explain it to you when you weren't there. One thing just led to another.'

'Oh my God! Tanner really *is* my brother.' Rosie dashed to the sink and began to rub her mouth frantically with water from the tap as the realisation finally sank in.

'Rosie?'

'Tanner Bryant is my brother. I've kissed my brother. I had *thoughts* about my brother. Oh, Mum, what a mess.'

As Rosie turned back from the sink, Frances was shaking her head. Rosie, although angry with her mother, recognised she needed to calm things down if she wanted to get any more information.

'I'm going to make a hot drink and get you some biscuits. We've both had a big shock.' The steel came back into her voice. 'But, Mum, you need to tell me everything – and I mean *everything*.'

Even the rituals of making tea did little to soothe Rosie's mind. She couldn't get over the enormity of the fact that she wasn't who she'd thought she was for all of her life. The revelation of who her real father was had rocked the foundations of her world, her identity …

Despite the turmoil, she took time to select the cups, load a tray, warm the pot and put milk into her mother's favourite jug – almost clinging with her fingertips to the rituals of normality, or that's how it felt.

Frances had more colour in her cheeks when Rosie finally placed the tray on the table between them.

'In some ways it's a relief, Rosie. I've kept this secret for so long ... I'd almost convinced even myself that John was your father.'

'Did you sleep with Michael Bryant to get back at him for having an affair with Georgia?'

'Sort of. It wasn't like that. I felt lost when I found out about the affair, but I still loved your father and always suspected Georgia was the instigator of ... "things".'

'Hence your frosty conversation at the funeral?'

'Yes, of course ... I ... I didn't anticipate how Michael's passing would remind me of how ... fragile ... life is. It seems as if I'm grieving for your father all over again, and the younger man Michael Bryant once was.'

'Mum!'

'I feel so guilty about deceiving you. I mean you could have easily slept with Tanner, married him in secret even – although I did try to warn you, but I didn't say enough. I'm so sorry.'

Rosie's mind was working overtime. *Did Tanner know? Would that explain how cool he'd been towards her? Why he'd wanted to meet her? Why he'd run off after she'd kissed him?*

'Rosie, I didn't have an affair with Michael Bryant. It wasn't like that at all …' Frances put up her hand to stop Rosie from interrupting her story.

'Lord knows, I thought about it. I considered long and hard how to get my revenge, mainly on Georgia. One evening I was feeling particularly low. I went to discuss the situation with Michael ... but when I was leaving and turned to get my coat, he …'

'He what, Mum?'

'He kissed me and … well, one thing led to another.' Frances had tears streaming down her cheeks yet again. 'I think we were both curious. But it didn't feel right at all. Very wrong, actually. Afterwards, I had such terrible regrets and nightmares about letting it happen.'

Rosie was trying to take in what her mother was saying. 'Was it just that once then?'

'It only takes once, Rosie. You'd do well to remember that. Yes, we only had sex once. I kept my distance after that evening. It wasn't even a particularly pleasant experience. I did wonder if, for his part, Michael saw the act as a revenge for his wife and my husband's behaviour, rather than wanting to have sex because he was attracted to me in any way.'

'So were you and Dad—John…' Rosie stuttered over calling the man she had always thought of as her father by his first name. 'Were you and John still "together" when you realised you were pregnant?'

'Michael must have given Georgia an ultimatum after that evening because the affair seemed to be over. John tried to be a loving husband again – even the Bryants appeared united for a while.'

'A while?'

'I don't think it was ever much of a loving union again, but they stayed married until Tanner was five … until just after John died …'

'You didn't consider an abortion?'

'I won't lie to you, Rosie. Of course I thought about it, but John and I had been trying to conceive for a while, which is why his affair was all the more painful. It suddenly didn't seem to matter whose child it was. I was pregnant, and there was no way I was going to give up that chance, no way I was going to give up you.'

'Were you and Dad happy after all of this?'

'We were reconciled, but I'll be honest and say that it was never quite the same. Trust is a difficult thing to define, but once you've lost it … and, of course, I never realised then that John and Georgia must have still seen each other for quite a few years afterwards.'

'Would you ever have told me any of this if the will hadn't mentioned it?'

'I don't think so, darling. John Phillips is the man named on your birth certificate. I guess if you'd got serious about Tanner, I would have been forced to tell you, but otherwise there would have been absolutely no reason ever to do so.'

'So, how did Michael Bryant know that I was his daughter?'

'He suspected, but I never told him either way. He came to the hospital when you were born and asked me if you were his child, but I didn't confirm or deny it. I never spoke to him about it again after that. So however he decided you were his, it didn't come from me.'

'So, somehow he confirmed I was his daughter. I wonder how he did that ... some sort of DNA test?'

'I wouldn't put anything past him.'

'And Dad didn't suspect I wasn't his?' Rosie couldn't believe she was crying again.

'We had lots of ... well, I suppose you would call it "make-up" sex.' Frances blushed. 'He loved you so much when you arrived, I don't think it ever mattered to him, even if he had worked it out. I got you and you're the best thing that's ever happened to me. One lapse in my otherwise blameless existence – how could I regret it?'

'What a tangled web ...'

'Can you ever forgive me?'

'I suppose the only thing I'm sure of right now is that you're my mother.'

Frances brandished the funeral service programme that she'd kept on a side table. It had a photograph of Michael Bryant on the front. 'You just need to look at this picture to be sure who fathered you. The resemblance alone may have convinced Michael to put you into his will.'

Rosie took the piece of paper and peered at herself in the mirror with the sheet held next to her face. On first glance, the resemblance wasn't striking, but when she looked more closely, the shape of Michael Bryant's face and the set of his neck were definitely echoed in her own.

Frances came across the room to put her arms around her daughter and they both clung to each other.

'I'm so sorry, Rosie. I should have told you sooner. I thought the need to tell you had died with Michael, especially as things seemed to have cooled with Tanner. I was wrong.'

Rosie broke out of her mother's embrace. She planted a kiss on her cheek. 'I wonder how many people never actually know their true parentage?'

'More than we imagine, I would think.'

'There is one thing I still don't understand. You said the other day that Michael Bryant waited to foreclose on some loans he'd given Dad until I was about five. Why did he wait for all that time?'

Frances gulped. 'I think Michael left things as they were because he was getting a good return from his investment in John's company, but then ...'

'Go on,' said Rosie.

'John and Georgia must have resumed their affair, or maybe they'd never actually stopped seeing each other after all. Around then, Michael delighted in telling me they were at it again.'

'Wow. You were right when you said he was cold.'

'Yes.' Frances' face was a picture of misery.

She stayed with her mum until mid-afternoon. They watched a comedy film on the television, although Rosie didn't really pay attention to any of it. When the film finished, Rosie got ready to leave.

'Mum, I understand that it was hard to discuss the past, but I feel as if I've been overloaded with difficult information. Right now, I think I need some time by myself to come to terms with all of this. I'll be in touch soon.'

As Rosie drove away, she could see her mother watching her from the front step of her house. Rosie's emotions were in turmoil. On one hand, she was annoyed that her mother hadn't told her these family secrets before, on the other, she could understand why Frances would have found it almost impossible to do so.

# *Chapter Sixteen*

The next morning, Rosie drew up outside her mother's house very early. She turned off the engine, squeezed her sleep-deprived eyes tightly shut and blinked rapidly in an effort to wake up. She realised that she couldn't remember anything about the journey from her own house, five miles away. Her eyes were sore, not just from lack of sleep, but because for the first time ever she hadn't removed her eye make-up before getting into bed. She had resembled a panda when she'd looked in the mirror first thing that morning.

The thought-wracked hours of the night were punctuated with feelings of guilt for leaving her mother in such a way yesterday, together with anger at herself, Michael Bryant, Frances and Tanner.

Rosie's mind was clearer about the chain of events in the past. It was not a pretty picture, full of betrayal and secrecy, but she was glad that she knew the truth. She was annoyed that she'd begun to judge her mother when they'd had their frank conversation. Rosie had found herself in enough difficult situations to understand that life was often not straightforward or easy. You could only act in the moment from the information you had at that point – judging with hindsight didn't work.

Frances had painted a picture of two young couples bound together by friendship, and then blasted apart by infidelity, betrayal and revenge.

Rosie wanted to check that her mother was all right, so, against all her normal principles, she had rung into work claiming to be sick when she wasn't.

Frances was weeding around the roses in her front garden. She stood up at the sound of Rosie's car and came to the gate. No one watching the mother and daughter would have realised that this was not a normal everyday visit. They passed the time of day and ambled around the garden, neither keen to broach what was really on their minds.

Eventually, they went indoors and Frances produced some ginger cookies from the cupboard to go with their coffee. Rosie took this as a peace offering.

It wasn't until they sat down that the real business of the day began.

Rosie's anger was by now directed at Michael Bryant, her unknown father until yesterday.

'How dare he, Mum? How dare he turn my life upside down? Why did he plot this great revelation after his death?'

'Only he would know what was in his mind and why he decided to do things this way. Maybe if he hadn't fallen ill, he'd have tried to meet you.'

'I guess we'll never know now ...'

They sat in silence. Frances gradually moved to the edge of her seat and appeared poised to reach her hands over the table to Rosie's.

'You know the worst bit, the worst bit …' Tears began to escape Rosie's eyes. 'The worst bit is my job at Borden Glass. Here was me, thinking I'd been head-hunted for my ability, for my skills and personality. But no, I was recruited for Michael Bryant's own agenda so that he could look after his DNA. *Aaaagggghhhhh.*' Rosie ran her hands through her hair, dislodging the clip that held it back.

'Did you ever meet Michael at Borden Glass?'

'Not that I recall. I think I said yesterday, I've seen him at a distance at events, heard him speak at a couple of corporate presentations, but that's it.'

'Rosie, I'm worried about you.' Frances put her cookie back on the plate, untouched.

'Mum!'

'I am and yes, I *am* your mum. You've had a lot of shocks lately. Breaking up with Ollie, moving back here, Tanner, the will ...' The words "my deception" hung in the air, but were not spoken aloud. Frances finally reached across the table and took Rosie's hands in hers.

'I am reeling a bit. No sooner have I got over one thing, than there's another hit. It really annoys me that Michael Bryant has tried to tie me together with Tanner.'

'His two children together.'

'Thanks for reminding me, Mum. What happened to a simple life where people are exactly who you think they are and have no surprises to spring?'

'Most families have secrets.'

'Yes, but whopping big ones like this?'

'I want you to be reassured that I love you, Rosie. I would never have put myself through all of these years of guilt unless I had thought it was for the best.'

'I know. I've had time to think about that overnight, and I can't judge you for the choices you made. I'd never have known, or had any doubts about my father, if it wasn't for the will. It must have been a very scary time for you, when you realised that you were pregnant with me and that your husband wasn't the father.'

They sat in silence for a while.

'Maybe you need a holiday.'

'A holiday? Wouldn't that be running away from things I need to confront? I've been wondering if Tanner would give me some money for my half of the estate and business, and then I could just walk away. I don't care if I have to wait for the year, but one thing is clear … I need a new job. I can't work at Borden any longer … not now.' Rosie picked up a cookie and began crumbling it into pieces, heedless of the crumbs showering over her jeans and the floor. Dusty was delighted, as Frances and Rosie were too distracted to tell the dog not to hoover up the sweet crumbs.

'I imagine Tanner won't be feeling too brilliant at the moment either, having just lost his father. And, remember, he most likely thought he was going to inherit the whole estate. It must be a shock.'

'I still don't know the full story, but I get the impression that Tanner knew, or at least suspected something about all this. It explains some of his behaviour, especially the fact that he ran off after I kissed him.' Rosie turned an anguished face to her mother. 'Why did he have to be someone I liked?'

'You can still "like" him ... just only as a brother.'

Rosie pulled a face, got up and went to the sink to tip away the dregs from her tea cup.

She hugged her mother, said her goodbyes and left her sitting in the kitchen. Just before she left the room, Rosie turned and mentally took a snapshot of Frances at the table with the dog at her feet.

'So, you're rich?'

'Trust you to think of it like that, Lucy. This is about much more than assets or money.'

Rosie had asked Lucy and Connie to meet her at the wine bar in Borteen to tell them what had been going on.

'And Tanner is your brother?' Connie had a bewildered look on her face.

'It appears so. Half-brother, if we're being precise.' Rosie laughed, but not with any amusement. 'My job was a sham, my mother has lied to me for thirty-one years, my father wasn't my father, my real father is dead and I never knew him, the first man I've fancied for ages is my brother, my whole life is turned upside down. It sounds like the script for a soap opera. I don't think a writer could make it up.'

'We're still your friends, aren't we, Connie? You rebuilt your life after Ollie, you can do it again. We'll help you. And for the record, you are good at your job.'

Connie nodded her agreement.

Rosie knew that she had the support and sympathy of her friends, but they couldn't really imagine the extent to which her world had been rocked, or the fallout she still had to deal with.

'Thank you, girls. I feel that I need to pay a visit to my real father's grave, and then speak to Tanner. But, right now, I could do with a glass of wine ... maybe even a bottle.'

# *Chapter Seventeen*

This time her footwear was sensible boots, but that didn't stop her remembering the feeling of her heels sinking into the grass on the day of the funeral. The churchyard was still enveloped in the dewy wetness of the early morning and the air smelled of damp earth. A solitary blackbird chorused his welcome to the day.

Rosie walked purposefully up the drive and turned left on the path through the moss-covered older gravestones. The single red rose that she clutched in her hand had been picked from the potted rose bush outside of her back door at dawn. It lost a petal as she walked.

It was easy to locate the grave. She stopped in front of the mound of newly dug soil, marvelling at its rich brown colour. The top of the mound was adorned with family wreaths. Rosie and her mother hadn't sent flowers. They'd given a cheque to the chosen cancer charity instead.

She couldn't quite pin down how she felt as she stood there. The very foundation of her existence had been shaken. *Who was she? Was she still Rosie Phillips?* She put her rose at the bottom of the pile away from the other flowers. It looked small and insignificant, and the tears came readily even before she had placed it.

Her real father lay here. A man she had not even met properly. How different would her life have been had she known him? Her beloved John Phillips had died when she was five, leaving her to grow up without a male role model. Could this man have plugged that gap? How would she and Tanner have got on, growing up as half-siblings? Would life have been better, worse or just different?

She tried to pray. Her relationship with religion had been shaky for many years – since she'd stopped going to Sunday school in fact. Despite this, she had always given thanks for the positive things in her life and directed her prayers at some vague deity in the sky. Now, she silently said both hello and goodbye to the father who created her. However, even saying that in her head seemed like a betrayal to John Phillips, whom she'd built up into a sort of hero figure in her mind over the years. It was a very confusing scenario and difficult to make sense of at all.

The tears kept coming. She didn't even know what she was crying about any more. Was it for herself? The little fatherless child inside her? For her mother, who had kept such a heavy secret for so long? For her genetic father and missed opportunity? For John Phillips and his tragic early death?

A prickling sensation on her skin alerted her to the fact she was no longer alone. When she raised her head, Tanner stood at the other end of the grave. He was pale, unshaven, with his hair, wild and untamed, curling around his face.

'Tanner?' Rosie felt her face redden. It was as if he'd been summoned by her thoughts.

'I never expected to find you here.' He half-smiled.

She couldn't read his expression. 'I had some things I needed to share with your father … my father. You knew, didn't you?'

'Not exactly.'

'But you suspected?'

'I found a file on my father's desk all about you. I knew there must be something, because my father was so fascinated to find out about you.'

'That's why you engineered for us to meet? Why you tried all of those jobs in the places I go to?'

Tanner nodded. 'Well, not entirely. I had an idea for an article. I just used the research as an opportunity to see if I could discover why my father was so interested in you.'

'I wish you'd said something that night at the pizza restaurant ... when I kissed you.'

'I know. I tried to pluck up the courage to broach the subject, but how could I when I hadn't a clear idea what was going on myself? I was worried about the possible dangers of letting us get too close. For all I knew, my father could have suspected you of fraud or something. The thought of a family link did sort of cross my mind, but it wasn't my main focus. I'm sorry.' He'd plucked a flower from one of the wreaths and was shredding it in his fingers.

'So, how do you feel now that you do know the truth?'

'Sad and happy all mixed together.' He looked up and the blue of his eyes sparkled. 'Happy I have a sister. Sad I didn't have you to share my lonely childhood with. I can continue. It all goes around in circles. I felt an instant connection with you too, so maybe I knew on some strange subconscious level, although I took it for something else …' He trailed off and looked at his feet.

'My head hurts with thinking too much too. And I got the instant connection thing as well. I thought I just fancied you.' She felt her face colouring with another blush.

Tanner put his hands in his pockets and looked away. Rosie suddenly recognised the coat he was wearing.

'Hang on a minute. That coat. Is it yours?'

'Of course it's mine.'

An image of the note she'd photographed drifted into her mind.

Rosie hadn't even realised Tanner's connections to Lucerne Lodge back then. She had so many emotions connected to this man in front of her. Anger. Suspicion. That connected feeling they'd talked about.

'I found a note in the pocket of that coat on the day we first met.'

Tanner rummaged around in his pockets and came out with a bedraggled piece of paper. His features tensed as he read it. 'Oops.'

'So you arranged my invitation to that party?'

'There's no point in denying it. Guilty as charged. Your poor dress. I still owe you a new one. I just wanted to meet the woman my father had shown such a great interest in.'

'That first meeting seems like a lifetime ago, instead of just a couple of months – it's been a summer I won't forget that's for sure – confusion, revelations and a change of identity,' whispered Rosie, musing on Tanner's choice of words.

As he moved past the grave, surprise made her powerless to stop him from taking her in his arms. His hug was warm but restrained – brotherly. They clung together for a few moments. They both had moist eyes when they finally pulled apart.

'Now, we need to work together to find a way to move forward with all of this, with our lives and our legacy,' he said, quietly.

Rosie wondered how wise it would be to discuss such big issues when both of them were so emotional. Nevertheless, when Tanner suggested they drive to a café close to the graveyard, she accepted. It was at least neutral territory and they really did need to establish a proper relationship – a working one.

By the time she'd driven the short distance, stewing on the subject of her legacy, her overwhelming emotion was anger. She found herself bubbling with it, more anger than she could remember feeling in all of her life, even during the break-up of her relationship with Ollie. She hadn't asked to be put in this situation and it wasn't fair.

Despite deep breathing whilst Tanner ordered coffees, Rosie knew she'd be unable to hide how she was feeling.

He sat down at the table. 'I've been watching you while I was at the counter. You look fit to burst.'

Rosie glanced up at him, shocked that he could read her so easily.

'Come on, now's the time for us both to be totally honest about our feelings. Share what's going through your head. It might make you feel better.'

'I'm not sure about that one. Are you sitting comfortably?'

Tanner exaggerated the movements of crossing his legs and arms, and moving forward. 'Go!'

She smiled despite the emotions coursing through her veins.

'I'm mad that I could have thought I was doing so well at work. I was so thrilled to be head-hunted, to be taken seriously and maybe in line for further promotion, but now I realise my real father was more than likely pulling the strings in the background. It was all fake, all engineered. Do you realise how that makes me feel?'

'Now, come on, I can assure you that my father wouldn't have taken you on at Borden Glass if you didn't have the right qualifications and experience.'

'But he must have engineered me moving back to Borteen. If he hadn't become ill, I wonder if he'd have eventually introduced himself and told me that I was his daughter?'

'We'll never know that one, I'm afraid. I don't believe even he was sure you were part of his family until just before he died.'

'*Arghh.*' She ran her hands through her hair, exasperated. 'So he was curious but not certain? Curious enough to influence my life and where I worked by making me a job offer I didn't feel I could refuse. How dare he think he could manipulate me? How dare he give me an advantage because of my possible links to him? I feel used and cheated. More than that, Tanner, I feel ashamed – a sham. How many of my colleagues knew that I was the golden girl, the preferred employee of the owner of the company?'

'I think you're probably blowing all of this completely out of proportion, Rosie. I doubt anyone knew anything, or even suspected, apart from Michael.'

'Before I left home today, I pressed send on an email to hand in my notice at Borden. It felt like the only thing to do in the circumstances.'

'Technically, you've just sent an email to yourself, seeing as we now jointly own Borden Glass.' Tanner was trying, without success, to hide a smile at this thought.

'Well, it's a symbolic gesture anyway. How can I hold my head up to ever go back into that building again? I don't feel I can even go in to get my things. I've been trying to remember if I'd left anything irreplaceable in the drawers of my desk.'

'I can go and get your personal stuff if you like. At least I know where you sit in the office.' This time he smiled properly, then drew her attention to the coffee going cold in front of her.

She took a large gulp from the mug. 'Did you know what your father was doing?'

He shook his head.

'Come to think of it, why don't you work at Borden Glass? Surely you would be the obvious choice as a successor for your father?'

'I chose a different path. Much to my father's disgust, I've spent my life rebelling.'

'I can't believe I was so flattered to be asked to join Borden Glass. I'm so angry with Michael Bryant. I'm also angry with Mum, you, myself and the world.'

Tanner sat back in his chair, hands raised in front of him in defence. 'Whoa! I bet it feels better to get that lot off your chest.'

She glared at him. 'Right now, I want nothing to do with the inheritance or the people who've kept me in the dark about my own life.'

Rosie's raised voice was attracting the attention of other people in the café. She forced herself to take a few moments to breathe before speaking again more quietly. She was relieved that Tanner seemed to have realised that she needed to vent her feelings, not necessarily to have a discussion.

'What else in my life isn't as it seems? My mother kept a secret from me for thirty-one years. If we weren't so close, I doubt our relationship could have survived the strain of this. My job was a lie, the man I thought of as my father didn't share the same blood and the man I …' She decided at the last minute that it was better to leave that comment unfinished. 'How much more can a girl take?' Rosie dabbed at her eyes with her pile of now damp tissues whilst Tanner calmly sipped his latte.

'Do I take it your mother has admitted my dad was also yours?'

'Yes, she says that I was the result of a one-night stand with your father. She swears it was only once and not in any way an affair.'

'So, there's no doubt that we're half-brother and sister?'

She looked into his eyes. 'It seems we're related.'

'Hello, sister,' he whispered. 'We'll need more meetings to decide how to proceed with our property, businesses and assets, but right now, Rosie, if you'll excuse me, I think I just need to go and walk my father's dog.'

'I'm sorry, I haven't given you a chance to speak.'

'It's fine. Next time, maybe.' He stood up and placed his chair carefully under the table.

'It's so overwhelming, and no doubt it's going to take time to adjust to the new reality of us. I think we both need plenty of thinking time.'

Tanner touched her hand briefly across the table, a strange look in his eyes. She watched him walk to his car, wishing at that moment that her half-brother was anyone other than Tanner Bryant. As he drove away, he raised a hand to wave to her. The sun chose just then to go behind a cloud.

As Rosie stared, unseeing, out of the café window, her thoughts crystallised.

What was keeping her here in Sowden or Borteen? Her two fathers were dead and buried, she'd resigned from her job, she hadn't a clue how to be with her mother at the moment, and then there was Tanner and her inheritance to face …

Where could she make a fresh start or at least have a break? Preferably somewhere where no one could find her and no one would know her. Her mind started to wander over possible scenarios, and she made up her mind to go on a holiday – her mother had even suggested it. She found herself repeating one of Frances' maxims – "things will look different with the passage of time". Well, it was time to test that one out.

Back at home, she browsed on the internet and it didn't take her long to find a huge static caravan by the coast in North Wales, which happened to be in a resort she'd visited many times as a child with her mother. It was late in the holiday season, so it was marked as available – she told herself it was fate. Booking was online and, within minutes, her bolthole was secured.

Picking up the phone, she dialled her mother's number. For once, she was pleased it went to answerphone. The message she left was brief, 'Please don't worry about me, Mum, I'm disappearing on holiday for a while. You suggested it, remember? Be in touch soon.'

She was guilty that, in her haste, she hadn't ended the message with "love you".

It was Friday, the caravan was booked from Saturday afternoon – just one sleep and then she was free. She could leave all of this unfinished business and baggage behind. Well, that's what it felt like – whether she could actually do that in reality remained to be seen.

# *Chapter Eighteen*

To fill the rest of the day, Rosie spent the time in Borteen, mentally saying a "goodbye for now" to the lovely seaside town.

Her rented cottage was in a row of whitewashed terraced cottages at the top of the high street. She deliberately set out to walk down one side of the road and up the other.

The Cancer Research charity shop had a lovely bright display of dresses in the window and it made Rosie smile. Mr Wong was washing the windows of the Chinese takeaway. He nodded to her. The craft shop had a display of watercolour paintings from local artists, and Rosie took the time to try and guess the locations before reading the labels beneath each picture.

Rosie skirted the estate agent's window. Normally she would browse the property for sale, as she'd been intending to buy a house before her next rental period was up. But now the boundaries of her life had shifted, and she was no longer sure where her future lay.

She was tempted to go into Polka Dot Paradise, the vintage shop, as there was a rather smart business jacket in the window. She'd almost reached for the door handle when she remembered that she wouldn't be needing business attire for a while. That thought had her walking past the next few buildings unseeing, as she tried to calm her troubled emotions.

She made her way along the promenade. The wind was brisk on the exposed area above the beach. Rosie toyed with popping in to Owl Corner Crafts to see the owner. Her friend Jenny had introduced her to Mandy Vanes, and Rosie often admired the art of her adopted son, Nick, in the craft centre. In the end, Rosie decided that in her current state of mind she might just cry and cry if Mandy asked how she was. Instead, she headed down the steps near to the craft centre and walked back the other way along the beach near to the sea wall. The tide was in and, at this time of year, it came up quite high.

Chilled a little from the sea breeze, Rosie left the beach by the steps at the other end of the promenade and passed the little beach café, wine bar, pie shop and chemist before stopping outside of a shop she'd never been into before. The shop window looked as if someone had thrown things into it and stirred wildly; a jumbled mix of crystals, jewellery, ethnic clothing and bags. But there, right at the front of the window, was a silver pendant in a dark blue silk-lined box. It was shaped like a crescent moon and the milky-white stone glistened and shone with iridescence. There was a tiny red stone in a silver star-like setting at one end. Rosie's eyes stood out on stalks, but she told herself just to admire it and move on. She didn't need any more jewellery. She held up her hand to look at her favourite flower-shaped ring as if to remind herself of that.

As she walked up the hill towards home, however, her mind had other ideas. There appeared to be moons and stars everywhere she looked, all reminding her of the pendant. Eventually, angry at the inevitability of it, she gave up and retraced her steps to the crystal shop, holding her breath in case the pendant had been sold in the short time she'd been away.

She looked into the display windows more carefully this time. They were so packed with items that it was difficult to see into the interior of the shop. The pendant was still there, seeming to wink at her. She exhaled thankfully. There was a sign above the shop door lintel that read, "Witches Welcome". She thought it must be a joke, but nonetheless a small shiver went up her back.

Inside the shop it was dark, almost womb-like. The first impression was of sanctuary and incense. The one wall had cabinets full of crystals and strange, to Rosie anyway, wands and pendulums. The other was hung with colourful ethnic clothing, rich velvets draped with crinkly skirts and wool coats. The rest of the wall space was bedecked with bags, pictures and mirrors. Other shelves contained carved wooden dolphins, jewellery, bells and incense burners. Rosie found herself feeling grateful that she didn't have to do a stock check for this place.

Her attention was drawn to the man behind the counter. She'd seen him around Borteen and knew he did charity events on the beach sometimes. He had a definite presence that filled the shop with a peaceful air. Physically, he was not your average pin-up, but his grey eyes and long grey hair gave him an attractive, friendly and almost teasing air.

'Good afternoon, fellow traveller,' he said, in a voice reminiscent of thick syrup.

'Hello.' Rosie smiled. 'I've come to ask the price of the moon-shaped pendant at the front of your window.'

'Ah, so you are the chosen one.'

'Excuse me?' The shivers had started up again at the base of her spine.

'I put that pendant at the front of the window first thing this morning, as it told me its future owner would be arriving today.'

*Did this man speak to necklaces?* Rosie was tempted to run, but something about his eyes was hypnotic and, although his words and manner of speaking were strange, he didn't feel menacing in any way. Besides, the necklace in question appeared to have been speaking to Rosie too.

'I think that the price will determine whether I am its future owner or not.' She smiled at him again. She told herself that his words were his sales patter, not a premonition.

The man walked past her and reached his hand deep into the window to retrieve the necklace. The pendant was suspended on a narrow black cord. He straightened it and put it into Rosie's outstretched hand. It felt satisfyingly heavy.

'What is the stone?'

'It's a moonstone.'

'Could I try it on please? I'd like to check how the moon hangs when you wear it.'

He took it out of her hand and stood behind her, waiting for her to lift her hair. As his fingers brushed the nape of her neck, Rosie experienced a strange sensation of heat. He brought a mirror out from behind the counter, so that she could see how perfectly the moon and star hung at her throat.

'Oh, it's absolutely beautiful. Please don't say it's too expensive.'

The price was surprisingly affordable, but she had the impression that he wanted her to own it and had maybe reduced the price so that she would buy it.

'Can I keep it on?'

'Of course, *cherie*. I'll just remove the label.' He touched her skin again as he removed the white tag. Heat surged from his fingers yet again. 'Take the label with you. It tells you what the stones are for.'

'What they're for?'

'Their meaning and purpose. The moonstone is a special stone for you at the moment, as it spoke to you today.'

'Yelled at me more like.' Rosie laughed. 'I couldn't get the pendant out of my head once I'd seen it. I actually walked half way up the high street and it felt like it called me back. It seemed like there were moons and stars all over the place to remind me to buy it.'

The shopkeeper smiled too. 'Signs from the Universe. The label says, "The moonstone energy balances and removes emotional tension. It helps restructure your life physically, emotionally, mentally and spiritually. It relates to new beginnings and is a stone to help you understand the next steps of your pathway through life's complications." Does that sound like the stone for you?'

'Wow,' said Rosie. 'Are you psychic?' She couldn't believe he had pinpointed the issues she was dealing with at the moment.

'Yes,' he stated matter-of-factly. 'I wrote out this tag first thing this morning, but the words are from this book.' He waved a dog-eared thick volume of a book entitled *Love is in the Earth*. Rosie made a mental note to tell Connie about it, or maybe to buy it for her friend as a gift.

She handed over her money and as he gave her the change, along with the prophetic label, he grasped her fingers and looked closely at her palm. The shivers were back, running up and down her spine. Rosie resisted the urge to pull away, her curiosity getting the better of her.

'Yes, this is absolutely the right stone for you. Wear it daily for the time being and try to walk in the moonlight wearing the pendant to enhance its powers. You are at a crossroads, but you do not need to make any quick decisions. Allow yourself to relax, let events unfold and the answers you seek will bubble to the surface.'

He paused and she gulped. 'You're starting to unnerve me and reassure me all at the same time!'

He released her hand and stared deeply into her eyes. 'I'm Buzz. Come and see me again. Next time I'll make tea or open a bottle of wine.'

It seemed a genuinely friendly offer.

'Rosie – and yes, I'll visit again.'

Long after leaving the shop, the wafts of incense clung to her hair and the energetic presence of the man lingered. She vowed to visit Buzz again, even though she was more than a little spooked by his words. She wondered vaguely if he had cast a spell on her. She fingered the pendant, tracing its outlines and the tactile surface of the stones. Right now, it felt like the most precious thing in the world she owned, and it would be a fitting reminder of Borteen as she prepared to go away, hoping to leave the town and her troubles behind at least for a while.

# *Chapter Nineteen*

The closer Rosie got to Wales, the more relaxed she felt, as if she was shedding her cares and worries along the roadside. There was something liberating about no one knowing where she was going. This feeling seemed to heighten her awareness of the countryside. She was delighted to spot buzzards in the skies over the mountains, or were they kites? She'd have to Google it when she stopped. Peacefulness crept into her bones and her driving style with each mile travelled.

When she reached her destination, she could be anyone she wanted. No one would know her or anything about her history, cares and worries. She spent a couple of miles imagining different personas for herself, each with its own way of dressing and acting in public. Some of her ideas made her laugh out loud in delight.

She only stopped once, to eat a cheese sandwich and drink a pot of tea at a little café with red-checked tablecloths. The café was on a major road junction and the other customers were lorry drivers and elderly couples. No one took any notice of her and it felt good to be anonymous. The journey was easy and uneventful, although the twisting roads made her feel a little dizzy at times.

As she approached her destination, trying to work out the directions the satnav was suggesting, she missed the lane down to the site and had to reverse. Back on track, she turned into the caravan park and experienced a leap of excitement. She hadn't stayed in a caravan since she was about fourteen. Stopping outside the office and shop, she collected her keys and a site plan from the pleasant girl who answered the bell on the desk. It didn't take long to locate number 52 and park her car alongside.

*Home for the next two weeks.* She sighed with pleasure and relief.

The green caravan had steps that led up to a platform with a wrought iron railing around it. Holding her car keys and handbag, she struggled to open the unfamiliar lock. It took her a few moments, but then the door opened outwards and she was inside. The van was huge compared to the caravans she remembered staying in as a child with her mother. There was a seating area with thick padded upholstery in a u-shape, a gas fire, a small flat-screen TV and a full-size kitchen with fridge/freezer and cooker. It all looked very modern and new. The corridor beyond had a twin room, with thin narrow bunks, and, opposite, a toilet and separate shower room.

At the far end, there was a double bedroom, easily the same size of the one in her rented house back in Borteen.

The whole caravan had a pleasing, if neutral décor of mainly beige with red accents in cushions, curtains and quilt covers. It smelled slightly musty, as if the door had been shut for a while. Rosie threw open all of the windows to let out the fustiness, while she unloaded her belongings. She piled everything in the twin bedroom, so that she could sort things out properly for her stay. The feeling that this was home for a couple of weeks was delightful, and a little glow of contentment ignited inside of her.

She felt unaccountably tired, but then she had driven a fair distance that day. Sinking down gratefully on the wide padded seating, she fell quickly asleep.

The sound of someone banging on the door brought her out of her slumber. Bleary-eyed and tousle-haired, she opened it to find a grey-haired lady in a green sweatshirt and jogging bottoms standing outside.

'Good afternoon. I'm Marjorie Owens. The office told me you'd moved in. I run the site social club, and I wanted to welcome you to the site and let you know about the events this weekend.' The woman thrust a large, flabby hand at Rosie.

Rosie managed to stay distant but polite. She'd come here to escape, not to socialise. The lady was very pleasant though, so she took the events timetable that Marjorie offered and smiled.

She closed the door, glancing at the piece of paper and making a vow to avoid the Saturday night bingo session. Her head felt muzzy, but she forced herself to begin unpacking and take a shower.

She wanted to explore and at least buy some milk, but after her long journey she couldn't face taking the car, so she walked instead. It occurred to her that shops might not be open late on Saturdays and maybe not at all on Sundays in this part of the world. As she walked away from the caravan park, she felt the pull of the sea and the unfamiliar beach to explore, but forced herself to turn the opposite way into the small seaside town to find supplies. There was one tiny Co-op store that was well stocked, and she bought wine, bread, milk, tea, pizza and salad, a packet of chocolate biscuits and a frozen fish dinner. She realised that she was not used to carrying shopping any distance. Normally, if she didn't order a home delivery, her car was parked next to the trolley bay at the supermarket.

She picked up the two carrier bags and decided that she could manage the walk back to the site with them. She didn't count on the phenomenon of things getting heavier the longer you carried them. Her arms began to feel twice as long and her steps slowed. A man walking his dog came up alongside her.

'Afternoon, Miss. You look like you're struggling with those bags.'

*State the obvious*, she thought.

'I'm not used to carrying shopping any distance. I didn't realise until I had bought all this.'

'Here, let me carry one for you.'

He held out a hand towards her bags and her first instinct was to refuse. Years of city living made you suspicious. A promise of help in London might lead to a thief running off with the bag. Eventually, Rosie smiled and gratefully gave the stranger one of the carrier bags, which had begun to cut into her hand.

'That's very kind of you. I'm going to the caravan site just down the hill, but even a few yards carrying my shopping would be a help.'

'Small world down here, Miss. My Marjorie told me a young lass had moved into van 52. I guess that's you. Am I right?'

'Bingo,' said Rosie. *So much for anonymity by the sea – that didn't last long*. 'I'm Rosie, and you are?'

'Alf Owens. I'd shake your hand, but I haven't one free at the moment. This is Griff.' His wiry-haired dog was pulling on the lead held in the hand with his stick, and Rosie's shopping bag was in the other.

'Have you been coming here on holiday long?'

'We live here most of the year. Marjorie and I feel much better by the sea, less aches and pains somehow, so we downsized to a first-floor apartment with a lift and bought the caravan. Best thing we've ever done.'

'I can see the appeal.'

He cocked his head on one side and looked at her. 'You running away?'

The colour rose involuntarily in her face. 'I did need to get away for a while, that's all.'

'Number 52 was free for you to rent as its owner has had to go and stay with her daughter to help with a new baby.'

That explained the caravan being free. They began walking down the sloping pavement. The views over the bay were breath-taking. Rosie spotted boats moored in a sheltered river estuary and, in the distance, mountains. The bay curved round, and she could see several sandy beaches close and further away. She looked forward to exploring them.

Alf Owens looked sprightly enough, but he had to be at least seventy. His face was weather-beaten to a permanent tan.

'So, you recommend life around here?'

'I love it. Lots of walks and beachcombing. We play bridge and bingo. Marjorie's an organiser. She hates being retired. It's given her a new lease of life, arranging the site's social calendar.'

'I'm here for two weeks, but I'm not sure bridge or bingo are my thing.'

'Oh, Marjorie will soon have you roped into something. I give you a week tops and you'll be joining in.'

Rosie smiled, secretly thinking *No way.*

Alf waited patiently while she opened her caravan door and put the bag she'd been carrying inside, and then he handed her the other one.

'Everyone is friendly here. You've no need to be wary.'

He must have read her earlier thoughts.

'We've loads of friends on the site and in the local area, but we're at that age where the women last longer than the men. The site is full of widows. Nice to have someone a bit younger in residence. A bit of eye-candy.' He laughed and winked, before ambling down the path with the dog.

After a cup of tea and a couple of biscuits, Rosie decided to explore the beach before it got dark. She'd been here many times as a child and it was just as she remembered it, right down to her favourite rock pool. It was a small one with sand at the bottom and seemed to look just the same as it had all those years before. Transparent prawns scurried around and anemones waved their tendrils at her. There were tears in her eyes as she mourned the carefree young girl who had holidayed here and gazed into the same rock pool in wonder. The one who had known nothing of life's complications.

The tide was coming in. Rosie couldn't resist kicking off her shoes, taking off her socks and rolling up her jeans to dip her toes in the water. It was icy cold, but it had been a symbolic ritual in her childhood to mark the start of a holiday, so had to be done. Before she had gone a foot into the surf, the tears began streaming down her face as she began to let out all of the tension of the last few weeks.

It was getting late and her tummy was rumbling, so she returned to the van to experiment with the cooker. The pizza was much too big for one, but somehow the salty air and a Saturday evening romantic film made her feel like eating it all. With the curtains drawn in the caravan, and the lamps throwing a soft light around the space, Rosie breathed a deep sigh of contentment as she snuggled up under the thoughtfully provided throw on the bench seat. After a glass of wine and a documentary about a singing celebrity, she was ready to curl up in bed with one of the new novels she'd downloaded onto her Kindle. It felt completely indulgent and relaxing.

She realised that lately she had got into the habit of rarely indulging herself or looking after her wellbeing. Her waking hours were normally targeted at some educational or work goal. Time off seemed naughty and wasteful, but she was determined to try it. She badly needed a break before making those momentous decisions about what she wanted to do with the rest of her life.

It was odd not having her mobile near to her, but she had deliberately locked it in the glove compartment of her car when she arrived. She was determined not to fritter away her time on social media and reading emails. She went to sleep, blissfully unaware of the mounting number of messages from her mother and Tanner accumulating on her phone.

# *Chapter Twenty*

Waking the next morning to a sunny day, Rosie emerged refreshed and excited. She had gifted these two weeks to herself and was determined to enjoy them.

It was already light when she opened her eyes, and a peek out of the curtains confirmed that the sun was high in the sky. She couldn't remember when she'd last slept so late or so long. Another thing she rarely allowed herself was a Sunday newspaper, only reading one when she stayed with her mother. Today, she tucked her nightie into some jogging bottoms, donned her coat and, after a cursory comb of her hair, she jogged to the newsagents and was back in bed within fifteen minutes. It felt blissfully indulgent, but she told herself that she deserved it. Back in Borteen, she had begun to feel like a pawn in a game that couldn't be won – a game that wasn't of her own making.

However, after a lazy day spent eating, beachcombing, reading, and then another early night, she began to feel rather restless. It was not going to be easy to get used to doing nothing. Maybe an adventure was called for. An enquiry in the caravan park office found her standing at the bus stop in the lane with an assortment of villagers the next day. A couple of young girls looked as if they were on the way to café jobs, judging by the little black dresses, leggings and flat shoes. There was also a gaggle of elderly ladies with shopping bags.

She could have taken her car but felt like trying something new. She was glad she'd decided to go by bus to Barmouth, as the route meandered around the coastal road and she was able to admire the view. It was lovely to enjoy the scenery in a way she never did when she was driving. The sea stretched out to the horizon, and she wondered if there were dolphins, turtles and seals out there.

Barmouth wasn't huge but could provide most necessities, even though it was blatantly geared up for tourists. Rosie meandered around the town, sizing up the shops for usefulness during her stay.

Tanner was searching for Rosie – he needed to speak to her urgently about their legacy, there were forms to sign, but, more importantly, he wanted to make sure she was all right after how upset she'd been at Michael Bryant's grave.

When he called into the solicitor's office, at the request of Justin Sadler, the solicitor told him that he'd been unable to get in touch with Rosie either. An icy chill crept into Tanner's body. The last time he'd seen Rosie, she had been very upset and shocked, but surely she wouldn't do anything stupid?

His worries grew when he went to Rosie's house. The curtains were half closed in the way they often were when people were trying to suggest that they were not away. An enquiry with a neighbour confirmed that Rosie had left with a suitcase. *Where had she gone?*

Tanner got back into his car and drove to Rosie's mother's house. If anyone knew where she was, Frances would. Tanner felt a bit ashamed that he only knew of this and Rosie's address because of the private investigator's research.

On the way, his thoughts resumed their turmoil. He was angry that his father could put somebody so prominently in his will without at least preparing his son for the consequences, or indeed poor Rosie. Now he also knew that Rosie was his half-sister, he felt betrayed by that too.

He'd known, of course, that his parents' marriage hadn't been perfect, but there was now the irrational thought that his childhood could have been so much better. He could have had the companionship of a sister growing up, instead of the loneliness and isolation that had framed his younger days. He'd almost been grateful to be parcelled off to boarding school aged eleven – at least he'd had companions of his own age, despite having to cope with bullies and brawlers.

'Sorry to just turn up, Mrs Phillips,' he said apologetically, finding Frances in her rose garden at the front of her house. To his surprise, Frances' face lost all of its colour and she clutched at her throat.

'It's not bad news about Rosie, is it?'

Tanner instantly felt even more concerned about his half sister, and also guilty that he'd scared her mother. He reached out a hand to steady Frances.

'I've been so worried,' croaked Frances. 'Even though Rosie left me a message to tell me not to be concerned, how could I not be? It's so out of character for her to just disappear without telling me exactly where she's going.' She rubbed her eyes with the back of her gardening gloves, leaving a smear of soil across her cheek.

'Have you heard from her at all, since she left that message telling you not to worry?'

'No. She told me she was going away, but she didn't tell me where and she's not answering her mobile. It is so unlike her to leave me a message to tell me something like that. She would normally have popped in for coffee first. Tanner, you don't think she's done anything stupid do you?'

'I'm sure she hasn't.' Tanner sent up a silent prayer because Rosie's mother's thoughts echoed his own. 'When did you last see her?'

'We saw each other two days running – the day your father's will was read on Wednesday and the day after that. I had to tell Rosie some difficult things, secrets from the past. She was very upset and unsettled.'

'I saw her at my father's grave on Friday.'

'She went to Michael's grave?' Her look showed her surprise.

'Yes, she seemed to be trying to talk to him when I interrupted her – well, talking out loud as if to him anyway. Our relationship has been a little bit strained since we found out we're related, to say the least. I don't think either of us knows how to be with the other at all yet.'

'Did your father ever tell you anything about Rosie?'

Tanner pulled a band out of his hair and shook his curls free. He put the black band on his wrist. 'No, my father wouldn't give away any information on the subject. I had my suspicions there was some link, because I found some notes about Rosie on his desk.' Tanner decided not to reveal he had a full private investigator's file and numerous photographs of Rosie, as that felt weird to say to her mother. 'Never imagined she was his daughter, though. So I got to find out like everyone else when the will was read. Hearing it like that was quite a shock, I can tell you.' He paused to put the band back into his hair.

'I never imagined Michael would do anything like that. I think we were all shocked, including me.'

'Rosie did tell me that you had confirmed things for her afterwards, and that she really is my father's daughter.'

Frances nodded. 'I should have prepared her. I feel so bad now, but you have to understand that I never imagined I'd have to tell her, especially after Michael had died.'

'I think she's upset that she didn't know before. Actually, I'd appreciate it if you could explain things properly to me too, even though I realise it might still be difficult to talk about.' He looked down warily at Frances. However, her face showed no reaction to his request.

'Come on, Tanner, let's go inside. I would like to tell you everything about Rosie and the past. Now the truth is out, it's time for complete openness. I probably should have tackled it with Rosie before, should have known that secrets always come out in the end.'

Tanner trailed after Frances into the house. She discarded her gloves, washed her hands and filled the kettle. She pointed to a photograph album high on the dresser shelves. Tanner reached for it. The cover was old and a little battered.

'Now, I'll make some tea and you have a look through those. I got it down from the attic when I started to get worried about Rosie. How do you take your tea?'

'Strong and a little milk, no sugar, please.' Tanner opened the album and began to study the images inside.

'Those are photographs from the good old times,' said Frances. 'Your mother and father, my husband, John, and I, were all close friends back then. Hard to believe now.'

Tanner turned the pages slowly. It was strange seeing photographs of his parents happy together, he'd only ever known them at loggerheads. Also, there was definitely something that looked distinctly like Rosie in the younger Michael Bryant in the photographs.

When he looked up, Frances was watching him.

'I keep wondering if that's what I initially recognised in Rosie – a similarity to my father. There was something I couldn't put my finger on. You understand, I only set out to meet her from curiosity. I'd found those notes about her on my father's desk just after he was admitted to the clinic when he became really ill.'

'Did you ask him about the notes?' Frances placed a mug of tea in front of him.

'I did, but by then he was so unwell and only mumbled something about a debt.'

'My condolences again for your loss.'

'Thank you. We were never close, but his death has left a strange hole in my life, particularly with all of these unanswered questions.' Tanner picked up his mug of tea.

'I thought you might like to see those photographs. Sad really, we four used to have such good times together. I remember it as a happy time of my life … before everything went wrong.'

'It's weird to see my parents looking happy together.'

‘I’m sure it is.’ Frances went on to explain about John and Georgia’s affair and about how Rosie’s conception was a result of the one and only time she’d slept with Michael.

They sat silently after that for a while, Tanner covering his thoughts by looking through the photograph album. His overwhelming emotion was sadness, sadness for the two happy couples torn apart by infidelity and betrayal. Sadness that his parents ended up divorced, leaving him as a lonely boy, brought up by a nanny.

Frances broke the silence and his thoughts. ‘Rosie does look a lot like the younger version of your father, doesn’t she? If you have any doubts about her being your sister, I think those snapshots show you the truth.’ Frances paused. ‘You do realise that she had the beginnings of an attraction to you?’

‘I did wonder and, if I’m truthful, I had a bit of a thing for her too. But I was cautious as I’d already seen my father’s notes. I’d had time to consider the possibilities and probabilities, although I definitely wasn’t expecting to gain a sister!’

‘You see, Rosie thought you were showing an interest in her as a woman.’

‘I can understand that with hindsight.’ He sighed and rubbed his hand over his face.

‘So you weren’t aware of Rosie being mentioned in Michael’s will?’

‘My father seems to have changed his will to include her after a visit from my mother in the last few weeks of his life. I wasn’t there, but the nurses told me Dad got very upset and my mum stormed out after an argument.’

‘Have you asked Georgia what the row was about?’

‘Not yet. I haven’t found the right opportunity, although I guess everything will become clear shortly. She’s challenging the will.’

Frances looked puzzled. ‘Georgia is questioning the terms of the will? Surely she got her cut of the estate when your parents divorced?’

‘You would think so, but the solicitor says she claims my father promised her much more if he died first. Did Mum know Rosie was Dad’s daughter?’

‘I don’t see how she would,’ said Frances. ‘I certainly never told her. I never ever confirmed her parentage to Michael, or John for that matter. As I said, we only slept together once. Georgia and my husband, John, had a much longer affair. Did you know about the affair before I said?' She looked uncertain.

'Sort of. I think I became aware of something over the years ... even if it was never openly spoken about.'

Frances stared out of the window, seemingly deep in thought.

Her dog came over to Tanner and nuzzled his hand. He was glad of the distraction. 'Hello, what's your name? I bet you can smell Trixie on me. I took her out for a walk this morning.'

'Dusty doesn't normally make friends easily, so you're honoured.'

'Hello, Dusty.' The dog had brought a toy over, clearly hoping Tanner would play. He obliged with a tug of war for a few moments and then threw the toy for the dog to fetch. 'I need to find Rosie to tell her about Mum challenging the will, and there are also some papers she needs to sign for probate.'

'I can relate to the fact that she needs to get away from all of this for a while. The last few weeks have been rather shocking and straining, and I feel so guilty that I've never prepared her for the possibility of this coming out … never told her about her real father. She's not answering her phone or text messages, so I'm not sure what we can do until she decides to surface and get in touch.' Frances rubbed a hand across her face, and Tanner realised how tired she was looking.

'Do you think we need to alert the police?'

'I'm hoping it won't come to that. I think maybe if she'd disappeared with no communication at all, I would have called them straight away. She asked me to give her space. I'll let her have a while longer ... it's hard, but she obviously needed to get away.'

'Will you please let me know if she rings you?' He took a business card out of his wallet and handed it to Frances. 'My mobile number is on the card.' He swigged the remains of his tea and stood up.

'I will, Tanner. I just pray she gets in touch soon. And you'll tell me if she contacts you first?'

'Of course I will.'

Frances stood up too. She scribbled her telephone numbers on a piece of paper and he put it into his pocket.

Tanner didn't quite know how to react as she moved closer to pull him into a hug. He stood limply as the smaller older woman pulled him close and reached up to squeeze his shoulders, her hair tickling his neck.

He had a sudden urge to cling on to her and to sob out his anxieties and feelings, but with practiced restraint, he didn't.

'You've had a lot to cope with yourself lately too, with your father passing away and finding out about Rosie being your sister – make sure you take care of yourself.'

Tanner pulled awkwardly out of her embrace. Frances' floral perfume had attached itself to his shirt, and he knew he would take her loving energy with him for the rest of the day. It made him miss his own mother, or rather, the fantasy image of his mother he'd built up to carry with him. The reality was far different, probably always had been and was likely to remain so. He sighed inwardly as he realised he had one more thing to tell her before he left.

'Frances, there's something I didn't mention ... you should be aware that the press appear to be taking an interest in the story of my father's will and my mother's challenge of its terms. I'm not sure if my mother is behind this publicity, but there will more than likely be coverage in the newspaper before long. It's another reason I wanted to find Rosie ... to warn her.'

# *Chapter Twenty-One*

Tanner found it difficult to settle after his visit to see Frances. The temptation to call the private investigator his father had used to compile the file about Rosie was growing. Surely the man had the skills to discover Rosie's whereabouts now?

Frances' words came back to him – *I can relate to the fact that she needs to get away from all of this for a while.* He knew Frances spoke wisely – he must try to be patient and allow Rosie her space. She'd been through an awful lot of shock revelations, and most of them were to do with his father.

He went to the kitchen and poured himself a large glass of water. He wondered if Rosie, wherever she was, would have read the speculative news reports about Michael Bryant's secret daughter, and about a challenge to the terms of the will, that had been published over the last couple of days. They hadn't made the headlines, but they'd been printed several times, and in all the tabloids. He still suspected that his mother was somehow behind the stories.

Where would Rosie go? He wracked his brains and sieved through the information he knew about her, both from the private investigator's file and things she'd said the few times they'd met each other. Back to London maybe? An image of Rosie dancing across the beach floated across his mind, and then he remembered something she'd said about her happy childhood holidays at the seaside. He knew that she had mentioned a resort where her mother had taken her for holidays every year. The name of the place was there in his head, just on the edge of his consciousness, but he couldn't bring it out. It began with the letter "H". *Harrogate ... no, that wasn't even by the sea, Hastings, H...?*

It was when he was showering it finally came to him – near *Harlech.* Now he was almost certain he knew roughly where to find her. Or if not, at least he was being proactive and trying to find her, rather than enduring this agonisingly passive wait for her to surface.

As he pulled the duvet over his head, he wondered how she would react if he just turned up after finding her whereabouts by chance. He was on his third version of a confrontation scene when he finally fell asleep.

Rosie's happy-go-lucky holiday mood nose-dived on the day after her trip to Barmouth. Misery enveloped her as soon as she opened her eyes, and drizzling rain outside didn't help. She decided to make a list of the questions she wanted the answers to and the areas of her life she needed to tackle. As the list grew longer, her mood grew blacker as everything still seemed so insurmountable.

A loud rapping on the caravan door pulled her from a blow-by-blow analysis of her encounters with Tanner. She tried to ignore the noise, hoping she couldn't be seen where she was sitting, but the knocking became even more insistent.

Rosie flung the throw around her shoulders to cover her crumpled pyjamas that she was still wearing, even though it was nearly afternoon. She turned the key, not bothering to remove the scowl that had settled on her features.

A tiny woman in a blue jumper, holding an umbrella, smiled brightly and began to nurse red knuckles from her pounding on the door. 'Oh, thank goodness.' Her sigh was heartfelt.

'Excuse me?' said Rosie.

'You're alive! We thought we might need to ring 999.'

'What?' Rosie was feeling more confused by the moment.

'You haven't been seen since the day before yesterday, and we knew you were on your own, so we feared the worst.'

'Oh … oh sorry.' Rosie didn't like the idea of being watched. 'I was out most of yesterday and I haven't got going yet today.' Why was she explaining herself to this nosy stranger? But then she felt herself soften as she realised that the woman could simply be concerned for her well-being. 'Thank you for worrying about me, but, as you can see, I'm perfectly fine.' She went to close the door, but the angel of mercy spoke again.

'Look, we're meeting at three o'clock in Beryl's van, number 17. Just the girls. We're having a Rummikub tournament, and we'd love it if you'd join us.'

*Over my dead body*, thought Rosie, and then realised that the thought was rather inappropriate given the woman's earlier fears. 'Thank you. I'll see what I feel like later, if that's all right. Number 17, you said?' Rosie beamed a big smile and the woman, whose name she still didn't know, backed away, nodding her grey curls.

Rosie locked the door and let the throw slip to the floor. She paused in the kitchenette long enough to grab two digestive biscuits and then went back to her list. This time she couldn't settle. The black spell had been broken, so she went to shower and get dressed at last.

At three o'clock, wondering what on earth she was doing, Rosie made her way to caravan number 17. The rain had moved away and the sun was trying to break through the clouds. The caravan door was open and laughter burst out in waves. It proved infectious, and Rosie had a big grin on her face by the time she tapped on the door.

The three ladies within were all giggling like young girls and gave Rosie an idea of what herself, Connie and Lucy might look like in forty years' time. Beryl, Betty and Anne announced very quickly that they were all widows.

Installed at the table with a glass of orange juice, as she'd refused the offered sherry, and a delicious piece of homemade cake, Rosie was soon absorbed with learning the unfamiliar game of Rummikub.

'Are you sure you've never played it before?' tutted Beryl, as if Rosie had a serious defect in her education.

They were patient and welcoming as Rosie studied the numbered tiles on her tray. They applauded her successes and cheered when she at last won her first game. Rosie was pleased that they didn't ask her questions about herself and her situation. However, the relief only lasted until after the fourth game.

'How come you're here all alone? A pretty girl like you.' Beryl's cheeks were flushed scarlet after another sherry.

'I just needed to get away from my everyday life for a while,' said Rosie, wondering whether to make a break for the open door.

She could tell that the third woman, Betty, who had knocked at her door earlier, was desperate to ask a question. When it came, the words burst out of her mouth in a torrent.

'Sorry dear, but we've all been speculating about whether you're the missing heiress mentioned in the newspaper. Please say you are!'

Rosie went cold and her voice shook when she found it. 'Missing heiress?'

'Yes, dear. I have the article here.' Beryl placed an article, carefully torn from a newspaper, on the table in front of Rosie.

Dots swam in front of Rosie's eyes, and she had a horrible feeling that she was going to faint, be sick, or both as she read the headlines. Somehow, she managed to maintain an outward appearance of calm and laugh at the suspicions of her new friends, but in reality she knew it might only be a matter of time before her whereabouts were discovered.

# *Chapter Twenty-Two*

When Tanner arrived on the coast near Harlech, he knew that it was a long shot that he would actually find Rosie. He booked into a small guest house, picking the one in the street with the neatest front garden. He was shown to a comfortable and clean room with old-fashioned heavy furniture and flowery curtains. There was a smell that combined cabbage and lavender in the air. The land lady, although very pleasant, showed a bit too much curiosity about his trip. He answered her questions without revealing anything significant and, ultimately, her interest gave him an idea – he was a journalist after all.

The castle, which he'd seen as he drove through the narrow main street of the town, drew him in. It was exciting to find a castle with nearly complete walls and tall towers. He had always enjoyed history and historical buildings. If he had his time again, he might have chosen a history or archaeology degree, instead of reading English at university. Although his main aim for this trip was to find Rosie, he decided to spend an hour exploring the castle. The views to the sea were mesmerising, especially as he knew, after reading the information boards, that the coast line had moved since it was built. The waves used to lap at the cliff below the thick walls. He spent his hour happily indulging his fantasies of being a knight in shining armour, wielding a sword and axe and rescuing a fair maiden who looked, in his mind's eye, incredibly like Rosie. He shook himself as he remembered she was his sister, but he supposed there was nothing wrong with rescuing his sister from a bad situation after all.

He suspected that the whole purpose of her trip was to escape, but maybe she was also re-living something from her childhood holidays, which she had said she remembered as idyllic. He tried to recall more about what she'd said when they'd discussed holidays, wishing he'd paid greater attention when she'd talked about her younger days while they were eating their pizza that night in Sowden – but back then he had been preoccupied with how to broach the subject of his father and their respective families.

Deciding to explore the beach next, Tanner laughed to himself that, up until a few weeks ago, he had rarely made time to set foot on the beach in Borteen, despite being near to the coast – but now he relished the idea of sinking his bare feet into the sand. He stood and worked his toes deep into the orangey-yellow grains and wondered how he could go about discovering Rosie's whereabouts. He had an inkling that she would be staying on a caravan site, as he was sure in their childhood holiday conversation she had definitely mentioned a caravan.

There weren't many people on the beach at the moment, but he scanned the scene, trying to see if anyone looked like his sister.

He was aware that if he started to ask direct questions about her, he might attract unwelcome attention. Falling back on his journalistic skills and the idea he'd had earlier, he decided to approach this as if he was writing an article on caravan holidays. When he thought about it, that seemed like a great idea anyway. He could cover the cost of his trip by selling several articles about caravans, castles and this coast.

However, he hadn't reckoned on the suspicion or closed communities of caravan park residents. Tanner wondered if they had all been schooled in scams and stranger danger. At the first park he went to, he approached the fifth person he met, but the man replied in cautious monosyllables. He warmed to his task once he'd decided on an angle for his first article – whether young people were taking caravan holidays, or whether it was a holiday option that would die out with the older generation. This slant also enabled him to ask residents questions to establish if there was anyone of Rosie's age staying on the sites. He'd never imagined that there would be so many caravan homes along this stretch of the coast. Lines of dark green corrugated metal stretched out before him. It began to feel like an impossible quest that would take forever.

Rosie was up and about early. Thankfully, she felt brighter today and more relaxed. Her mood had improved after she'd written her list of things she needed to tackle, and she had also rationalised that only the three ladies she had been with yesterday suspected she was the missing heiress from the newspaper article. It was almost funny to be described as an heiress and, although she knew she would eventually have to return to Borteen, she was in Wales right now and was still determined to try and enjoy it.

She didn't seem to need as much sleep here. The face looking back at her from the mirror appeared different and slightly tanned already. The birds were chorusing a tribute to daybreak as she pulled on her old tracksuit and trainers. She'd taken to walking along the shoreline as early as possible, before anyone else was about. It was interesting to see what had been washed up by the tide, and she wanted to get there first. It was fascinating to notice the differences to back home in Borteen. She enjoyed beachcombing there too. *I didn't do it as often as I should have, though,* she thought. Her life before all this had happened had always been very much focused on her work and career.

She had a bag slung across her shoulder for special finds to add to her growing collection of holiday shells, stones, seaglass and driftwood. The plastic rubbish distressed her, so much so that she had vowed to collect a carrier bag a day to put into the bin at the top of the beach while she was here.

She wasn't the only early beach scavenger today. A couple with a small dog that was yapping excitedly at the waves were heading towards her along the edge of the surf. It went through her mind that back in her old life she would have been irritated by the repeated bark, but here, in her relaxed state, it didn't cause a ruffle. She was so chilled this morning that she was more tolerant and less judgmental – definitely something she wanted to continue when she returned to normality, whatever that might mean and whatever the new challenges would be. She tried to ignore the lurch in her chest at the thought of returning home, as she had no idea what, or even where, that would be for her now.

The air was fresh and the breeze brisk and chilling. The grasses in the dunes sang their own particular tune as the wind whipped through them, and the horizon line was inky blue. Rosie's thoughts were somehow more peaceful after committing her worries to paper. A list could be worked through after all.

*Your soul has a new skip in it.* She giggled. Good food and sea air were beginning to help her to heal. She hadn't worn her watch since she arrived. It languished unwanted with her mobile phone in the glove compartment of the car. A timeless existence was so much more restful. It must have been like this in bygone days when people flowed with the seasons and the sunlight. *Clocks have a lot to answer for*, Rosie decided.

The couple with their dog passed her by with hearty "good mornings" and now she had a clear beach in front of her. She smiled as she took in lungfuls of sea air. She was almost, but not quite, ready to contact the "real" world again. How were Tanner and her mum? They had been the people she had thought of most in her isolation. She hadn't known Tanner long, but he was definitely logged as an important person in her future life. A brother-sister relationship needed to be built so that they could sort out their legacy. She wondered who had put that story in the press about the missing heiress. She couldn't believe it would have been Tanner or her mum.

'Rosie!' The yell dragged her out of her thoughts and she turned. She could hardly believe her eyes to see Tanner jogging over the sand towards her. *How?*

As he reached her, he looked so overjoyed that Rosie couldn't help but smile back. Tanner looked as bouncy as the little dog she'd encountered earlier. He hesitated a few feet from her as if checking she was all in one piece, and then grabbed her hands and swung her around in a circle.

'I'm so relieved to find you! I've been having nightmares.'

'Nightmares?' Guilt overwhelmed Rosie. 'Oh, Tanner, I'm so sorry. I've maybe been a bit selfish. But how on earth did you manage to find me?'

After her initial elation at seeing Tanner's face, Rosie suddenly felt uneasy and even a little annoyed with him appearing in her new world. He was invading her precious sanctuary and bringing her jolting back into reality before she was ready. All of the reasons she'd run away in the first place began to rise up in her thoughts, and she felt the smile begin to fade from her face.

Tanner seemed pleased with himself for finding her. 'Come on, I'll race you to the café over there and tell you everything over a coffee.'

She played along and began to jog to the end of the beach, but her attitude to him had definitely changed.

Tanner ran along next to Rosie. Her hair whipped into her eyes. She ran a little harder and then turned into Tanner's path, making him do an emergency stop.

'Why did you feel the need to find me? Why couldn't you let me have some space?'

'I got the impression that you were pleased to see me just now.' His expression was the picture of bewilderment.

'That was before I'd had time to think about it. I'm starting to believe my very first impression of you must have been right. You *are* a stalker! You're trying to control me and where I am. How long have you been watching me here?'

'No, no, Rosie, you have it all wrong.'

'Have I? Have I really?' Rosie felt her eyes bulging with indignation.

Rosie saw the light in Tanner's eyes extinguished by her words. What was she doing? *Stop it.* But she couldn't. She unleashed the full force of her anger on him. He held up his hands as if to ward off the onslaught, which caused her to pause.

'Okay. I'm sorry, maybe I shouldn't have come. I only wanted to be sure that you're well and happy. Your mum is worried and things have happened since you went away that I thought you should know about. It's taken me a few days to find you, and it was only by chance that I did. I haven't been stalking you, I promise.'

'Is there a problem, Rosie? Is this man bothering you?'

Rosie turned to see Alf Owens brandishing his stick in front of him like a sword. She was touched that the old man was ready to fight for her.

'It's fine, Alf. This is my half-brother, Tanner. I'm just annoyed with him because he's found me here and ... I'm not ready to talk to him about some family issues yet.' She put her hand on Alf's arm and he lowered his stick. 'Thank you for being ready to defend me, but there's really no need.'

'I was just leaving anyway,' said Tanner, looking meaningfully at Rosie.

When Rosie didn't reply, he turned abruptly and began to march back across the sands.

Rosie burst into hot tears.

'Rosie, love, he's really upset you.' Alf moved towards her, but Rosie waved him away.

'I'll speak to you later and explain, Alf, but right now I need to catch up with my brother. I think I'm being unreasonable.'

Tanner was disappearing into the dunes, as she began to run frantically after him. He'd clearly come all this way because he cared about her, and she had just slammed it back in his face.

She arrived at the door of his black sports car as he fired the engine. She was breathless and unable to speak. She could feel her skin reddening. Tanner wound down the window but didn't get out.

'I'm sorry, I was out of order. I was just annoyed that you'd found me when I thought I'd managed to hide away.'

'Let's forget it happened, shall we? I'll see you again when you decide to reappear in Borteen. Just be aware that there is a lot we need to sort out and some things you should know.' His tone was curt and he didn't look at her.

Rosie watched helplessly, her emotions all over the place, as he drove away.

# *Chapter Twenty-Three*

Unsettled by Tanner's surprise appearance in Wales, Rosie knew that she needed to do something different to clear her head and decided to go into Barmouth again. All the way on the bus, she was replaying what had been said on the beach and her thoughts about it all. She tried to put questions about what Tanner had meant by the "things she should know" to the back of her mind. She shrugged off a shiver of doubt about Frances' well-being. Surely Tanner would have made her listen if it was anything like that? It was more than likely the newspaper articles and legal stuff about the inheritance.

She made her way out of the shopping part of the town and on to the sand at Barmouth, marvelling that each beach had its own characteristics, right down to the colour and texture of the sand. She remembered hearing about a wooden carving in the sand dunes, almost like one of those on far away Easter Island in the Pacific. She found it and took a selfie with the figure in the background, but she could recognise a new tenseness in her face in the photo, just after she'd started to relax. Despite enjoying a mooch around the shops afterwards, her mood had irrevocably changed.

Rosie had stayed in her caravan for a week and a half so far. It was booked for two, but when she returned from Barmouth, she knew it was time to pack up and go home. She was surprisingly sad to be leaving. She'd mostly kept to herself during her time at the caravan park, apart from several games of Rummikub and one picnic, but she had known that the more permanent residents were unobtrusively keeping an eye on her, not to be nosy, but to make sure she was safe and in good health. She'd lost count of the number of cakes and home-baked loaves that had been left outside her caravan door.

She went to the local store, bought boxes of eggs and packs of apples, and left them at the top of the steps of each caravan whose occupants had helped her. They wouldn't be sure where they'd come from, but they'd no doubt guess when they discovered she was gone. It was satisfying to know that she had at least said her thanks, albeit in a small way. She couldn't face proper goodbyes.

The journey home was uneventful. She broke her trip in a little market town, had a coffee and a wander around the shops to stretch her legs. She had no intention of buying anything, but she knew that she was mentally preparing for going home, easing herself gently back into reality and what awaited her in Borteen.

As it was on the way, she stopped off at her mother's house in the late afternoon when she reached Sowden. Frances was in the front garden with Dusty running around her. When she turned, Rosie caught a flash of pain crossing her mother's features just before Frances schooled her face into a smile.

'The prodigal daughter. How are you, Rosie?'

Rosie and her mother didn't habitually hug, but Rosie thought that this was an appropriate time to show some affection. Frances clung on to her just a second longer than Rosie had been prepared for.

'Coffee? Nice necklace. Where have you been?'

'Yes, thanks, and Wales.'

'Ah, I should have guessed. Childhood haunts?'

'Yes, even the rock pools are still the same.'

'Goodness, I'd forgotten about the rock pools. You used to spend ages feeding the anemones with biscuit crumbs.'

'I swear they were the same anemones, Mum – and still as hungry.'

'At least some things don't change. Did you have a lovely time? You certainly look healthy.' Frances held Rosie at arm's length and looked her up and down.

'Amazing what beach walks can do. It was a mix of enjoyable and sad times, but I think it did me the world of good. Generally restored my spirits and my faith in human nature. Gave me time to think and to get things into perspective.'

'Everything here has been much the same, apart from I had a frantic visit from Tanner last week. He was really worried about you.'

'Tanner turned up in Wales.'

'I knew he'd found you because of a quick message he left for me about you being safe and well, but how did he know where to look?'

'We had a conversation once about childhood holidays over pizza. He must have made a lucky guess, or else he's been busy visiting seaside towns up and down the country.' She laughed.

'He was obviously meant to find you.'

'You say he left you a message?'

'Yes, on my answerphone saying that I'd been right and we should leave you to come back in your own time, but he wanted to reassure me that you were okay.'

'I'm surprised he did even that after my reaction in Wales when he turned up.' Rosie sighed, feeling slightly guilty again.

'Let's go and get a coffee, and you can tell me all about it.' Frances set off up the path and into the house. 'I did laugh when I saw his article in the newspaper about how the young are turning their backs on caravan holidays. It makes sense now.'

'He must have taken the opportunity to do some research while he was trying to find me.' She laughed again.

Rosie waited until her mother had put steaming cups of real coffee on the table. Her whole life had revolved around issues being settled over a hot drink, with Frances always seeing tea or coffee as essential to any troublesome conversation.

'Did you speak to Tanner about me and what happened in your past?'

'A little.' Frances rubbed at a small drop of spilled coffee on the table with her finger. 'I showed him the old photograph album I found in the loft. You might like to have a look yourself. It actually shows very clearly that Michael Bryant was your biological father.' She pointed to the dresser and Rosie went over to pick up the album. 'It was tricky to know how to share some of it with him, Rosie, as it doesn't always reflect well on his parents. I think it made him sad to see Michael and Georgia happy together. I suppose he's never seen them like that.'

'I guess so, but I still think he needed to know what happened back then.' Rosie brought the album back to the kitchen table. Did she imagine that she could feel Tanner's energy on the surface? She'd obviously been more influenced by her encounter with Buzz, the mystical man from the shop where she'd bought her necklace, than she'd realised.

'Maybe it would be better if you discuss it all with him.'

'I'm not sure he'll be speaking to me after I got so angry with him in Wales.'

'Why did you get angry with him?'

'It felt as if he'd disturbed my peace, invaded my space and not respected my need for a complete break. I'm ashamed of myself now, as I'm sure he was only trying to give me some information and was worried about me, but, Mum, my feelings around him are so complicated and confused right now.'

'Sounds like you have some bridges to build with your brother.' Frances emphasised the word "brother". 'You two have got to establish a working relationship – that is, unless Georgia is successful in her attempt to overturn the will and inherit most of her ex-husband's estate. Oops ... do you know about that?'

'I do, actually.' Rosie grimaced. 'When I was in Wales, I got sort of adopted by the elderly residents of the caravan site. They successfully guessed that I was the missing heiress mentioned in newspaper articles, and they showed me newspaper cuttings about Georgia's attempt to overturn Michael Bryant's will. I denied being the heiress, of course, but I don't think they believed me. They were really sweet people and so protective. I think Alf Owens was ready to call Tanner out for a duel at dawn when he saw that I was upset by his appearance in Wales.'

'It sounds as if you've been well looked after.'

Rosie thought she could detect a note of envy in her mother's voice. 'Why don't we go back there together sometime?'

'Maybe, but I  sort of feel responsible for you needing to run away to Wales in the first place. I gave you a lot of scary information last time we met. I was worried that I had traumatised you, perhaps even pushed you over the edge. You'd never have got close to Tanner if I'd come clean about my secrets earlier.'

'Mum, you can't help things that happened in your past. As far as I can see, you've been the victim here too. You were virtually used and discarded by Michael Bryant and had to live with the consequences. You lost Dad when you had a small child and struggled to bring me up on your own.'

'Strange, I never thought of it as a struggle. I enjoyed your childhood and your auntie helped too. I've always thought I was lucky. I got to build the sandcastles and fly the kites. I've noticed that in families where there's a mother and a father, the man usually gets that privilege.'

'In case you are wondering, Mum, I never felt deprived, or that anything was missing in my childhood. Of course, I built Dad ... John ... into a mythical superhero. What child wouldn't? He is the only father I'll ever know, and I'm grateful that he was a great one. I'm sort of glad I didn't know he'd had an affair with Georgia before now, though. It would have been much more difficult to deal with knowing that when I was younger.'

'I was worried you might never speak to me again after I told you he wasn't your father.'

'Why did you never find anyone else to share your life with, Mum?'

‘I figured I was better off relying on myself. I still carry the hurt of John’s betrayal to this day and, to a certain extent, the memory of Michael and our disastrous one night. I made a conscious decision never to put myself in that situation again, and I’ve no regrets.’

‘Maybe I should follow your lead and keep away from men altogether.’

‘Rosie, don’t base your life on mine. I can hardly claim to be an ideal role model.’

‘I wasn’t even thinking that. I had a bad time with Ollie, I began to fall for Tanner and then found out he’s my brother! Now I’m confused about how to handle our joint inheritance, whether to go into business with him, whether to stay around here at all, whether to run away to the seaside again.’ Rosie drew in a huge breath as she had run out of air during her speech.

Frances reached forward to place her hand on her daughter’s arm. ‘So, despite your argument in Wales, you’re going to talk to Tanner, aren’t you?’

‘In one way, I don’t want to see him again, but if we are going to move forward then we have to make a fresh start, build a relationship as brother and sister. I’m just not sure I’m strong enough. What am I going to do, Mum?’

‘Just take it one day at a time, love.’

‘Maybe Georgia will be successful with her challenge and I won’t inherit anything after all, then I can be free again.’

Rosie opened the old photograph album and turned the pages. There was indeed no doubting that Michael Bryant was her father. Part of her felt pleased that there was no doubt, but sad too.

She claimed fatigue after her journey from Wales and left Frances shortly afterwards with another big hug.

Her little rented house was just as she’d left it, if a little dusty and musty smelling. She sat pondering everything for a long time, stroking her moonstone pendant thoughtfully.

# *Chapter Twenty-Four*

The next morning, Rosie made a phone call to the solicitor, Justin Sadler, to request a meeting be set up on a formal basis with Tanner to talk about the future and the challenge to the will by Georgia.

Leaving the legal wheels to turn, she headed out to retrace the steps she had taken before she'd gone away to Wales. She went into Polka Dot Paradise, tried on and bought the formal business jacket – which miraculously was still there and was the right size for her. She decided it would give her courage for the serious meeting ahead.

It was as if the seasons had changed while she'd been in Wales. The leaves on the trees were turning to autumn colours and the air was definitely colder.

When she reached the beach, a crowd had gathered further along the sand. Intrigued, she meandered over to see what was going on. Someone had marked out a labyrinth in the sand. People were taking turns to weave around its intricate paths.

Rosie noticed a pink heart-shaped bucket placed at the start. A notice asked for donations for a homeless charity. Then she saw who was running the event: the man who had sold her the moonstone pendant, Buzz. She took some coins from her purse, joined the queue and stood watching a freckled-faced man walking the labyrinth. Determination was written into every line of his face as he concentrated on each footstep.

'Ah, moonstone lady. Are you in need of inner peace and direction?' The shop owner's grin was broad and somehow challenging.

Rosie smiled back and unconsciously grasped the pendant nestled beneath her scarf. He had remembered her. 'Rosie, and yes – desperately in need of both peace and direction.'

He threw her proffered coins in the bucket and, grasping her hand, looked closely at her palm. 'You have cried many tears and have agonised over choices. Now you need to be at peace and let your destiny unfold,' he announced.

'It's easier said than done to be at peace and let destiny unfold when you feel so confused.' She dug a small hole in the sand with the toe of her boot.

'Why don't you come and see me again at the shop for a tarot reading? The tide is coming in. I won't be here much longer.'

'I might just do that.' Rosie mused again about this man's attention and intentions. 'Now, how do I tackle this labyrinth and what is it supposed to mean or do?'

Buzz's distinctive incense smell caught at her nostrils as he spoke. 'Follow the path and concentrate on your feet. Wait and see if it helps you. Keep an open mind.'

Rosie walked around the meandering circular paths of the sand maze and wondered if she was imagining growing ever calmer. It was as if the troubled thoughts she'd had that morning were washing away with each step.

Not long after she'd finished walking the path, the tide reached that part of the beach and, along with the rest of those standing nearby, she watched the pattern in the sand wash away. Was it that simple? Could her troubles be washed away so easily?

People dispersed and Rosie wandered around the Borteen alleyways, window shopping. She bought herself a cheese and coleslaw sandwich and a takeaway coffee from the pie shop, and sat on a bench overlooking the beach in the sun to eat.

At two o'clock, she made her way to Buzz's shop. The wind chimes tinkled as she opened the door and a cloud of incense wafted out to greet her. She allowed herself to be enveloped by the shop's dark, cosy interior.

Buzz didn't show any surprise at her arrival – she could have almost believed he'd predicted the exact time. He sat down by a wooden table which was deeply carved with strange symbols, and gestured for her to sit in the chair opposite to him. The deck of cards, which he put into her hands, was heavy and well-worn at the edges. He asked her to shuffle them. When she returned the pack to him, he placed several cards from the top of the deck onto the table in a pattern.

'What do you really need to know, Rosie?' His expression had taken on an otherworldly look, and she could suddenly understand where some of the popular shape-shifter stories had come from. His nose became beak-like and his eyes seemed hooded, as she imagined they searched her soul.

She took a few moments to consider. 'At the moment, I need to be sure whether to return to my life in Borteen or to leave and go somewhere new, and whether to go into business with my brother. I'd also like to know whether I will ever find a special love.'

'Not much then.' Buzz laughed softly.

‘Sorry, is that too much?’ Uncertainty and shyness crowded in her mind.

‘No, no, I will see what can be revealed.’

Buzz touched her hand briefly and heat flared on her skin, just like when she’d had her Reiki treatment at the health fair. She shifted a little uneasily in the chair. Did she really want the answers to her questions in this way? The incense smell was getting deep into her nostrils, but she thought sneezing right now might ruin the atmosphere.

Buzz looked up and smiled at her. ‘You are wondering right now what you are doing here and whether I’m going to tell you a load of rubbish.’ He didn’t wait for a response. ‘Okay, let’s see what we have in the cards.’

He began to turn over the colourful rectangles of cardboard, displaying their bright pictures. ‘Confusing information ... but I’ll say it anyway, as sometimes the message will only mean something to the person for whom it is intended. Running away won’t help you, you’ve tried it before. Stay and face the music. Make the best of things. You will have a business helping others, but that won’t be with a brother. As to love, yes, there is a man coming very close to you right now. Listen to what your guardian angel whispers into your ear and you can’t go far wrong. Oh, and I have a key word for you – Star. Interesting. That means that you have moved on in the couple of weeks I have known you. You have moved from moon to star. Does that jumble help you at all?’

‘I’m not sure.’ Rosie was busy scribbling notes into her handbag notebook. ‘I’ll have to think about it. Does that mean I need a new pendant with a star rather than a moon?’

‘No, no. There’s a star on your pendant too.’ He pointed to the silver talisman swinging free from her T-shirt as she leaned forward.

‘And here was me thinking this might be an elaborate marketing tool.’ Rosie laughed.

‘No, if I was that clever I wouldn’t be sitting here.’ He winked. ‘And I’m wondering if I’ve already met the man the cards foretold for you.’

‘Really? You think you have met the man?’

‘Time will tell, my dear. Time will tell.’

Rosie thanked him, but as she was preparing to leave, she asked him, ‘Why are you called Buzz? Is it short for something?’

‘When I did my Shaman training I was given a new name – Buzzard.’

# *Chapter Twenty-Five*

Rosie was at the solicitor's office once more. She had decided to keep her first contact with Tanner on a formal basis and had asked for this meeting with him and his father's solicitor. She glanced at Tanner as Justin Sadler explained Georgia's challenge to her ex-husband's will. Tanner was either writing notes on the pad of paper in front of him or doodling. She wasn't close enough to him to work out which.

'Georgia King, formerly Bryant, claims that her late ex-husband promised her a further settlement to add to the one she received at the time of their divorce in the event he pre-deceased her. I have, however, been unable to find reference to this promise in writing, and therefore suggest that the challenge to the legal will is more than likely to fail. Unless, of course, she has a personal letter or other paperwork from Michael Bryant detailing this further bequest that can be proved to be valid and genuine. Have you any knowledge of your mother's claim, Tanner?'

'Pardon? Sorry, I was miles away,' replied Tanner sheepishly.

That answered her earlier question – he must have been doodling.

Justin repeated his question for Tanner's benefit.

'The relationship between my parents has always been a complete mystery to me. I'm not aware of any post-divorce promises made to my mother, but am I allowed to ask, Justin, if my father's original will contained a slightly different bequest for her?'

'We're on slightly dodgy grounds here, but no, the original will left Michael Bryant's entire estate to you, Tanner.'

Tanner glanced over at Rosie. 'I would love to know what my mother said to my father that day. They argued and then he altered his will afterwards. She's refused to talk about it the couple of times I've managed to have a conversation with her. I think I probably need to be more persistent.'

'My advice to Georgia King would be, and I presume she has her own solicitors working on her behalf, that she is unlikely to succeed with any challenge and would be wasting her money continuing with her claim. The challenge will, of course, delay probate.'

Rosie spoke for the first time at the meeting. ‘Given your thoughts on the will and Georgia’s challenge to it, it’d be good for me to know exactly what I stand to inherit and also any conditions associated with that.’

‘Let me start with the items to be jointly inherited by yourself and Tanner.’

She had to hide her surprise at the amount Michael Bryant had left to her. He had clearly been a very successful business man. She waited until Justin completed his report.

‘As you probably realise, this legacy has been a complete surprise to me, and I’m struggling to come to terms with it, to be honest. My … erm, father appears to have assumed I’d just step in and manage his interests alongside Tanner, but I’m not sure I can, or even want to do that.’ Justin seemed able to hide any reaction to this statement, but Tanner’s face was full of surprise. He went to interrupt her. She waved her hand to silence him. ‘Let me finish, Tanner.’

He sat back in his chair; his brow furrowed.

‘I wondered if there were any possibilities for me to walk away with a financial settlement instead of a hands-on involvement?’

*Did she imagine the sharp intakes of breath?*

‘You wouldn’t want to work with me?’ Tanner spluttered.

‘If I’m totally honest, I’d like to walk away from this, even if it means I inherit nothing. My life has been turned upside down. I’ve given notice at Borden Glass, I couldn’t work there now, especially as I don’t even know whether I earned my job on merit rather than because I’m Michael’s daughter. So, there’s really nothing to keep me in this area. If there was the possibility for a settlement, I could start again, maybe do some of the things I’ve never had time for before, treat my mum …’ Rosie’s voice tailed off.

Tanner jumped in to the silence. ‘Is there any scope for a settlement for Rosie?’

She smiled her gratitude for his support.

‘The will clearly states that Tanner Bryant and Rosie Phillips are to jointly hold the items named in the will for at least a year before considering any sale of the assets,’ explained Justin.

‘He may have intended this and I have no idea why, but he doesn’t have to live with the consequences, does he?’ Rosie knew her voice had a steely edge.

'But we just have to keep everything going for a year before we have the option to sell the lot?' Tanner looked thoughtful. 'Then, we can *both* start again.' When no one spoke, Tanner continued. 'I've been standing in for my father for the past six months while he's been ill, but his businesses are not of my choosing. I've had to virtually abandon my own career to keep everything going.'

Justin nodded. 'That about sums it up. You need to work together for a year. It seems that he wanted you to get to know each other. However, Michael did put another substantial sum into a trust.'

'I don't remember this being mentioned before.' Tanner looked at Rosie and she shook her head.

'Did either of you read the personal copies of the will I prepared for you?'

Rosie felt her face redden slightly. Her copy was still screwed up at the back of the fireplace in her cottage, where she'd thrown it in disgust on the day she'd found out that Michael Bryant was her father.

'The trust will release these funds to you both if you continue to run the businesses or, indeed, any part of them selected by you jointly for a further period of five years.'

'Why was he so keen to keep us together?' asked Rosie faintly.

'No idea,' replied Tanner. 'So what happens to this trust money if we don't "comply"?'

'The whole lot goes to charity.' Justin turned his computer to reveal a figure in an online account to Rosie and Tanner. Tanner swore under his breath, and Rosie gripped the edge of the table in shock at the sum.

'What do you think of all this, Rosie?'

'I'm not in this for the money. It would suit me very nicely to get a cash equivalent, even if I have to wait a year for it. In fact, anything is better than nothing, because if you think about it, up until recently I didn't even know anything about an inheritance.'

'So, what happens if we don't work together for the specified year?' asked Tanner.

'All of the assets are to be sold and added to the charity trust.'

'Then we'd inherit nothing at all?' Tanner looked thoughtful.

'But that's totally unfair,' exclaimed Rosie. 'And I don't mean for me, I mean for Tanner.'

‘So the bottom line is that we need to manage my father’s assets and businesses between us for a year from his death, and then we can sell the lot?’

‘Not from the date of his death, rather from the date probate is settled,’ explained Justin.

‘I have a few ideas of how we could achieve this, Rosie.’

‘And you’d be happy to sacrifice the rest of the money, by not doing the further five years?’ asked Rosie.

‘Let’s see how our compulsory year goes …’

# *Chapter Twenty-Six*

Tanner had appreciated Rosie's point of view at the meeting and tried to support her, but he still hoped they could salvage their legacy by working together. The danger was that she could just walk away. When he suggested a drink at a nearby pub as neutral territory that evening, she'd accepted.

The country pub was a bit run-down and had not been refurbished for many years. Tanner wrinkled his nose as he sat on the bald velveteen bench and sipped his shandy. He felt nervous but kept telling himself it was ridiculous. He needed to see if he could preserve the fledgling friendship they'd been developing before they found out that they were related. Trouble was, it was still difficult to see her as his sister … yet – he'd have to get used to the fact.

The bar was empty as it was early, and he found himself relieved that their conversation would not be overheard. Rosie was wearing jeans and a cream blouse. Tanner was fascinated by the glint of a necklace at her throat. She asked for a diet coke in response to his question about what she would like to drink.

'How have you been?' He regretted asking her as soon as he'd said it.

'I'm still very confused about all of this. It's as if I've landed in an alien world, not of my choosing.' Her tone was sad, her face pale.

'Sorry, silly question.'

'But how have *you* been? Sorry, I was a bit tactless. You've just lost your father after all.'

'And so have you.' He quirked an eyebrow and wondered if he'd been wise to remind her.

'The difference being, I didn't know I'd lost a parent until he was already gone. Tell me, did he ever say anything to you about me?'

'No. I don't know if your mother mentioned it, but he had collected some information about you and I found it on his desk. I tried to ask him about it but by the time I did, he was already very ill and out of it on heavy medication.'

'Is that why you kept turning up in my life?'

'Yes, I was curious about his link to you, especially when all I could get out of him was something about a family debt. I guess I should say that my father and I didn't get on too well a lot of the time, so we didn't talk much anyway.'

‘But you were his only child!’

‘Guess he wasn’t too happy with what he’d produced.’ Tanner felt the familiar dissatisfied and inadequate feelings creep over him in response to thinking about his father’s opinion of him. ‘I guess I was a bitter disappointment.’

‘But how so? You seem to have achieved a lot to me, your articles are sought after and ... you’re handsome and tall.’ Rosie reddened in embarrassment, presumably because of what she’d just said.

‘Hardly a chip off the old block, though.’

‘I’m so sad for you, at least I know that my dada loved me, even if he wasn’t my biological father. When I think of him, I can only feel love radiating from him towards me.’

Tanner watched Rosie drift off into some remembered scene. ‘What will you do with your half of the money in a year’s time? Twelve months will go very quickly, I think.’

She shook herself. ‘Rebuild my life. Maybe buy Mum a house nearer the sea, write a novel. You?’

‘Move back to London and get my journalism career back on track.’

‘Let’s drink to new beginnings then ... after twelve months working together, of course.’

Tanner couldn’t help a glimmer of regret as they clinked their glasses and drank. He decided that he needed to tell her about his idea.

‘We can just keep everything going as it is for the next year, or … Rosie, before we think of just turning the handle then giving it all up, I’d like you to have a proper look around Lucerne Lodge ... I’d like to float a couple of ideas about how this inheritance could work for both of us, maybe longer term beyond the first year. Please, just humour me.’

They stood in front of the huge façade of Lucerne Lodge. Rosie mused that it was nearly the exact spot where Tanner had first spoken to her after he’d caused the accident that had resulted in her being dowsed in prawn cocktail. She shook herself to sponge out the memories of how seeds of attraction had stirred inside of her that day – attraction to Tanner, before she’d known he was her brother. *Yuck*! She still shuddered when she thought how they could have become too close without knowing they were even related.

‘So, what did you have in mind for the Lodge? It sounds as if you have an idea.’

'I was thinking that if we start a new business here, we could maybe keep it running and make it work for both of us. We could start small and then when we're able to sell other assets – probably Borden Glass – we could invest some of the money here. Lucerne Lodge would make an ideal luxury venue for weddings and parties. It could be quite a money-making venture.'

Rosie was quiet as she thought about this. A glimmer of excitement began to build, despite her misgivings. 'I agree, it could be a great venue for weddings ... but what about it being something like a retreat centre?'

'Like a spa?'

'Not exactly, more somewhere offering people an escape from their normal lives with extras such as alternative therapies, meditation and yoga. Maybe even writing and art courses, that sort of thing.' Rosie began to feel more animated as her thoughts crystallised.

Tanner was smiling now too. 'So we'd offer peace and tranquillity for burnt out executives with therapies, and art courses to get them de-stressed and creative again?'

'Yes, that's exactly it.'

'Not sure we could do the weddings and parties too. Wouldn't it break the peaceful atmosphere?'

'Maybe, although we could have that business as an alternative.' Rosie didn't like him to think she was dismissing his idea entirely. 'So, am I right in thinking you're reluctant to part with the house?'

'Not sure. I'm not exactly sentimental about it, just looking for something more positive for us to spend a year doing. The other businesses are already set up to be managed by others. At least we meet the stipulation of working together if we do this, and then who knows? Do you think we could start this business together, given everything that has happened?'

'We'll see.' After her initial enthusiasm, Rosie began to feel uncertain, but then what else was she going to do now that she'd given up her job?

'Don't say that, please.'

'What?'

'"We'll see"'.

'Why not when it's the truth?'

'It's what my parents said a lot when they were about to disappoint me. "We'll see if we can go to Disneyland", "We'll see if I've time to read you a bedtime story", "We'll see if I have time to come to graduation".'

'Oh, Tanner, you poor thing.'

'I survived. In fact, I think I'm a pretty balanced individual given my upbringing.' He laughed.

'When I said, "we'll see", I meant ... well ... I still don't really know you as a person very well, Tanner, so how can I say with any certainty if I could work with you?'

'You're right, of course. Maybe we should take some time to become friends ... err, siblings even, and then make that decision.'

'Maybe.'

Tanner went quiet, and Rosie could see he was probably imagining new futures for Lucerne Lodge.

'I also have a bit of a weird feeling here now I know that my dad, John Phillips that is, died down by the lake.'

'I suppose only you can decide if you can get over that one and work here. I can understand why it would affect you.'

Rosie looked over to the large stone building. The clouds had parted and it was bathed in sunlight. Rosie wondered if this was a sign she was on the right track. She needed some of Buzz's foresight.

'Perhaps you should take me on a tour. I haven't seen much of the house yet.'

'It's half yours – feel free.'

'But it's still your home. I really would prefer it if you gave me a guided tour.'

'It's not really my home any more. I haven't lived here for over ten years. I moved back when Dad was ill, but my main home is my apartment in London.'

'Okay, so do I need to factor in living quarters for us in the house?'

'Probably a good idea. It would make sense for at least one of us to live in on-site to keep an eye on things.'

'We could have a self-contained apartment each ... if there's room, of course.' She eyed the building. 'Possibly on the top floor.'

'There should be plenty space for that – the old servants' quarters are vast.'

'Come on, show me.' Rosie began to walk quickly towards the house. Her enthusiasm to get on with the project was bubbling through her veins again. Despite any misgivings about the location and her worries about working with Tanner, she began to feel more alive than she had in a long time.

The ideas kept coming. Maybe the therapy retreat wasn't compatible with the weddings and parties idea, but that didn't stop them hosting alternative therapy fairs. She realised she needed to assess the house properly. How many guest bedrooms could they offer? What insurance would they need? Would she want to train in therapies herself? Would Connie want a job? After all, if she hadn't dragged Rosie to those courses and fairs, she wouldn't have had the idea. Rosie kept remembering a retreat she'd attended herself in Somerset when the strain of splitting up with Ollie had worn her down and how much it had relaxed her.

'Even if you say you aren't totally sure, your face tells me you're starting to enjoy considering the possibilities of this.' Tanner was grinning at her as they reached the back door.

'I will admit that my mind is whirling off in all sorts of directions.'

'It's nice to see you enthusiastic.'

'Maybe I do need a project to get my teeth into.'

'I can always go back to London and leave you to it.'

'Oooh, not just yet. It would feel scary doing it all on my own. Moral support at least, please!'

Rosie realised she was having fun, and she could tell that Tanner was enjoying it too – his face was lit up with a huge smile. It was lovely to be able to talk and joke with him without all of the heavy stuff getting in the way. Maybe they could work together as brother and sister after all.

'Come on, let's take this grand tour.'

Rosie laughed and curtseyed, as she entered into the role play. 'Lead on, kind sir.'

Lucerne Lodge was huge and rambling with glorious views from every window. Rosie was amazed as they wandered the corridors and peeked into slightly dusty room after slightly dusty room. The house had a faded grandeur, and Rosie resolved not to modernise it too much. As it stood, it was comfortable and relaxing without the forbidding nature of the contemporary interior of some modernised grand houses she had visited. The layout of the building was very suitable too, with the bedrooms arranged on the first and second floors, and reception rooms on the ground.

Rosie followed Tanner around, taking in as much as she could. She knew she would have to make a more detailed analysis of each room and what needed to be changed in every one, but she could see that the building would adapt itself to her proposal almost effortlessly.

'Do you have ghosts?' she asked, as they reached a particularly dark landing.

'I don't think so, but then I wouldn't imagine I'm particularly sensitive to stuff like that.'

'I often think that I sense my father around me.' Rosie hesitated. 'I mean Dada, not your father.'

'It sounds as if he was a good man.'

'What I can remember of him is all good, but he died when I was very young – I worry that I've built up an overly rosy picture of him.'

They reached what was obviously the library, and Rosie couldn't help getting excited over the dusty books. 'Now, if I was a ghost, this is the place I'd choose to haunt.' She flitted amongst the shelves, examining titles.

Tanner laughed. 'Do you truly believe in ghosts?'

'I've never seen one, but I do feel strange sensations sometimes. I believe that we all have a spirit, which is different from the physical body, and so I don't see any reason why that can't linger after death.'

'I've never really given it that much thought.'

Rosie decided to shut up and concentrate on the job in hand.

Tanner finished off his tour with a look around the formal gardens of the house, including a lovely walled area full of roses. He introduced Rosie to Trixie and seemed pleased that the two girls struck up an instant friendship. Trixie whined as Rosie walked away from the pen.

The tour over, Tanner led Rosie to the kitchen. It was strange to be back in the familiar room. Rosie glanced into the Belfast sink, half expecting her ruined dress to still be there. It wasn't, of course.

'Okay, to summarise.' Tanner leaned against the marble counter and collected his thoughts. 'I propose that we keep Borden Glass and its subsidiaries going for the year using the business managers and try to find buyers to take over eventually, but I think we should hang on to Lucerne Lodge and give this project a chance, at least for the stipulated year.'

'Agreed,' said Rosie with a smile.

The future suddenly seemed brighter. Tanner settled Rosie on a kitchen stool and proceeded to make toasted teacakes and hot chocolate.

Rosie looked thoughtful. ‘You know, I really believe this idea could work and I’m even more convinced of it after the tour of the house. It’s perfect, almost as if it was purpose built for it.’

‘I can see a way to link it into other things too.’

‘Such as?’

‘I think we need to do some research about what’s out there in the market already.’

‘Research sounds fun.’

‘Yes, but more than that. I can write articles on the places we visit for the research, and an article comparing them too.’

‘Ahh, the journalist is coming out now.’

‘Hang on, I haven’t finished yet. Those articles could lead to other features about our refurbishment of Lucerne Lodge and our business launch. It would make perfect advertising.’

‘Great idea! You could also do in-depth articles on the therapies we propose to offer, and maybe even profiles of the therapists we hire to work here too?’

‘You have a clear vision of how this will all work, don’t you?’

‘I’m surprising myself, because you are totally right – I do.’

‘We just need it confirmed that we are actually going to inherit it, I guess.’

An inner glow began to build in his chest and, from her face, he could tell Rosie had a similar feeling. He decided it was time to give her something he’d bought for her a while back. ‘I’m hoping you don’t bite my head off, but—’ Tanner mock ducked ‘—before you go, I have a present for you. In fact, I wouldn’t have even suggested this meeting if the salesman – if you can call him that – hadn’t said something when I bought it.’

Rosie’s expression was understandably puzzled.

Tanner handed her a tissue paper parcel. The familiar looking paper had yin and yang signs on it.

‘What have I done to deserve this?’

‘I bought it on a trip into Borteen, just before I came to Wales. I had rather a strange encounter with the shop keeper.’

‘Don’t tell me, a grey-haired mystic guy?’

‘Tall guy, creepy eyes, grey hair, incense-laden shop.’

‘That’s Buzz.’ Rosie’s hand flew to her throat to hold her pendant.

'Why don't you open it?'

'I need to hear what Buzz said first.' She squeezed her pendant in anticipation.

'He took my hand when I held out my money, which you can probably imagine totally freaked me out, and he seemed to read my palm. If he wasn't so hypnotic in his mannerisms, I might have decked him for touching me before I realised what he was doing.'

'And?' Rosie was getting impatient.

'He said that the present I was buying matched something that the person I was going to give it to already owned, and that I needed to give it to her when we had decided to run our business together.'

'Have we decided?'

'I think we are close to it, and I couldn't wait.'

Rosie laughed and tore open the tissue paper. Inside was a bracelet with two hanging moonstone charms – a moon and a star. She looked up in surprise. 'It's so lovely! Thank you. Did you choose it, or did Buzz?'

'I saw it in the window of his shop and went in to ask about it. It sounds so stupid, but it seemed to call to me. Can you imagine that I would be tempted to venture into that sort of shop otherwise? Now, come on, I'm intrigued. Does it match something you own?'

Rosie pulled her moon and star pendant out from under her blouse. 'Look at this.'

'Whoa, that *is* totally spooky.'

'Thank you for my lovely present. Buzz is a pretty special guy. He got one thing wrong, though. He told me the person I'd run a business with wouldn't be my brother.'

# *Chapter Twenty-Seven*

Rosie returned home in the late afternoon. She kept looking at the new bracelet on her wrist with wonder, but also strange mixed feelings that she couldn't quite put her finger on. Her head was full of ideas and plans for Lucerne Lodge, and she decided that she had better write some of them down as soon as she could.

She walked from the car up the short grey-paving-slabbed path and looked, as if for the first time, at the cottage she was renting. It appeared so tiny compared to the building she had just come from. She would soon have the money to buy a much bigger house if she chose to, but this little cottage had represented a new start when she'd moved from London.

She could vacuum the whole house in thirty minutes, and that included moving the furniture. The tiny porch led into a lounge, beyond this was a kitchen, with just room for a small half-circle table and two chairs against the radiator. There was a door to the yard outside. Rosie had struggled to find a washing airer tiny enough to fit in the space. She'd put two trough planters against the fence to indulge her love of bright flowers. If the washing wasn't out, she had a folding chair and table so that she could sit outside.

Upstairs was a main bedroom with a mere foot width all around the bed, a shower room and a box room. Rosie often marvelled that a family of four lived in the house next door. *Needs must*, she supposed. At least the lack of space made her better at giving away things she no longer used or needed. If she had learned anything living in this cottage, it was that accumulating possessions was not what made you happy.

If the plans for Lucerne Lodge were to go ahead, she would need to live on-site for a while, at least to begin with. She reached for a pad of paper and began to note down ideas, questions and the skeleton of a business plan. There were still circling doubts, but their chatter seemed to be diminishing. A year would pass very quickly, and then she would have so many more choices with her legacy funds.

Tanner was full of questions, ideas and some doubts too. He started two spreadsheets on the computer. One covered the ideas and questions he had for Rosie, and the other was a list of articles he could write and sell based on the journey they would have to go through to create the retreat and therapy centre.

He felt happier than he had in a long time. He didn't think for one minute that his father would be pleased about their proposed use for his house, but there was a certain satisfaction in the continuation of a sort of rebellion, even after Michael Bryant's death.

He pondered Rosie's plans for apartments for both of them on the top floor of Lucerne Lodge. He guessed that at least one of them would need to live there to keep an eye on the business. Maybe he should volunteer to move back to his London flat to stop any awkwardness and let Rosie take the lead on this?

Lucy and Connie squealed as Rosie walked into the restaurant a few days later.

Lucy rushed to embrace her. 'It feels as if you've been away ages, but it's obviously been good for you. You look *so* healthy.'

'So, come and tell us all of your news,' said Connie.

Rosie had thought long and hard about exactly how much to tell the girls. 'Potted version, and then you can ask me more if you feel the need – met a clairvoyant. Stayed in a caravan in Wales. Tanner came to find me over there and I got very angry with him. The will is being challenged, so I might not inherit after all. If we do inherit, Tanner and I are considering setting up a retreat at Lucerne Lodge offering therapies, yoga and courses.'

'Oooh, can I have a job?' asked Connie excitedly.

'We will definitely need therapists, so you'd better finish your diplomas. After all, you dragging me to those courses and health fairs made me think of the idea in the first place.'

'How is the lovely Tanner?' asked Lucy. 'He was very worried about you when you went missing. I gave him a big hug.'

Rosie had to swallow down the feelings Lucy's question produced. Could she cope with Lucy showing an interest in her brother?

# *Chapter Twenty-Eight*

Rosie and Tanner had decided to pick an outing each, so that they could get to know each other better before finally deciding whether or not they could be business partners.

'Have you got walking boots?' Tanner asked her.

'Yes,' lied Rosie. She didn't want to admit to Tanner that she hadn't done any serious walking for a long time, just her meandering beach walks in Borteen and recently Wales.

'Okay, let's go and spend a day walking in the hills. I'll pick you up at eight tomorrow morning.'

'Eight on a Saturday?' Rosie wailed. Why did Saturday still feel like a very different day even when she wasn't in a regular working routine?

'Come on, it'll be fun.'

Tanner's lopsided grinning face on the video call was hard to resist, so Rosie agreed, before grabbing her coat and bag and zooming down to the shops. She didn't normally buy outdoor clothing, so it took her a while to locate the camping shop. The lady behind the counter was very helpful in kitting her out with a small rucksack, waterproofs, walking boots and socks. Rosie went for a snazzy pair of purple boots, although, in truth, the blue ones she'd also tried on had been more comfortable. She had vague memories of an Outward Bound course in Wales when she was in her teens, but she hadn't really been hill walking since. She confessed her inexperience, and the shop assistant managed to get further money out of her for a penknife, insect repellent and a hat.

Back at home, Rosie carefully removed all of the labels and hoped that her purchases didn't look too new.

When Tanner turned up just before eight the next morning, Rosie was downing a coffee and desperately trying to wake up. He looked very comfortable in combat trousers and a sweatshirt.

They drove for what seemed like miles over the moors, roads and then the motorway, before Tanner turned off and navigated down a labyrinth of country lanes. The landscape got more hilly all the time. He parked the car in a lay-by near a brook.

His walking boots showed obvious scars from being used a lot, with their scuffs and muddy soles. Rosie tried to hide her feet, so that he wouldn't see her pristine boots.

By now it was starting to drizzle, and she secretly hoped that Tanner would call the whole thing off as she jammed her new hat dejectedly over her hair. Tanner had a map pre-loaded on what he said was a GPS unit and set off with a loping gait towards the brook. He traversed the waterway using two stepping stones and then, after looking back and finding Rosie wasn't following him, he came back over the water to hold her uncertain hand. She teetered alarmingly on one stone, with the water rushing past seemingly ready to claim her.

Tanner raised an enquiring eyebrow when they were on dry land. 'Do you go hill walking often?'

Rosie blushed. 'Er, no, not often.'

Tanner set off along a path that looked as if a sheep had made it. Before long, they were faced with big boulders arranged where she guessed the ice age had left them at the side of a waterfall. Rosie immediately began to struggle. Tanner, with eyebrows raised again, turned to haul her up the rocks. The noise from the waterfall was deafening and, in some places, the water made footing very slippy. Rosie knew that she was well and truly out of her depth.

Tanner took pity on her after a while, and they sat in the shelter of an overhanging rock to share a piece of cake and a bottle of water that he produced from his rucksack. When she stood again, Rosie's legs felt like jelly.

'So, tell the truth now, how often have you *really* been hill walking?' asked Tanner.

'I did an Outward Bound course in my teens.'

'And you haven't done this sort of walking since?'

'No.' She blushed again.

'You must tell me if I'm going too fast then.'

Rosie looked around her at the scenery. Every fibre of her being was screaming with the exertion, but the views were amazing. They had reached a ridge and Rosie could see the trail stretching for miles in each direction. The thing she couldn't believe was how many other people were on the top of the hills too. It was like a motorway for walkers. People of all ages, on their own, in twos and threes or larger groups were striding confidently over the hillside. Rosie felt anything but confident, but she marvelled at a lake below, which looked more like an image from a map as they were up so high.

'Where are the toilets?' she asked Tanner.

He looked at her and laughed. 'You are kidding, right? You'll have to find a bush.'

Rosie glanced warily around at the barren landscape and the torrent of walkers. 'There don't appear to be many bushes ... or much privacy.'

'I just hope you're not desperate to go then.' He was so obviously trying not to grin.

Rosie began to feel rather miserable. She was damp from a recent short shower of rain, bedraggled, hungry and she needed the loo. To top it off, her new boots had rubbed blisters on the backs of both heels and the sides of two toes.

Tanner seemed to sense her mood. 'There is a quicker way down over here. We'll take that, and then I'll treat you to a nice snack in a warm café.'

'Sounds marvellous. Lead on.' Rosie smiled.

Tanner paused to smile back and then walked over what looked like the edge of a cliff. Beyond, there was a steep scree slope. He set off at a blistering pace, running and sliding on the slippery stones. He was as sure-footed as a goat and didn't pause until he appeared to realise that Rosie wasn't behind him.

She was picking her way cautiously through the scree. She hated the feeling of being out of control and let out a little scream each time she slipped. Progress was painfully slow, as she inched her way in a zigzag motion down the slope.

Tanner ran back up the hill and tried to encourage her to use his own "devil may care" sliding run motion, but this was totally alien to Rosie, even if he held her hand. She could sense his exasperation, and tears began to form in her eyes.

'It's a good job we're not proposing a mountain walking business,' he joked.

'If we were, I'd have to be in the office and you could be up on the hills. It could work.' This outing was making Rosie feel totally inadequate, and she wasn't sure if her self-confidence needed another bashing. 'Tanner, go down at your own pace and leave me to it. I'll catch up eventually.'

He was sitting on a rock playing with his GPS unit as she arrived at the bottom of the slope twenty minutes later. Her blisters were now bleeding, but she was determined not to let him know. Tanner must think her hopeless enough.

He looked up and smiled. Rosie hoped that he couldn't tell that she'd been swearing under her breath at him and had shed a few tears on the way down the slope, as each yard had felt like a painful mile.

'Not far now. I'm sorry, Rosie. I really shouldn't have taken you on such a challenging walk. Come on, let's get back to the car and I'll treat you to an ice cream or a big cake. Or both!'

'Sounds wonderful,' said Rosie.

'You're limping. I'd better have a look at your feet.'

She reluctantly took off her boots when they got back to the car, and Tanner exclaimed over her bloodied feet. He had blissfully comforting padded plasters in his first aid kit. Rosie was grateful she didn't have to put the boots straight back on as she wasn't driving.

Tanner appeared to be very familiar with the area, and soon they were ensconced in a café with blue lace-edged table cloths. For once, Rosie didn't worry about the calories. She ordered a massive slab of coffee and walnut cake, which matched Tanner's chocolate cake in size and stickiness. The coffee was hot and strong with delicious milky froth. She began to feel more human and the circulation returned to her numb toes.

'I'm sorry, Rosie. I should have realised you weren't up to that walk. I was selfish.'

'No, Tanner, stop apologising. I wasn't totally honest with you in the first place. I didn't want to admit that I hadn't been walking for years. I only bought these boots and equipment yesterday afternoon. I should have known that I'd be found out.'

'Maybe this is a valuable lesson. If we're going to work together, we need a strict rule that we're honest with each other at all times, both about our feelings and our skills.'

'Deal.'

'Deal.'

They clasped hands to seal the promise.

'Anyway, it's my turn to choose the next outing.'

'Should I be scared?' He laughed.

# *Chapter Twenty-Nine*

Rosie took off her sandals and ran giggling across the sand. What was it about being on a beach that brought out the child in her?

The sky was blue and the clouds were like cotton-wool balls. The tide was on the way out, leaving smooth golden sand speckled with shells and seaweed. Rosie inhaled the unique seaside smell and filled her lungs with salt-laden air.

Tanner had seemed surprised when Rosie had chosen a trip to Trinam beach just down the coast from Borteen. The siblings were getting more at ease in each other's company and had both sung aloud to an album of old pop songs on the journey. Rosie had insisted on driving. She explained that Trinam was another of the places she'd enjoyed as a child.

Rosie was curious about Tanner's reaction to the beach. He seemed very cautious when they arrived and paused to roll up his jeans with a strange expression on his face. By the time he caught up with Rosie further down the sand, she was drawing patterns. He walked carefully around her lines, circles and zigzags.

'What is it?' He tilted his head to look at her drawing.

'Just a random outpouring.'

'Oh, okay. I thought you were drawing something in particular.'

She looked up and noticed the same strange expression on his face. He had his hands shoved deep into his pockets and there was a stiff set to his shoulders.

'Don't you like being on the beach?'

'I'm getting used to it. This is the third or even fourth time I've ventured onto sand lately, my second visit here actually. Not sure about the fishy smell, though.' He wrinkled his nose. 'I came here on the day my father died.'

'I'm sorry, Tanner. I hope it doesn't make you feel sad and stir up too many awful memories. I wish I'd known – I'd have chosen somewhere else.'

'It's fine. A lot has happened since that day. It almost seems like a dream that I was here before.'

'I love it on this beach. I know we live right by Borteen beach, but this one reminds me of childhood. Doesn't it do that for you?'

He shook his head and she couldn't read his expression.

'Are you telling me that your mum and dad didn't take you to the beach for holidays, or even take you down to Borteen beach?'

'My mother and father barely spoke to each other.' He was digging a hole in the sand with his toe.

'I'm sorry. What did you do for holidays then?' Rosie felt perplexed and upset for the younger Tanner.

'The best holidays were the ones I spent with friends, usually skiing or sailing.'

'That's sad. We didn't tend to go to Borteen beach when I was young, but we came here some weekends, and Mum and I always rented cottages or caravans at different seaside places for holidays and spent our time trawling rock pools, beach combing first thing in the morning, flying kites and playing King Canute.'

'King Canute?'

'You know … building castles and trying to stop the tide from coming in.'

'I must have some serious gaps in my experiences.' He smiled, but looked so lost and wistful that Rosie knew she had to try to break the dismal mood. She dropped her stick and raced off, her pink cardigan billowing out behind her. 'Catch me if you can.' She left wet footprints in the sand that showed the high arches of her feet. She squealed as Tanner began to chase after her.

It didn't take long for him to overtake her, and then he turned back and barred the way. They stood in the shallow surf laughing. It was at times like these that Rosie felt a little strange with Tanner. She hadn't had many male friends who weren't also lovers, and it was still weird to know that he was her brother.

They had caught the attention of two children who paused in their task of dissecting a crab to stare at them. Rosie broke free and, running up the beach a little, she began to trace the letters of Tanner's name with her toe.

He took her lead and began tracing Rosie's name beneath his own. It was just like something a brother and sister would do when they were younger.

Rosie held her breath, wondering if he would link their names in some way, but he didn't.

After an hour pottering around the shops in the little seaside town, they had lunch and then set off for home.

'Well, what do you think?' asked Tanner.

'About what?'

'Us as business partners? I'm happy if you are.'

Rosie didn't reply for a moment as she concentrated on manoeuvring her car past a lorry.

'Rosie?'

'Yes, I'm happy to work with you. Let's go for it. We've still got a lot to learn about each other, but I'm happy to do that if you are. Lucerne Lodge Retreat and Therapy Centre is in business.'

'It is ... as long as my mother's claim on the estate isn't too huge.'

They sat in silence for a while, each lost in their own thoughts.

# *Chapter Thirty*

Rosie and Tanner travelled together to the next solicitor's meeting. Tanner picked her up at her cottage on the way into Borteen.

'We've been making all of these plans for Lucerne Lodge. What if your mother's challenge to the terms of the will has been successful?'

'Justin Sadler seemed to think it was unlikely, but hopefully he'll know more about that today.'

'I just hope that it can all be resolved and we can finally settle down to our new reality.'

Rosie marvelled that she could already feel so possessive of the Lodge. She guessed it was because she had now filled out ideas for the place in her head. What would it mean for their plans if Georgia inherited some of the estate? They might have to sell the beautiful old house after all.

While she'd been pondering, Tanner had parked the car and must have realised that she was miles away. 'Come on, Rosie, we need to go and sort this out. Deep breath and off we go.'

Rosie had only had a brief encounter with Tanner's mother at Michael Bryant's funeral. She'd been protective of her own mother and hadn't liked the way Georgia had spoken to Frances, or indeed how she'd looked at Rosie. When they got to the solicitor's, the secretary hurriedly informed them that Georgia and her solicitor had requested a brief meeting with everyone together.

Tanner embraced his mother, but in a wary way. She air-kissed either side of his face.

'Surprised to see you, Mum. You could have called to let me know you were around.'

Rosie thought Tanner sounded hurt. She got a brief nod of acknowledgement, but the older woman's face left her in little doubt of Georgia's opinion of her. Georgia smoothed down the jade-green sheath dress that showed off her petite figure beautifully, as if she was brushing off Rosie at the same time, and turned away.

Justin Sadler's office had its usual big flower arrangement on the side table. Today the main flowers were lilies. Rosie could feel her nose tickling at the pungent smell.

'I wasn't aware you were even in the country, Mother,' called Tanner as she walked away.

Rosie couldn't imagine not having the closeness that existed between herself and Frances. How could he not know his mother was in the country?

'I had business to take care of in London, darling, and I want this will thing cleared up once and for all.'

Rosie felt for Tanner. His mother didn't seem to need him or show any interest in his life at all. In contrast, Rosie knew that Frances would be distraught if she didn't see her daughter for a long period of time.

Justin Sadler soon took control of the meeting. 'Madam, perhaps you could tell us what your counter claim on the estate of Michael Bryant is based upon.'

Rosie watched, fascinated, as Georgia's face changed and she positively flirted with Justin, looking at him from underneath her lashes. If she'd been a younger woman it might have seemed sweet and endearing, but she looked like a comedy actress doing an impression. Justin Sadler visibly moved his chair back, but the expression on his face was the same as before – professional and deadpan.

'Michael always said he would make sure I was looked after following his death.'

'I can understand that he might have said that, but unless you have written evidence of an actual bequest, I'm afraid we can't help you.'

Rosie wondered why a woman who appeared successful in her business life would effectively beg for money in this way.

'He said that he would leave a letter with his solicitor – you,' Georgia continued.

'I'm afraid that didn't happen. I have no such letter associated with Michael Bryant's will.'

Georgia sighed and got up. 'Well I suppose that means Michael has let me down yet again. Typical.' She turned aside and had a whispered conversation with the suited man who accompanied her.

Justin spoke next. 'Can I be clear about whether you will still be mounting a challenge to the will of Michael Bryant?'

Georgia glanced at her own solicitor. 'If Michael didn't do what he said he was going to, then I'll have to accept the will and rely on the charity of my son in my old age.' Her mouth was set in an angry line. She grabbed her handbag and walked to the door, not even looking at Tanner or Rosie.

'Justin, I'll just see my mother out and be back in a moment.' Tanner followed Georgia and her solicitor out of the door. The atmosphere in the room lightened immediately. Rosie let out an involuntary relieved sigh and realised that Justin had just done the same.

'There was no need to see me out, Tanner. Go back and enjoy your inheritance with that little minx, Rosie Phillips.'

'Mum, don't talk about Rosie like that. None of this is her fault. And, as for seeing you out, you don't get it, do you? It would be nice to spend some time with you sometimes. Maybe we can have dinner while you're over here?'

'Sorry, Tanner. I've a plane to catch.'

'Mum, be honest with me. Are you in financial trouble? Is that why you needed some of Dad's estate?'

Georgia sighed again. 'Tanner, he promised me money if he died before me. I don't necessarily need it, but you can never have enough in your old age.'

'You're not old!'

'No, but I will be. Do you know how scary that thought is?'

'You will always have me to look after you,' said Tanner. He genuinely meant his words but also knew his mother was unlikely to ever turn to him. He breathed out heavily. 'Can I ask you a question, Mum?'

Georgia glanced pointedly at her watch. 'Yes, dear, but make it quick. As I said, I have a plane to catch.'

'What did you say to dad, that day in the clinic? What made him angry enough to change his will and put Rosie in it as a beneficiary?'

Georgia visibly jumped and her face went very pale.

'I need to know what you said – not words just to pacify me, but the facts.'

Georgia sighed yet again and looked at the floor. 'I finally told your father the truth about *your* parentage.'

Confusion flooded Tanner's mind. 'Rosie's parentage, you mean?'

'No, yours.' She put her hands on her hips and stared at him, eyes bulging slightly.

'Mum, you're not making any sense at all.'

'Oh, all right, I'll say it straight – I finally told your father that you weren't his. That you aren't Michael Bryant's son.'

Tanner felt something akin to an avalanche inside of him. He flopped down onto one of the reception hall chairs, and before he buried his face in his hands, he caught sight of the wide-eyed stare of the receptionist.

His mother's voice seemed to reach him through a thick fog. His heart was racing and his ears buzzed.

'I'm sorry, Tanner. I never meant to tell you like this, but the truth needed to come out sometime.'

He lifted his head to look at his so-called mother. Why was he surprised that she had blurted out such a momentous truth with no care for his feelings or where they were? 'So, Mother, who exactly is my father if it wasn't the man I treated as my dad for all of these years?' The words echoed around the high ceiling of the room and hung there expectantly.

'Your father was John Phillips.'

# *Chapter Thirty-One*

When Tanner came back into the room and sat down in the chair next to Rosie, she was instantly on alert. Something was odd about his body language. She turned and tried to read his face, but he was looking away from her. She became even more alarmed when she saw Justin Sadler's reaction to his return.

'Tanner, are you all right? Can I get you a drink maybe?'

Tanner sat up straighter. 'A whisky would be good, or brandy if you have it.'

'I might manage a strong coffee,' he said apologetically.

'Maybe just a glass of water, please.'

Justin hurried to a cupboard on one side of the room. Rosie watched Tanner's hand shake as he took the glass from the solicitor. Whatever his mother had said to him outside of the door, it had shaken him to the core. Tanner took a sip of the liquid and shuddered. He was still refusing to look at Rosie.

'Justin, can we get this meeting over as soon as possible, please? I really need some fresh air.'

'You look awfully pale, Tanner. Are you sure you don't want to reschedule this meeting for another day?' Justin was shifting uneasily, passing his sheet of paper from hand to hand.

There was silence. Rosie had heard the expression "you could have cut the air with a knife" and thought it strange, but that was exactly what it felt like in this room. The lily-laden air was trapped in her throat to the extent she thought she might choke. She wished she hadn't waved away the offer of a coffee.

As if in answer to her thoughts, Tanner coughed and it turned quickly into a painful choking. Rosie tried to pat him on the back, and the solicitor came rushing over with another tumbler full of water.

'Sorry. I've had a bit of a shock, that's all. If we could discuss things another time, as long as you and Rosie don't mind, I'd appreciate it.'

They both said they didn't mind at all. Tanner put the glasses down on Justin's desk and mumbled a goodbye.

Rosie, now quite alarmed by Tanner's behaviour, struggled to keep up with him, as he strode quickly along the corridor and out into the car park, seemingly gasping huge lungfuls of air when he emerged from the door.

'Are you sure you're okay, Tanner? Is there anything I can do?'

He shook his head, but the expression on his face did nothing to calm her concern.

*What had Georgia said to him?*

Tanner was utterly bewildered. He felt like a teddy bear whose stuffing had been forcibly removed. The lynch pin of his life, the very foundation of his identity had gone. He was not Michael Bryant's son.

'Sorry, Rosie, I think I need to go on a long walk, and then I need to speak to your mother. Could you perhaps meet me at Frances' in a couple of hours?'

Rosie nodded. He could tell she wanted to say something else, but he couldn't take anything in right now, not until he'd made sense of his jumbled feelings. He now understood why she had taken off when she'd discovered Michael Bryant was actually her father, because that was exactly what he wanted to do – run away. The whole thing was like a nightmare, and he just wanted to escape reality.

'Are you sure you don't mind walking home?'

'Of course not. It isn't as if it's far.'

He nodded and turned away from her. Questions kept bubbling up to the surface with no possibility of getting any answers. As he began to walk, something else hit him full force. *He and Rosie were not brother and sister after all.*

A little while later, Tanner found himself outside Frances Phillips' door without having taken any wrong turns, despite his overwhelming distraction. He'd purposely arrived earlier than he'd said to Rosie, and leaned against the door until he had centred his thoughts a little. He knocked and Frances soon answered. The concern, which immediately clouded her face as she peered out, told him that he must look as bad as he felt.

'Tanner, whatever is the matter? Come in, come in. Has something happened to Rosie?'

'No, no. She's fine. She's meeting me here in a little while.'

He sat heavily in the squashy conservatory chair Frances guided him to whilst she went to make coffee, after he'd reassured her again that her daughter was in good health. He ruffled Dusty's ears and stared out of the window.

Tanner was appalled, when Frances put the warm cup into his hands, that tears had begun to spill down his cheeks. The tension, which he had been trying to button up inside, was somehow released by the tender gesture.

Frances didn't ask him questions or make a fuss. She took the cup from him and put it on the table, then just sat close by and allowed him to pour out the layers of grief and confusion, which burst out from the depths of him. Eventually, she offered him a box of tissues.

'Emotion like that is better out than inside in my experience. Are you feeling up to telling me what has happened?'

He snivelled into his tissue, wondering what on earth Frances would think of him. 'I'm sorry. I don't know why I'm acting like this.' It was so out of character for him to cry.

'Tanner, I can't second guess what you are going through, but you must have thought I was the person who could help you, or you wouldn't be here.'

Tanner took a sip of his coffee thoughtfully and tried to regain his composure. Eventually, he felt strong enough to voice the questions he'd come here to ask. He sat forward, perturbed to notice that his hands were still shaking from the shock.

'My mum came to the solicitor's office today. I sort of cornered her as she left about why my father had changed his will to include Rosie. I knew that he and Mum had a terrible argument the day before he drew up the new will. The nurses told me how much the shouting had upset Dad.' Tanner took a big shuddering breath. 'Mum told me … she told me that ... that … Michael Bryant wasn't my father after all.' Tanner was aware that he was babbling in his confusion. For someone who prided himself on his communication skills, he couldn't believe how inarticulate his state of mind had made him.

It was Frances' turn to gasp, and she reached out a hand to touch his arm.

'I feel so confused and bewildered right now.' He put the cup back down on the table before he dropped it.

'That must have been an awful shock to be told such a thing. Did Georgia tell you who your father actually is?'

'Yes. Did you know?'

'Not for certain, but I may have had suspicions. It was John, wasn't it? John's your dad.'

'That's what my mother says now.'

The colour had drained from Frances' face. 'With John and Georgia's affair, Tanner, it makes perfect sense, I'm afraid.'

'I'm sorry. I've shocked you too.'

'Not shocked me, just confirmed something that I knew, if I'd actually let myself admit it in my heart of hearts. Self-preservation not to, I suppose.'

'And can I ask you to confirm once more … Michael Bryant is definitely Rosie's father?'

Frances paused and squeezed his arm. 'Yes, Michael fathered Rosie. I'm one hundred per cent sure of that.' Frances took her hand away and crossed her arms tightly across her body. 'Tanner, I was not your mother's confidant while she was pregnant. Sad really, as we'd been such good friends before. The relationship between me, my husband and your parents had broken down by then. We went from being inseparable to not being able to be in the same room. I cannot categorically say who your father was – I wasn't there when you were conceived – but I'm sure Georgia wouldn't lie about something as important as this.'

'But she has lied. For thirty-one years …'

'As I did to Rosie …'

Tanner was surprised as Frances abruptly got up and began clearing away the mugs of coffee. She went off into the kitchen and left him alone in the conservatory. He realised that he'd reminded Frances of difficult issues and had been asking her something she could only speculate on, something that, because of her husband's betrayal, would more than likely cause her pain.

Frances was crashing the mugs around in the washing up bowl in the kitchen, and something told Tanner that she perhaps knew more than she was telling him. He went after her. She had tears pouring down her cheeks.

'Hey, hey, I'm sorry. I've upset you.' He wasn't sure whether to try and give her a hug or not.

'No, Tanner, the upset really happened many years ago. This has just brought it all to the surface again.'

'I'm sorry.'

'Thirty-two years ago, Tanner, when I found out that my husband ...' Frances stopped and took a great gulp of air. 'Found out that my husband was having an affair with your mother, it felt as if my world exploded. I don't think it's truly been the same for me ever since.'

Tanner put his arms around the obviously distressed Frances. She clung to him for a moment and then shook herself free.

'Having said that, if the affair had not happened, if I hadn't gone to bed with Michael, I would never have had Rosie, and she's been the best thing that ever happened in my life. I just hate the thought that the two of us ending up in bed made us just as unfaithful as Georgia and John. Until you came here today, I didn't think John could father a child. We never had any success having a baby together. It somehow makes John's betrayal feel even worse.'

'I'm sorry.' He knew he'd already said the words at least once, but he had no idea what else to say.

For the second time that day, Tanner felt drained, almost as if someone had punched him in the chest, by hearing everything confirmed and feeling Frances' distress. He turned and went back into the conservatory. The doors were wide open to the garden, and he walked up the path, hardly seeing the beautiful cottage garden and totally oblivious to the dog trying to get him to play ball. His mind was reeling with the enormity of everything.

Eventually, he calmed down. He knew he was more at peace because the scent of the roses on the bush next to him began to drift into his consciousness. He turned and returned to the house, bending down to pet Dusty before he went back inside.

Rosie had arrived at the house while he was in the garden. Frances must have told her what had happened, because she was handing her mother a large mug of coffee and looking concerned. The women in this family seemed to associate hot coffee with sorting out traumas.

Rosie turned to him, her eyes brimming with tears. 'I'm so sorry, Tanner. What a mixed-up mess.'

'It's hardly your fault,' said Tanner. 'But you do realise what this means? After all of this, I can't believe that we aren't brother and sister after all …'

# *Chapter Thirty-Two*

A reasonable night's sleep helped Tanner put things into perspective. His life had been totally rocked on its axis, but it wasn't the end of the world. The fantastic news was that he was not related to Rosie … and he supposed, with a measure of sadness and regret, not to the man he'd previously believed to be his father either. Michael Bryant and Tanner had never been on the same wavelength really, and now he knew why. This latter thought made him feel horribly guilty. Michael had believed Tanner to be his son almost until the day of his death, and the revelation of his ex-wife at the eleventh hour must have been devastating to the sick man. He was grateful that Michael Bryant had still included him in his will, but, having said that, he wasn't certain how he felt about that inheritance now.

He ran around the lawn with Trixie until she needed a rest. It helped to do something to take him out of his cyclical thoughts. He put her back into the dog run and gave her a treat, as a mad but irresistible compulsion took hold of him and wouldn't let go.

*Rosie.* He had to get to Rosie. They were free. They could be together. They could, they could … Rosie wasn't his sister, wasn't related at all! Finally letting the repressed feelings he'd had about Rosie surface and blossom, Tanner launched himself in the air with a jubilant punch to the sky.

He almost fell over his feet as he rushed back to the house. He was still buttoning a clean shirt as he dived into his car. Besides a shower and fresh clothes, he'd only paused to retrieve a small leather box from his desk drawer, something his grandmother had once said was his to use.

Music full blast and top down on his sports car, despite it being a cool day, he zoomed along the country lanes. He didn't feel the chill. He was glowing, on fire, on top of the world.

Where would Rosie be on a Saturday, mid-morning? He whooshed confidently into a parking space near to The Sunshine Restaurant.

The girls appeared to be avidly listening to Rosie when he walked in the door and didn't notice him at all. Tanner realised that she was more than likely relating the tale of their parents and the complicated family relationships that had finally come to light the day before. This thought was confirmed when Rosie's skin flushed as she caught sight of him.

He had to make a concerted effort to continue with his mission, as doubts suddenly began to invade his previous certainty. Was he being too impetuous? Too presumptuous? He hurried over to Rosie's table, trying to maintain, even if falsely now, the spring he'd found in his step earlier.

Connie and Lucy exchanged glances and giggles, which Tanner tried to ignore.

'Rosie, I'm so excited about our future together ...'

Rosie looked meaningfully at the other restaurant tables. His tone and volume were already attracting attention.

'And I don't care who knows it,' he declared in an even louder voice. He dropped to his knees in front of Rosie and groped for her hand. She looked absolutely horrified, but now he'd started, he had to finish.

'I was going to wait, but I can't. Rosie Phillips, will you marry me?'

There was a round of applause and a couple of cheers from those nearby who had overheard.

'No. No! Stop it, Tanner. No!'

Tanner sat back on his heels, registering hurt and surprise at her reaction – maybe his doubts had been totally justified. His hand now limply held the ring box.

'I'm sorry, Tanner. I have to go.'

She left him kneeling on the floor and ran for the door. She didn't look back and Tanner, by now feeling a complete idiot, bent over double and pressed his forehead on the cool floor tiles.

The restaurant had fallen completely silent, almost as if those who hadn't overheard still knew that something momentous had occurred.

Tanner didn't move for a few moments. He felt rather silly on his knees in the busy restaurant as the volume increased once more. Everyone was probably talking and speculating about him and what had just happened.

One of the waiters he'd worked with in his short time at The Sunshine came over to ask if he was all right and pulled him to his feet.

Lucy and Connie were staring at him. The other diners were now studiously studying their meals or menus. The shock of Rosie's rejection turned to acute embarrassment, and Tanner muttered apologies and bolted for the door. He didn't stop until he was safely locked inside his car.

How could he have been such an idiot? He truly believed that Rosie cared for him, but, with hindsight, he could see that he had been insensitive; he'd rushed her, cornered her.

What did he do now?

Rosie was still shaking by the time she closed the door at home. Splashing water onto her extremely pale face, she tried to compose herself. Up until yesterday, she had thought that Tanner was her brother. She still hadn't got used to the fact that they weren't related, couldn't actually trust it to be true, even though her mother had explained it all to her yesterday. They were setting up a business together. In her mind, there was no way they could even have a romantic relationship, let alone get married. It felt so weird to contemplate as she'd only just got used to them being friends.

Looking at herself hard in the mirror, every imperfection stood out as pain stabbed at her heart. She could still smell the delicious scent of Tanner's aftershave. There was no doubt that she was attracted to him, always had been ... but marriage?

'Rosie Phillips, get a grip,' she said aloud to her reflection, just as there was a loud hammering on the front door.

To begin with, she feared that it was Tanner, but instead Connie and Lucy stood outside the cottage with matching concerned faces.

'Rosie, what are you playing at?' Connie exclaimed.

'I can't marry him!'

'Why can't you? You've just told us that you don't share his blood. We know you have feelings for him. So why not?'

The girls followed her in, and she automatically set the kettle to boil. Rosie went to the kitchen sink to splash water on her face again and managed to soak the front of her blouse. She dabbed at the mark with a towel.

'He's as good as my brother. I'll always think of him as my brother. Our families are too entangled. I can't marry him, I just can't. It's all too complicated.' The tears began to flow unchecked, adding to the wetness of her blouse.

Connie hugged Rosie to her ample bosom and Lucy put her hands on her back, so that she was totally enclosed in the love of her friends.

# *Chapter Thirty-Three*

After her disastrous encounter with Tanner, Rosie almost didn't go to their pre-arranged meeting that afternoon at Lucerne Lodge. However, she decided that they had to see each other sooner or later, and she might as well get the first meeting post-proposal over with.

She was surprised to be greeted at the door of the Lodge by Demetri, the security guard. She'd never come into the house through the main entrance and felt completely overawed by the Grecian columns of the huge doorway. Demetri was chatty but in a professional way. He led her upstairs into the study with its huge desk, without seeming to have any awareness of the tension coursing through her, which she felt must be obvious.

The room was well used, as there were lots of personal items on shelves and table surfaces, and little sign of dust. Rosie felt like an intruder, but she reminded herself that she now owned half of all this. She continued looking around, but then stopped dead.

There was a photograph on the wall which looked remarkably like the picture that she'd used as a screen-saver at work, minus the Bryants. Rosie could recognise a younger Georgia and Michael. She stared at her real father curiously.

Tanner flew into the room, unbuttoning his shirt. 'Oops, sorry, I didn't know you were here yet. Just changing. I'll be two minutes.'

She had no chance of a reply as he dashed out again. It was only when he'd gone that she wondered why he had rushed here half way through getting ready. Her suspicions aroused, she went to look on the desk surface. A folder lay open and spewing out from it were photographs of her – and lots of them. She picked up a couple of shots and tried to identify where they'd been taken. Underneath the pictures was a typed sheet. Reading the words made her feel sick. It was a report about her, her work place, her skills, qualifications, even Ollie and her mother's addresses. Rosie's blood began to boil.

Tanner chose that very moment to re-appear. He stopped just inside the door when he realised exactly what she was looking at. 'I can explain.'

Rosie dropped down in the large leather armchair. Tossing her hair back over her shoulder, she gave Tanner the benefit of her best scowl. 'It better be good.'

Tanner sat in the chair facing hers with the desk between them. He shifted uneasily as if she was interviewing him and had just asked a particularly difficult question.

'Well?'

'I've had that file since before I actually met you. I did mention that my father had some notes about you, I just didn't tell you the extent of the information he'd collected. Look at the dates on the reports if you don't believe me. It's how I decided some of the places to work when I was researching for my article on low-paid jobs.' He paused and ran his hands through his hair and then down his face. 'Put yourself in my position, I found this file on my father's desk when he was very ill. I didn't know who you were, or what your connection was to my father. I was going to shred it all before you arrived.'

'It might have been better if you had. I mean, I originally suspected that you were stalking me when we first met, but, to be honest I'd rather not see the proof now that we are *business partners*.' She emphasised the last words.

'Rosie … about earlier … I'm sorry I embarrassed you.'

'Yes, well, let's say no more about *that* episode and maybe get on with setting this place up as a viable business.' *Could she do this now?* The words were coming out of her mouth, but could she really be in business with Tanner after this?

'I'm not sure what my father would think about the house being used as an executive retreat.'

'Do you honestly think I give two hoots about what Michael Bryant would think? He was never my father, whatever anyone says.'

'Nor mine, it would seem.'

Rosie hitched her breath after realising what she'd said. 'Sorry, Tanner, that was insensitive.'

'No it's fine. I've come to terms with it. It actually makes perfect sense.'

A look of misery passed across his features. Rosie tried not to notice how his hair was curling around his ears.

'Now I know the truth, it explains so much.'

'About your childhood?'

'Yes, and about how dad always was with me. We never really connected.'

Rosie searched on her phone and bought up her favourite photograph of her parents –well, her mother anyway, and John Phillips. Goodness, this was so complicated. She stood up and moved closer to Tanner so she could hold the phone up next to him, taking her time to examine his face and the image on the screen together. 'Absolutely no doubt about it, though. I don't know why we didn't realise you were John Phillips' son before. After all, we both looked through Mum's photo album.'

Tanner quirked an enquiring eyebrow and when she nodded, he took her phone from her hand to look at the picture more clearly himself. He gestured over to the other half of the image framed on the wall. 'To think that the other half of this picture has been here all this time. I guess there weren't many photographs of my parents together, but goodness knows why dad left it on the wall, given everything that happened back then. We could do with the complete photograph framed really – a photograph of both sets of our parents, just not in the expected mix.'

'Well, Tanner Bryant, it would appear that we don't share any blood relatives after all, but I do wonder if the similarity to Dada sparked my interest in you in the first place?' Rosie suddenly realised what she'd said and coloured to the roots of her hair.

She and Tanner had begun to show signs of working well together, but that was as brother and sister. Now that she knew that they weren't related, would that change everything, especially after he'd declared his feelings? She thought back to the time they had first met and their subsequent meetings. There was always a frisson of attraction and flirtation. Would this news sabotage their budding business relationship?

She concluded that the best way forward would be to lay down some ground rules, so that Tanner knew exactly where he stood with her … so they both did. *And so that I don't get carried away, too.*

'Tanner, although we're pretty certain that we're not related, I think we should maybe have some proper tests to make absolutely sure, to have irrefutable proof. Otherwise, I think I will always see you as my brother on some level. It's just a very confusing situation.'

Tanner looked once more at Rosie's phone screen, although she could see it had returned to the locked image now. He handed her the phone, and his face changed as he did so. The person who looked up at her was a cool-headed business man who proceeded to go through the plans for Lucerne Lodge as if the previous conversation and his botched marriage proposal had never happened.

Rosie was surprised but somehow relieved that they were back to discussing their business idea, even if it did take her brain a few moments to catch up with the change of pace.

Once they had examined the plans and proposals, and decided exactly what needed to be done in what order and the budget they would work to, Tanner stood up. He looked almost like a robot as he packed a briefcase that had been lying nearby. The last thing he loaded into the bag was the photograph of Rosie getting out of her car from the open file on the desk. He then closed the private investigator's folder and handed it to Rosie.

'Here, this is yours now, do with it what you like. I'll arrange for a DNA test pack to be sent to you at the cottage and I promise to do a test too. If you need funds for the refurbishment, email me. I'm going back to London for the time being. I think we both need some space to settle down and decide who we actually are, but you can reach me on my mobile to discuss anything, anytime. Would you please make sure that Trixie is walked regularly?'

He didn't wait for her to reply. He just walked out of the room, leaving Rosie stunned and not quite sure what to think, or how to react. *Had he really gone, just like that?*

# *Chapter Thirty-Four*

Tanner didn't seem able to settle in his apartment and wasn't happy at all in London. Everything seemed to have changed. The city was noisier and smellier than he remembered it. His flat was pristine because he had a lady who came in to clean regularly, but she had unfortunately left behind a pungent smell of synthetic air freshener.

Strange how this flat and the world in the city had once been his ideal way of living. No longer, it seemed. It felt synthetic and false too. Tanner didn't really know who he was or what he wanted any more.

He looked around his apartment as if it was the first time he'd been there or he was viewing it from an estate agent's particulars. It was small, but perfectly formed. The bathroom, gleaming with chrome and marble, although tiny, had been designed so that everything was exactly in the right place. His bedroom was decorated in harmonious neutral tones, the silk coverlet on the bed gleamed in the sunlight streaming through the floor-to-ceiling windows. The spare room was again neutral, but with sapphire-blue accents in the cushions and bed cover.

The rest of the flat was one large open-plan room, with floor-to-ceiling windows on two sides. The kitchen was in the windowless corner. The amber marble work surfaces were similar to those at Lucerne Lodge. Two white leather settees fronted a long black coffee table. There was a computer desk, sited so that the view when Tanner was typing his articles was across the London rooftops. In the past, he'd loved working there in the dark evenings when the city was bright with a million lights. Near the kitchen, there was a dining table with seats for eight, just in case he needed to entertain. In truth, he couldn't remember the last time anyone had sat at that table.

His father had called this flat an extravagance, but Tanner had thought it a triumph, as he'd financed it from his own earnings. Earnings gained from a job Michael had called "tin pot". Now, when he looked around the flat, he saw an empty shell with little sign of his personality reflected in the fixtures and fittings.

Could he have changed so much in the months he had been back in Borteen? What was different?

Was it meeting and being attracted to Rosie? Then having his world changed by finding out she was his sister, and then rocked again when they were not related after all?

Was it his father dying? And then discovering that Michael wasn't actually his father?

Why had he run away now and left Rosie to deal with Lucerne Lodge on her own? He'd felt an idiot about his botched marriage proposal, yes, but he also needed to have some space to decide who he was after all of these huge changes. It was almost as if the gods were pouring challenge after challenge on his head, and he just couldn't process any more for now, which is why he'd had to get away.

He'd retreat to familiar ground, throw himself into writing articles and networking. After all, they would need the right contacts when they came to launch Lucerne Lodge Retreat and Therapy Centre, wouldn't they?

Rosie was also soul searching after Tanner had left for London. She went to Lucerne Lodge and wandered into the large kitchen, feeling very alone in the big house and still a stranger here. That would have to change.

The housekeeper was around somewhere and the security guard would be monitoring the grounds. She and Tanner had already spoken to these two, together with the head gardener, and agreed that they would all still have roles at the house for the new business. All three had seemed enthusiastic about staying on.

Despite everything that had happened, Rosie was certain that she wanted to be involved in this project and resolved to pour herself into getting everything up and running. There was a lot to do before the retreat centre could open. She felt the need to prove to both herself and Tanner that she could do this successfully. As the will had allowed for a generous monthly allowance for her, she had the freedom to spend time here without any money worries despite having resigned from her job at Borden Glass.

However, today the project seemed empty like the house, because Tanner was missing. He'd gone before she'd even had chance to articulate her feelings, let alone explain them to him. Maybe space was what both of them needed. There had been a lot to cope with in a very short time.

She couldn't help wondering why she wasn't "normal" and married with three children by now. Despite that thought, she took a moment to thank her lucky stars that she and Ollie had never had kids. She could be a single parent struggling to make ends meet by now. And Ollie had never proposed. Tanner had …

Whilst there was no way she could have accepted him, she knew she could have handled the proposal much better, told Tanner she'd think about it, given him time to explain why he thought he wanted to marry her so suddenly when they hadn't even been dating, hadn't even known that they were free to consider anything other than a platonic relationship until the day before.

An unbidden image came into her head of walking down the aisle of a church decked in a white dress and veil. She could see Tanner waiting for her, and the expression on his face in her imagination was so full of love that Rosie found tears streaming down her face.

She took a deep, shuddering breath and gave herself a good talking to.

*Come on, Rosie, count your blessings. One, you have a lovely mum. Two, you have lovely friends. Three, you will soon be living in this beautiful house with money in the bank. Four...*

She somehow couldn't finish her list.

# *Chapter Thirty-Five*

Rosie had spent an hour walking Trixie. She'd come to adore the dog and the feeling appeared to be mutual. She had made it her own personal job to see that Trixie got exercise and play time because it was the last thing Tanner had asked her to do before he left for London. Whenever she was at Lucerne Lodge, she had the dog by her side and got used to Trixie's gentle snores from the vicinity of her feet as she worked. Trixie seemed to appreciate not being in her pen.

The plans to convert Lucerne Lodge were gathering pace after so many months solidly working at it. A quiet Christmas with her mother had come and gone. Rosie had sent Tanner a Christmas card and aftershave, but somehow it didn't feel satisfactory. Tanner had sent cards and luxury chocolates for them both, but had not been to visit.

Rosie, encouraged since childhood to make Christmas and New Year wishes, fervently asked for at least a resolution of the relationship between herself and Tanner. She tried to be smiley for her mother's sake over the festive season but inside she was desperately sad about the loss of what had been growing into an easy friendship.

The main aim in her life was now to fulfil the plans they had made for Lucerne Lodge. As promised, she'd made two lovely light and airy apartments for herself and Tanner on the second floor of the house. She did find herself wondering if Tanner would ever stay in his.

The first floor housed the ten beautiful guest bedrooms. In the majority of cases, the existing furniture, curtains and bedspreads had been perfect for their new purpose. Many of the bedrooms already had en-suite bathrooms, and those remaining were large enough to add en-suite shower rooms.

On the ground floor, the main reception rooms had been left intact for the guests to use. The newest wing of the house had a gym room already, which was perfect for a yoga studio, or else could be filled with chairs and tables for courses and presentations. The space above this had been converted into the therapy suite. Rosie had managed to fit four rooms with sinks into the area. Each was decorated in pale eggshell colours. It was all looking perfect for the purpose they'd intended, at least from Rosie's point of view.

While she had dealt with the fitting out of the house, Tanner had sorted any red tape from London. He'd charmed the council into giving planning permission for the new venture, kept an eye on the budget and paid the bills.

After an initial awkwardness, they'd begun to speak on the phone almost every day, then every day, then several times a day, sometimes with video calls when Rosie wanted to show Tanner something in particular. She was sure she wasn't imagining that their conversations were becoming easier and more friendly as the weeks went by, and that made her very happy.

She'd been so busy that the months were flying past as she worked to make Lucerne Lodge Retreat and Therapy Centre a reality. She'd lost count of how many tradesmen had been through the doors of the house, painting, plastering, installing. She thanked heaven for her attention to detail, as it enabled her to keep to budget and project time. This was now a matter of pride and something she needed to prove to Tanner.

Rosie had finally moved completely into her flat at the Lodge with mixed feelings. It was bigger than her rental house and filled with light, but the little cottage had been her safe haven close to the beach in Borteen, and had offered a very different way of living to this. But this was the future wasn't it …?

She'd spent today playing with layouts and themes for an initial marketing brochure and website. She wanted it ready to show to Tanner, along with the rooms and his flat, because he'd finally agreed to come and visit soon. He'd been careful to emphasise that it really would only be a "visit", but it felt like a huge step forward.

She took a last look at the graphic she'd created: a picture of the house, framed by the profusion of flowers in the garden, the sky blue and the slogan "Summer at Lucerne Lodge" flanked by a pair of great tits – the birds that fed at the bird feeder outside the main lounge window every day. It looked summery and appealing.

She had the beginnings of a headache and decided to take a break. The little cottage garden at the back of the house had become her favourite place to walk and sit. She loved the old roses and the herb beds.

The gardener, a vital employee of the new business, was busy dead-heading, and Rosie paused to watch him for a moment and speak to him about the garden. Patrick's hands were covered with soil. His face was as crumpled as his clothing. She was about to move away, when he looked up and spoke more seriously.

‘Don’t want to speak out of turn, Miss Rosie.’ He hesitated. ‘I knew your father. I was gardening here even then. Yes, don’t ask how old I am!’

‘I was only five when he died, so my memories are pretty hazy. You probably remember more about him than I do myself.’ Rosie decided not to try to explain that John Phillips was actually Tanner’s father and Michael Bryant her own. She was surprised that Patrick hadn’t read one of the newspaper articles about the will, but maybe he was wary of upsetting her.

Rosie sat down on a bench. She was torn between brimming curiosity about what Patrick could tell her about her father and a wish to maintain her illusions. The elderly gardener had moved to another border where he was wielding his hoe. She shouted over to him.

‘Patrick, did you want to tell me something about my dad? As I said, I only have my own hazy memories and what other people have told me. Do you know anything about what happened that day … the day he died? Even Mum doesn’t really know. Would you tell me what you remember?’

Patrick came closer. He took off his gloves and leaned on the hoe in front of her.

‘It was a tragic, horrible day. I was mowing the lawn at the front of the house, so I didn’t hear what was said, just saw the body language.’

‘I don’t follow you.’ Rosie felt confused.

‘Your dad, John, and my boss, Michael Bryant, had an argument on the front steps. It got quite heated. They were both very upset. Your dad started yelling and pointing, and then Michael flounced back into the house and slammed the door.’

‘What happened next?’ Rosie found herself holding her breath.

‘I went round the back of the house and the next thing I knew we were being called to help get Mr Phillips out of the lake.’ Patrick’s face contorted with something that looked like pain.

‘So, there wasn’t much time between the argument and dad dying then?’

‘I’d say twenty minutes at most.’

Rosie wondered what on earth Michael Bryant could have said to John Phillips. It must have been something to do with money and the loans her mother had mentioned, she supposed.

‘I bet it was all a shock.’

‘You can imagine what we all thought,’ he said, now looking decidedly embarrassed.

‘That he’d deliberately drowned himself in the lake after the argument?’

‘Exactly that. Although I do know that it was later proved he’d had a heart attack before he went into the water. Michael Bryant made a point of gathering the staff together to tell us that.’

‘How did Michael react when it happened?’

‘He was distraught. I guess he felt responsible. The old security guard, Sonny, Michael and I dragged John out of the water. Sonny tried to revive him. Michael phoned for an ambulance, but I think we all knew it was too late to do anything to save him.’

Rosie looked over to the lake. She could picture the scene clearly. ‘And Mr Bryant’s wife?’

‘She was away in America at the time.’

‘Thank you for telling me this. It just helps to fill in the blanks.’

She said her goodbyes to Patrick and went to lie down on her bed, to think and grieve all over again.

Afterwards, she couldn’t settle and decided to go into Borteen for a walk on the beach. However, it was a lovely day and the beach felt too full of day-trippers for the aimless wandering that Rosie had in mind.

After a coffee in the little beach café, she had the idea to visit Buzz at his shop, Crazy Crystals, just a short walk away.

Buzz looked up and smiled as she walked through the door. ‘Moon and star lady!’

‘You must have an amazing memory,’ said Rosie, flabbergasted that he would remember who she was.

‘I don’t suppose you’d believe me if I told you that my spirit guides told me you’d be dropping by today?’

Rosie smiled. ‘I’m not sure I know what to believe any more, but it was sort of the subject of beliefs I came to talk to you about.’

‘Sounds like I’d better make us a cup of tea.’

‘Have you time?’

‘The shop bell rings up in my flat, so it’s really no trouble. Come on, let’s see if we can sort you out.’

Rosie was soon sitting at Buzz’s kitchen table nursing a cup of tea.

‘So, what can I help you with?’

Rosie was alarmed at the tears which appeared in her eyes.

Buzz, unfazed, put a box of tissues within her reach, next to some delicious looking biscuits. He patiently waited for her to be ready to explain.

'I just wanted an opinion really, maybe a little guidance if you have it.'

Buzz nodded and so she continued, explaining to him about the death of the man she'd known as her father, how young she'd been and how she'd now ended up living and working in the very place where John Phillips had died.

'So, what do you need help with?'

'I just sort of wish I knew if he's happy with me being there, or if he'd prefer I kept away. It sounds silly to say aloud.'

Buzz reached a hand part way across the table but didn't make connection with her. 'Let's get something clear – if something is on your mind, it's a genuine concern. Have you tried talking to him?'

'Talking to him?'

'Yes. Just go to a place that feels right at the property and ask your questions. You might be surprised to get answers coming into your mind, or at least a kind of knowing.'

'But how would that work?'

'I can't claim to understand what happens when we die – I think you can only understand that when you die yourself – but I do believe in the spirit world, heaven if you like, and I certainly think that you can get answers from those who have passed over into the afterlife if you ask clear questions.'

Rosie grabbed one of the biscuits, suddenly feeling the need for sugar as she pondered what he was saying. Buzz was patient to let her process his words.

'You could also try asking for a sign.'

'A sign?'

'Make a request for something to appear in your life after asking your questions, sort of as a confirmation that your dad heard you.'

'Okay. This all feels a bit weird, but I'll try what you say and maybe report back.'

'That would be lovely. I genuinely would like to know how you get on.'

Rosie decided that she would like to speak to Buzz some more, but for today he had given her enough to work with, and she wasn't sure her brain could cope with anything else right now.

'Do I pay you for a consultation like this, Buzz?'

'Absolutely no need. If when you return to tell me how you got on, you feel I have been of value, you could put a donation in my tin for the homeless charity.' He smiled and walked back down the stairs to the shop with her.

Rosie gave him some money for the homeless charity anyway, made her farewells and went back to Lucerne Lodge with a lot on her mind.

# *Chapter Thirty-Six*

Tanner was returning from London for his promised visit. Rosie had been overjoyed when he'd finally said it was time for him to come back, as she was excited for him to see the changes she'd made to the house. She also needed his help to recruit therapists and get other necessary staff organised, and to brainstorm the marketing and a launch event. Plus she couldn't wait to see what he thought about his new apartment.

Despite the passage of time and their numerous conversations, she still wondered how they would react to each other back under the same roof at Lucerne Lodge.

Rosie knew there was something she had to do before he arrived. It had been on her mind after talking to Buzz. First, she checked the finishing touches to the decoration and furnishing of the guest bedrooms. She wanted everything as perfect as possible before Tanner saw what she'd done.

When she was satisfied, she made her way down to the lake and laid a picnic blanket on the ground. Despite her intentions, her courage deserted her and she spent ten minutes examining the pattern on the rug. It was a blue tartan, and she found that by tracing a line with her finger she could mesmerise herself with the movement.

Having lived through the aftermath of John's untimely death as a child, she'd missed her dada terribly, but hadn't really understood the implications for her mother of his death because she'd been so young.

She took a deep breath. 'Dada,' she spoke aloud, quietly to begin with and then louder as she became confident that there was no one around or near enough to hear her. 'Dada, I know you didn't mean to leave us when you did. You must have been very worried about money and how you could look after Mum and me that day when you came down to the lake after your argument with Michael Bryant. My adult self is sad that you missed out on so much of my life, but I know that you loved me. It feels very strange to be doing this, but I wanted you to know that I'm living here at Lucerne Lodge now, Dada.' She still used the pet name she'd given to her father when she'd learned to talk.

'I need to know that you're okay about me being here. Can you send me a sign? Send me a sign that all of this will be for the best. I'm confused, and I hurt in so many ways about your passing and the circumstances around it. Help me, please help me to know I'm on the right track.'

There didn't seem to be any answers, or the "knowing" Buzz had talked about.

She tried again. 'What if I choose a sign? How about two herons flying together over the lake? If I see that, I'll know you approve and are all right with all of this. Please. I think it would help me to settle down at Lucerne Lodge.'

Rosie's voice had reached a crescendo but she still couldn't feel any connection to John. Hopelessness crowded into her heart. Maybe she needed to get closer to where he was when he died. Maybe his spirit couldn't hear her here ...

Tanner made his way down the drive. He was looking forward to a cup of tea after a rather difficult trip from London. He had a complicated mixture of feelings about the thought of seeing Rosie again. It had been quite a while since he'd last been here, over six months in fact.

They had spoken on the phone many times, but those conversations had been about their business, the building, red tape and money. Both had been careful not to stray to anything too personal, although their conversations had become easier as time went by. Rosie had updated him about the refurbishments and the budget, but they had not spoken about their feelings at all, particularly not about each other.

Now the building was taking shape, it was time to finalise what therapies they would provide and which therapists they would employ. Tanner needed to start researching for his marketing articles, and he and Rosie had agreed to take a couple of courses each so that they had a greater understanding of their new business venture.

As he drove around the sweep of the drive, he saw something bright red down by the lake. It took a few seconds to realise that it was Rosie in a red top. Almost as soon as he recognised her, she seemed to slip down the bank and into the water. He did an emergency stop, sending gravel flying in all directions. He flung himself out of the car and raced across the lawn. His heart was pounding with fear.

When he reached the lakeside, Rosie was flailing around in the water, unable to stand up in the thick reeds. Tanner tore off his trainers and jumped in. It wasn't as deep as he'd thought at the edge. He grabbed hold of her top and pulled her upright. By now, he was furious, mainly as a reaction to his fear that she could have drowned.

'Rosie Phillips, what on earth are you doing in the lake?'

'I was talking to my father.'

'You were what?'

'Talking to my ... our father ... or trying to, before I slipped.'

She'd begun to shiver violently. Although the afternoon was warm for the time of year, it was still freezing cold in the water. Tanner put his arm around her and helped her out of the lake. He heard distant shouts. The security guard and the gardener were running towards them across the lawn. Tanner retrieved the picnic blanket from the grass and wrapped it around Rosie's shaking shoulders.

She seemed disorientated as if the cold water had numbed her senses. Tanner knew better than to ask her to explain herself right now, but he was so angry with her.

Patrick had sat down on the grass after the exertion of running across the lawn. 'Are you all right, Miss Rosie? I thought for a moment history was repeating itself.'

Rosie lent down and patted his shoulder. 'I'm sorry I scared you.'

'This is my fault, isn't it? Because of what I told you?'

'No, no. I was fine until I lost my footing. I'm sorry …'

Tanner was trying to breathe more deeply as this exchange with the gardener took place. His heart was racing. As if he'd needed reminding after being away, this incident reinforced, with a bluntness that was almost painful, that he cared about Rosie.

He led her back to the house, and a warm bath was run for her by the housekeeper in her new flat.

Tanner wouldn't let her completely shut the outside door, as he still wasn't convinced about what had happened at the lake. Could she actually be a danger to herself? He hadn't seen enough from a distance to be sure if she'd actually slipped or deliberately gone into the water. And he knew the stories about her father and his death, of course.

His head was spinning by the time he'd corrected himself that John Phillips was actually *his* father, not Rosie's. And it had been proved he'd had a heart attack rather than taken his own life, but still …

He sat by the partly open door, trying to ignore his cold, wet body, and talked to Rosie about the therapy centre plans, listening for her answers to his questions. His hair was plastered to his head and he was making a wet stain on the carpet in the corridor, which would not please the cleaners.

As soon as she was out of the bath and dressed, he went to try out his new shower and then returned to sit in a chair opposite to Rosie in her small but comfortable lounge, fixing her with a searching stare. 'Great flat. You've done a really fantastic job with this and mine. I'm truly impressed. Now, tell me what on earth you were doing down by the lake – no, make that actually *in* the lake. The truth, mind. I won't be fobbed off, not this time.'

'Why won't you believe me? I was trying to talk to Dada.'

'Then have a séance. Don't go near deep water.' He knew his tone was sarcastic, but he couldn't help it. She had given him such a scare when he'd seen her disappear into the lake.

'It wasn't deep,' protested Rosie.

'But it is deep about a foot away from where you were standing. There's a ledge all the way around, and then a deep hole.'

He could see Rosie's mind working. 'You do know that my father – or make that your father, John – was found in the lake?'

Tanner nodded.

'Patrick told me the other day that at first they thought he'd taken his own life. But the inquest said a heart attack was to blame for his death. He'd had a row with Michael Bryant and gone down to the lake. He was probably trying to calm down, do you think?'

'We won't ever know, I'm afraid.'

She put her head in her hands and then peeked out at Tanner. 'Tanner, please don't mention this to Mum.'

'I won't. Poor woman. Goodness knows what she would think.'

'I'll tell her about it when I'm ready. You didn't really think I meant to drown myself, did you?'

'I will admit that it was my first thought. What else would I think seeing you disappear into the lake like that? It terrified me. The muscles in my legs still hurt, I ran so fast across the lawn. And poor Patrick …'

'I'm sorry.' She pushed her damp hair back out of her eyes.

'Did he say anything?'

'Who?'

'Your dad ... my dad. Yikes, this gets so confusing.'

'No, I couldn't make a connection, but I did ask him for a sign, so we'll see.'

'Rosie Phillips, are you seriously saying that you asked a dead man to leave you something in answer to a question?' It was Tanner's turn to put his head in his hands.

'Yes.'

Tanner made a snorting noise and unsuccessfully tried to turn it into a cough. 'Sorry, I couldn't help that reaction.'

'You're entitled to your opinion. It sounds mad, but I wanted to ask, I wanted to know that he approves of me living here … where he died. I went to see Buzz to ask about all this, by the way.'

'The mystic man in the crystal shop?'

'That's the one. The guy you bought my bracelet from.' She lifted her wrist to show him she was still wearing it.

'And what was the sign you asked for?'

'I'm not going to tell you.'

'Then I won't believe you if you say he's given the sign, will I?'

'Oh, okay, I asked him for two herons flying together over the lake.'

'Right!'

They spent the rest of the afternoon and early evening looking around Lucerne Lodge. Tanner was astounded by the way Rosie had bought their plans to life and very proud of what she had achieved. He also loved her initial brochure design, and after a light meal of cheese, bread and fruit, they had fun playing around with a website template.

He'd been unnerved by the lake incident, but at least it had broken through any initial awkwardness of being with Rosie, and they seemed to have drifted back into a friendly way of being together.

Rosie yawned. 'I'm going to say goodnight., but it's good to have you back to discuss things with.' She smiled.

'I'm still worried about you. You're not going back to the lake tonight, are you?'

'No, I'm going to sleep. I'm suddenly very tired.'

'Good, I need my sleep too. Rosie, we haven't spoken about our DNA test results either – I have the results in my bag.'

'There are a lot of things we need to discuss, Tanner, but I don't think tonight is the right time.'

Tanner left her, resisting the urge to barricade her door. He slept fitfully as he tried to listen for any creaking floorboards. He wasn't sure if he actually had cause for concern and, as Rosie had forbidden him from mentioning the episode to her mother, he had no one to discuss it with either. The burden felt very heavy on his shoulders.

# *Chapter Thirty-Seven*

Tanner was scared. He couldn't ever remember feeling this afraid. It ranked with the first day at school, the first visit to the headmaster or the first time he'd told his father 'No'. The room was predominately populated by women, one in particular he recognised – Lulabelle Martin. He hadn't seen her since the embarrassment of having to lift her up to the crowd as a lot at the charity auction, but he could see by the glint in her eye that she had recognised him.

Lines of therapy couches filled the room and there was a pervading smell of lavender in the air. Rosie and he had agreed to do basic courses in a couple of therapies, just so that they were more informed about the therapists and therapies they chose for the business. Rosie had dabbled in alternative therapies for quite a while, instigated by her friend Connie's interest, but Tanner was totally new to it apart from the treatments he'd had when he was writing his article about therapies from the point of view of a newbie.

The massage tutor, Natalie, split Tanner and Rosie up. Natalie must have assumed that they were together as their booking had been a joint one. She said that couples knew each other's bodies too well for this exercise. Neither Rosie nor Tanner contradicted her. Later, Natalie referred to Rosie as "your wife" as she spoke to Tanner, and he countered with the word "sister", for want of a better description. He realised the moment he'd said it that business partner might have been more accurate ... and would have made him feel less weird.

The tutor was addressing them. 'The best way to learn massage is to do it,' she declared.

She divided the group into two and asked one half to lie face down on the couches arranged around the room. Tanner struggled to get comfortable on the unfamiliar bed with a face hole. He was so tall that his feet dangled off the end.

'The rest of you – choose your victim and go and stand by their couch.'

Tanner's heart began to thud, and he contemplated sprinting for the door. He opted instead for closing his eyes and not looking up.

The tutor spoke again in her authoritarian tone. 'Right, put your hands on the shoulders of the person on the couch and press. This exercise is all about getting used to the feeling of a body beneath your hands. As you work, ask your patient how the pressure feels and for any comments on the sensations they get as you press different parts of their body. Client, in other words the person lying on the couch, if it hurts, yell. Don't just endure it in silence. Oh, and, of course, no inappropriate touching please!'

Tanner couldn't help but open his eyes at that phrase. He caught sight of legging-clad ankles and had a horrible feeling he knew who had chosen him for a patient. He was helpless, when nails that were a little too long, pressed into his back. Lulabelle had her hands on him.

At half time, Tanner scurried over to ask Rosie how she was getting on. She had chosen a small lady in a vivid purple tracksuit. She told him in hushed tones that when she put her hands on her patient's shoulders, she realised that her clothing hid a body that felt fragile. Rosie said she had been scared to press too hard in case she broke a bone.

The students swapped over, with the people who had been massaging taking the role of client, and Tanner decided that there was just one thing worse than being pressed all over by Lulabelle and that was having to press Lulabelle all over. It felt like the longest thirty minutes of his life.

He knew by the end of the course that he could no more do this for a living than fly to the moon. *Management roles only for him at Lucerne Lodge Retreat and Therapy Centre.* Although his experiences today would, of course, make for a great article.

Rosie and Tanner took a long time mulling over the wording of advertisements for therapists to place in local newspapers. They spent most evenings and any spare moment during the day going through the applications to shortlist applicants for interviews.

They planned to offer hypnotherapy, Reiki, reflexology, aromatherapy, Swedish massage and acupressure massage to begin with. There would also be yoga, tai chi and meditation classes in the gym space.

Rosie looked up from her pile of application forms. 'When are we going to hold these interviews?'

'We'll need a few days.'

'Especially as the best way to interview these people would be to get them to treat us.'

'Do we have to do it that way?'

Rosie could see the panic in Tanner's eyes, and a vision of him lying on the therapy couch with Lulabelle bending over him at their recent course came to mind.

'I don't see how we can do it any other way. I mean, they may be skilled at talking to us, but can they treat the clients and, more to the point, can they do it to a very high standard?'

'I see what you mean. Couldn't we shortlist them first and then ask the best back to do treatments?'

'Yes, I can see that would work. These positions have been very popular, even though they are part-time and the therapists will only be called in when we need them.'

'I suppose most therapists are self-employed and have to get their clients themselves. A contract like this must be like gold dust.'

'We're going to have to advertise for a cook and a receptionist too. Finalising those initial brochures and advertising are next on the agenda.'

'I have some celebrity contacts. Maybe I could charm them into giving us their endorsement? *And* I could include them in my articles.'

'That would be super.' Rosie blushed, wondering what the "charming" would involve.

'We need to decide on a name.'

'I'd assumed we'd call it "Lucerne Lodge Retreat and Therapy Centre".'

'I suppose that sums it up really.'

'If you're happy, I thought I'd invite Connie and Lucy to come and stay for the weekend. We need to try out the guest bedrooms, just to make sure everything is up to scratch, and it would give some independent views.'

'That sounds like a brilliant idea, but can I cope with the three of you for a whole weekend?'

'It'll be fun,' said Rosie, laughing and feeling pleased that she and Tanner were back to an easier, more relaxed relationship and that he hadn't mentioned returning to London lately.

# *Chapter Thirty-Eight*

*It will be fun,* Rosie had said, so why did Tanner feel like escaping back to London when Friday night arrived?

Even though it would mean a lot of cleaning and washing, Rosie wanted the four of them to stay in a room each on Friday and then a different four rooms on Saturday night, so that things like the new bathrooms got well tested.

Connie and Lucy took their roles as venue testers very seriously and asked lots of questions about how the retreat and therapy centre would operate. Tanner was glad that Rosie took the lead in answering the questions, even though he suspected that she might be making up some of the answers as they went along. At least it was making them both think about what might be asked by prospective clients and the people staying at Lucerne Lodge.

Tanner cooked a mild curry and served it with fluffy rice, naan bread and poppadums. They ate in the dining room, again to test if it would work for guests.

'I'll try out your therapy rooms tomorrow if you like? I can give all of you a treatment maybe?' said Connie.

Tanner knew that Rosie was worried that Tanner would think it favouritism if she gave Connie a job – she'd said as much – so he decided to head the worry off straight away. 'That sounds great, Connie – and it can serve as your interview trial for a job here if you like.'

Connie squealed and embarrassed Tanner by darting round the table to give him a kiss on the cheek.

Rosie smiled at him, and her obvious delight made him pleased that he'd suggested it.

When they'd finished their meal, they sat in the lounge. Rosie and Lucy shared one sofa, Connie sat on another and Tanner took the chair by the fireplace.

'This house is almost too lovely to be open to guests,' commented Connie.

'It is rather grand,' said Lucy, standing up to have a look at some of the paintings on the wall. 'Is this Michael Bryant?'

She was looking at two portraits: one stuffily posed one, and a more relaxed portrait that Tanner told Lucy had been done by Nick Crossten, who lived with Mandy, the owner of Owl Corner Crafts.

Lucy had moved to the other side of the fireplace. 'And a lovely portrait of you, Tanner.' She flashed a smile at him.

'Again by Nick.'

Tanner stood up and took Lucy through the other downstairs rooms to look at the numerous other pictures and portraits. He reasoned that this might be something other guests could show an interest in, and even found himself wondering if he should produce some sort of laminated guide to the Lucerne Lodge art.

Rosie was deep in conversation with Connie about therapies and the cost of them when they returned. He noticed that Rosie had started to make notes in a notebook and asked her to add a note about the art guide so that he didn't forget.

He offered to make coffees and took himself off to the kitchen to sort them out. Rosie's friends were very pleasant, but it was a little intense entertaining them, especially when they were taking their role as centre testers very seriously. For the first time, he questioned whether he could cope with strangers at Lucerne Lodge.

Rosie was also finding it weird entertaining her friends at the house. She felt ultra-conscious of Tanner and his reactions too. She didn't know if he had noticed that Lucy was trying to spend time with him. While he was away making the coffee, she decided to find out what was happening with Lucy's eventful and changeable love life.

'Lucy, I haven't heard you mention any new dates lately.'

'That's because I haven't had any. I've taken myself off all of the dating sites, and I've decided to have a break from ... most ... men for a while.'

'*Most* men?'

Rosie didn't get an answer, as Tanner came back with brimming coffees that smelt so divine. He'd also put some mint chocolates on the tray.

Connie surprised Rosie by taking custody of the chocolates.

'You're all going to have to earn these,' she said with a mischievous look on her face.

'How do I earn a chocolate then?' asked Tanner. Rosie knew him well enough by now to realise he was playing along but wary.

'I get to ask you a question, and if I'm happy with the answer you get a choc,' explained Connie.

'Go on then,' said Tanner.

Rosie felt the hairs standing up on the back of her neck, wondering what on earth Connie would ask. She also realised how protective she felt of Tanner. Almost imperceptibly over the last few weeks, they had become closer, like family even. Was she still thinking of him as a brother? She got her answer to that question when Lucy sat next to him on the third sofa where he'd positioned himself after returning with the coffees so that he could reach the table. Rosie felt a dart of something when Lucy sat closer to him than she felt was necessary. It wasn't exactly jealousy, more a spark of anger that he was *hers*, not Lucy's. *Now where did that come from?*

She brought her attention back to Connie, who had been deciding what question to ask of Tanner.

'Best ever job?' asked Connie.

Tanner sipped his coffee and made a show of pondering her enquiry. 'I love writing articles, so I suppose being a freelance journalist.' He smiled and Connie threw him a chocolate.

'My turn,' said Lucy. Rosie wondered if she imagined her moving even closer to Tanner.

'So difficult to know what to ask you,' mused Connie.

'Nothing embarrassing, please,' pleaded Lucy.

'Oooh, how much is that worth?' Connie laughed. 'Favourite ever present?'

'My Kindle. My parents got it for me a couple of years ago and I use it every day.'

Connie threw her a chocolate.

'Same question to Rosie,' said Connie.

Lucy was by now really annoying Rosie with her ever-increasing closeness to Tanner.

'My bracelet,' she said quickly, holding up her wrist and displaying the moon and star bracelet wrapped around it.

'Oooh, when did you get that?' asked Lucy.

'Tanner bought it for me.'

Tanner smiled, and Rosie couldn't help being pleased when she saw Lucy move away from him slightly. Connie threw Rosie her chocolate before starting to unwrap her own, drawing immediate protests from the others.

‘One rule for you and another for us,’ said Rosie indignantly. ‘You haven’t answered a question.’

Tanner cleared up the now empty cups and declared that he would leave the girls to chat and see them in the morning.

In one way, Rosie was glad he’d escaped Lucy and her not-so-subtle advances, but on the other hand, she missed his presence in the room.

The rest of the weekend passed pleasantly enough. The guest rooms all seemed to work well, apart from the shower in the bathroom of the room Tanner used on the Saturday night which leaked terribly. It seemed like the project was well and truly coming together.

‘Have we got some interviews this afternoon?’ asked Tanner a couple of days later.

‘Yes, a massage therapist and a reflexologist. So, do you fancy having your back or your feet done?’

‘Do I have to?’ Tanner didn’t find either option particularly appealing. ‘What time, so that I can get cleaned up?’ He was sorting through papers in his father’s study.

‘First one at two o’clock, second at three-thirty.’

‘Okay, I’ll just finish up here.’

Tanner had a last-minute dash to appear in the dining room, where they had taken to conducting therapist interviews. He rushed in and nearly straight into the arms of Lulabelle Martin. It was difficult to make his body language not reflect his inner “*Oh no*!”

‘Ah Tanner, darling, I was trying to tell the delightful Rosie that we’re old friends.’

‘Erm, hello, Lulabelle. You were on the massage course the other week, but I didn’t think you worked as a therapist?’

‘I’m just starting out. I’ve had enough of cleaning for a living, so I’m training up in therapies.’

Rosie had her annoyed face on – he guessed it must be because he was late. Or maybe Lulabelle was getting to her too. She couldn’t be jealous of her over-familiar way with him, could she?

The interview droned on with Lulabelle evading many of the answers. Then it came to the practical demonstration.

‘Tanner, are you going to be Lulabelle’s massage subject?’

‘Actually, Rosie, I can already vouch for Lulabelle’s massage talents, so there’s no need for her to demonstrate.’

Rosie showed Lulabelle out, whilst telling her the procedure they had established for letting people know about their decision. Tanner sat idly picking at a piece of skin on his thumb.

Rosie had a taunting tone to her voice. 'Tanner and I are friends. Tanner already knows *all* about my massage talents.'

'She was on that taster massage class at the same time as us. I can't believe you didn't realise it was her when you read her application.'

'So, she has no more experience at massage than we do?'

'Exactly. She must have decided to blag her way through the interview as I've got a horrible feeling that she has a crush on me.'

'Do you want to employ her so you can avail yourself of her talents anytime you wish then?'

'Please! I'd rather train as a dragon tamer.'

'I'll take that as a no.'

Tanner thought he could detect a note of relief in Rosie's voice.

He was not enjoying the interview process, but it was good to be sharing fun and laughter with Rosie. The shortlist was predominantly women, and he didn't understand too much about therapies yet. He was busy reading up on the techniques and their uses for his forthcoming articles to promote the new business.

He talked to Rosie about reflexology, which was the specialist therapy of the next interviewee. They had a coffee in the kitchen, and then the doorbell was ringing once again.

This candidate was an olive-skinned gentleman with a wide smile. He ignored Tanner throughout the interview and concentrated on flirting with Rosie. Her simpering was getting on his nerves. He'd never seen her in the girly, giggly mode, and he didn't like it. He definitely *was* jealous and he was annoyed at himself that he was.

# Chapter Thirty-Nine

Rosie decided to spend Saturday night at her mother's house in a bid to relax and recharge her batteries ready for the final push before Lucerne Lodge Retreat and Therapy Centre opened its doors. They had chosen the last day in June for the opening, and it appeared to be approaching faster than either of them had anticipated.

Her mother found the tales of the therapist interviews and last-minute panics over the centre highly amusing. Rosie began to realise that she used Tanner's name an awful lot. Did she imagine her mother's raised eyebrow every time she mentioned him?

On Sunday morning when she returned, Tanner emerged from the front door of Lucerne Lodge just as she pulled up in her red Fiesta. He was carrying a lurid pink holdall.

'Rosie, you're early …'

Whatever he was going to say was drowned out by squeals and then a cry of "darling" as Lucy came out of the house, launched herself at Tanner and wound herself around his neck.

Tanner shrugged at Rosie with his eyebrows raised.

Rosie fought to maintain her composure as her mind freewheeled around various possible reactions to the scene in front of her. She'd told Lucy that she wasn't interested in Tanner, and her friend had witnessed the disastrous marriage proposal, so there was no point turning possessive now, but she mentally tore Lucy away from Tanner and clawed at her, imagining leaving nail marks down her face and smudging the perfect make-up. Things must have developed while she'd been away for the evening. Her reaction to Lucy entwined with Tanner made her realise that her own feelings had undertaken a dramatic turn too.

Torn between braving things out, walking past them into the house or getting back into her car and driving off, she allowed confusion and uncertainty to battle inside her. *Hang on a minute*, said a voice in her head, *you own half of this house legitimately*. She pressed her remote-control key fob, which caused a decisive sounding beep, and strode past the entangled couple into the lodge.

'Morning, Lucy, Tanner.'

It didn't take long for Tanner to follow her up the stairs. She was already in the study when he reached her.

‘Lucy stayed over last night. She’d had a nasty argument with her latest boyfriend. I thought she said she was off men, but apparently not.’

‘No need to explain. I’m sure I don’t need the details of your love life. It has nothing to do with me.’ Rosie was exasperated that her tone sounded glacial even to her own ears.

‘No, Rosie, you’re misunderstanding. She stayed in a guest room, of course.’

‘I bet she did.’ Rosie was in no mood to listen. She needed coffee and a headache tablet, and not necessarily in that order.

Tanner panicked that Lucy had made it look as if they had a thing going on. He could imagine the scene through Rosie’s eyes and it made him groan. He couldn’t help wondering if Lucy had thrown herself at him deliberately, but then she couldn’t have known that Rosie would arrive at that exact time. Maybe it was for the best that Rosie had turned up. Goodness, what would he have done if she’d made a pass at him? *No*, he reasoned, *if she was going to make a pass, she would have done it last night when he was comforting her through her tears about her boyfriend’s unreasonableness.*

He was now faced with trying to convince Rosie that there was nothing going on. Things had been going well lately with their working relationship, so he didn’t want anything to jeopardise that.

He followed her to the kitchen. Rosie was standing at the window staring out at the landscape. The park had been designed with views from every window. This room looked out over the woodland at the back of the house. It was one of Tanner’s favourite parts of the estate because it was wild and not manicured. The woodland was left mostly to its own devices. He hated it when they had to cut trees to allow the strongest ones to grow and mature. Sometimes he wondered whether he preferred trees to people.

Rosie had obviously heard his approach. ‘Tanner, do you think it would be better for both of us if I go back to live in Borteen?’

‘Why would you want to do that?’ He panicked even more. ‘You can’t just leave our project. It will never get finished without you. Besides, I’d miss you.’

She turned and looked directly at him.

He could tell by the sudden movement of her shoulders that she’d reached a decision. ‘We need a review meeting to decide what last minute things need to be done before the launch.’

Tanner sighed in relief but also some consternation at her changed tone. 'Let me make us some coffee, and then I'm all yours.' He gulped at the possible double meaning of the expression, although he realised that even if Lucy had draped herself over him, he had felt nothing, not even an ounce of attraction. Whereas being near Rosie ...well, that was a different story.

The rest of the morning went by in a blur, as Rosie and Tanner examined and redrafted check lists and reviewed progress or, in some instances, lack of it. Tanner found himself presented with a "to do" list, but he was grateful for it. It was better to be busy than thinking.

When they had finished, Tanner suggested they take Trixie for a walk. He was amused that the aged dog was more pleased to see Rosie than himself.

'This is the best part about living here.'

'The grounds?' he asked.

'Yes, the freedom to roam in so many acres.'

'It's lovely, but also a big responsibility.'

They stopped together on the hillside opposite the house. This was the best place to appreciate the architecture of the building and understand why the house had been sited here.

'Shall we sit?' asked Tanner.

Rosie lay back with her hands behind her head. Tanner didn't think he'd seen her look so lovely. He hated to destroy the mood, but he had to discuss something with her.

'You've never asked me about our DNA test results.'

'I've thought about them, but it's never seemed the right time, and we had so much to do.'

'The tests prove categorically that we can't possibly be related.' Tanner turned to gauge Rosie's reaction.

Apart from a sharp intake of breath and a subdued 'Oh', she didn't give much away. 'Where's Trixie?' Rosie sat up and looked around.

Tanner spotted the dog down by the lake. 'Oops, we'd better catch her. I'm not sure she's strong enough for a swim in the water these days.

They ran down the bank together. Trixie had a short lead attached to her collar, although most of the time it trailed behind her as she trotted along beside them. Tanner and Rosie reached for it at the same time and, as they straightened, their heads were very close together.

Tanner couldn't resist the opportunity. He brushed his lips on hers. The light pressure sent tingles down his spine. Rosie didn't pull away, but he didn't want to push things, so he stood up and resisted the urge to deepen the kiss. *Take things slowly, Tanner. Don't scare her.*

There was a noise above them and Rosie squealed as two herons flew overhead.

'My sign!'

'I've never seen two at the same time before.'

The herons landed on the far side of the lake.

'Wow, do you think they might nest?' said Rosie, a look of complete joy on her face.

'It's a fantastic place to live, and to raise a family,' said Tanner, not thinking of the birds at all.

# Chapter Forty

The following Tuesday was Rosie's birthday. When she got up, she peered through the curtains. The day had dawned bright and clear with a strong breeze. *A proper birthday*. She always thought it wasn't the same if it rained on your special day.

She threw on her dressing-gown and went down to the kitchen. Tanner, complete with voluminous white apron, was cooking pancakes. He hadn't tried to kiss her again, but their friendship seemed to have moved to a different level.

'Oooh, my favourite,' she exclaimed.

Tanner looked up with a grin. 'Happy Birthday, Mademoiselle Rosie.'

He looked younger than normal, his hair tightly curled and damp from the shower. She couldn't help admiring the view of his taut backside as he concentrated on the pancake in the pan.

Smiling to herself, she sat at the table as her mobile phone erupted with her current distinctive ring tone, 'Freedom' by George Michael.

'Happy birthday,' yelled Lucy when she answered the call. Rosie chatted for a few moments, making Lucy laugh about Tanner the chef. There had been no further awkwardness about Lucy staying over at Lucerne Lodge, because by the next time Rosie had seen her friend, she was in raptures about a fireman called Dave.

Just as the call finished, Tanner presented Rosie with a pancake on a plate. It looked less than perfect, with a little charring at the edges and a hole in the middle, but it was special because it had been made just for her.

It tasted wonderful. She liked pancakes with lemon and sugar, and enjoyed every bite of this one.

Her phone rang again. Connie this time. Another pancake was waiting for her by the end of the call.

When her mother rang, Rosie was feeling satisfyingly full. Tanner indicated that he'd like to speak to Frances, so she passed the handset over.

'Hi, Frances. I'm cooking this evening, so would you like to join us?'

Rosie was pleased that Tanner had invited her mother. They were feeling their way into this new phase of their relationship.

When the call had finished, Tanner handed her a gold envelope. Her heart thudded as she opened the card. She was disappointed that it was a plain card with a bunch of flowers on the front and a very stark message.

*To Rosie, Happy Birthday. Tanner.* There was one kiss. She chastised herself inwardly, before smiling her thanks.

'Now, as soon as you're dressed, I'm taking you shopping for a new dress. I still owe you one and I hate not paying my debts.'

'Well, I will need something special to wear for our launch day here,' mused Rosie.

They parked in Sowden and as they walked into the town, Rosie caught sight of them together in a shop window. Walking side by side, she thought that they looked well matched as a couple. She couldn't believe she was thinking that, but the fact she was gave her a message that her feelings about Tanner were deepening once more. Fear lurched into her stomach. *Dare she allow herself to dream again?*

'Won't you find it boring shopping for dresses?'

'Not with you inside them.' He winked suggestively.

The simple reply produced the first blush of the day. She guessed that it would not be her last.

'Have I got a budget to spend?' she asked cheekily.

'Just find a great dress to replace the one I ruined. It's so long ago now since that charity auction at Lucerne Lodge that I think you can legitimately add interest to the cost of the dress I spoiled.'

'It's dangerous not to give me a budget.'

'I'll rein you back, if necessary.'

Tanner sat on a pink leather sofa outside of the changing rooms. The department store had so many sections of clothing in a full rainbow of colours that his head had started to hurt as Rosie sorted through the dresses. An assistant had quickly latched onto them and begun to hang likely purchases in a changing room ready for Rosie to try on. Tanner knew that he would have to grit his teeth to get through this experience, but he was determined to be supportive to Rosie in her search for a replacement dress. Even though it had been almost a year ago, he could still visualise the original, both with Rosie wearing it, and then wet and pink-tinged in the sink after the prawn cocktail incident.

She emerged from the curtained corridor numerous times, wearing a succession of red silk, cream polka dot, emerald taffeta, and he lost count of the little black dresses. He had an irrational hatred of black dresses, so tried to steer her towards the red and green, encouraging her to twirl in front of him. *Wow, she was gorgeous*. Rosie became bolder as she tried on more clothes and got used to Tanner making encouraging noises. It reminded him of scenes in a couple of films he'd watched.

Other women, whose husbands had more than likely sensibly gone into the sanctuary of the electronics shop down the street, began asking for his opinion on their attire too. By the end of his time sitting on the awful pink sofa, he felt he'd used up all of his imagination to make diplomatic comments about women of all shapes and sizes in all manner of clothing.

Rosie emerged in the red dress for the third time and, as she disappeared to put on the green yet again, Tanner wearily told the shop assistant that he would pay for both dresses.

When Rosie found out what he'd done and protested, he said, 'You'll need more dresses anyway for the events we have planned at the Lodge.'

They left the store with Tanner holding huge colourful carrier bags and Rosie smiling. Hopefully his brownie points were worth the discomfort of all of the time sitting outside that changing room.

'Thank you for being so patient, and I didn't realise you were so practised at tactful comments. I wouldn't have known what to say when that one lady asked for an opinion on that awful brown suit.'

'I was honest. The suit was the same colour as her eyes.' He laughed.

'Hmm, just as long as you didn't think the green or red dresses matched mine.'

They both laughed this time.

'I've bought you the dresses, but don't you need shoes, handbags and jewellery to match?'

'Goodness, no. I've got things that will go with them already. Thank you.' She planted a chaste kiss on his cheek, and he resisted turning his head so that their lips would fully meet.

'Are you going to be having a red or a green evening today?'

'For my birthday meal?'

'Yes, you may as well dress up on your birthday. So will it be red or green?'

'I haven't decided yet. I'll surprise you.'

Later, after an unusually lazy day of reading and a walk around the park and gardens with Trixie, Rosie dressed for dinner. She decided on the green dress and had to look at herself twice in the mirror – she couldn't quite believe how elegant she appeared.

She knew that Frances would feel uneasy about her trip to Lucerne Lodge. She had so far managed to avoid visiting the house. Rosie could understand it, because of her uncomfortable past associations with the Lodge, but she *so* wanted to show her mother what she had achieved here with the new therapy rooms and the guest bedrooms.

When she got to the kitchen, Tanner was working over the stove as if he'd been there all day after cooking the pancakes. He turned as she came in.

'Your dress looks lovely – really, *really* nice.' He smiled.

She felt another blush rising and so diverted attention to his cooking. 'I'm impressed, Tanner. More culinary talents?'

'Cheeky! I like cooking, but it isn't much fun cooking for yourself. Much better to have an occasion and someone special to cook for.'

She digested the *special* comment and then answered her mobile phone's sudden insistent beep.

'Rosie, love, I don't think I can do it. I don't think I can come over to Lucerne Lodge.' Frances' tone was tense and sharp.

'Hey, Mum. It doesn't matter. Would it make it easier if I fetched you?'

'I don't think I can face being there ... sorry.'

Tanner whispered, 'Is everything all right?'

Rosie shook her head.

'Tell your Mum to put the oven on and lay the table. We'll be there in an hour with the food.'

Frances' voice sounded relieved when Rosie told her Tanner's plan.

Rosie put down the phone and went over to hug Tanner. She didn't mean to linger over the hug – it just happened. Before she knew it, he'd lowered his head. He paused above her lips, as if he was about to question if it was all right to kiss her, but she reached up and made the connection. His lips were firm and his tongue produced sparking sensations on hers. Longing filled her body as she relaxed into the kiss.

When they parted, Tanner still with his arm across her back, he spoke first. 'I did wonder if Frances might find it difficult to come here.'

'Thank you for being so thoughtful. What can I do to help with the meal?'

'Mmm, I'm sure I can think of something. Maybe treat the chef to more kisses?'

He lowered his head again for a second lingering kiss. He found another apron to protect Rosie's dress, and they worked as a team for the next half hour.

They arrived at Frances' cottage laden down with bags and containers. The way she looked from Rosie to Tanner and back again, told Rosie her mother had not missed the new hint of friendliness between the two of them. She admired Rosie's dress and Rosie told her the tale of its purchase. Tanner raised his eyes heavenward in appropriate places to make Frances laugh.

Her mother's dining table was spread with a cheerful cloth covered in roses that Rosie recognised from her childhood, and the cutlery shone in the light of several candles.

Rosie, despite having helped prepare the food, was shooed off into the living room as Tanner and her mother put the final touches to the meal.

Melon with Parma ham, a delicious salad and a moussaka – Rosie thought she hadn't tasted better food in a restaurant. For dessert, he produced a blackberry cheesecake with cream. Rosie was in heaven.

After they had eaten, Frances made coffee and they moved into the dusk-lit conservatory. Rosie had eaten so much that she hoped that her dress would fit the next day. She sat next to Tanner on the wicker settee and allowed her leg to rest against the black denim of his jeans.

Frances presented her with a thin white box. Inside was the gold locket, which Rosie recognised from when Frances had worn it to Michael Bryant's funeral. She raised her eyes to her mother in question.

'I figured it was time for you to have it,' she breathed.

'It has special significance, doesn't it?' asked Rosie.

'Your father, real father that is – Michael Bryant – gave it to me when you were born.'

'I thought he never knew for certain I was his?'

'He was suspicious, curious. He came to see me in the hospital and voiced his thoughts. He kept asking me "is she mine?". I didn't confirm it one way or another. It seemed easier at the time. He gave me the locket and said I was to pass it to you at an appropriate point in your life. I think that time has come.'

Rosie had a huge lump in her throat. How different would her life have been if her mother had told Michael Bryant that he was the father of her new born baby? She picked up the locket and examined it closely. It was solid gold and appeared to be very old.

Tanner, who had been very quiet during the exchange between mother and daughter, spoke. 'I have a picture of that locket.'

Rosie couldn't read his expression. 'Really?'

'When you get back to Lucerne, look at the portrait at the top of the first flight of stairs. I think it belonged to my father's … erm, I mean *Michael's* grandmother.'

Rosie put the locket carefully into her bag. She wanted to think about its significance a little more, and she was already wearing her moon and star necklace with the matching bracelet.

Frances produced a cake from the pantry, complete with candles. Tanner lit them with a taper. Rosie waited until they had chorused, "Happy Birthday", before blowing out the candles with one breath. She silently made a wish as was traditional, and this time it concerned her hopes for her future happiness. Frances and Tanner applauded and then both hugged her.

As Tanner embraced her, her mother was mouthing suggestively behind his back. Rosie had to concentrate very hard not to giggle.

Frances insisted she didn't want any help with the clearing up, and she left them talking in the conservatory. As they spoke about their plans for Lucerne Lodge, Rosie realised that they had gradually slipped into an easy working relationship, friendship and, now, maybe more, and it felt good. Not for the first time, she cursed herself inwardly for having refused his offer of marriage, but it had been too much too soon. She wondered how Tanner felt about his proposal now, but it didn't seem a subject she could raise easily without making an implication that he should repeat his question and risk their new-found harmony.

When Rosie and Tanner returned to Lucerne Lodge, they decided to watch a film together. Rosie excused herself to change out of her dress and put on leggings and a slouchy top instead. Tanner told her that she could choose the film as it was her birthday. She promised Tanner that he could make the choice the next time. The implication that there would be a next time felt exciting.

They sat close together as one of her favourite films, *The Wedding Date*, came up on the screen, and, for the first time, they held hands. She was pleased that Tanner appeared determined not to rush things between them this time. Sure enough, as soon as the credits started, Tanner released her hand, got up from his seat and stretched.

'That film was a bit too romantic.' He laughed.

'I think it's lovely.' Rosie sighed, remembering the look in the hero's eyes as he finally claimed his girl.

'Is that what women really want – heroes and romance?'

'If a film can't transport you to another world, even an unrealistic fantasy one, then it isn't worth watching.'

'So, how would I measure up as a hero?' He paused. 'I probably shouldn't open that can of worms.'

Rosie stood up too and pretended to survey him with a critical eye. He wore his hair long, but neatly tied at the back of his neck most of the time. She'd always had a thing for men with long hair.

'I think you'd do very nicely: tall, moody, long hair …'

'Stop it, you're making me blush. I wish I'd never asked. Moody? I'm not moody.' He pulled a face. 'But seriously, what type of hero do you go for? Robin Hood?'

'Oh, yes.'

'Pirates?'

'Oooh, yes.'

'Vikings?'

'Yes.'

'Highwaymen?'

Rosie nodded.

'Musketeers?'

She nodded again.

'Dashing rogues.'

'Every time.'

'I really don't understand women. So, honest answer now, what do you think of my long hair?'

'It suits you and it has a certain charm. How come you never cut it off?'

'Another rebellion. My father hated it, but I needed one thing that was mine and mine alone to distinguish me, or else I'd have just become another one of his clones.' Tanner ran his hand over his hair.

Rosie hadn't spoken her mind completely, of course. She was beginning to get a vivid picture of the lonely boy and young man who had become Tanner Bryant the loner.

She moved to give him a big hug, thanking him for making her birthday special. The hug ended with another delicious kiss, before they said goodnight and went to their own separate flats.

# *Chapter Forty-One*

'Come on, we need to practice massage for our exam tomorrow.'

'Can't you ask the gardener to be your victim? I've got so much to organise for the launch day,' said Rosie, hardly lifting her head from the papers in front of her.

'He'll think I'm coming on to him, besides you could do with relaxing for a moment,' said Tanner, feeling embarrassed at the thoughts and images that went through his head. "*Hey Patrick, fancy a massage?*" might come across in totally the wrong way and, no, it would be far too awkward to have the elderly gardener on his massage couch.

He could tell that Rosie was reluctant, but she lay face down on the couch. The acupressure massage they had been learning was carried out over clothing. He began some moves to warm up Rosie's back, but found it difficult to concentrate as his body kept reacting to the fact he was touching her. Her body felt warm and firm, and each press released a waft of subtle floral perfume. His saving grace was that she was face down, otherwise she would have surely noticed his discomfort. He fervently hoped that certain parts of his anatomy would calm down as he massaged, but, at the moment, he was having difficulty remembering even the basic moves.

'Tanner, are you okay?' Rosie's muffled voice came from under the face hole in the couch.

'I am. Just trying to remember how to do this.'

He tried to make his movements more fluid, but a sigh from Rosie made his body react once more, resulting in him forgetting what he was supposed to be doing yet again.

'That feels so good and you're right – just what I need.'

Then it happened. The very air around them changed. Experimentally, Tanner allowed a finger to stray under the bottom hem of her T-shirt. When she didn't protest, he moved so that his whole hand was touching her skin. Her body was smooth and silky under his fingers. He was becoming hypnotised by the circular movements he was making as he worked up the muscle groups of her back, his moves nothing to do with the course they had done or the impending assessment. Her shirt was riding higher as he worked. When he encountered the resistance of her bra strap, his heart rate accelerated. Rosie appeared to be holding her breath.

'Okay if I undo this?'

She hesitated for a fraction of a second. 'Carry on.'

The breathiness of her voice led him to increase the pressure of his hands slightly. Soon the T-shirt and bra lay crumpled on the floor as he moved over her skin, pressing and smoothing as he went. He'd worked all of the way up her back slowly, concentrating carefully. Now he came back downwards, dwelling on each inch of her skin, feeling each muscle, and tentatively beginning to edge his fingers underneath the waistband of her trousers.

'Well, Tanner, I don't remember these moves, but they are good ... so good.' She sighed and her voice now seemed to have a different tone. 'You'll have to teach them to me … later.'

Emboldened by her words, Tanner reached beneath her to undo the trouser button and zip, and he eased the fabric away to join the rest of her clothing on the floor. He gasped when he saw her black lace underwear. He massaged her bottom slowly over the top of the silky garment and then slipped slowly and tentatively beneath. Rosie groaned and his body reacted to the sound.

All of the time he'd been massaging, she'd been lying still and passive apart from appreciative sounds and comments, but now she arched her back as he massaged deeper. He took his time, marvelling at his restraint, although by now he'd given up trying to conceal the reactions of his own body. He removed her underwear inch by inch, so that he could concentrate fully on giving her pleasure.

He used his other hand to clumsily remove his own clothing. She gasped as he lay full length on top of her and began to nibble her neck.

'Tanner, should we be doing this?'

'I think it's the perfect time, but if you're not ready, just say and I'll stop.'

'No! Don't stop. I want you to carry on … please.'

He got up for a moment to remove the rest of his clothes. She turned over to watch him slip on a condom and then he was savouring the warmth of her body as he nibbled and kissed her lips. His excitement built to such an intensity that the movement of their bodies didn't take long to push him to a crescendo of climax, and from the sounds Rosie made it seemed she was more than happy too.

Rosie wondered if she had imagined what had just happened. She'd been deliciously seduced on a massage couch. She opened her eyes to find

Tanner searching her face with questioning eyes. She wrapped her arms around his neck and kissed him long and deep, wrapping her fingers in his hair. She took his hand, scooped up their clothing and led him through the house to her bedroom.

He had gone from her bed when she woke, but there was a slight depression in the mattress to show he really had been there. Rosie hugged herself and rolled into his space in the bed to savour the memories of the night before.

She washed and showered ready to go to the massage test, wondering if she would be able to keep the grin from her face. She was sure that everyone would know that she and Tanner had finally given in to their mutual attraction and made love.

Rosie and Tanner both passed the massage tutor's test, despite Tanner's unorthodox methods the day before. They skirted around one another for the next few days and didn't spend much time alone. Rosie came to the conclusion that Tanner must regret them giving into physical desires. She didn't have much time to dwell on her disappointment, as there was so much to arrange for the Lucerne Lodge Retreat and Therapy Centre launch party at the end of the week. She parcelled up her complicated feelings about Tanner and tried to put them to one side until she had space to deal with them.

She had to make sure the therapists' uniforms and those of the catering and administration staff had been sent out. The caterers rang with queries. The florist couldn't get white roses, so asked for her approval to use white carnations instead. The marquee floor wasn't as clean as she would have liked, so a clean-up operation was organised. The gardener mowed the lawns and the noise began to give her a headache. *Rush, rush, rush.*

Tanner was confused. He couldn't read Rosie's reactions to their intimacy. She looked at him shyly from under her eyelashes and seemed to avoid direct eye or body contact. Did she regret what they had done and their new-found closeness?

His job for the launch had been to co-ordinate the celebrity and press invitations, and his phone rang non-stop with acceptances, queries and others begging to be included on the guest list. He was particularly pleased with these calls, as they showed that word of the launch and the retreat centre was spreading.

He opened the morning newspaper to an article he'd written announcing that Lucerne Lodge Retreat and Therapy Centre was opening its doors on Saturday. The graphic Rosie had prepared for "Summer at Lucerne Lodge" was prominent and colourful on the page. He went into the new office near to the front door where Rosie was working.

'Hey, Rosie, look at this. They've published my article and your advert. Hopefully it will bring bookings flooding in.'

'The telephone's been ringing steadily already this morning. Well done, you.'

'And you!'

He wanted to hug her, but unsure of her reaction, he high-fived her instead.

'Is everything on track for the launch party? Anything I can do?'

'I think it's just about under control.'

He could see furrows on her brow. 'You still friends with me?'

'Why wouldn't I be?'

'I don't know. I got the impression that you were avoiding me, after … you know … I thought maybe your feelings had cooled?' He sat on the stool by the photocopier.

'Not avoiding you at all, just suddenly shy around you now for some reason.'

'So, I haven't done anything wrong?'

She got up from the desk. The phone began to ring, but she pointedly ignored it and walked over to him. 'Of course you've done nothing wrong. Everything right more like.' She put her hands on his shoulders and bent down to kiss him.

He closed his eyes, putting his hands on her waist. She shuddered and groaned as his tongue touched hers and he pulled her closer.

'Maybe it's time for a break?'

They went up to Rosie's apartment, and afterwards the grin didn't leave his lips for the rest of the day.

# *Chapter Forty-Two*

The day of the launch party for Lucerne Lodge Retreat and Therapy Centre dawned bright and clear. The white canvas of the marquee undulated in the breeze, but the sun was shining.

Caterers were busy arranging the table cloths on the buffet tables. They were burgundy to match the therapists' uniforms and contrasted with the white flower arrangements. The tables would be loaded with delicious food in a short while. The wine merchant, who had been engaged to supply and serve the drinks, was unloading his vans with a chorus of clinks and clanks, as bottles and glasses jostled.

The guest list included celebrities and politicians, thanks to Tanner's connections. Rosie's mother had at last agreed to come to the launch event on the understanding that she would leave quietly if she became too uncomfortable with being at Lucerne Lodge. Frances had stressed that Rosie was not to be worried about her on such a big day.

Rosie couldn't wait to introduce her mother to her caravan friends from Wales, who had all accepted her invitation and would be staying in the guest rooms for one night. Marjorie and Alf Owens had left Griff with another friend on the site and travelled with Beryl, Betty and Anne in the backseat of their car – an experience, Alf had told Rosie, he didn't want to repeat too often due to their noisy singing.

Lucy was bringing Dave the fireman to meet Rosie, Connie and Tanner. Rosie was overjoyed that her friend at last seemed to have met someone more compatible.

Rosie had visited Buzz and given him an invitation after explaining that he'd been right about everything – Tanner wasn't her brother, and when she'd asked for a sign signifying John Phillips' blessing for her venture and living at Lucerne Lodge, the two herons had appeared shortly afterwards and were now regular visitors at the lake. Buzz had been absolutely delighted, especially when he noticed that she was wearing her matching moon and star bracelet and necklace. 'I haven't lost my touch,' he said, and then staring into Rosie's palm once more, he declared that her pleasant surprises weren't finished yet.

It would soon be time to change out of her tracksuit and into the special red dress that Tanner had bought for her birthday. Rosie couldn't resist twirling around in the large canvas-covered space. Despite her childish actions, there was a dull ache of worry in her stomach about whether she'd remembered everything.

At that moment, Tanner walked into the marquee and Rosie stopped twirling – instead, she melted. He looked so handsome in a dinner jacket. His hair was caught back in a matching black tie and made him appear as if he'd time travelled from another age. In fact, he looked exactly like he had the first time Rosie had set eyes on him at the charity auction, right down to his jet cufflinks.

'You're not ready,' he exclaimed.

'Just finishing a few last-minute things.'

He raised his eyebrows and laughed. 'Dancing? Tell me what needs doing and I'll carry on while you change.'

Rosie gave him her half-completed check list and pen. Impulsively, she reached up to peck his cheek. 'Good luck for today.'

'Good luck to you too.' He went to grab her waist, but she whirled away laughing and ran to the house to get ready.

A short while later she checked herself over in the mirror and was pleased with her appearance. She looked slim and elegant in her red dress. The weight had dropped off her whilst she was engrossed in preparing Lucerne Lodge for today.

As she emerged into the sunshine, her mother arrived and gave her a huge hug. Rosie was pleased that, in the last few days, she'd finally explained to Frances about her chat with John by the lake, and the fact that she'd received her sign that he was happy for her to be living and working at the Lodge. She thought that this had finally made Frances' mind up that it was okay to come to the launch after all.

The photographer hired for the day was marshalling the therapists for a photograph in front of the house. Connie gave her a wave, a look of pure joy on her face to be included in this line up. Clad in their burgundy uniforms designed by Rosie, they looked so smart and perfect that emotion caught in her throat.

As the photographer finished and dismissed them, several of the women rushed up to greet Tanner and he was soon wiping lipstick from his cheeks. An irrational dart of jealousy shot through Rosie. Connie came to give her a hug and thanked her for taking a chance on her as a new therapist.

Tanner caught Rosie's eye over the heads of the therapists. His adoring expression, aimed solely at her, warmed her heart and confirmed that she looked great in her dress. He pushed his way through the group and led her a little way onto the lawn.

'Rosie, you look absolutely beautiful.'

'This almost reminds me of the first day we met.'

'A lot has happened since; I don't think either of us could have imagined back then that so much in our lives was not as it seemed.'

'And yet, I feel at peace with it all at last. I feel at home here, and with you …' she trailed off, feeling suddenly shy again.

Tanner took two steps towards her, but Rosie moved back out of his reach.

'I love you, Rosie. I think I have since the moment you turned your angry blue eyes on mine when I tipped that tray of prawn cocktail over you.'

'I certainly didn't love you at that moment. By the way, I've made sure prawn cocktail isn't on the menu today, just in case.' Rosie winked, but Tanner's expression was serious and unreadable.

He pounced on her words. 'So you do love me back? Do you think you love me enough to marry me? I asked you once before, but you didn't seem very keen on the idea.' He grinned in that endearing way that made her heart turn over.

Rosie moved closer. She wrapped her arms around his neck, plunging her fingers deep into his blond curls. She pulled him in close for a lingering kiss, forgetting they had spectators, including her mother. 'Of course I love you, Tanner Bryant and, yes, I'd love to marry you, if you'll still have me.'

The therapists all cheered as Rosie and Tanner kissed, and the photographer caught the moment with a photograph that would be framed and treasured on the wall of their beautiful old house, alongside the other family photographs, for many years to come.

Now, they could truly look forward to summer at Lucerne Lodge.

* The End *

# *Thank You*

Dear Reader,

Thank you for reading the sixth book I have written for Choc Lit, set in my fictional seaside town of Borteen on the East Coast of England.

Writing is a continuous journey, an apprenticeship even, and the characters of Rosie and Tanner have come along on that trip with me almost from the first day. I'm so pleased that their story is finally published.

If you did enjoy their story, please let me know by posting a review on the retail site where you purchased this book. Just a few words in a review can make a real difference to the profile and sales of a book.

Details of my other Borteen books, all stand-alone stories, are given in the next few pages. If you would like to keep in touch with me, my social media links are listed at the end of my author profile.

Thank you for reading my words.

Morton xx

## *About the Author*

Morton lives with her husband, two sons and Lily, the little white dog, in Worcestershire, UK. She has been reading and writing fiction for as long as she can remember, penning her first attempt at a novel aged fourteen. She is a member of the Romantic Novelists' Association and The Society of Authors.

Her debut novel *The Girl on the Beach* won the Choc Lit's Search for a Star competition.

Morton previously worked in the electricity industry in committee services, staff development and training. She has a Business Studies degree and is a fully qualified Clinical Hypnotherapist and Reiki Master. She also has diplomas in Tuina acupressure massage and energy field therapy. She enjoys crafts, history and loves tracing family trees. Having a hunger for learning new things is a bonus for the research behind her books.

**For more information on Morton visit:**

https://twitter.com/MortonSGray

www.facebook.com/mortonsgray/

www.mortonsgray.com

www.instagram.com/morton_s_gray/

# *More Choc Lit*

*from*

*Morton S Gray*

***The Girl on the Beach***

*Who is Harry Dixon?*

When Ellie Golden meets Harry Dixon, she can't help but feel she recognises him from somewhere. But when she finally realises who he is, she can't believe it – because the man she met on the beach all those years before wasn't called Harry Dixon. And, what's more, that man is dead.

For a woman trying to outrun her troubled past and protect her son, Harry's presence is deeply unsettling – and even more disconcerting than coming face to face with a dead man, is the fact that Harry seems to have no recollection of ever having met Ellie before. At least that's what he says …

But perhaps Harry isn't the person Ellie should be worried about. Because there's a far more dangerous figure from the past lurking just outside of the new life she has built for herself, biding his time, just waiting to strike.

Available as an eBook, audiobook and paperback.

Visit: www.choc-lit.com for more details.

***The Truth Lies Buried***

*Two children in a police waiting room, two distressed mothers, a memory only half remembered…*

When Jenny Simpson returns to the seaside town of Borteen, her childhood home, it's for a less than happy reason. But it's also a chance for her to start again.
A new job leads to her working for Carver Rodgers, a man who lives alone in a house that looks like it comes from the pages of a fairy tale – until you see the disaster zone inside …
As Jenny gets to know Carver she begins to unravel the sadness that has led to his chaotic existence. Gradually they realise they have something in common that is impossible to ignore – and it all links back to a meeting at a police station many years before.
Could the truth lie just beneath their feet?

***Christmas at Borteen Bay***

*Christmas has a way of bringing family secrets to the surface ...*

Christmas is a bittersweet time for Pippa Freeman. There are good memories, of course – but some painful ones too.

Then her mother is implicated in a mysterious occurrence in their home town of Borteen, and Pippa wonders if she'll ever experience a happy Christmas again – especially when a family secret is revealed.

But when police officer and old school friend Ethan Gibson offers his support, Pippa begins to realise that even though her life has been turned upside down, a happy and hopeful Christmas isn't impossible …

Available as an eBook and audiobook.
Visit: www.choc-lit.com for more details.

***Sunny Days at the Beach***

*From party nights at the pub to sunny days at the beach …*

Craft shop owner Mandy Vanes has always enjoyed a commitment-free singleton lifestyle — in fact, she's well-known for her wild ways in her small seaside town on the coast.

But when local teenager, Nick Crossten, turns to her for help, Mandy has the opportunity to prove she can be a responsible adult. Although things get tricky when gin distillery owner Graham Frankley comes to town with some unexpected news.

Could this mean that Mandy the party girl is finally ready to grow up?

Available as an eBook and audiobook.
Visit: www.choc-lit.com for more details.

***Christmas at the Little Beach Café***

*Run away to the little beach café this Christmas ...*

Five years ago at Christmas, solicitor Justin Sadler made the decision to leave his comfortable existence behind and move to the coast. Since then, he's tried his best to ignore the festive season and, as he sits in the little beach café and reflects on that fateful night when his life was turned upside down, he expects his fifth Christmas alone to be no different to any of the others since he made his escape.

But when he encounters a mystery woman on the beach, he soon realises he may have found a fellow runaway and kindred spirit. Could Justin finally be ready to move on and let Christmas into his life again?

Available as an eBook, audiobook and paperback.
Visit: www.choc-lit.com for more details.

# *Introducing Choc Lit*

We're an independent publisher creating
a delicious selection of fiction.
*Where heroes are like chocolate – irresistible!*
Quality stories with a romance at the heart.

***See our selection here:***
**www.choc-lit.com**

We'd love to hear how you enjoyed *Summer at Lucerne Lodge.*
Please leave a review where you purchased the novel or visit:
**www.choc-lit.com** and give your feedback.

Choc Lit novels are selected by genuine readers like yourself. We only publish stories our Choc Lit Tasting Panel want to see in print. Our reviews and awards speak for themselves.

**Could you be a Star Selector and join our Tasting Panel?**
Would you like to play a role in choosing which novels we decide to publish? Do you enjoy reading romance novels? Then you could be perfect for our Choc Lit Tasting Panel.
Visit here for more details ...
www.choc-lit.com/join-the-choc-lit-tasting-panel

***Keep in touch:***
Sign up for our newsletter Choc Lit Spread for all the latest news and offers: www.spread.choc-lit.com.

Follow us on:
Twitter: @ChocLituk
Facebook: Choc Lit.
Instagram: ChocLituk

Printed in Great Britain
by Amazon

38315677R00121

# A LAYM…
# AT THE
# LOVE OF GOD

## *Also by W. Phillip Keller*

*Splendor from the Sea*
*As a Tree Grows*
*Bold Under God—A Fond Look at a Frontier Preacher*
*A Shepherd Looks at Psalm 23*
*A Layman Looks at the Lord's Prayer*
*Rabboni—Which Is to Say, Master*
*A Shepherd Looks at the Good Shepherd and His Sheep*
*A Gardener Looks at the Fruits of the Spirit*
*Mighty Man of Valor—Gideon*
*Mountain Splendor*
*Taming Tension*
*Expendable*
*Still Waters*
*A Child's Look at Psalm 23*
*Ocean Glory*
*Walking with God*
*On Wilderness Trails*
*Elijah—Prophet of Power*
*Salt for Society*
*A Layman Looks at the Lamb of God*
*Lessons from a Sheep Dog*
*Wonder O' the Wind*
*Joshua—Man of Fearless Faith*

# A LAYMAN LOOKS AT THE LOVE OF GOD

*Devotional Study of 1 Corinthians 13*

W. PHILLIP KELLER

Marshall Pickering

*All author earnings from the sale of this book go to Bethany Fellowship for missionary training.*

Scripture verses are taken from the King James Version of the Bible unless otherwise noted.

Pickering and Inglis
Marshall Pickering
3 Beggarwood Lane, Basingstoke, Hants RG23 7LP, UK



First published in 1986 by Pickering and Inglis Ltd
Part of the Marshall Pickering Holdings Group
A subsidiary of the Zondervan Corporation



ISBN 0 551 80682 8

Printed and bound in Great Britain by
Anchor Brendon Ltd, Tiptree, Essex

To
"CHERI"—
My happy companion
who reflects
the love of God.

## *A Word of Thanks*

A note of appreciation is due to Mr. Dave Thomas of Montecito, California, who provided me with tapes of the talks I gave to the Montecito Covenant Church on the topic of The Love of God.

Again I am genuinely grateful to "Cheri," my wife Ursula, for the time and care she devoted to typing the manuscript.

Also a great debt of love is owed to those dear people across the continent, who, in the early hours of the morning, pray for me as I write. Their loyal faithfulness is a precious honour.

Most important is the distinct direction and guidance given in this book by Christ Himself. In a very personal way His Love has been manifested to me in this work. *What an honour!*

## *Table of Contents*


Chapter 1 — The Character of Christ ..... 9
Chapter 2 — The More Excellent Way .... 19
Chapter 3 — Prophecy, Knowledge and Faith, Without Love, Are Simply of No Account ... 29
Chapter 4 — Social Service Without God's Love ................ 39
Chapter 5 — The Qualities of Christ's Character ............... 49
Chapter 6 — The Love of God Is Not Arrogant or Abrasive ....... 59
Chapter 7 — Christ's Character Is Free of Guile, Irritability and Malice . 69
Chapter 8 — God's Love Finds Joy Only in Truth ................. 79
Chapter 9 — The Love of God Endures All Things in Hope ........... 87
Chapter 10 — The Character of Christ Is Constant—His Love Never Fails 97
Chapter 11 — The Perfection and Maturity of God's Love ............ 107
Chapter 12 — Knowing and Understanding the Love of God ........... 117
Chapter 13 — The Enduring Aspect of Faith, Hope and Love ...... 127
Chapter 14 — Follow Christ—He Is Love He Is Greatest ............ 137

# 1

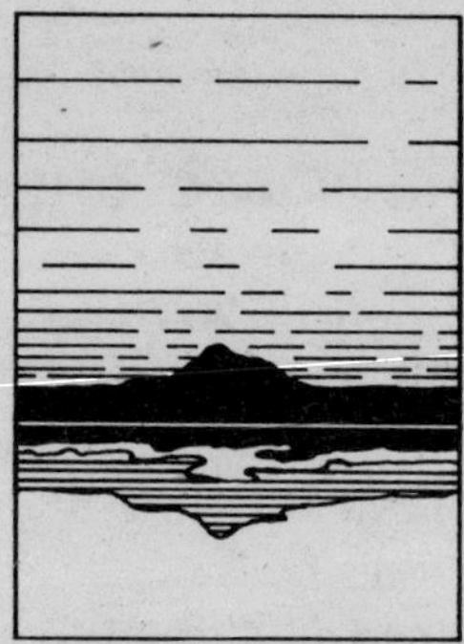

*And yet I show you a more excellent way.*

*Though I speak with the tongues of men and of angels, but have not love, I have become as sounding brass or a clanging cymbal.*

*And though I have the gift of prophecy, and understand all mysteries and all knowledge, and though I have all faith, so that I could remove mountains, but have not love, I am nothing.*

*And though I bestow all my goods to feed the poor, and though I give my body to be burned, but have not love, it profits me nothing.*

*Love suffers long and is kind; love does not envy; love does not parade itself, is not puffed up; does not behave rudely, does not seek its own, is not provoked, thinks no evil; does not rejoice in iniquity, but rejoices in the truth; bears all things, believes all things, hopes all things, endures all things.*

*Love never fails. But whether there are prophecies, they will fail; whether there is knowledge, it will vanish away.*

*For we know in part and we prophesy in part.*

*But when that which is perfect has come, then that which is in part will be done away.*

*When I was a child, I spoke as a child, I understood as a child, I thought as a child; but when I became a man, I put away childish things.*

*For now we see in a mirror, dimly, but then face to face. Now I know in part, but then I shall know just as I also am known.*

*And now abide faith, hope, love, these three; but the greatest of these is love.*

*PURSUE LOVE. . . .*

**1 Corinthians 12:31–14:1, NKJV**

# THE CHARACTER OF CHRIST

For roughly fifteen years various earnest people, eager to know God, have asked me to write a book on "The Character of Christ." Some of these thirsty, seeking ones have been ordinary lay people like myself. Others are scholars, pastors and teachers.

This book is my third serious attempt to respond to that compelling inner cry of the human spirit, "Oh, that I might know God, Whom to know is life eternal" (see John 17:3). For when all else is said and done, a man's greatest and highest goal in life is to enjoy intimate communion with Christ.

The keen companionship which can be developed and cultivated between Christ, who is God very God, and a humble human being is based upon a clear understanding of His character. Not until we come to perceive clearly with our spirits the true nature of Christ and what a sublime person He is do we ever actually draw near to Him or allow Him to draw near to us.

The first book I wrote to portray the true character

of Christ was *A Shepherd Looks at Psalm 23,* based on the Spirit's revelation in the Old Testament of Christ as our Good Shepherd. The second earnest endeavour to convey this theme to the reader was the book *Rabboni—Which Is to Say, Master,* based on the Gospel records given to us in the New Testament. It is perhaps by far the most important book I have ever written. It reveals Christ as God, very God, in human garb.

This book is based largely on the teaching of God's gracious Spirit given to us in the New Testament Epistles, with special emphasis upon the statements made so emphatically in the "Love Chapter," 1 Corinthians 13. Before we go further, we must clarify a few fundamental truths.

The first basic concept is that *the character of Christ* is essentially *the life of God*—or, to use an ancient term, *the very nature of God.* If we wish to know God as He really is, then we must perceive Him as portrayed in the person of Christ. "Christ is the visible expression of the invisible God" (Col. 1:15, Phillips).

The second foundation truth is that *the life of God* revealed to us in *the character of Christ* is in essence *the love of God*, "for God is love" (1 John 4:8). Or to put all of this in the most fundamental terms, we can understand something of the intrinsic character of Christ as we comprehend more clearly the love of God.

The third point to grasp with our spiritual understanding is that the phrase *love of God* does not refer to our love for God but rather *His love for us*, that quality of His own divine life which emanates from

Him to us in a wondrous outpouring. There flows eternally to the family of men a stream of self-giving from God. It finds expression in a thousand generous gestures all intended for our good. "Every good gift and every perfect gift is from above, and cometh down from the Father of lights, with whom is no variableness, neither shadow of turning" (James 1:17).

The fourth basic truth is that this generous, gracious self-giving of God to us in Christ by His Spirit becomes for the Christian the greatest and most important reality in all of life. In point of fact, the realization that *God is with me . . . Christ is in me . . . His Spirit occupies my spirit* becomes the compelling relationship, the divine impetus, that causes my character to change and transforms me into someone of His own likeness. "For it is God which worketh in you both to will and to do of his good pleasure" (Phil. 2:13).

The fifth foundation truth to grasp is that not only does God's Spirit reveal to us the fact that He resides in us, but also that *it is possible for us to live in Christ.* A Christian comes to the comprehension in very practical terms that it is "in him [God] we live, and move, and have our being. . ." (Acts 17:28). The child of God recognizes that his entire life is bound up in the enfolding goodness of God, expressed to him in the love of God.

The sixth basic concept is that as one comes to commune with Christ in this intense interrelationship, *His presence becomes increasingly more precious.* To know Him, enjoy Him, obey Him, serve Him and love Him becomes the ultimate fulfillment in life. Paul, in his letter to the Philippians, put it this way: "I count all things but loss for the excellency of the knowledge of Christ Jesus my Lord . . ." (Phil. 3:8).

The seventh and last truth is that for our life in Christ to prosper and His life in us to flourish, *our attention must be focused upon Him.* He simply *must* occupy the prior position in all our interests. Time, thought, prayer and meditation in quiet interludes with Him are imperative. Then this scripture will become a reality in our lives: "If anyone is in Christ, he is a new creation; old things have passed away; behold, all things have become new" (2 Cor. 5:17, NKJV).

This total transformation of our lives is an ongoing process. This means having the very character of Christ transmitted and transferred to us. It is to actually know and experience the incoming of the life of God into our tiny, human lives. It is to sense and know the very love of God shed abroad in our spirits by His Spirit (Rom. 5:5).

There is no doubt whatsoever that ultimately this is the most intense inner desire of anyone who earnestly longs to know God. Therefore, it is without apology that as a lay person I undertake to share with the reader some of those insights which God's gracious Spirit has given to me on this magnificent subject.

I am fully aware that perhaps more sermons in this century have been given on "The Love of God" than any other theme. More books have been written about it than any other spiritual subject. More emphasis has been given to it than probably any other aspect of Christian life within the church.

Yet, despite this deluge of material, both oral and written, it is my simple prayer that Our Father will see fit to honour this little book with His smile of approval. My desire is that through it the reader will come to a clearer comprehension of Christ's character, and that in reading these pages, God's Spirit will impart the very life and love of God to the reader.

For this to take place there is a sense in which a person must literally plunge into and drink deeply from the stream of life that flows to us from God Himself. This is not mere figurative language. If we are to know Christ and experience His love in daily reality, we cannot stand at a distance and simply discuss it doctrinally. We must come to Him and drink of His divine life, partake of His very nature.

This book, written in simple layman's language, using word pictures and the most practical terms possible, endeavours to help the reader to know the love of God. The "knowing" of which I speak is both in the wondrous expression of the life of Jesus Our Lord and in His winsome operation within our own souls and spirits. It is both an outward, objective observation and a profound, personal, inner, subjective experience. It is both the love of God as revealed in His own conduct and character and the very life of God worked out through our lives in this weary, sin-stained world.

To know this love of God is to be totally immersed in the stream of life which flows to us from Him. In human society we speak freely of being in "the stream of life," the area or discipline in which we choose to involve ourselves. It may be in business or science or music or the arts or the humanities or travel or athletics. To plunge fully into the interest or vocation of our own choosing and to drink deeply of all it has to offer is part and parcel of succeeding in any given arena of life.

Likewise for the Christian, if we are to find complete satisfaction in Christ, there is no other way than to submerge ourselves in the stream of His life. We need to come to Him and drink deeply of His love. We must find our refreshment, our constant reinvigoration, in His consistent character. Here lies the secret to quiet serenity, confident strength and sure stability amid all the changing circumstances which face a Christian in today's world.

In Psalm 42 we are given a beautiful word picture of a deer in distress. It is being pursued by the hunters and their hounds in the hills. For safety and survival it rushes down the slopes and into the stream.

There in the cooling, refreshing current that flows from the snow-mantled mountains its thirst is slaked; its safety is assured; its survival is guaranteed. This dramatic poem written under the inspiration of God's Spirit portrays precisely the elements inherent in the picture of a man or woman plunging fully into the refreshing, protecting fullness of God's life and love, finding total salvation amid life's strains and stresses.

It is a vivid metaphor that will be developed in much greater detail in a later chapter. It is the basic background against which this devotional study of 1 Corinthians 13 has been written. So I invite the reader to carefully and prayerfully peruse the pages which follow. Please do not hold yourself aloof, examining what has been written with only academic and objective interest. Instead, allow God's Spirit to so immerse you in Christ's love that His very life shall become your life, His character your character.

This is what it means to come to Christ, to drink of Him, to know Him, to relish Him.

As I pen these lines I am vividly reminded of an incident that took place during my early teens, roughly fifty years ago. My dad and mother were literally laying down their lives to try and establish a strong group of Christian believers in the bush country of Kenya. But after working tirelessly for sixteen years in that difficult territory, they decided a special, deeper work of God was needed. Only God's Spirit and God's Word could inspire and lead men and women to immerse themselves in the very life of Christ.

With this goal in mind, a conference was held. Every one of the Christian leaders, pastors, teachers and elders was obliged to attend. In preparation for the week's conference, each one was to read and meditate on 1 Corinthians 13. The entire chapter was to be prayed over carefully every day for a full month! It was also to be completely memorized and repeated whenever the Holy Spirit brought it to their attention. The leaders were to submerge themselves in these scriptures.

When they came to the conference, held in a very simple, sheet-iron chapel on the crest of a high hill, it was to study and examine and understand what God's Spirit was conveying to the church in this profound passage. For seven days and seven nights that group of African Christians dwelt in the truths of this so-called *Love Chapter*. In doing so, they came to Christ; they drank deeply of His life; they were satisfied; their thirst was slaked. And they went away revitalized.

The results of that event were absolutely dramatic. In the lives of the leaders there came an acute and unique awareness of Christ within. It began to change the whole character of the African church. There was a tremendous new thrust in the work of God's Spirit among those who longed to know God. A great sense of earnestness and devotion to Christ developed. Perhaps most profound for me as a lad was to see the beginning of an enormous change in my dad's character. Where before he had been rather rough and tough, there began to steal over his life a winsome, mellow tenderness. He became one dearly beloved. He was approachable, understanding and patient in ways never known before.

This was the unique impact of the character of Christ upon his character. In awe and gratitude I saw in living terms what the love of God could do. My most earnest prayer is that the pages which follow may be used of God in the same way for you.

# 2

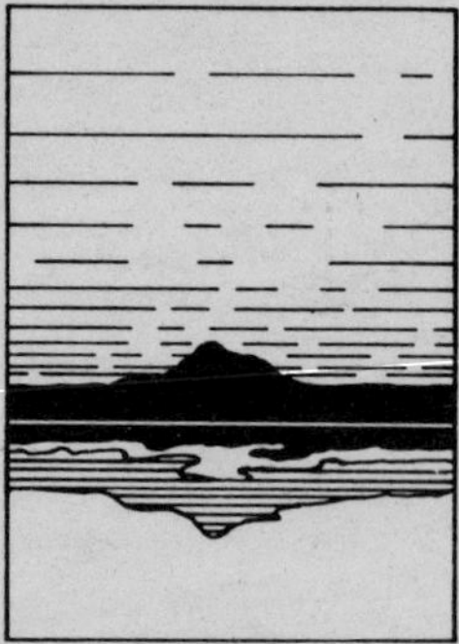

***"Yet I show you a more excellent way. Though I speak with the tongues of men and of angels, but have not love, I have become as sounding brass or a clanging cymbal."***

**(1 Cor. 12:31; 13:1, NKJV)**

# THE MORE EXCELLENT WAY

God Himself has given us a remarkable revelation of His own love in Scripture. It comes with startling significance in the very center of the Spirit's most detailed discourse on God's special "gifts" to the church. It stands there with towering grandeur as a call to all Christians: *the more excellent way in which the church can know Christ and live for Him in this world is through His love and by His life.*

This thirteenth chapter of the first letter to the carnal church at Corinth is a compelling description of Christ's character. Here is the divine declaration of Christian attitude and behavior, the way in which Christ Himself calls us to conduct ourselves as His followers—His people, His Bride. It is the great central theme around which all other considerations in the church are of secondary consequence and peripheral importance.

This dazzling revelation of Christ's divine love, like a diamond, outshines with burning brilliance all the other precious gems of God's gifts. With enormous power and value it transcends all other unique capacities given to the church for service. It is Christ Himself—His love—His life that is "the more excellent way."

The sensual, self-serving Corinthians were challenged with this message. And the Spirit of God speaks the same heart-stirring word to the sensual, pleasure-seeking church of the Twentieth Century.

Today's church worldwide, as in the days of Paul, has become unduly preoccupied with the spectacular. It pursues power and growth and social acceptance without purity. It is eager for miracles and manifestations, often with very wrong motives. It revels in the sensational, often being diverted into that which is grossly sensual, all in the name of "spiritual gifts."

It is the age-old tendency, present in Corinth as well, to become more attracted to the "gifts" than to The Giver of those gifts . . . of being busy rather than being bountiful . . . of being "on the go" rather than being godly.

The consequence for the church has been to forget that it is The Lord Jesus Christ who is its Head. He it is who stands supreme amongst us, yet who so often has become almost a stranger to us.

Writing on this theme, David Wilkerson makes this solemn, yet valid observation: "I say to you, it is possible to gather Spirit-filled people in one place, praising and lifting up their hands—and still have Christ walking among them as a stranger. . . . We make Christ a stranger—by giving the Holy Spirit preeminence over Him."

It is for this very reason that God's Gracious Spirit speaks emphatically to this point, declaring unequivocally at the end of 1 Corinthians 12: *"Yet I show you a more excellent way."* He calls us back to the love of God, exemplified for us in the character of the living Christ.

Using the persuasive power of contrast, He then proceeds to compare the gifts bestowed with the life of The Giver. He holds up to full view our folly in being so taken up with our gifts that the very life of God is lacking in our activities and conduct.

Sensational, blood-stirring, nerve-tingling services filled with "faith," "prophecies," "miracles" and "tongues" all amount to nothing . . . nothing . . . *nothing* without God's love.

This is a most serious indictment! It should pull us up short. It shatters and pulverizes our pride in performance!

This solemn call to examine our own characters in the intense light of the love of God is almost as solemn as Our Lord's cataclysmic statement in Matthew 7:21-23: "Not everyone that saith unto me, Lord, Lord, shall enter into the kingdom of heaven. Many will say to me in that day, Lord, Lord, have we not prophesied in thy name? and in thy name have cast out devils? and in thy name done many wonderful works? And then will I profess unto them, I never knew you: depart from me, ye that work iniquity."

We begin with a basic understanding of what God's Spirit means when He speaks of God's love.

As many readers no doubt have heard explained, there are three types of love. Each of them has its origin with God. It is He who devised and designed these expressions for the benefit of mankind. Yet it must be understood that of these three, only one (the third point discussed in the following list) is referred to in the thirteenth chapter of 1 Corinthians.

1. There is filial love, so-called "family" love, the affection that flows freely throughout the family of man. It is sometimes called the "milk of human kindness." We see it reflected and displayed in the intimate bonds of love between parents and children, brothers and sisters, friends in sports, business partners, or even soldiers in war.

It is that element of loyalty, devotion and concern which enables one human being to lay down his life for another who is a friend or family member. Jesus Christ referred to this as the greatest love there is in the human family ( John 15:13).

This fraternal love is found even amongst pagan people.

2. Then there is erotic or so-called sexual love. This is the profound and powerful attraction between people of opposite sexes. It, too, was designed and arranged by God for the preservation and intimacy of the family of man. It was intended for the perpetuation of the race.

This kind of love is to be found amongst all people all over the earth. In its proper role as the instigator and protector of the family, it is a beautiful bond of human behavior. Within the framework of a home and in the cherished intimacy between true life mates it is beautiful beyond words to describe.

Unhappily, it has been eternally prostituted and perverted by the sordid minds of unregenerate men and women. Consequently, many modern references to this sort of love tend to be more beastly than beautiful.

3. Lastly there is the profound love of God referred to

so often in the New Testament. As pointed out in the previous chapter, this love of God does not denote our human "love for God," as we sometimes state so glibly, "for love of God and country." Rather, this love of God is uniquely and amazingly *His love toward us.* It is His care and concern and affection for us even while we were still His enemies. (Please take a moment here to read and meditate on Rom. 5:5-11.)

Human beings with filial love lay down their lives for their friends and family.

But Our Father in Heaven, the source of divine love, lays down His life for His *enemies*, we who were alienated from Him. In Christ we see this love poured out for men who hate Him and vilify Him, who are determined to destroy Him. Despite their animosity, He in love comes to seek and to save.

This *agape* love, as it is called in the original Greek, is vested only in God. It comes only from Him. It is epitomized in the very character of Christ. It can only be imparted to us by His Own Spirit.

This love of God is essentially His utter selflessness as opposed to our self-centeredness. It is His self-giving as opposed to our self-getting. It is His generous self-sharing as opposed to our self-gratification. It is His self-sacrifice as opposed to our self-indulgence.

In His generous, gracious manner, Christ longs to convey this quality of His own life and character to us. But far too often we are so preoccupied with our own personal pursuits and selfish pride that He is given very little opportunity to bestow His own life on us. There is little stillness or solitude in which His Spirit can shed abroad such love within our spirits.

We of the busy, boisterous and clamorous Twentieth Century would much rather get on with the glitter and excitement of our own interests and special gifts. After all, who is interested in laying down their lives when all around us people are shouting, even from the pulpit, that we should be "living it up," "living life to the full"?

This is the very first contrast that God's Spirit draws for us in the almost formidable language of the opening verse of this wonderful chapter: "Though I speak with the tongues of men and of angels, but have not love, I have become as sounding brass or a clanging cymbal" (1 Cor. 13:1, NKJV).

What a commentary on contemporary society, both inside and outside the church! At no time in human history has there been so much emphasis on communication—on human and celestial "tongues," breaching the barriers of known and unknown language. The power and impact of the media to bear a message, no matter how "brassy," is unsurpassed in history.

People with all sorts of destructive propaganda, the most blatant deception, have their followers. Inspiring leaders can capture the attention of the masses by their eloquence and magnetism alone.

Both within the family of God and outside, multitudes are lured into believing lies by the smooth eloquence and clever use of the tongue. People are led to think they are receiving truth when in fact it is often false teaching.

It is significant that the first aspect of the Christian life to be addressed by God's Spirit in this passage is the use of language without love. It is the question of our conversation without the accompanying quality of Christ's genuine, self-giving courtesy. It is the manipulation of others with words which carry no sincerity. It is the absence of integrity in our communication with others. Christ states emphatically: "Either make the tree good, and his fruit good; or else make the tree corrupt: for the tree is known by his fruit. O generation of vipers, how can ye, being evil, speak good things? for out of the abundance of the heart the mouth speaketh. A good man out of the good treasure of the heart bringeth forth good things: and an evil man out of the evil treasure bringeth forth evil things. But I say unto you, That every idle word that men shall speak, they shall give account thereof in the day of judgment. For by thy words thou shalt be justified, and by thy words thou shalt be condemned" (Matt. 12:33-37).

Few Christians today take these statements seriously. Much of their conversation is double-tongued, double-edged, with more than one meaning, a carryover from our own corrupt society. It is alarming how often those who claim their special spiritual gifts from God as a sign of His infilling actually defame His name with their own duplicity. Both in their personal conversation and in their business transactions, this pernicious double-standard of speaking and acting brings shame to Christ.

Christ Himself used the metaphor of a fruit tree to make this fact clear to His generation. And through a vivid experience with a wild apple tree I, too, learned this important principle as a young man.

On the first ranch I owned, there was an ancient homestead. The early pioneers had planted an orchard. All the trees had ultimately perished before I had come on the scene. But near the rough, old rock foundation of the original frontier house I found a single, vigorous apple tree crowded in by dense brush and wild brambles.

The discovery that first year excited me, though the tree bore no fruit. So I got busy and cleared away all the encroaching undergrowth. In the winter I took hours to prune the tree with painstaking care. In the early spring it was sprayed against disease.

The magnificent-looking tree burst into a billowing cloud of exquisite pink and white blossoms, many of which set fruit. And as the summer progressed the whole tree leafed out into a magnificent display of green glory. Never had I seen such a majestic apple tree so laden with a promising crop of fruit.

As summer moved on into the golden autumn, I could hardly restrain myself from immediately gathering some of the apples. They formed into large heavy fruit that weighed down the branches in their abundance. What a sight! What a show!

At last the time came to sample the crop. To my utter chagrin and total dismay, the fruit was worthless! It had no flavour; it was unfit even to cook or preserve. We never were able to eat one of the apples! It was but a wild seedling!

All the work, the care, the pruning, the spraying was of no avail. All the size and strength of the tree, its beauty, its blossoms, its abundant crop was but a "show," a sham.

God's Spirit used that wild, untamed tree to teach me a cardinal Christian principle I have never forgotten: "It is by their fruits you shall know them."

It is not by our eloquent language, not by our capacity to communicate, not by our charm or charisma, not by our special gifts of "tongues," whether natural or supernatural, that we shall be known as God's children. Rather it is by our conversation—what we say and how we say it—when it conveys the integrity of Christ's own character.

The mark of the person whose spirit is laden with the fruit of the love of God is a wise tongue, a trained tongue, a tempered tongue.

Such a person's conversation will have complete credibility. He will speak in honesty, wisdom, and with transparent sincerity.

Communication with others should be a benefit and benediction. It should be used to build up the weak and to encourage the strong. It will be courteous and kind.

Our language must not be tainted by indecent frivolity or worldly foolishness. It should convey healing humour, wholesome laughter and good cheer for heavy hearts.

The tongue of a true child of God will speak often of the goodness of God, Our Father, the presence of Christ, and the sure guidance of God's Gracious Spirit along life's tangled trails.

Any such "word fitly spoken is like apples of gold in pitchers of silver" (Prov. 25:11).

# 3

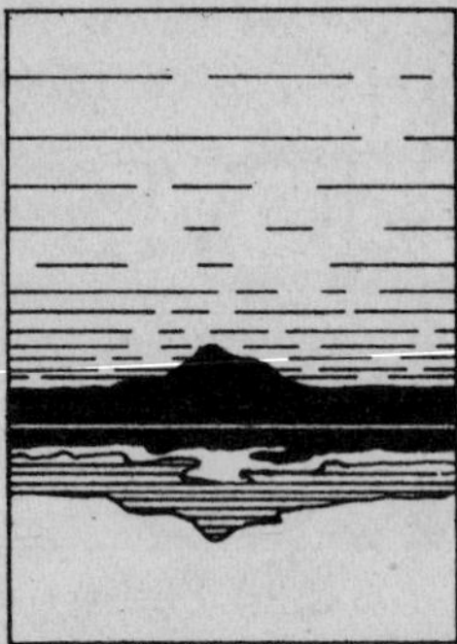

***"And though I have the gift of prophecy, and understand all mysteries and all knowledge, and though I have all faith, so that I could remove mountains, but have not love, I am nothing."***

**(1 Cor. 13:2, NKJV)**

# PROPHECY, KNOWLEDGE AND FAITH, WITHOUT LOVE, ARE SIMPLY OF NO ACCOUNT

The next three great gifts of the Spirit with which God's love is compared are prophecy, spiritual knowledge, and faith. In the evaluation of most Christians, these three would stand supreme in the service of the church.

It would be helpful if we look at each of these in detail. We should understand their role in the modern setting of Twentieth-Century society. Most importantly, we must see the enormous prominence given to them by our contemporary church leaders.

Yet ever in the background there stands this solemn statement of God's Spirit of Truth: all prophecy, all knowledge, and all faith are of no value without love. This startles us. It should stir us to ask, "Why?" It should stab us wide awake as to what is of greatest worth in God's view. Perhaps our priorities and spiritual emphasis in the pulpit have become reversed and confused when compared with what Christ considers to be of primary importance.

Before doing this, however, it is essential that the reader should grasp the great difference between (a) the "gifts" of God's Spirit and (b) the "fruits" of God's Spirit. There is genuine confusion in many Christian circles over this matter; this is the reason they are especially contrasted here.

1. The fruits of God's Spirit—love, joy, peace, longsuffering, gentleness, goodness, faith, meekness, temperance (Gal. 5:22-23)—are each a dynamic, living function of the very love of God. Each is active, growing, benefiting the life of the believer in whom Christ resides, as well as all those whose lives He touches through that believer.

We only have the fruits of God's Spirit to the extent we have the presence and person of Christ's life within. The degree to which we allow Christ to control all of our character, conduct and conversation will determine the abundance or scarcity of the fruit of His life produced in us.

To put it in the plainest possible terms, *the fruits of the Spirit are the character of Christ made visible in me by His presence at work in me.* It is literally the life of God governing my character, the love of God shown to others through my conduct and conversation.

The actual expression of these fruits in our daily lives stands as the supreme test of whether or not Christ lives in us, filling us for fruit-bearing by His Spirit.

2. The *gifts* of God's Spirit are not indicators of a divine life *within,* as the fruits of the Spirit are. Rather, the gifts are special capacities bestowed *upon* a believer for special service to the church.

The gifts of the Spirit are not an integral part of the character of Christ. Though they can be used to give expression to His work within, they are not an essential part of the love of God. Yet they are sometimes the vehicle used to demonstrate that love. They are not the very life of God's Spirit, but rather the capacity bestowed on a believer to manifest that life.

These "gifts," these capacities for service, are bestowed as a unique responsibility to each Christian to make a valuable contribution to the corporate body of believers. Some gifts are considered by God to be much more useful and more important to the whole Body than others. Some benefit everyone. Others benefit only the recipient. The gifts may or may not be used. Some who have them never discover that they do. They may lie inert for years, unused.

In my case, it was not until I was about 47 years old that it became evident God had given me the gift of teaching. Before that I believed my only gift was "helps."

Lastly, it must be mentioned that these gifts can be misused and abused. They can be exploited by counterfeit forces in the spiritual realm. They can be used to deceive others. They can be employed for destructive ends and selfish personal gratification.

Let us consider now the gift of prophecy. Contrary to what most Christians believe, this "gift" does not deal with just foretelling future events. That is one of its true functions, but its most important role, by far, is the capacity to speak on God's behalf to men. It is the noble ability to take divine, supernatural truth revealed by God and transmit it to human beings. "God, who at sundry times and in divers manners spake in time past unto the fathers by the prophets. . ." (Heb. 1:1).

In God's estimation this is one of the greatest of all gifts. It can be such a great benefit to so many. By it mankind can clearly understand not only who God is, but also what His will and intentions are for His creation.

We are urged to both desire and seek to receive this gift (1 Cor. 14:1). Astonishingly, one seldom hears a Christian pray for this capacity. Most people are paralyzed with apprehension about it. They would rather die than speak out boldly as a prophet for The Lord.

In startling contrast, thousands upon thousands deliberately seek the gift of tongues. Whether through personal ignorance or the persuasion of men, this is not the gift which we are told by the Spirit to desire and seek. Many Christians pray and plead and insist on being given this least beneficial of all capacities, the one which usually edifies only the recipient. Essentially, this becomes a self-centered desire which can provide the enemy with a beachhead of delusion in a life.

We have few prophets of God in our pulpits today. But we do have predators with only the trappings of a prophetic gift, making much of their so-called prophetic utterances. They shout about the frightening future that faces the planet. They play upon the fears and emotions of their audiences. They cater to the insatiable curiosity of the human mind regarding the unknown future. They entertain the masses with their sensational predictions.

But we long for the true prophets of God who in

brokenness of spirit and burning tears of travail call their generation to repentance from sin.

We yearn for modern counterparts to men like Ezra, Elijah, Jeremiah and John, the flaming Baptist. People perish for lack of brave spokesmen prepared to lay down their lives for the sake of God's Word, and God's people, in a wretched world of wickedness.

So the declaration of God's Spirit is stern and severe in this thirteenth chapter: "Though I have the gift of prophecy, but have not the love of God to lay my life down for those I address—it is all of no account" (author's paraphrase).

Spiritual leaders endowed with the great persuasive gifts of prophecy, eloquence and oratorical language need to examine their motives carefully before God. Are they in the pulpit because of its power, its prominence and prestige? Or are they there because they are ready to lay down their very own lives to feed God's flock, to bring the lost and the straying to Christ, The Good Shepherd?

Do they prophesy for personal gain? Or does their proclamation of divine truth come out of hearts consumed with compassion for perishing people?

What is true for our leaders is equally applicable to us, the lay people in the pews. If Christ's Spirit has bestowed upon us this capacity to speak clearly to others regarding God, it should be always in humility, mercy and truth.

We do not prophesy to impress people with our eloquence or persuasiveness. We do not declare God's Good News of salvation to pander to our ego but rather to bring men from death to life, from despair into the wondrous love of God.

One vivid and indelible memory from my early

childhood is bound up with the copious tears shed by my mother and dad in their travail over the tribes-people around them in Africa. They would spend hours on their knees in anguish of spirit over the lost. This travail eventually led to a mighty awakening amongst the Africans. We need that kind of love in our lives, too, whether we are ministering to heathen overseas or reaching out to a next-door neighbor who does not know Christ.

In this verse The Spirit of God also deals with the whole range of knowledge, with mysteries and their understanding. This covers both secular and spiritual education, enlightenment and comprehension. It embraces the entire realm of learning upon which modern man puts so much emphasis. The acquisition of diplomas, degrees and human credentials upon which we put so much store is here put into divine perspective.

He tells us plainly that no matter how great our qualifications, unless accompanied by love, they are of no value. This comes as a rude shock to a world where one's relative worth is often measured by academic credentials or factual knowledge.

Again the classic comparison is made between what is important to man and what is of value to God. Human beings, conditioned by a scientific society that largely ignores God, bases behaviour on the standard of technology and human philosophy.

Christ, on the other hand, calls us to live our lives according to the standards of truth, love and compassion revealed to us in His life and by His Word.

For many this leads to tremendous tension within, "Because the foolishness of God is wiser than men; and the weakness of God is stronger than men" (1 Cor. 1:25).

People do not really believe this concept!

Individuals who for years gladly submit themselves to the demands of their chosen discipline in the arts, humanities, sciences, business or athletics often will refuse to come under the discipline of God's love. They will gladly abide by the standards established in other fields of human knowledge in order to advance, yet they reject the standards of Christ's love as a guide to godliness.

It is ironic that although order, progress and mutual understanding depend on adhering to specific laws and principles in every other area of life, men reject this concept in their code of personal moral conduct. It is as if to say, "In engineering I will abide by the laws of engineering, but in loving either God or man I shall do as I please—each person is a law to himself."

Are we surprised then at the chaos and confusion in human conduct? Are we startled by the selfishness in society? Are we alarmed at the growing anarchy around us?

The love of God, contrary to what most Christians think, is not some sweet, sentimental emotion that seeps into their lives from God's Spirit. The love of Christ is a powerful, profound setting of man's will to do God's will in this wretched world. It is that tough and uncompromising determination of a man's entire soul to submit to God's Spirit in complying with His wishes and carrying out His commands. (Please read John 14, 15 and 16 prayerfully.)

This is the very practical way whereby we demonstrate that we do in actual fact have God's love, "for love worketh no ill to his neighbor: therefore love is the fulfilling of the law" (Rom. 13:10), that is to say, God's wishes.

If a person misses this vital truth he has missed the whole meaning to his existence on the planet. All else is pointless, a mere mockery, for it all passes away.

Finally, God's Spirit, in a single shattering sentence, contrasts faith with love. Again He reveals that even mighty faith sufficient to move mountains is of no worth without love.

This strikes us as an enigma. We of the West put so much emphasis upon a person's capacity to make things happen. We idolize the "doers," the "movers" and "shakers" amongst us. But God does not.

In fact, the use of faith amongst Christians purely for the purpose of self-gratification and self-improvement has become a formidable fad. From pulpits across the country, people are taught that all they need do is "confess it, then possess it." No matter what it is they desire, be it health, wealth, power or pleasure, all of it is available on demand.

The doers, movers and shakers are more preoccupied with what they can claim from Christ than in laying down their lives in service for Him and the suffering around them. In the name of God and with flambouyant faith, mighty miracles are purported to happen. Prophetic utterances are declared. Evil spirits of all sorts are exorcised. Various wonderful and stunning projects are paraded for public view.

Yet the searching question which always must be asked is, "Was this done in selfless, self-giving love in compliance with the will of God, or is it merely the spectacular, selfish aggrandizement of man to flaunt his faith?"

Again, the final criterion is not one of mighty works. It is not a question of achievement or accomplishment. It is not even one of stunning society with the spectacular. Rather the ultimate determination from Christ's viewpoint is, "Was this His will, done in His love, for the sake of others?"

If not, the most grandiose display of faith will be a farce, a show, but nothing more. Though it may produce a measure of self-gratification, that does not mean it satisfies God or brings pleasure to His person. He may even disclaim having any knowledge of the performance. If it was carried out apart from Him, who is love, it is all for naught. (With humility read Matt. 7:21-23.)

# 4

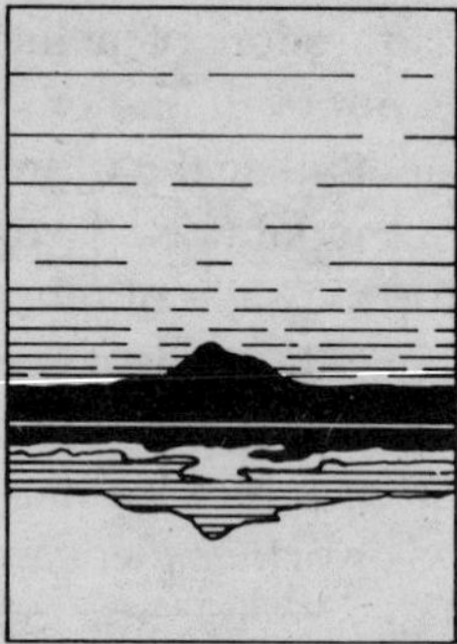

***"And though I bestow all my goods to feed the poor, and though I give my body to be burned, but have not love, it profits me nothing."***

**(1 Cor. 13:3, NKJV)**

# SOCIAL SERVICE WITHOUT GOD'S LOVE

This verse is one of the most difficult to consider. It stands in contrast with the character of Christ, with divine love, because it deals with our human motives. Human nature being what it is in its unregenerate condition, much of that which passes as "charity" in society, though of merit in man's estimation, may be less so in God's economy.

Since the whole question of social service is so much debated in Christian circles, it is vital that we look at it with intense integrity. Always the questions must be asked, "*Why* am I bestowing my goods to benefit the poor?" "*Why* do I involve myself in social service for underprivileged people?"

It is true this type of ministry has been considered one of the main missions of the church. Some groups consider it of greater importance than proclaiming the good news of Christ's redemption. They prefer to feed hungry stomachs rather than hungry spirits. They are quick to cry out for the poor in body, slow to see the need of the poor in spirit.

The Spirit of God speaking here through the Apostle Paul does not specifically define whether the poor are such in their physical needs or spiritual poverty. Nor does it matter. For to minister to either class entails the outlay of time, energy, strength, skill, money and material assistance of one sort or another.

The crucial question is, do I really *love* the poor? Do I truly care with Christ's compassion for those who need to be fed, whether it is earthly or spiritual food?

If not, any activity I may engage in to succour those who are underprivileged becomes an empty endeavour. In fact, though it may benefit the recipient to some degree, it may be pointless and of no profit whatever to me, the donor.

Why? Simply because a great deal of the charity carried out in our culture is done for one of three reasons:

1. As an insidious form of self-satisfaction. Somehow it panders to a personal desire for self-gratification. These people give not because they are deeply concerned about the deprived, but because they just want to "feel good." These are the so-called "do-gooders."

2. To contribute to charity whether for feeding hungry mouths or feeding hungry hearts is too often merely a "sop" to one's conscience. God's Spirit may speak to us to go personally to the poor. But we choose to "go" vicariously through our donations in a detached way. This is much less costly in terms of personal discomfort and involvement.

3. Many give generously to the poor simply to dodge paying excessive taxes. There is virtually no personal concern for the terrible and terrifying plight of the millions who perish in the earth.

We in the Western world have serious and well-nigh insurmountable difficulties in dealing with our "poor." So many forms of social services are available, both in government agencies and church relief programs, many Christians have not encountered personally the earth's truly poor.

I grew up amongst some of the most poverty-ridden people in East Africa. They lived in crude mud huts, barely subsisting on corn meal and bananas. Many were riddled with despicable tropical diseases. They lived at a level of degradation very little above the animals around them. They were plunged in the darkness and despair of spirit worship. Poor, poor people! Hungry for food, hungry for health, hungry for bread from Heaven, hungry for love.

As Dad often said, "You don't just come to such people with the Gospel. You come with bread and cups of cold water in one hand, and the great Good News of Christ's love in the other. You pour out all of yourself to serve the whole man!"

And the only possible motivation that will prompt a person to do this in total, unselfish self-giving is the love of God. It is the unashamed, profound caring for others that characterized the life of Our Lord when He was here amongst us. "And Jesus went about all the cities and villages, teaching in their synagogues, and preaching the gospel of the kingdom, and healing every sickness and every disease among the people. But when he saw the multitudes, he was moved with compassion on them, because they fainted, and were scattered abroad, as sheep having no shepherd" (Matt. 9:35-36).

For those unable to go to the poor in person, it is still possible to express the compelling love of God in very practical ways. One very important key is prayer. It is nearly impossible to pray for someone without loving him. We can pour out our souls in prayers of intercession for the poor; we can pray for those who are ministering to their needs. We can so discipline our own lives in simplicity and moderation that we have an abundance to share with them. We can give and give and give with glad generosity, loving others as God Our Father first loved us.

Living this way, with a vivid impression of the perishing and needy clearly before us, we will be blessed beyond measure. There will flow through us rivers of refreshment, strength and support to a host of materially and spiritually poverty-stricken people to the ends of the earth.

We can be a part of God's great relief plan for the world. It will be a stirring experience to share in lifting the woes of the world. But to do it aright, we must truly care in God's generous way of love for them.

In speaking of giving our bodies to be burned, the Spirit of God is again dealing with the inner motivation for our actions. What prompts me to "burn out" for others? What underlying cause makes a man or woman willing to be made a martyr?

When I was a lad, a phrase often used by Christians but seldom heard today, was, "I would much rather burn out for God than merely rust out!" It sounded very heroic and noble, but I often wondered who the speaker was trying to impress.

In the days during which these profound principles stated in 1 Corinthians 13 were written, it was not uncommon for Christians to be burned at the stake. The formidable price many paid for their confidence in Christ was to be consumed in flames in order to satisfy the evil debauchery of the cruel Romans. Nor across the ensuing centuries has there been any diminution in the ranks of unknown followers of Christ who have been done to death for their faith.

The Spirit of Christ casts no reflection on the brave men and women willing to lay down their lives in martyrdom. Often it is intense persecution of God's people that produces an enormous impetus to the church. Again the issue is one of the purpose behind it all.

Sometimes pagan people and non-Christians deliberately burn themselves up to make a public statement of protest. What sort of statement is the Christian making by his or her "burn out"?

Is this a means of attracting attention to one's self, or is it a genuine willingness to be consumed for others without public recognition?

Are we trying to impress others or to please God?

Do we engage in self-sacrifice for subtle reasons of self-aggrandizement, or are we sincerely concerned for the welfare of our fellows? The line of demarcation between the two is often hazy and sometimes obscured by our own lack of objectivity.

To be honest before God Himself, to be honest with those we serve, and to be honest with ourselves, it is necessary to allow God's Spirit to search our hearts and make clear to us what our motives are.

The tragic truth is that often those we serve can detect more quickly than anyone else whether or not our actions are done in love or not. The unfortunate of the earth have an acute capacity to distinguish quickly between the person who offers them help in a patronizing way and those who come with compassionate love.

The genuine, selfless love of God, active in a person's life, speaks so clearly and with such concern that it is unmistakable. Its winsomeness is louder than any human language. Its warm, transparent integrity surpasses any eloquence. Its wholesome aura transcends any expertise or education.

This quality of love that is prepared to give and give and give to others without any thought of return is a gift from God Himself. It is part of His own life being expressed through the common clay of our humble humanity.

This humble aspect of love which will allow a man or woman to gladly burn out on behalf of others without grudging, in total obscurity if need be, is nothing less than the life of Christ. It comes into our daily conduct as we learn to love others as He first loved us. Such love comes by practice, not by whimsy.

It is an aspect of life which we actually learn from living with Christ. It is a way of life which finds ever increasing expression as He lives out His very life through us.

It is not a matter of theology or doctrine.

It is not a question of biblical knowledge.

It is not the exercise of a gift or gifts.

Rather it is cups of cold water given to the needy with compassion. It is setting the prisoners free with the chain-shattering power of the great Good News of God's love for them in Christ. It is offering comfort, encouragement and a listening ear to those with heavy, pain-filled hearts. It is the clothing of the naked both with apparel to keep out the cold as well as the new garments of the righteous goodness of Our God.

This loving self-giving comes through seven specific steps. Understanding them clearly can transform our lives. Our life with God will become one of enormous benefit to those in physical, material, emotional and spiritual need as well as a benediction to Christ Himself.

Here are the basic principles for learning to love:

1. *We can only learn to love those to whom we have been introduced.*

If we are to care for the poor, we must see them in their poverty. If we are to care for God, we must see and meet Him in Christ (John 14:9).

We do not love—we *cannot* love—the one we have never encountered. Sometimes it requires perseverance, time and effort to meet those whom we will love.

2. *There must be a positive response within the soul and spirit to the one met.*

It has been said that "Our friends were once all strangers." So it is likewise true both with God and man. We must be drawn to those afar off from us.

It is the specific work of God The Holy Spirit to elicit a personal response within our spirits to Christ, and out of that to the poor and needy around us. He it is who quickens our conscience, enlivens our faith and enables us to be drawn to them.

For the fact is, all of us have been strangers to Him. And for many in our affluent western society, the truly poor and bereft of the earth are still unknown strangers.

3. *Having seen and met the Saviour in His Word, through the revelation of the Holy Spirit, or in the poor, we must give them our attention.*

If one is to truly love God or man, neither can be held at arm's length. We must not have a mere nodding acquaintance. We cannot act as mere spectators.

Instead, we find our attention being focused on the newfound friends. We are drawn into the circle of their lives. We are no longer distant and detached.

4. *Our time, our thoughts begin to center on this person to the exclusion of others.*

By the choice of our own wills we begin to spend more and more time in communion with Christ. Out of that relationship we give increasing attention to the needs of others.

In a remarkable manner, other competing interests begin to fade away.

5. *Because of a growing affection and true concern for Christ and His suffering ones, we are prepared to suffer with them.*

It matters not what the price is we are asked to pay, be it in time, strength, labour, money, discomfort or even mortal danger, we gladly give and give and give. This is the laying down of one's life in love for another.

This is the beginning of a valid expression of God's love in our experience. It is the character of Christ in our conduct.

6. *The daily decisions we make to devote ourselves to Christ and to His interests in the earth are evidence of His love in us.*

John, the dearly beloved old Apostle, wrote with such impact, "My little children, let us not love in word, neither in tongue; but in deed [action] and in truth [integrity]" (1 John 3:18).

As we learn to love both Christ and His own children in the earth, that devotion will be much more than mere rhetoric. It will be shown in tears, in toil, in sharing, in giving, in earnest intercession—in a thousand little ways in which we do God's will in this weary world.

7. *As this love is learned in the crucible of life, it is demonstrated with joy and wholehearted delight.*

To love with the love of God is not martyrdom. It is not to feel put upon or exploited. It is not to be deprived of joy. Quite the opposite! For the person who has found that which is much greater than himself, in which to invest all of life, has found the secret to serenity.

The greatest good to which any individual can give his entire being is God Himself, in Christ. And God is love. So to give ourselves to Him is to give ourselves to loving Him, in person and in His people.

Where do we find God? We find Him in Christ. We find Him in the poor, the needy, the lost, the people whom He brings across our path. For by His own definite declaration He has said, "*Inasmuch as you have done it to one of the least of these my brethren, you have done it to me*" (Matt. 25:50).

# 5

***"Love suffers long and is kind; love does not envy. . . ."***

**(1 Cor. 13:4, NKJV)**

# THE QUALITIES OF CHRIST'S CHARACTER

The process of "learning to love" described in the preceding chapter is of long duration. It does not happen in a single day or overnight. It calls for fortitude, perseverance and endurance over long spans of time. It calls for fidelity in practice and faithful devotion to the object of love that lasts a lifetime.

This principle has been proven over and over again. Whether that which we learn to love is something as exciting as tennis, as stirring as music, as complex as chemistry, as romantic as a life mate, as needy as the poor, or as noble as Our King of Kings, Jesus Christ Himself.

The seven steps set out in the previous pages apply to all of life. A person becomes a fine tennis player, a remarkable musician, a superb scientist, a fine life partner, a wondrous benefactor to the poor, a devoted child of God by patient, and at times painful, perseverance. This is the meaning of long-suffering.

The remarkable point that escapes most people is this: no matter what area of life we are active in, loving demands that we learn to obey the rules and "go by the book." Again, this is as true for music as for God Himself. The path to success and perfection in learning love requires implicit obedience to the laws and principles that govern every sport, art or discipline in life.

Strange as it seems, we humans do not hesitate at all to invest our whole lives in learning to obey the laws of athletics, art or science. Yet we rebel against learning to obey the laws of God for loving Him and for loving others.

There is an amazing statement made by God's Spirit in Hebrews 5:8-9 regarding Jesus Christ: "Though He was a Son, yet He learned obedience by the things which He suffered. And having been perfected, He became the author of eternal salvation to all who obey Him" (NKJV).

Many modern Christians deeply resist the idea that love and obedience are intertwined in our relationship to both God and men. The assertion that these attitudes so inherent in Christ's character should also be a hallmark of a Christian raises inner resistance in the Western mind used to democratic ideas of "freedom" and "doing our own thing." They retort that to so live is to be "under the law," to be legalistic, to be bound.

Yet the answer to all of these charges is simply to read quietly Christ's last great discourse with His disciples in John, chapters 14, 15 and 16. He iterates and reiterates that "if you love me, you will keep my commandments—you will abide in my word—you will do what I direct you to do."

In layman's language, we will learn to love God and man, just as Christ learned it, by obedience and suffering and patient perseverance. We will begin to "go by the book," the Book of Life that contains all the rules necessary for successful loving.

It always astonishes me that men and women who will suffer anything for their love of sport, art, science or success in business refuse to suffer at all in succeeding at love. They flippantly brush off any suggestion that God Himself, who is love, has provided us with a rule Book for learning how to love Christ and man.

It is as if to say, "I will play and live by the rules in every other area of life. But when it comes to love, each of us can do as we wish."

What an absolute absurdity! Are we surprised at the chaos, the confusion in contemporary society? Are we startled by the corruption and degradation in our culture? Are we abashed by the immoral behaviour of some within the Christian community?

The love of God does not give us the freedom to behave as libertines. It calls us to commitment, to live in complete decency and integrity. The laws of God's design demand that we shall care for others and respect others and suffer for others as much as we do for ourselves. (Prayerfully read Gal. 5:13-14.)

This is not easy or comfortable or natural for us to do.

It entails some suffering—long-suffering.

It demands self-discipline under adversity.

Just as He puts up with our perverseness, often Christ calls us to put up with some unlovely characters. He puts us into situations where the only healing that can come to others is through our "putting up with" their wretchedness in long, strong, unshakable suffering.

It will cost something to be *a long-suffering soul.* It costs heartache, grief, inconvenience, disappointment, tears and loneliness to help bear the burdens of this woebegone, tired world.

But if the very life of Christ is at work in us, we will patiently comply with His wishes. We will be closely identified with His interests in society. We will share actively in His long-suffering on this earth. Only thus can the loads of others be lifted in love.

Yet it is essential to point out here that this long-suffering must be endured with kindness, not resentment. We *must* do it with compassion and mercy for lost men!

God's love to us is oh, so kind, so generous, so very merciful, so patient! Where would we be but for the lovingkindness of Christ! What hope would anyone have of Heaven, our Home with Him, were it not for His kind concern?

Without apology I here repeat my own testimony of God's enduring kindness in my own life as stated in my book *A Gardener Looks at the Fruits of the Spirit.*

"His merciful kindness is great toward us" (Ps. 117:2) is a refrain that never dies. It is repeated in the Psalms scores of times as a reminder that the mercy, compassion and kindness of God flow to us freely, abundantly every day in refreshing rivers.

The kindness of God has drawn me to Him with bonds of love stronger than steel. The mercy of my Lord has endeared me to Him with enormous gratitude and thanksgiving. The generous compassion and intimate care of His Gracious Spirit are an enriching refreshment, new every day!

It is extremely difficult to convey on paper in human language the incredible kindness of my Father, God. It seems to me that anyone who attempts to do this falls short. There is a dimension of divine generosity that transcends our human capabilities to clearly convey to one another. It can be experienced, but it cannot be explained.

It is the kindness of God expressed in Christ and revealed to us by His Spirit that supplies my salvation. His kindness makes provision for my pardon from sins and selfishness at the cost of His own laid-down life. It is His kindness that forgives my faults and accepts me into His family as His dearly beloved child. His kindness enables me to stand acquitted of my wrongdoing, justified freely in His presence. God's kindness removes my guilt, and I am at one with Him and others in peace. It is the kindness of God that enables Him to share Himself with me in the inner sanctuary of my spirit, soul, and body. His kindness enables me to be remade, refashioned, reformed gently into His likeness. His kindness gives enormous meaning and dignity to this life and endless delight in the life yet to come.

As this kindness flows into our lives from the life of Christ, it must in turn be passed on to others around us. It is an integral part of the rivers of refreshment that can spring up from within us to run out and refresh others.

Those whose lives it touches may not always return or reciprocate that love. Some may even spurn it or react in anger as they did with Christ. He warned us it might even mean being hated (John 15:17-19).

The divine principle of sowing and reaping still

applies. In due course we may be sure that others, from whom we never expected it, will show us great kindness. Our God is not only the God of all consolation but also all compensation.

Show kindness and in due time you will receive it back in abundance. Sow a crop of compassion and you will harvest a field of goodwill. He will surprise you with spontaneity and unexpected delight.

Some of the most memorable moments in life can be those flashing interludes when kindness stole softly into our daily round of duty. I call these times "My Master's bonuses." They come as a joyous surprise. They come unannounced. They come to cheer us along our way.

We are also told in our text for this chapter that the "love of God" is not envious. Some modern translations use the word "jealous" instead of envious. That is not quite accurate. There is a subtle but profound difference between envy and jealousy.

One envies that which another achieves or owns. We envy that which does not belong to us. Jealousy, on the other hand, is an inflamed sense of personal possession. It is self-centeredness and self-preoccupation with what I already own and am unwilling to share with others.

Next to the sin of self-pity, which is without doubt the most heinous of all human sins carried out against God by Christians, jealousy is perhaps the next most despicable. Self-pity implies God has failed me and cannot care for me. Jealousy implies that I am so self-centered I cannot share what is entrusted to me.

It is obvious neither attitude ever occurs in the impeccable character of Christ. The statements made in Scripture that God is jealous would be much better translated *zealous.* For example, He is zealous for His name, for His reputation, for His presence amongst His people. Being God very God, supreme and sovereign in the universe, there is no reason He should envy or be jealous of anyone, for He has no equals.

We humans with our limited comprehension of God's character tend to overindulge in anthropomorphism. We attribute qualities of human personality to Him which at times are very erroneous. These are a caricature of His true likeness. To say He is jealous or envious as we are is very misleading and wrong!

On the other hand, the love of God is exceedingly fair, generous and well-intentioned toward others. Christ is delighted when He sees others succeed. He is elated when His people triumph. He loves to know that because of His poured-out life to us we too can enjoy life abundantly.

We never ever see Christ caught up in the wretched, self-centered role of a rival. We do not see Him debasing Himself with envy, ill-will or any hint of personal jealousy. Even when abused and despised by His detractors, He remained silent and refused to respond with railing against railing. (Meditate on 1 Pet. 2:15-25.)

This is the greatness of Our God.

It is the surpassing generosity of His Spirit.

It is the character of Christ unclouded by discord.

Christ calls us, as His followers, to live our lives on this same lofty plane. He sheds His great love abroad in our characters to keep us from getting mired in the cruel criticism and mud-slinging that is all too common in some Christian circles. Too many are envious of the success or blessings or benefits bestowed on their brothers and sisters in God's family.

Instead we should be glad and cheer for those who are doing well. We should rejoice for any ground gained by those who love The Lord. We should thank Our Father for every inch of territory taken by any Christian in his contest with the enemy.

Our Master calls us to be large in spirit. He is delighted to see us become generous and greathearted toward others engaged in the same work we are doing. He is more impressed with our gracious goodwill, expressed in mercy and kindness, than any other impressive sacrifice we may make. "But go and learn what this means: 'I desire mercy and not sacrifice.' For I did not come to call the righteous, but sinners, to repentance" (Matt. 9:13, NKJV).

Why? Simply because the greatest personal sacrifice one can offer to Him or to one's fellowmen is selfless love—a love that smiles when others succeed; a love that cheers when others triumph; a generous love that does not envy or become jealous.

# 6

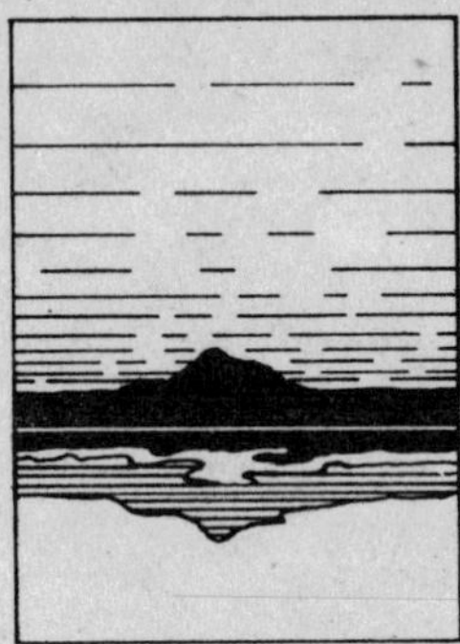

***"Love does not parade itself, is not puffed up; does not behave rudely. . . ."***

**(1 Cor. 13:4, 5 NKJV)**

# THE LOVE OF GOD IS NOT ARROGANT OR ABRASIVE

If anyone had a good reason to be proud, it was Christ!

Pausing but a few moments to consider His great and mighty achievements throughout the universe, we are struck with awe. He is the *Supreme Creator of all.* He is the sublime sustainer of the biota. He controls the cosmos.

Yet, wonder of wonders, He is also our *Suffering Saviour.* He, the *Everlasting God,* was willing to become a babe in Bethlehem, prepared to work as a carpenter in Nazareth, glad to live in poverty and minister to multitudes in humility. By a clear choice of His own will, He determined to go to His death at Calvary to bear the awful burden of sin for us perishing earth people.

This is He who rose in mighty power from the rock tomb, ascending in splendor to His previous position of power. In majesty and power, He has been crowned Monarch of the Eternal Realms—King of Kings—Lord of Lords—Maker of all!

He has no equal!

He has no peer!

He has utter supremacy!

But such majesty, such power and magnificence has never corrupted His character with arrogance. He has never been tarnished with conceit, pride or abrasive behaviour.

His great strength is shown in His incredible gentleness.

His gracious conduct displays His remarkable might.

He is *The Perfect Gentleman* in the truest sense.

It startles us proud, self-centered earthlings to be told by His Spirit that we, too, should have the same humility of heart, the same servant spirit, as our Master. "Let nothing be done through selfish ambition or conceit, but in lowliness of mind let each esteem others better than himself. Let each of you look out not only for his own interests, but also for the interests of others. Let this mind be in you which was also in Christ Jesus" (Phil. 2:3-5, NKJV).

The human mind has enormous problems with this. Our pride asserts itself with formidable energy in the form of self-esteem, self-assertion, self-interest, or self-aggrandizement. It pulses through our souls and surges through our personalities with ferocious power.

From childhood, human pride parades itself in a thousand subtle disguises. It "struts its stuff" with a subversive vanity that feeds on its own deplorable self-importance. It is pandered to in a hundred ways by the corruption of our sophisticated culture and the gross cynicism of our human society.

Beginning with the first syllables we learn to speak, "me"—"I"—"mine" become the center of our focus, the circumference of our self-centered interests. From our first faltering steps we are urged by parents, teachers, associates and now even preachers in our pulpits to "stand on our own feet"—"make your own way"—"fight for the top"—"assert yourself"—"become self-sufficient"—"discover your self-identity"—"fulfill yourself."

Modern false teaching by the "predators in our pulpits" asserts that we can demand whatever we wish from God. Though we are but dust and less than dust upon our puny pedestals of pride, we are taught to insist that *we* be served by *The Most High!* (Carefully read Isa. 40:12-26.)

What an affront! What brazenness! What audacity!

Little do most Christians realize that such proud people are actually an abhorrence to God. He resists them! (See James 4:1-10.)

Show me the person who is humble in heart (will), desiring only to do God's bidding, who is contrite in spirit and seeks to comply with Christ's Spirit, and I will show you the individual with whom God loves to reside. "The Lord is nigh unto them that are of a broken heart; and saveth such as be of a contrite spirit. Many are the afflictions of the righteous: but the Lord delivereth him out of them all" (Ps. 34:18-19).

We as His people are not in this world to extract all we can from it for our own ease and selfish ends. Life is not our oyster to pry open and plunder in pride and arrogance. That is the world's gross and deplorable philosophy. But it should not be a Christian's. The world's aim is self-aggrandizement. Christ's aim is service to others.

The two are set in diametrically opposite directions. The powerful stream of Our Father's will at work in the universe flows against the mindset of a society interested only in self-gratification—the so-called "me" syndrome.

Are we surprised that many moderns are so jaded? Are we taken aback by the cynicism of our age? Are we astonished by the weariness and boredom, the general discontent of our generation?

God made us for Himself, to learn to lose ourselves in the majestic grandeur of His incomprehensible greatness. He formed us to be conformed to His image in the pure joy of pouring ourselves out in the stream of His goodwill for the planet. He urges us by His Wondrous Spirit to find our total fulfillment in complete identity with Christ and His cause in the redemption of human society.

We are not here to play our little private games.

We are not here to pass our little lives in pleasure.

We are not here to lounge around in ease and luxury.

We are here to walk humbly with Our Master and, working with Him, see great and wondrous changes wrought in the world around us. Not because we are great Christians, but because He is Our Great God!

How then, one must ask, is a person to become humble in attitude, contrite in spirit, gracious in character? These are valid questions. Our confused world with its twisted emphasis on self-love demands clear, concise answers.

1. *Read the Word of God* intelligently, sincerely and with an open, receptive attitude. Ask Christ to speak truth, life and spirit to you from its statements.

Soon the clear revelation will come to you that, contrary to all you have been taught and told, you are not a "self-made" person. Every faculty you possess of body, person, mind or spirit is a gift from God Our Father. Every capacity you own for life, learning or earning is a direct bequest from above. They are His benefits entrusted to you for a brief sojourn here.

This will pulverize pride and bring a proper perspective into your outlook.

2. Spend days, weeks and months meditating quietly in the four Gospels. *Carefully consider the character and behaviour of Christ* revealed to us there in such clarity.

Think about the life and language of The Master. Make Him your model of behaviour. As you expose yourself to His presence in those pages, there will begin to be a metamorphosis in your own character. We become like those we emulate.

3. *Pray earnestly* that His Gracious Spirit will fill your mind, emotions and will to overflowing. Actually allow Him to have His way and wishes in your life and experience. Submit deliberately to His sovereignty. Comply with His commands. You will be changed into a humble and contrite soul.

The choice is ours whether we shall be haughty, arrogant people or those who walk humbly with The Master. If the former, then we shall have grief and difficulty in our relationship to Our Father. If the latter, we shall enjoy an intimate friendship with Him that far transcends any human companionship. His constant comradeship then becomes our most precious possession on earth.

The person who so lives with Christ does not behave in an abrasive or rude manner. He is courteous and considerate toward others. He does not treat his associates with contempt or disdain.

One aspect of the Christian community which has deeply grieved me is the harsh, tough, worldly way in which so-called Christian business people abuse others. It is as though in the church they are very proper, courteous people, but in their business transactions their behaviour is quite unseemly.

This duplicity of conduct has been a difficult burden to endure in dealing with all sorts of self-styled Christians in nearly half a century of business. The inclination to drive a hard bargain, to pull off a sharp, shady deal, to throw up a smoke screen of excuses to cover injustices has often dismayed me beyond my ability to explain.

So the declaration made here by God's Spirit is not just some super-spiritual hypothesis. It is the plain statement of practical truth applied to our very ordinary lives. We are to be polite people who deal with others in decency, integrity and courtesy.

Often the world puts Christians to shame in this regard. Some of them are far more considerate and courteous than their Christian counterparts.

Therefore the question has to be asked, "How does a Christian come to have the character of Christ in the rough and tumble of the business community?" We cannot claim to be God's people, yet live as speckled birds, spattered with the world's ways. The excuse will not do that it is a rough world and the only way to survive in the jungle of commercial competition is by being tough.

The basic truth is we must be transformed people (Rom. 12:1-2). We have to become those who allow Christ to control us. Not just in the area of our spirits, but also in the whole realm of our persons—our minds, our emotions and our wills. It is a case of actually being converted in *the way we think* so we come to have the mind of Christ. It means being transformed in our emotional responses so we react to others as Christ does. It involves a profound capitulation of our wills to the control of Christ so that our deepest decisions are in accord with His will and wishes.

All of these principles for proper living have been dealt with in detail in my book *Walking with God.*

Of course none of this will ever happen unless we see ourselves as we are and decide we need to change. So much of the preaching handed out in our pulpits today is like dishing up pablum to pacify irritable children. Most pastors and ministers are too intimidated by the seemingly successful, tough business people in their churches to ever warn them of their wrongdoing. They are too timid to call a spade a spade or bad behaviour what it is—a sin against both God and men.

If indeed the love of God indwells us, we will not exploit other people, even when there is a chance to do so. We will not take undue advantage of our business associates in our transactions. We will not be rude and demeaning to those we consider less privileged or less "sharp" than we are.

This is a difficult order to fill in the setting of a

society that pressures us to push for the top of the heap; that is drunk with the "success syndrome" measured only in dollars, sales and profit sheets; that shouts at us to be first and foremost, while all the time Christ insists it is best to be last.

Again, the choice is ours as to what our conduct will be. So many who appear so placid in the church, so affectionate to their families, are "tough tigers" in the concrete jungles of our business communities. This is no credit to them. Nor should pastors be afraid to tackle this dichotomy in their congregations.

As Christ's followers, our characters should be above reproach. We cannot claim to be Christians and behave like brutes. For the love of God does not behave unseemly. It behaves like a gentleman and a gentle lady—always!

# 7

***"[Love] seeketh not her own, is not easily provoked, thinketh no evil."***

**(1 Cor. 13:5)**

# CHRIST'S CHARACTER IS FREE OF GUILE, IRRITABILITY AND MALICE

*Love does not demand its own way!*

What an astounding statement! So simple to say. So difficult for us to do. So characteristic of Christ!

This concept diametrically cuts across all our self-centered concepts of what constitutes complete and full achievement. It smashes into atoms all our vaunted human vanity of total self-realization. It is the spear plunged into the heart of our egocentric preoccupation.

These words embody the true meaning of the cross in the life of the Christian.

Unless we clearly understand this idea, there will be a never-ending controversy in our relationship to God Our Father. We will have conflict with Christ Himself. There will be inner subversion against The Spirit of God who endeavours to guide us.

In our arrogance most of us are very sure we know what is best for us. We too often choose our own tangled way through life. We insist on achieving our own ends.

Then we wonder why our lives become snarls from

which only God Himself can extricate us. Oh, such awful agony we endure because of our own self-willed behaviour! What wasted years we forfeit chasing rainbows of our own devising, goals that have no end but an emptiness that mocks us!

The simple truth is we do not know what way is best for us. Only God does. The sooner we agree to follow in His footsteps, the sooner our grief ends. "There is a way which seemeth right unto a man, but the end thereof are the ways of death" (Prov. 16:25).

The "death" spoken of here is not only that of ultimate despair or defeat, but also ultimate alienation from Christ who all along has our best interests in mind. He constrains us to come to Him and live new lives, set free from the fretful pursuit of self-fulfillment. But we resist His overtures. We resist self-abasement. We repudiate the idea of giving up our own ideas.

It all goes against the grain of our contemporary lifestyle.

We insist we will be our own boss.

We demand our own desires.

And the startling, sobering, terrible truth is God will let you go on your own. He will grant you your own selfish wishes. He will never override your will or impose His lofty, noble life upon you. Ultimately, it is your choice at which level and in what way your few years on earth will be spent.

Israel insisted on her own decision not to enter Canaan, the Land of Promise. So for forty years this obstinate nation wandered in the wilderness and perished in the desert wastes.

Israel insisted on having her own king rather than

submit to the monarchy of Jehovah. So they were given Saul and all his terrible, tragic acts.

Yes, God will give you what you insist on. One reaps what is sown. It can be His good and gracious goodwill or it can be our own tragic way.

Christ chose always to do The Father's will. He chose always to do His work. He chose always to speak His words, no matter the cost. The end was total triumph.

The same opportunity is open to us.

*Love does not demand its own rights.*

We of the Western world with our powerful and often repeated emphasis on the democratic rights of our people have enormous problems here. We insist that as free citizens of the community we have, under our constitution, certain inalienable rights. We call these civil rights.

It is a very ancient tradition, well-nigh sacred to the British people and passed along to their American cousins, that a man's home is his castle. Within the sanctuary of his own domicile he enjoys enormous personal privileges which no one can invade or violate with impunity.

So it is natural for us to jealously guard our own rights. In fact most of us, either consciously or subconsciously, have acquired a fortresslike mentality about standing on our own authority. Like the tough Texas motto symbolized by a coiled rattlesnake ready to strike, we warn others *"Don't tread on me!"*

The net result is a people bent on striking out at any intruder. We are a nation quick on the trigger, fast on the draw. Only now in our more "civilized" era, it is done more often through endless lawsuits and formidable litigation.

So it comes as a shock to be told that Christ did not live that way. It is noteworthy that when He was taken prisoner by the mob on the Mount of Olives, then charged before a kangaroo court, He never once asked for the services of an attorney. He never resorted to revenge. (Read 1 Pet. 2:18-25.)

No, He did not insist on His own rights.

And if in truth His life is real in us, neither will we.

Rather we will believe implicitly that Our Father, in His own good way, will settle the scores of life with justice.

My personal testimony here is that He has proven Himself utterly reliable in this way all my life. Put in colloquial terms, "He laughs best who laughs last." Let God be your judge. Let Him settle the scores. Give Him your rights even in the small issues of life. This is the path of serenity of soul.

*Love does not insist on its own aims and aspirations.*

If we are going to have great ambitions in life, let them be of The Master's arrangement. God Our Father gives us great dreams. His Vital Spirit can impart to us stirring visions of what His best intentions are for us.

May they not be our own design.

The person caught up in the great, ongoing purposes of God for the planet knows and senses the thrill of living and moving in God's will. It is not a hardship to endure. It is a dynamic stimulation of spirit. Our motivation is not self-interest but enormous gratitude to God for sharing His wonderful generosity with us mere mortals.

We can love in His way and live in His way, only because He loved us this way first and now lives in us this way.

His aims become ours. His ambitions become ours. His name and reputation are at stake in us. His love is on the line. Let us live up to His noble standards, yet in lowliness of attitude.

*Love is not easily provoked.*

It is the haughty spirit, the arrogant soul obsessed with its own ways and wishes that is readily aroused. Anger flashes out at any adversary. Temper rises to react to any transgression against its owner. Belligerence breaks out in angry provocation against any opponent.

For lack of a better description, I have called such proud individuals, *porcupine people.* Every deadly quill is tense and ready to impale those who dare to endanger its self-interests.

Quick temper is an attitude passed over too often as being of no great consequence. Actually it is a most serious evil in the disposition. It not only blights the character of the one who is angry, but casts gloom and injury over those who feel its wrath.

There is a place, and there are appropriate times, when Christians should express rightful indignation over wrongs done to others. We are too often silent when we should stand and shout for justice to be done to others.

But angry outbursts of abuse against associates to express hurt over our own interests have no helpful role in our conduct. They shame us. They becloud cordial relationships. They tend to alienate even those who might excuse us.

As a young man I had a terrifying, hair-trigger temper. It would erupt in devastating violence like an unpredictable volcano blowing its top. At times even I was alarmed by the horrendous heat of my awful anger. It would convulse my whole person, body, mind and spirit in ferocious fury.

At the age of 27 I read Henry Drummond's classic essay, "Ill Temper." For the first time I saw what my anger really was. It drove me to my knees before Christ in contrition. In His gracious way His Spirit flooded into mine to flush out the filth and pollution of a soul stained with "self-righteous rottenness."

Here are excerpts from Professor Drummond's remarkable insights:

> "Jealousy, anger, pride, uncharity, cruelty, self-righteousness, sulkiness, touchiness, doggedness, all mixed up together into one—ill temper.
>
> "It is the intermittent fever which tells of unintermittent disease; the occasional bubble escaping to the surface, betraying the rottenness underneath.
>
> "One of the first things to startle us about sins of temper is their strange compatibility with high moral character."

If we are to be truly Christ's people, we cannot endure such contamination of our character. We must be put right within by His righteousness. We must be cleansed by His incoming. We must be purified by the presence and power of His Wholesome Spirit.

There is no other way.

It is the expulsive, explosive newfound power of His love flooding into our experience that can expel the debris of our own desires. And this Christ does for the one who wants it to happen.

*Love thinketh no evil.*

An entire chapter could be devoted to this one phrase.

Its standards are so high. Its values are so lofty. Its motives are so pure. This is the love of God, the attitude of Christ, the stance of His own sweet Spirit.

How completely opposite from our own perverse outlook on life! Too often we see only the mud, not the sunshine after the showers. We too frequently find fault instead of looking for the lovely. We too easily are suspicious and cynical instead of being bouyant with good cheer. Our minds are clouded with evil intentions when they could sing with innocence.

Oh, that our inner attitudes were as gracious as God's! "For I know the thoughts that I think toward you, saith the Lord, thoughts of peace, and not of evil, to give you an expected end" ( Jer. 29:11).

Being a very practical man, I have come to the conclusion that in large part a person's thoughts are the product of his intellectual diet. We simply reflect back that to which we expose our minds. If we feed on filth and falsehood that pours from the media and corrupt culture of our generation, we will think in evil terms.

If we choose corrupt companions, associate with perverted minds, absorb lustful lyrics, read passionate literature, watch suggestive television programs, accept deceptive human philosophy from our schools and universities, and allow materialism to mesmerize our minds, we will become persons with wicked intentions.

It is a simple, straightforward equation, "As he thinketh in his heart, so is he" (Prov. 23:7).

The alternative is a deliberate choice on the part

of the Christian to develop a pure and wholesome outlook on life. As we set our wills deliberately to do this, God's Spirit will honour our decision to devote ourselves to that which is noble and great. He will actually *work in us* to will and to do of His own good pleasure.

Spend time in the Scriptures. Get into good books. Learn to appreciate fine music. Relish great art and participate in it. Make friends with true Christians—noble, loyal people. Enjoy the beauty of trees, flowers, fields, sea and sky. Look for the strength and goodness in others. Give hearty thanks to God for all the joys of life. (Read Phil. 4:4-9.)

In His wondrous love Christ will change your character as you continually expose yourself to companionship with Him. You will begin to see the touch of His presence in all the world around you. You will become beautiful in your heart and mind.

Give generous gratitude for His grace and love that allow you to live and move and have your very being in Him.

# 8

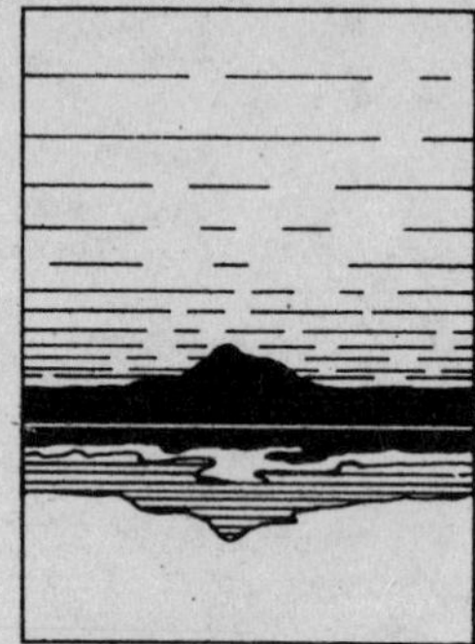

***"[Love] rejoiceth not in inquity, but rejoiceth in the truth."***

**(1 Cor. 13:6)**

# GOD'S LOVE FINDS JOY ONLY IN TRUTH

For the earnest Christian, the sixth verse of this "Love Chapter" of the New Testament is one of the most important in all of God's Word. It goes to the very heart of the issue, *Where lies joy?*

The Spirit of The Most High, speaking to men across the great spans of human history, speaking through the prophets and apostles of His own choice, speaking directly to us through the life and teaching of Our Lord Jesus Christ Himself, refers constantly to the "joy of the Lord."

The oft-reiterated theme of "rejoicing" is one of the great hallmarks of the life of God Himself. Our Father by special revelation shows us that His character is distinguished by joy. He assures us again and again in scores of scriptures that it is possible for God's dear people to be impelled and sustained by His unique joy. We are urged and encouraged always to find our joy in Him, who is love.

If we are to understand this joy of the Lord, the joy in the Holy Spirit, as it is sometimes called, we must first see how it relates to happiness.

The word "happy" as used in God's Word was originally an ancient Anglo-Saxon word which meant "fortunate" or "well-favored." For example, "Happy is that people, whose God is the Lord" (Ps. 144:15).

Unfortunately some modern translations of the Word of God have interchanged joy and happiness rather freely. This is a grievous error, for they are not the same.

In its modern understanding, happiness is very much a worldly word. It is a passing, transient sensation that depends upon what is "happening" around a person. It has to do with the people, events or circumstances that touch our lives from outside.

If my family is fond of me, if my friends are loyal, if my associates are faithful, I can be happy. If not, I may well be in deep distress.

If my health is flourishing, my career is prospering, and I am financially secure, I may be happy. But if the opposite happens I may be very unhappy.

If people or circumstances make possible the acquisition of special little gifts or delights which bring personal pleasure, I may be happy with them for a few hours. But if I am bereft of any or all, I may feel unhappy.

This simply is not the equivalent of joy.

Yet increasingly the modern-day church aims toward happiness; it has allowed the world's value system of happiness to become equated with God's unique attribute of joy. It promotes human happiness as an end in itself to be sought by souls really looking for fulfillment in joy.

The result has been chaos and confusion in the lives of many Christians. For, to be very blunt, to look only for happiness in life is to look for the same thing the world looks for so intently. And because happiness is based on transient things, it can never satisfy the eternal spirit of man.

The classic proof of this can be found in the gloomy disillusionment of millions of successful people who have attained every aim and ambition in life only to be mocked by all they attained. They dreamed they would find joy and satisfaction only to discover all their aspirations turned to dust and ashes. They had missed the mark in life!

This was true in my own career as a young man. By the time I was forty every goal I had ever set myself had been gained, every ambition had been attained, every dream had been fulfilled. Yet I was an empty shell of a man, knowing full well that the achievements of my own selfish aspirations had brought no lasting joy.

Why? Because, like uncounted millions of other human beings, I had been deluded to believe the dreadful, ultimate deception that joy could be found in loving the transient elements of earth's short sojourn. It cannot! It never will be! This is the great delusion under which men apart from God struggle and strive, all for naught. It is the terrible evil which our enemy, Satan, has perpetrated on the planet. It is the awful iniquity of the ages which has led billions of blinded, deceived souls to end up in utter despair.

This is the dilemma of the human race.

This is the paradox of life itself.

This is the mystery of iniquity.

What we thought could bring joy brought sorrow.

What we deemed to be success is but sadness.

What we supposed we owned had become our cruel master.

So men and women stand shattered, bewildered and lost.

In the midst of man's mayhem and confusion, Christ comes to us and declares boldly: "Your life does not consist in the abundance of things you possess" (Luke 12:15, author's paraphrase). (Read also Luke 12:13-21.)

The love of God as seen in the life of Christ makes no attempt whatever to find its fulfillment in loving the passing pleasures of the earth scene. It does not, *cannot*, rejoice in the iniquity of deception and disillusionment perpetrated on the planet by the "god of this world" and the gross folly of human philosophy.

The character of Christ is grounded in the unchangeable goodness of God. It is founded on the eternal faithfulness of Our Father. It is based on the enduring reliability of His mercy, love and justice.

These indestructible, unshakable qualities in the life of God Himself are the eternal ground of all joy. The tremendous truth which seems to escape most Christians completely is that this unique disclosure comes only from Christ. It simply cannot come from man, the world or any other spirit beings.

He and only He is truth. Without apology He stated emphatically, "I am the way, the truth, and the life. No man cometh unto the Father, but by me" (John 14:6).

And that quality of joy which transcends the turmoil of our times, which stands calm and sure when all else is shaken around us, which reposes in strength and surety amid the disasters of our days, is founded in Our Father's love. The eternal truth that He is ever with us, enfolding us in His wondrous care is the ground of our joy.

This is the stirring truth that makes our spirits sing in the darkest night. This love of God for us is the unshakable truth that enables us to face the greatest frustrations with firm courage. This love of Christ empowers us to carry on no matter what calamities cross our paths.

Oh, the unchanging, unshakable stream of God's love that without diminution flows to us from the unbounded fountain of His own wondrous person and life! It has its source in Him. It finds its true fulfillment not in the world nor in men's ways, nor in the transient scenes of time, but in the truth that He is with us, His people, calling out a chosen church, bringing sons and daughters to the full glory of His own character.

This is the great ongoing purpose of Our God.

This is the eternal project He has for the planet.

This is the supreme truth in which both He and we rejoice. (Read Eph. 1:3-10, Phillips.)

This is the love of God finding full expression in a joy that sees common men and women changed into the very likeness of Our Lord. This steady transformation becomes actual reality in the daily experiences of God's children.

This joy does not lie in possessions, achievements, accomplishments, fame, success, wealth or health. This joy resides in that wondrous, indescribable relationship of knowing God as Father, of knowing Christ as Friend, of knowing The Holy Spirit as Constant Companion through all of life. *Oh, what joy!*

Just as a giant gyroscope, whirling silently deep in the center of an ocean liner provides stability in stormy seas, so our joy in God's love for us gives us serenity in the stresses of our days. The profound inner assurance "I am His and He is mine" brings surety and repose in the storms of life.

Turning briefly now to the broader world view, it is important to see the distinction drawn here by The Spirit of God. He recognizes clearly that the vast majority of human society does delight in iniquity, does rejoice in evil. He faces the fact that we live on a planet where wrongdoing and selfish behaviour is the accepted way of life for multitudes. The "fun thing" is to taunt that which is righteous, to scorn that which is gracious and noble.

In a word, the world loves what is wrong.

It does not naturally rejoice in what is right.

It prefers deception to truth.

So the Christian is confronted with hard choices.

We simply cannot love the world and revel in its wicked ways and also claim to love Christ who embodies all truth.

John the beloved Apostle was very plain about this. "Love not the world, neither the things that are in the world. If any man love the world, the love of the Father is not in him" (1 John 2:15).

This does not imply that as God's people we are to be dour and dull, finding no delight in the experiences of life. Quite the opposite! As we view life through the perspective of Christ's life within us, we see living evidence of the truth that His wondrous love is everywhere at work in the world, not just in us.

We rejoice in the astounding beauty of mountains, oceans, forests, fields, birds on wing, flowers open to the sun and ten thousand other touches of His integrity and creativity in the earth. We rejoice in the grandeur of His grace and mercy and truth at work upon the spirits and souls of stubborn, wayward men. We rejoice in the strength of character and honesty of life displayed by His own followers determined to live for Him at any cost.

Yes, oh, yes indeed, the tremendous thrust of the truth as it is in Christ is very much at work in this sin-weary world. And we who claim His name, who are being conformed to His character, who are urged and motivated by His life and love find enormous joy in aligning ourselves with His way, His truth, His life.

The odds against us may be staggering.

To stand for truth may be to stand against the surging current of corruption that swirls around us.

To revel in what is right may be to invite the contempt and ridicule of the majority.

To be the purveyors of God's love and honesty may be to suffer loss and endure hardship in our society.

So what? Did not The Master carefully alert us to the cost of walking in His way? Did He not tell us only a few would choose this path through life?

We are not permanent residents of the planet. We are pilgrims passing through, headed for home. May our steps never become mired in the mud of the world's wretched paths. We *can* travel the high road of excellent, righteous conduct. Living in truth and integrity we can spend our few short years here in joy, love and laughter. Our pure delight is walking with Our Father's hand upon us all the way.

# 9

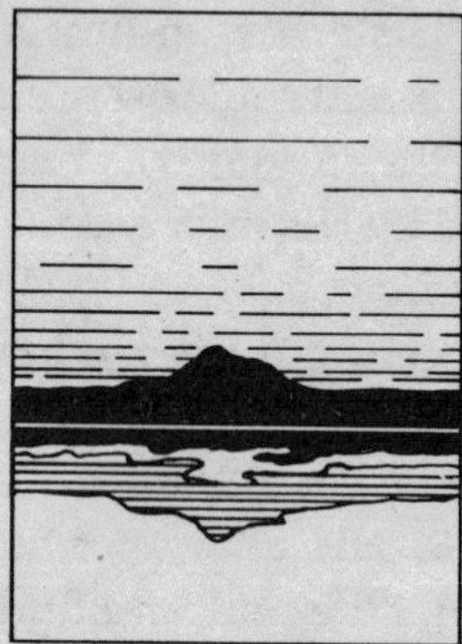

***"[Love] beareth all things, believeth all things, hopeth all things, endureth all things."***

**(1 Cor. 13:7)**

# THE LOVE OF GOD ENDURES ALL THINGS IN HOPE

We are startled by this categorical statement that God's love is so majestic it is unbreakable. The character of Christ is so strong it can withstand any shock. The life of God is so grounded in hope that it outlasts every situation in radiant optimism.

Placed at the very end of this remarkable chapter is a second supporting statement: "And now abide faith, hope, love, these three; but the greatest of these is love" (1 Cor. 13:13, NKJV).

In the church literally thousands of messages are given on the subject of God's love. Almost as many are delivered on faith in the life of the Christian. Yet, hope is scarcely ever mentioned, except maybe occasionally at funerals.

I recall, on several occasions, asking congregations if they had ever heard an entire message on "Hope." To my surprise only one or two people could ever recall such a sermon.

This is doubly surprising since God's Word makes clear to us that just as He is the God of all joy, so likewise He is the God of all hope. In fact, His forbearance with us fallen men, His patient endurance with our perverseness, His deep belief that we can become *the children of God*—all are grounded in this remarkable quality of *hope* which is uniquely His.

Unfortunately for all of us moderns the word hope, like the word love, has changed in its meaning across the centuries. It no longer has the same strong basis in reality as it did when first spoken to the church at Corinth under the unction of God's Spirit.

Today in the English language we flippantly and rather facetiously use the word in a casual form—*hopefully*. Hope in this sense merely implies wishful thinking. One supposes something might possibly happen. It carries the vague impression that one might assume something to be so without really being sure.

In this subtle and insidious way, the strength, power and might of this remarkable word *hope* has been eroded away. This is a tragic loss for Christians.

*Hope,* from God's perspective and in the clear context of Christ's character, is the exact opposite of the indecisiveness described above. *Hope in God is as unshakable as rock.*

It means absolute assurance.

It implies utter confidence in Christ's own impeccable character.

It denotes composed stability and strength in any situation no matter how drastic.

It is overwhelming optimism in the darkest hour.

All of this energy is grounded in the eternal goodness of God Himself. It flows to us from the impeccable character of Christ. It stands sure in the power and person of His Wholesome Spirit.

Hope is the antithesis of despair. It is that quality of God's life available to us which dispels the darkness of the world around us. It is that assurance which enables us to bear any difficulty, which empowers us to believe the best in any situation, which helps us to transcend the strain of our times no matter how difficult they are to endure.

Yet all of this is predicated upon us drawing upon the very life of God that flows to us in a constant stream from Christ. I sometimes refer to this as the Christian's "inner stream." It is that very outpouring of God's love to us by His own Spirit that makes real in us His own life.

The non-Christian knows nothing about this inner life of serene hope that is hidden from view in the character of Christ. He has never tasted the thrill or known the delicious delight of having quiet confidence in Christ. Even though the pennies in his pocket may bear the motto "IN GOD WE TRUST," it really means nothing of spiritual significance to him as a person.

Actually almost the same may be said for most people found in the pews of the church every Sunday morning. For the moment difficulties arise or disaster threatens, they do not hope in God. Rather they immediately seek help from their bankers, lawyers, doctors, business associates, or other professional people who can "hopefully" deliver them from their dilemma.

God calls us to live our lives in a different dimension from that of the world around us. He quietly invites us to find our hope in Him. He urges us to plunge into the inner stream of His life, there to find the help and wholeness we need amid our distress. Our hope should be in God, not in man.

To help us understand this, His Gracious Spirit has given us a vivid word picture in Psalm 42 which portrays a hunted deer in distress and how it finds hope.

Next to Psalm 23, Psalm 42 is, beyond doubt, my favourite. It opens with an arresting cameo of exquisite poetry: "As the hart panteth after the water brooks, so panteth my soul after thee, O God" (v. 1).

A magnificent stag, a buck deer, pursued in the hunt, flees for safety to the hidden mountain streams. Pressed for its very life, it plunges into the surging current of the stream to survive.

The poem concludes with the shout of assurance, the challenging cry of one who has overcome, "Why art thou cast down, O my soul? and why art thou disquieted within me? hope thou in God: for I shall yet praise him, who is the health of my countenance, and my God"! (v. 11).

In the days of David and Solomon, the countryside of Israel was very unlike what it is today. It was terrain covered with lush vegetation, flourishing forests on the hills, and singing streams that flowed from the high country.

There was a large wildlife population. Deer were abundant, both red deer (roe deer) and fallow deer. The latter are now virtually extinct. But at the period in history when the Psalms were composed, venison was a favourite dish. In fact, King Solomon insisted that it be served at his royal table every day (1 Kings 4:23).

So deer hunting was common. The quarry was

pursued by dogs, driven into nets, hunted with bows and arrows, or pursued on horseback to be killed with spears and swords. This Psalm portrays a hunted hart fleeing for its life, seeking safety in the swift-flowing coolness of a mountain stream. Deer—all deer, no matter what species—seek water to survive.

The reader may not realize the size and extent of the deer family worldwide. The largest are the moose, elk and caribou of North America. Then there are the various species of mule deer, black tail deer, white tail deer and others native to Europe and Asia. They all love water. They are all strong swimmers. They all frequent streams, rivers and lakes for safety.

I have watched moose plunge into roaring rivers in the northern Rockies to escape predators. I have seen elk and deer swim across lakes to evade wolves and coyotes. I have observed bucks wounded in hunting rush for the nearest stream.

Why? Why run to water? Why plunge into the flowing current? Why is this their hope of survival?

There are four reasons. Each of the four has an exact counterpart in our lives as God's people. These are precise parallels which can give us great hope in God.

1. *Plunging into the stream provides immediate safety from the pursuer.*

The deer is very familiar with every foot of its own home territory. This includes every water course. It knows every pool, every riffle, every expanse of water that provides protection.

The predator does not. The pursuer will pull up short at the water's edge. Here is a foreign element. Here are deep running currents and rushing waves that spell safety for the deer but imminent danger for the hunter (Ps. 42:7).

Likewise in the life of the Christian, there are times when we feel the very hounds of hell are upon our heels. We feel harried and driven by events over which we have no control. There seems, at times, no place to turn, no spot to escape the onrush of the enemy of our souls.

But there is! There is a place of safety! There is sure hope! That spot of quiet help is in the inner stream of Christ's life flowing to you, around you, over you.

Plunge into His very presence. Immerse yourself in Him. Surge buoyantly into the swift-flowing, deep, still waters of His love that flow to you so freely.

The sure, serene rest and repose that will come to you from Him is, *"All is well."*

2. *Plunging into the stream cools and calms the panting, heated deer.*

Because deer do not have sweat glands to cool the body as some animals do, they have to pant through their open mouths, the same as dogs. Consequently, deer when pursued, quickly become overheated and dehydrated.

The cooling effect of a stream or lake quickly restores the animal's composure and normal body temperature. Almost immediately it dispels its panic and dissipates its frantic fear.

The same is true for us when we come to Christ in our emergencies. Amidst the continuous pressures of our artificial "pressure-cooker" society, there is real repose in the constant love of Our Lord.

Speaking from firsthand experience, I am not

ashamed to say that again and again I come to Christ and literally fling my whole being into His embrace.

It is He who can cool the fever of our furious lives. He can restore serenity to our souls. He can give hope amid our hurried days.

3. *Plunging into the stream slakes the deer's thirst and refreshes its life.*

It is from the stream that the deer must drink. Here its thirst is quenched. Here the body fluids are restored. Here there is beautiful refreshment that brings repose.

Some of us know the fierce and burning thirst that has driven us to seek God. No other source of drink could satisfy the inner yearning that shriveled our spirits and scorched our souls. Empty, parched and dry, we wandered in a wasteland of despair until we came to the river of life that flows to us from Christ. Oh, the refreshment of His life! Oh, the delicious delight of His love streaming to us!

To whom else shall we go? *Thou hast the words of life!* And therein lies our satisfaction. We drink deeply from that inner spring and we live!

He is our hope, always!

4. *Plunging into the stream erases every scent, every spoor, every hint of the past.*

In this way the predator is thrown off the track. He gives up the hunt. His prey escapes in the swift-flowing current of the stream.

Likewise with us as God's children. We can plunge freely into the current of cleansing, forgiveness and full acceptance that flows to us from Christ. It is His deepest desire to wash away the spoor, the tangled tracks, the guilt of all that has gone before. He removes our sins from us, washing them away into the sea of His forgetfulness.

No longer can the enemy pursue us from the past. No longer can he harry us with his charges of wrongdoing.

We have found our hope in God. Our souls are at rest. Oh, the love of God!

In the midst of the stresses and strains of our earth days, there remains this inner stream of the life of God flowing to us in abundant hope. Come to Him often, come to Him daily, to endure and bear with all of life in buoyant optimism. Christ is here. All is well. I am made whole. He is the very health of my countenance amid life's hardships.

*Bless His name forever!*

# 10

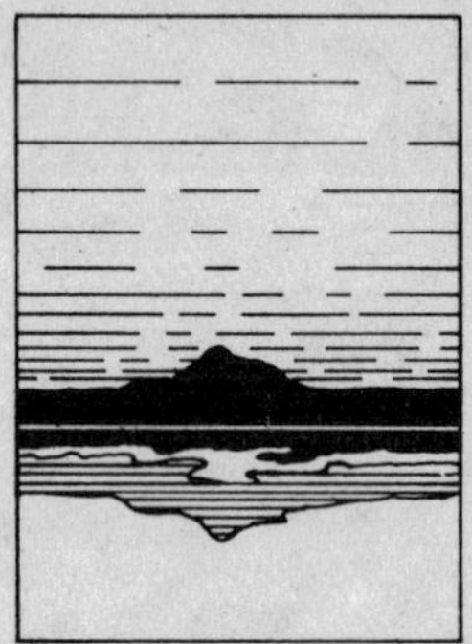

***"Love never fails. But whether there are prophecies, they will fail; whether there are tongues, they will cease; whether there is knowledge, it will vanish away."***

**(1 Cor. 13:8, NKJV)**

# THE CHARACTER OF CHRIST IS CONSTANT— HIS LOVE NEVER FAILS

No other quality in the character of Christ elicits our awe or stabilizes our souls in the same way as His constancy. It is the remarkable consistency of His conduct that makes Him stand out as a symbol of strength and integrity above the chaos of human history.

All around us the earth scene is one of never-ending confusion, change and calamity. Civilizations emerge, rise and then collapse. Human society stumbles along from failure to failure. The best-laid plans of governments fail. The sophisticated schemes of economic well-being fail. The hopes of nations and people fail. All is change, all is in flux, all is in transition and turmoil.

Amid the ruins, in great, unchanging consistency, Christ stands serene and sure and unfailing. Oh, the majesty of The Monarch of the Universe! Oh, the grandeur of Our Lord! Oh, the splendor of Heaven's Royal Sovereign!

What assurance He brings to our spirits. What

calm repose He bestows upon our souls. What sure strength He injects into our puny lives. He does not fail! He cannot fail! He *will not* fail His followers!

This basic truth should put steel in our spines. It should put fire in our faith. It should put peace in our hearts.

Even in the privacy of our personal lives we are, apart from Christ, confronted with never-ending change. Our physical well-being rises and wanes. Our families come, then pass on. Our financial affairs are ever in flux. Friends share our brief life sojourn, then fade away. Deterioration and depreciation erode and destroy our goods and possessions. We discover everything is subject to failure. Even churches rise, flourish and then fall.

So life is ever an increasing challenge to adapt to change. The tension of our times is one of adjusting to a world void of stability. As Our Lord put it, sufficient to each day is the trouble that comes with it (Matt. 6:34).

It has been said facetiously that the only two sure things in life are death and taxes. Actually this is not true. Both Enoch and Elijah bypassed death, and for those who remain at Christ's return, with hope in Him, there will be no death.

As for taxes, many primitive societies simply do not have them. Neither is this form of levy required from the poor even in our own country.

No. The only two sure things in the universe are "change," which happens again and again, and God Himself.

It is to these that man must make some sort of essential adjustment. The changes and fluctuations of the earth scene are at best temporary. The character of Christ never alters. The glory of God, which is of course the splendor of His person, never fluctuates. The inherent love of His Spirit of goodwill to us men never diminishes.

It is only as we open our own souls to Him and receive His as Heaven's Royalty can we ever hope to share that same enduring quality of His constant care.

The Word of God is very clear and specific about the constancy of Christ's character. If we read the Psalms in a modern translation, it is astonishing to discover how the consistency of God's conduct and love is their main theme throughout.

Here are several categorical statements from other portions of Scripture:

> "I am the Lord, I change not" (Mal. 3:6).

> "And, thou, Lord, in the beginning hast laid the foundation of the earth; and the heavens are the works of thine hands: they shall perish; but thou remainest; and they all shall wax old as doth a garment; and as a vesture shalt thou fold them up, and they shall be changed: but thou art the same, and thy years shall not fail" (Heb. 1:10-12).

> "Jesus Christ the same yesterday, and today, and for ever" (Heb. 13:8).

Thus it comes home to us amid the changing scenes of our days that here is One who endures, One who can be counted on always, One who ever remains truly steadfast.

Wonder of wonders, this applies not only to our

fleeting few years upon the planet but also beyond them into the long avenues of eternity that stretch out before us. This thought, this hope, stirs me to the depths. There is no other concept which gives such dignity to me as an individual. "I am His and He is mine forever." No other truth can so encourage a man or woman to face the unknown future as this: *Christ is here. He never changes. He never fails.*

Oh, what a consolation to His children!

Oh, what an encouragement to His people!

Oh, what a stronghold for our faith, feeble as it may be, for it is grounded in His total integrity!

For in essence, when a man truly has God in all His goodness, it matters not what fails around him.

As Paul put it, "I count all things but loss for the excellency of the knowledge of Christ Jesus my Lord" (Phil. 3:8).

It is this awareness of Christ, His very presence pressing in upon us, His love being disbursed to us as a divine dynamic, His character impinging upon our characters, which changes us.

We are, in our humanity, actually changed and remade from our character to His character, from glory to glory, by the influence of The Spirit of God (see 2 Cor. 3:17-18).

So it is that we in some small, feeble, yet shining way become reflectors of His life. We in turn show something of the constancy of God's love to a sickly world. We become in effect candles of hope and light and good cheer in the darkness all around us.

There will be about us a quality of credibility that does not fail. We will be people who are truly consistent in our conduct. We will carry out our commitments to others and to God. We will refuse to fail those who trust us. We will become disciplined individuals of bold courage on whom others can rely. We will be strong enough in Christ to carry on even when *we* don't feel like it. We will not fail to live in dignity and decency. We will be people of our word who bear the name of Christ without fanfare, but in great honour.

Those within the church who claim to be born again and filled with God's Spirit should be totally different from their worldly counterparts. In their conduct and conversations there should be an element of decency, integrity and reliability not found in a society that fails to exhibit these qualities.

God is not impressed by people who pompously boast of being spiritual while behaving like the world. He is calling out of human society, with all of its gross corruption and fallibility, an unusual, special people to be known for their incorruptibility. He is looking for Christians who have the very character of Christ displayed in their deportment.

It is a high calling.

It is a noble life He sets before us.

It is an enormous honour to walk worthy of Him.

Unless a man or woman comes to feel comfortable in the select company of Christ here on this earth, it is not the least likely that they would ever be at ease with Him in the expanses of eternity.

It is sheer humbug to hope that one will be contented with conditions in Heaven if one has never been accustomed to keeping company with Christ here. And a large part of this preparation is learning the utter integrity of the love of God.

We cannot manipulate Him the way we do other

human beings. We cannot deceive or delude Him. We cannot put pressure on Him to bow to our preferences. We cannot play our little games with One who does not change, who is so consistent He never fails to come through.

Some Twentieth-Century Christians are too flippant with Christ. The modern church and its soulish leaders treat Him as though He were just another human being. Even the music they play and almost meaningless lyrics they sing about Him reflect a lack of proper respect for Heaven's Royalty. Too often He is merely regarded with the same low, crude esteem given to a rock star or Hollywood celebrity.

Whereas the latter all fade away into oblivion, He endures forever. Yet, He is not given the great honour and respect His character deserves, His glory demands.

We deceive ourselves if we believe that somehow our spectacular displays of prophecy, tongues or knowledge can compensate for our lack of credibility. We are totally deluded if we think that special miracles, great gifts or enormous understanding of the Bible can be offered as a substitute to Christ for conduct which is contemptible in failing to honour Him.

Hyperactivity is no substitute for the quiet, strong love of God evident in a life that knows Christ and loves the company of His Spirit.

In fact, in this verse under consideration, God's Spirit makes clear to us that all the prominence of prophecy will one day come to an end. All the spectacular means of communication, language, tongues and their interpretation, will cease. The emphasis and importance we attach to knowledge, understanding and information will simply vanish into oblivion.

Yet, is it not strange that we are constantly being deluded to believe that these are the things to which we should devote our time? We are told by preachers and teachers that these are the supreme attainments of life. We are urged by our religious leaders to believe that the greatest thing in all the world is to be totally immersed in the gripping activities of prophecy, communication or acquisition of knowledge.

Not that these are not good and desirable. They are. The trouble is, they simply do not last. Nor are they the loftiest purposes to which we can give ourselves.

Perhaps the most important single sentence written in this whole book is contained in the next few lines. *A person can give his life to no greater good than Christ Himself. God formed us for Himself. We only find our fulfillment in Him.*

To devote ourselves to anything less or anyone else is to actually deprive both ourselves and Him of His highest purposes for us. It is to settle for less than His grandest aspirations for us. It is to come down to the end of our brief lives, only to discover in dismay that in failing to truly love Him, we have failed altogether.

At the risk of annoying the reader, I simply must repeat here that this is precisely why Our Lord Jesus Christ was so very shattering in His earnest statement made in Matthew 7:21-23. I urge you to read this passage quietly and sincerely, in private, allowing Christ's Spirit to speak to you from it.

No matter how highly we may esteem prophecy and all that it means, including the proclamation of the Gospel, no matter how skilled we may become in mass communication or personal persuasiveness, no matter how remarkable and extensive our accumulated knowledge, either secular or biblical—none of them will last throughout eternity.

All are passing—all are transient—all fade away.

Yet God Our Father goes on in glory.

Christ continues in His magnificent constancy.

His Holy Spirit remains ever the same.

This is the durable, eternal, never-failing life of the everlasting One. It is the love of God being continually imparted to those of us open to receive Him and know Him daily. And this in essence is life eternal—without end (see John 17:3).

## 11

*"For we know in part, and we prophesy in part. But when that which is perfect is come, then that which is in part shall be done away. When I was a child, I spake as a child, I understood as a child, I thought as a child: but when I became a man, I put away childish things."*

(1 Cor. 13:9–11)

# THE PERFECTION AND MATURITY OF GOD'S LOVE

These three verses disclose that man's knowledge at best is only partial. The most brilliant human intellect only dimly comprehends the complete scope of what can be known. The most esteemed scholar understands but a fraction of the full knowledge available to God.

Obviously this concept applies to both secular and spiritual verities. It is a universal principle that applies to all men of all time. There is never an end to the new discoveries which are to be made, either in the laws that govern the cosmos or the love of Christ that ultimately consummates God's plans for the created universe.

This remarkable revelation given to us by God's Gracious Spirit is valid not only for the great ongoing purposes of Our Father in the immensity of the universe but also in the intimacy of my own inner spirit as His child. The eventual completion and consummation of His good intentions for the entire cosmos, for both heaven and earth, are just as potent for my own personal perfection and maturity as His child.

In other words, God's great work that is underway, in the majesty of the whole universe, is likewise in progress within the soul of a single man. It is inevitable that this be the case. All is change. All is in transition. All is moving towards final perfection within the generous purposes of God's grace.

Often we look around us, both at the world scene and the private lives of God's people, and wonder if this can be so. We tend to doubt, sometimes, the sovereignty of Christ in the cosmos. There are occasions when our faith in the sure Word of God's Spirit falters at the sight of sin and sorrow so prevalent in the human experience.

Part of the reason for our dismay and our doubts is our incomplete knowledge of God's great and good intentions. We are ill-informed about His pure and majestic purposes both for the planet and His people upon it. Too often the pastors in our pulpits are not attuned to the stimulating intentions of Our Lord in the divine dimension. All they see is the sickness, the despair of a sin-cursed society.

Dismayed and almost hopeless, many Christians struggle with the sordidness that surrounds them. Grappling with the evil of their world, they are discouraged by the constant conflict with the enemy of their souls and the downward pull of sin.

Yet the great good cheer given to us here is that God's love changes all of that. The life of Christ at work within us is re-creating us into mature men and women of God. The relentless Spirit of the Most High is everywhere active in bringing history to its supreme conclusion—whether that history be for the entire cosmos or the story of a single soul saved by God's grace. "For God has allowed us to know the secret of his plan, and it is this: he purposes in his sovereign will that everything that exists in Heaven or earth shall find its perfection and fulfillment in him. And here is the staggering thing—that in all which will one day belong to him we have been promised a share (since we were long ago destined for this by the one who achieves his purposes by his sovereign will), so that we, as the first to put our confidence in Christ, may bring praise to his glory!" (Eph. 1:9-12, Phillips).

*This is all great good news. It is good cheer for Christians. It is Christ's view of coming perfection.*

God's great love for us, His children, for His own amazingly created universe, for all His unseen ministering spirits is such that it must find its ultimate fulfillment in perfection. He would not be God very God if it were less!

This should give us enormous encouragement. It is an assurance, a hope, an anticipation that stirs us to the depths. It quickens our confidence in Christ, stimulates our trust in Our Father's faithfulness, makes our spirits sing with joy as we "see" with spiritual vision what God's Spirit is achieving.

He is at work in us changing us from glory to glory. He is re-creating us to be conformed to the character of Christ. He is actively leading us to follow in His footsteps.

All of this is part of growing up into the maturity which He has purposed for us, a progressive process. It is a life of moving into the godliness of Our Father.

This is His best intention for us.

This is His great love for us.

This is His life in us.

Many Christians are alarmed and dismayed by the idea of perfection. They need not be. It is an inspiring and wondrous design intended by Our Loving Father for our completion as His people.

It was never His intention that we should remain as mere infants, tiny tots, our nourishment only in milk, barely able to crawl around in a cradle. His profound longing, as with a human parent, is that we should grow up in Him. We should become strong in His Spirit. We should mature into men and women who have His mind, His will, His life, delighting to walk with Him.

Each of us are at different stages of development in our life with Christ. We may be just a newborn babe, or a happy youngster, an adventuresome teenager, a young adult, or a sedate senior. Still each of us can be perfect—complete individuals at our stage in life.

A tiny child in the cradle is a perfect human being for his particular level of life at that point in time. Yet we would never claim he is a mature man. So, likewise, in the spiritual realm, it is essential for us to see that each of us can be "perfect" in Christ as God's child, even though less than mature in understanding and judgment.

But it is never God's will that we remain small, weak and helpless. His desire is always that we will put away childish things; be done with childish behaviour and mature into well-developed characters of strength and courage in Christ. All of this is an integral part of God's love for us and just as surely an essential action of Christ's life in us.

The previous paragraph should not be misunderstood here. It does not imply that we are to reject our childlike attitude of faith and love toward Our Father. It does not mean that we lose our childlike trust in Christ. It does not infer that we forget our childlike readiness to follow the gentle leading of God's Holy Spirit. No indeed!

What is intended for us is to know and understand clearly that Christ calls us to change, to growth, in our conduct, our conversation and in our character. He expects that we will achieve our goals with Him. He longs to see us become strong in the power of His might. He looks for the same signs of spiritual maturity in us as a human parent looks for in his offspring.

There are seven of these. And if in fact a person claims to be born again into the family of God, it is appropriate and proper for us to see these sure changes in his life and behaviour. If they are lacking, we have no option but to doubt the validity of a person's claim to be a child of God.

1. A newborn infant must immediately begin to inhale air from the new atmosphere around him. The doctor who delivers the child may even slap him to compel the newborn to draw in oxygen from the air in order for him to survive.

A born-again child of God immediately becomes aware that he is surrounded with a brand-new atmosphere of spiritual life. Through meditation and communion, the child must begin to draw new life from above, from the very wind of God's Spirit that enfolds it.

2. A healthy, sturdy newborn child soon learns to cry out lustily to his parents. He has strong lungs, not

only to inhale fresh air, but also to give loud voice to all his needs.

Likewise with the newborn child of God. The inner longings, yearnings and needs find prompt expression in prayer, in cries to Christ. There is an immediate communication established between the two. The person who finds it well-nigh impossible, or unnecessary, to pray and beseech God as Father has not been born into His family.

3. The normal, healthy human youngster develops a hearty appetite. Every few hours he must be fed. He seems to have an almost insatiable hunger and thirst for constant nourishment.

The result is he clamors for food. He puts on weight. He increases in height. He begins to grow.

A person born from above by the Spirit of God also has an enormous appetite for spiritual food. There is an insatiable thirst for the Scriptures. God's Word becomes meat and drink. Before long young Christians are not satisfied with just the "mere milk" of early infancy. They crave strong meat for maturity.

Again there is good cause to wonder about the man or woman who claims to be a child of God, yet never takes the time to read God's Word, to fill heart and mind with spiritual truth. The Bible remains a closed book to such a person.

4. As a normal human child matures, he very quickly comes to distinguish his parents from others around him. He senses in a very special way the loving bond of "belonging" to his mother and father.

He revels in the warmth and affection shown by the parents. He smiles and snuggles comfortably into the strong embrace of the arms that cradle and surround him with security and love.

So it should be with the child of God, the one who comes to know and love Him as Father. Here there is no fear, no apprehension, no hesitancy at His nearness.

Those of us who truly enjoy the love of Our Father revel in the closeness of our relationship to Him. All through our day we sense His strong arms around us. We relax in His warm embrace. We sense His smile upon us. We are reassured. We are content. We cherish His affection. We smile back.

All is well!

God is not some remote deity far off in space.

He is my Father! He is here! He is at hand! He is attentive to my every need! I am His! He is mine!

Oh, the wonder of His love!

5. The maturing human youngster soon identifies his siblings. He recognizes brothers or sisters. He learns that a special bond of common heritage binds them all together in a single family.

Likewise for the maturing Christian. We soon see that we are not the only child in the family of God. We have become part of a very large and privileged group. Not only is Christ our Saviour, Our Lord, Our Sovereign, He also deigns to call us His brothers and sisters. He is the eldest brother. We have a special affinity and respect for Him.

Beyond this we feel a special kinship and fellowship with other children of God whom we learn to love deeply.

6. The healthy, growing young person in a human family wishes to get past crawling on the floor. He wants to walk. He learns to run. He even becomes strong enough to leap, jump, climb mountains, and keep company with his strong father.

So for the growing child of God. It becomes a special joy to walk with God Our Father. There is enormous excitement in keeping company with Christ. There is a wondrous adventure in being led to new heights by the loving guidance of God's Gracious Spirit.

7. In this constant exposure to a human parent, the young person actually takes on the traits and characteristics of the parent. We become like those we live with.

It is precisely the same in our life with Christ! We actually *become like Him.* We take on His very character. We are matured by exposure to His company. We are conformed and perfected in His companionship. It is all a part of the perfect union of His life and love. What a wonder!

"('The Lord' means the Spirit, and wherever the Spirit of the Lord is, there is open freedom.) But we all mirror the glory of the Lord with face unveiled, and so we are being transformed into the same likeness as himself, passing from one glory to another—for this comes of the Lord the Spirit" (2 Cor. 3:17-18, Moffatt).

# 12

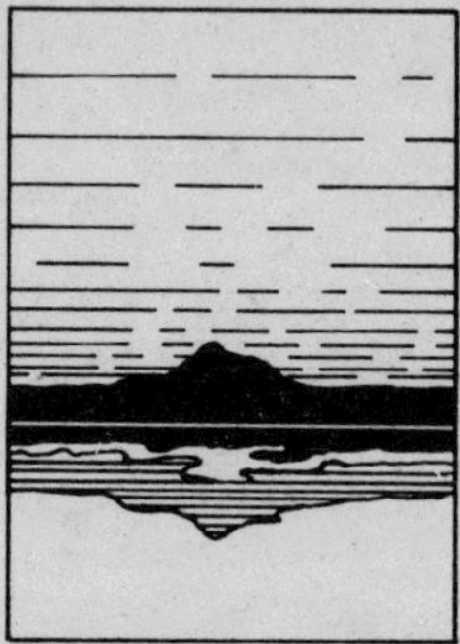

*"For now we see through a glass, darkly; but then face to face: now I know in part; but then shall I know even as also I am known."*

(1 Cor. 13:12)

# KNOWING AND UNDERSTANDING THE LOVE OF GOD

Again and again the point has been made in this book that our comprehension, either secular or spiritual, is at best limited. Most emphatically is that so when it comes to a clear understanding of the true character of Christ.

His life, His love, His awesome attributes of integrity, strength, compassion, mercy, justice and righteousness outshine our human condition like the midday sun excels the darkness of night. His glory and His grandeur are of such magnificence that we dare not gaze upon them in their full-orbed splendor without being blinded by their intensity.

Our human eyes, our human understanding, our human spiritual awareness is veiled by our hardness of heart, and dullness of spirit, our stained souls. And the nearer we draw to Him, the more acute becomes our awareness of our own undone condition.

The closer any child of God comes to Christ, the more he realizes how desperately he needs to be purified, cleansed and searched to stand before The

Most High. The utter intensity of His impeccable person bows our haughty hearts, crumbles our proud spirits, sending us to our knees in humility to cry out as Isaiah did, "Woe is me! for I am undone; because I am a man of unclean lips, and I dwell in the midst of a people of unclean lips; for mine eyes have seen the King, the Lord of hosts" (Isa. 6:5).

It is this acute awareness of the matchless purity of Christ's person which is a hallmark of the man or woman who walks in close communion with Him. There is an aura of awe, respect, reverence and great regard for God. He is spoken to with enormous deference. He is treated with the utmost honour. He is held in the highest esteem.

This does not preclude loving Him dearly. It does not mean His companionship cannot be cherished. But it does imply that He is supreme and I am at best a mere man upon whom His bountiful grace has been bestowed in making me His child.

Because of all this, it is only dimly that I can perceive the supreme perfection of Christ's character. At times I can catch fleeting glimpses of His true glory reflected as it were from the mirrored events of life that He has arranged around me.

Here and there startling shafts of light glance off the walls of my world to illuminate the darkness with His splendor. Yet, even then, the light is only dimly perceived because in the very nature of things whatever we see comes to us in reverse, left to right, and right to left, as in a mirror. Always, ever, our human limitations require that an adjustment be made and compensation allowed for our fallibility.

As long as our spirits are confined and restricted

by our human condition, our true comprehension of the greatness of God's love will be only a dim perception of Christ's perfection, blurred by our partial blindness, dulled by our doubting souls, distorted by our finite understanding and feeble faith.

Yet, in spite of all this inner struggle "to see Him" as He truly is, there burns bright the hope and assurance that one day we shall see Him face to face. It will be as if the opaque veil of our humanity is torn away. The encroaching cataracts of our spiritual blindness will be removed. Then we shall see Him without restriction in all His beauty.

Then, our spirits set free in wondrous adoration, we shall sense that incredible change that will conform us to His own character. Bless His name forever!

"As for me, I will behold thy face in righteousness: I shall be satisfied, when I awake, with thy likeness" (Ps. 17:15).

Then imperfection will have put on perfection. Oh, what glorious emancipation awaits the child of God! What stirring hope God gives His people! What a complete and sublime consummation for the Christian!

In the meantime, however, it is appropriate and proper that we should clearly understand the methods and means God uses to reveal Himself to us. While we are still here in the earth scene, it is essential for us to grasp precisely how we can "see God," even though it be dimly at best.

He has arranged four sets of mirrors around us from which there is reflected to us, like light from the walls, the very character of His own life and love.

On the one side there is the actual expression of

His person in the life of Christ, Jesus of Nazareth. "Christ is the visible expression of the invisible God" (Col. 1:15, Phillips).

In His conduct, His conversation and His character, we see without tarnish or inconsistency the love of God. From His life we get startling insights into the depths of divine nature.

As we meditate quietly over His short sojourn as a man amongst us, yet God very God, an enormous impact is made upon our spirits by His person.

Expose your poor soul to His life and He will change you so that you are never quite the same again.

The second great mirrored wall which God has put in place for us is His wondrous Word. It is the divine disclosure of His own self. It is a shining revealer of His true character.

As we look into it there glances from it bright beams of One who is totally trustworthy, utterly reliable, forever faithful. He is no mere man. We see instead, even if only feebly, the stirring grandeur of Our God, Our Father, Our Monarch arrayed in majesty, power and might.

Yet with all of that, we "see" Him who loves us with an unexplainable, unshakable, eternal love that draws us to Him.

The third wall of mirrors arranged around us to reveal something of the character of God is the natural universe. The beauty of trees, fields, streams, hills, forests and oceans reflect the pure loveliness of Our Lord.

In ten thousand life forms and uncounted myriads of spheres in space we "see" a dim reflection of the magnificent mind of Christ. In the expanses of ocean, the majesty of mountains and the exquisite artistry of flowers, we catch a hint of the beautiful heart of our caring Father. "For the invisible things of him from the creation of the world are clearly seen, being understood by the things that are made, even his eternal power and Godhead; so that they are without excuse" (Rom. 1:20).

If we are people contrite in spirit, humble in heart, free from human arrogance and its corruption of intellectual pride, we will pause before the wonders of nature and give hearty thanks for Christ's creative artistry.

The fourth wall of reflecting surfaces is made up of all those precious people in whom God resides by His Spirit. From their conduct and gracious words there flashes something of the very life of Christ who indwells them.

In a hundred kind deeds, in a score of selfless, generous gestures, in comforting actions, words of good cheer and hearty encouragement, we see something of the selfless character of Christ. Amid the selfishness and skepticism of human society there sparkles here and there a soul that shines to us a likeness of the love of God.

If men are to see God, even dimly, in this dark and dreary world, they can catch a fleeting glimpse from the wholesome lives of godly men and women in whom He is at work (see Phil. 2:13).

In all of this we can know, only in part, a small fraction of the full-orbed greatness of Our Lord. Yet it is enough to strengthen our spirits and set our souls to singing. We are assured on every side that Christ has come to us. He is here with us. He will not forsake us. All is well!

With this awareness there grows upon us a new dimension of confidence in Christ. It is the intense realization that not only is He here, but also that He fully *knows me.* Or, put in the plainest possible terms, *He completely understands me.*

It may well be that I shall never, ever, fully know or understand all of God's love and concern for me. I may never comprehend all the impeccable qualities of His character. But praise to Him for His great generosity, He fully knows me in every detail and deals with me in utter integrity.

For the child of God, *to be known by Him* should be the greatest encouragement in all the world. All of our lives we are interacting with people who do not really know us, much less understand us. Many of our problems in life arise from lack of knowledge and adequate understanding of one another.

People wear masks to conceal their true character. They live behind false fronts of propriety. They pretend to be one thing while living another. A veneer of culture covers crudeness, cruelty and deception.

It is frightening for most people to realize that *"God knows you through and through!"* They feel threatened by such knowledge.

But for the Christian this is great good news. And for these three special reasons:

1. God in Christ knows all the intricacies of my genetic makeup. He is fully aware of all the interrelated characteristics which were inherited from my parents, grandparents and former forebears. He knows precisely why I am the unique, special person I am.

No one else, not even my parents, knows this much.

In fact I am often an absolute enigma to them.

But God knows me in this intimacy. He understands exactly why my inherited features influence me to behave as I do. Consequently only He can treat me with utter integrity and complete understanding, tempered with compassion.

2. Only God in Christ, by His spirit, is fully aware of all the environmental influences which have been brought to bear upon my life since the day of conception.

No human being does, not even my own mother.

It is this infinite, incredible *knowing* that enables Christ to deal with me in dignity, forgiveness and love. He knows all the strains, stresses and pressures that shaped me.

He alone can properly appraise the impact made on me by my parents, my home, my siblings, my schools, my playmates, my teachers, my friends and all other human associates. He knows the experiences, the griefs, the triumphs, the adventures, the work, the impact of books and films and a thousand other influences that molded me as a man.

No one else does or can.

Not even I can fully know myself or understand my behaviour. Is it any wonder, then, He cried from the cross, *"Father, forgive them; for they know not what they do"?* (Luke 23:34).

3. Only God in Christ can clearly comprehend all my thoughts, all my hopes, all my fears, all my imaginations, all my emotions, all my deliberate choices, all my subconscious impulses.

And because He does, He deals with me in mercy, kindness, patience, long-suffering, justice and total integrity. Oh, the grandeur and graciousness of such a Saviour, such a Friend, such a *Father*!

It is this dimension of being known to the utmost depth of my being that has drawn me to Christ with unbreakable cords of love—*His love.*

For though He knows the best, He also knows the worst, knows the noble, knows the wrong, and He knows the deep yearnings of my spirit to be like Him. He treats me with utter truth and total understanding.

I dare not try to run a bluff on Him. Yet I can cast myself in fearless contrition upon His compassion. I dare not indulge in hypocritical duplicity. But I can come to Him, anytime, completely assured He fully understands me through and through.

Oh, the marvel of His love! Oh, the wonder of His care! Oh, the greatness of His grace! Hallelujah!

*He is mine and I am His forever!*

# 13

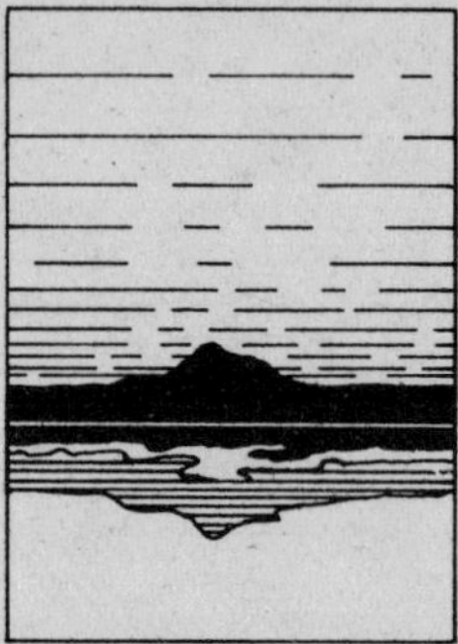

***"In this life we have three great lasting qualities—faith, hope and love."***

**(1 Cor. 13:13, Phillips)**

# THE ENDURING ASPECTS OF FAITH, HOPE AND LOVE

It has been emphasized repeatedly that everything in this life is transient—except God Himself. Only that which is grounded in God endures. All else is subject to change and disintegration.

For this reason, if for no other, man's life, unless founded upon the unchanging character of Christ, comes to nothing. It is a vain show. Like the morning mist, it vanishes into vapour. What remains is but an empty vacuum of no value.

Upon what, then, are we to build our eternal destiny? From what fabric will a man or a woman fashion his/her future? What qualities of life can one count on to outlast our little lives and see us safely into the eternal dimension?

Without hesitation, The Spirit of The Living God assures us that there are three beautiful building materials from which a Christian can construct an indestructible character. They are *faith, hope,* and *love.* All three have one common aspect to them—they last, endure, remain and abide until the dawn of eternity.

The reason they do so is simple to see.

They are essentially grounded in God.

They are basically centered in Christ.

They are ultimately established in His Spirit.

These are the eternal verities which endure.

If a man invests his short life in anything else, his days are spent for naught—wasted, gone with the wind.

Faith, hope and love are not competing qualities in life. They do not stand separately, detached and apart from one another. Quite the opposite! They are a tightly intertwined, three-strand cord, braided together to form the unbreakable line of Christ's character extended to us as our own lifeline of eternal duration.

Our faith in God, if it is to have any dynamic reality at all, is inextricably intertwined with the love of God. The basic reason is so obvious it scarcely needs mentioning here. But we can have confidence only in a totally trustworthy character. We can invest our reliance only in an utterly reliable person if we hope for lasting endurance. We can have quiet faith only in the love of The Eternal Christ if we expect to have it validated in an eternal dimension.

It is the character of Christ which validates our faith in Him. It is the essential integrity of His love which gives vitality to our trust. It is the sterling caliber of His commitments to us which assures us of His constant care.

Our Father's love, justice, truth and mercy are the basic bedrock upon which we build. All our hope, love and strong confidence as Christ's followers are fashioned from the unbreakable fabric of His own impeccable character. It is the raw material of the very life of Christ, the love of God Himself, which is dispensed to us by The Holy Spirit of The Most High in re-creating us.

In all of this, faith is a formidable force which He, The Gracious Spirit of God, imparts to us. It is a generous gift which bestows upon us the capacity to respond to the grace of God. It is, unfortunately, exercised by very few.

*Faith is my personal, private, positive response to the character of Christ and to the Word of God, to the extent I will act upon His wishes.*

This implies, of course, that I clearly comprehend the integrity of His character. This book has been an earnest endeavour to inform the reader of God's love and character as expressed in the very life of Christ.

It implies, too, that I clearly understand what My Father's will, His wishes, are for me as His child. Such information comes increasingly as one studies, examines and meditates over God's Word. Or to put it in the rather poetic language of the New Testament: *"Faith cometh by hearing, and hearing by the Word of God"* (Rom. 10:17).

The "hearing" spoken of here implies much more than merely receiving audio impulses upon the membranes of the ear. It means a powerful, positive response of my spirit to God's Spirit when He speaks to me.

There are three profound aspects to this process of "hearing" that lead to viable faith in any Christian's life.

1. *I recognize it is God speaking to me.*

The message communicated to me is not merely man's ideas. I am aware that Christ is communing with me. The words He speaks convey to me both *Spirit* and *Life* (see John 6:63).

2. *I respond to His disclosures in a positive action of my will.*

Keen attention is paid to what He says. A willingness to comply with His commands marks my behaviour. I set my will to do His will no matter the personal cost or inconvenience.

3. *I run instantly to do His bidding—always.*

"Hearing" in this way not only builds enormous faith in the daily life of the believer, but also, even more importantly, brings inexpressible pleasure to Christ. For without this faith of active obedience it is impossible to please God. And surely, surely, *surely* if we claim to love Him, the very least we can do to demonstrate our devotion to Him is comply with His wishes.

Our Lord made this entire concept clear to His disciples in His last great discourse with them just before His death. It is iterated and reiterated in John 14–17. This is a passage which every seeking soul who longs to understand the love of God should read and re-read.

There we discover something of the remarkable love of Christ which enables us to invest our faith in Him without fear or hesitation. Such faith, no matter how feeble, will never fail simply because it is grounded in the impeccable character of Christ. It will abide because He abides forever the same. It is constant because His love is constant. It is filled with hope because He is our hope.

It is not the caliber or quantity of our faith that matters. Rather, it is the content of His loving character that counts.

This is why Jesus said that even if we only had as

much faith as a grain of mustard seed, it would be possible to move mountains. Few can truly understand this kind of faith.

I sometimes use the illustration of a young lady falling in love with a handsome young man. She invests enormous faith in him. She builds her hopes of a happy marriage around him. She dreams her dreams of a fine family on the basis of his behaviour during their courtship. She is sure all will be bright and beautiful.

But after the wedding bells have rung and the honeymoon is over, she discovers that her handsome "Prince Charming" is really a rotten rogue. He is unfaithful to her. His character is corrupt. He is full of falsehood and duplicity.

All her dreams crash into rubble.

All her hopes are blown to the winds.

All her longings are swept into oblivion.

Her heart is broken! Her home is a shambles! Her happiness is gone!

Why?

Because she lacked faith in the fellow? No.

Because she was not sincere? No.

Because she did not love him enough? No.

*Simply because his character was no good, was false.*

She had invested all her confidence in the wrong person. She had put her trust in the wrong place. She had built her hope and love on the wrong kind of character.

Eventually her husband dies. The years go by. She is sure she can never have faith in men again. She is uneasy about them all.

One day a second stranger comes into her life. He seems a much more simple man. He is not pretentious, proud or vain. His sincerity and earnestness attract her.

A tiny spark of faith is ignited within her. Almost in fear and trepidation, she finally decides to try once more. She trusts this one. With no more faith than a grain of mustard seed, she agrees to share life with him.

It turns out he is a person of commendable character. He is honest. He is trustworthy. He is loving and kind.

Her heart is healed. Her home is a bit of heaven. Her fondest hopes come to life. Her happiness is complete.

What made the difference?

Was it the amount of faith she had? No!

Was it her sincerity? No.

It was the superb character of the second man that validated her tiny particle of faith in him. It was his character that guaranteed and totally insured her future contentment.

It is exactly the same with Christ!

He is our bridegroom. We are His people, His church, His followers, His Bride.

Our love, our hope and our faith are and should be grounded only in Him. It is His impeccable character, His perfect conduct, and His utterly trustworthy commitments to us in His Word which honour our hope, validate our faith and confirm our love for Him.

It is for this reason and only for this reason that our faith, hope, and love for Him endure. They abide because He abides faithful. They endure because He endures ever trustworthy. They remain ever sure only because He remains steadfast, the same forever.

Once we see this tremendous truth we will no longer fasten our attention on our own feeble faith. Instead we will lift our gaze upon the glory of Him who is totally trustworthy. Our hope instead of being set upon those things which can be seen will be centered in the consummate character of Christ who will never fail us. Our love, rather than being lavished upon the transient things of time, will be poured out in overflowing gratitude to Our Father who loves us with His everlasting love.

At last our lives will have found their sure, strong, peaceful resting place in the companionship of Christ.

As I have said before and must repeat here, *"The great glory of Our God is His character, and His character is His glory!"*

We simply *must* grasp this truth if we are ever to become the triumphant people of God who will make an indelible imprint on our generation. Our faith, our hope, our love—yes, indeed our very life—has force, power and impact in direct proportion to the extent we clearly comprehend the character of Christ.

He and He alone is the object of our faith. He is the bedrock of our hope. He is the epicenter of our own love. We are in Him. He is in us. Therein lies our endurance amid all the changing scenes and circumstances of this unpredictable life scene.

Down to the very last day that we tread the tangled trails of our earthly sojourn we will find that *"faithful is he that calleth you, who also will do it"* (1 Thess. 5:24).

Then when the call comes to us "to come home," even through the door of death and beyond the grave, our sure and serene confidence will be in Him. For then, and only then, will our faith be turned to spiritual sight, for we shall see Him face to face. And then our hope shall be turned to the living reality of heaven and home for we shall be in His visible presence forever and ever (see 1 Thess. 4).

Such stirring and thrilling expectations set before us as His people are but a part of His gracious, generous love for us. Not only for all of this life does He supply us with faith, hope and love, but also far beyond. Into the endless avenues of eternity His love never fails us.

*Praise His wonderful name!*

# 14

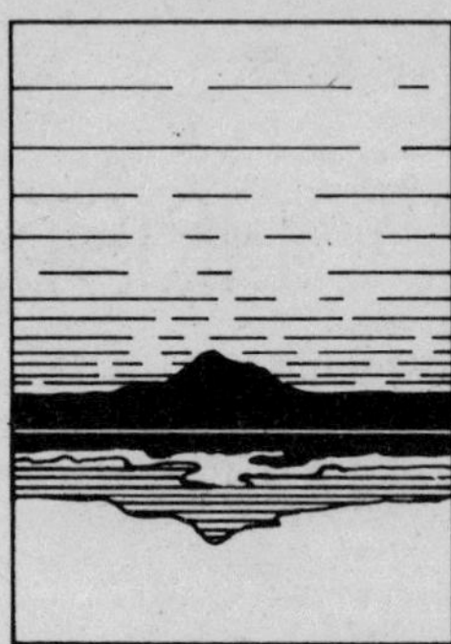

***"But the greatest of these is charity* [love]. *Follow after charity* [love]."**

**(1 Cor. 13:13–14:1)**

# FOLLOW CHRIST—
# HE IS LOVE
# HE IS GREATEST

The final, quiet conclusion to which God's Spirit leads us in this discussion on God's remarkable love is simply this: *love is the greatest of all.* There is no fanfare about it. There is no bugling of trumpets or blaring of brass.

It is one of those calm, categorical statements of truth that are so typical of Christ. Either we accept this as fact or we reject it as folly. Most people prefer to believe that money, wealth, success, pleasure, adventure or fame are the greatest.

Within the church itself, people may not be quite so crass. Still multitudes prefer to devote most of their time and attention to more spectacular and sensational activities than living quietly in sincere love.

It is fascinating to have huge building projects under way. It is exciting to hold large conventions with thousands in attendance. It is fantastic to have loud music with a powerful beat that attracts crowds of young people. It is great to see faith healers performing miracles. It is magnificent to watch gifted speakers storm up and down the platform shouting into microphones and television cameras. It is terrific to tell of the millions of miles traveled on tours to the most remote ends of the earth.

Amid all of this self-centered behaviour the still, small voice of God's Spirit reminds us—*love is the greatest.*

Why? Why is this so?

Simply because *God is love.*

We do not have His love unless we have Him.

It is a most grievous mistake, often perpetuated by preachers and teachers, to think God dispenses His love to His people apart from Himself. Many labour under the false delusion that Our Father sits aloof, far off in His Heaven, dropping down little gift-wrapped packages of love to those who request it.

Not so!

We only have the love of God in our lives to the extent we have God in our lives. We only have the character of Christ reflected in our conduct to the extent we have Christ resident within us. We only have the fruit of God's Gracious Spirit born within our attitudes and actions to the extent God's Spirit actually indwells our minds, emotions and wills.

This is the basic, inescapable concept that eludes so many Christians. Yet it is the secret to experiencing God's love.

*To know God in Christ is the greatest thing in all the universe.*

There is no greater good in all the world.

There is no greater end to which we can give ourselves than to abide in Christ and allow Him to abide in us.

There is no greater life than that of laying down ourselves in love and gratitude as He laid down His life for us.

"For God so loved the world, that he gave his only begotten Son, that whosoever believeth in him should not perish, but have everlasting life" (John 3:16).

"Hereby perceive we the love of God, because he laid down his life for us: and we ought to lay down our lives for the brethren" (1 John 3:16).

He made us for Himself in love. He chose us in love to be His children. He longs over us in love to be conformed to His character. He delights in us in love as His sons and daughters who walk with Him.

*From the world's viewpoint there is nothing remarkable or earth-shaking about this. It is to be despised.*

Nor is the world alone in its wrong evaluation of what is man's ultimate end and aim. Within the community of Christendom, there are many discordant voices and false teachers who would divert God's people to other purposes.

From their pulpits, their media broadcasts, their magazines, books and pamphlets, a host of leaders insist on other priorities. They scream loudly or suggest very subtly that the greatest issues in life are:

Peace! Peace! Peace! at any price.

Political reform.

Social concern.

The exercise of faith in many forms.

Mass evangelism.

Feeding of famine-ridden people.

Mighty miracles.

The gifts of the Spirit.

It was no different in A.D. 55-60.

The church at Corinth was totally absorbed in sensuality. It was a body of believers preoccupied with the sensational. It was caught up in following every new fad that was spawned by false teachers in the spiritual realm.

So, amid God's clear and explicit instructions as to the role of His gifts to the church, the startling and sobering command is given: *"Follow love! Follow me!"*

It is as if in the midst of all the flighty ecstasies of the moment, a direct appeal is made to all men to come back to the ultimate reality; to come back to the consummate concern of God Himself; to come back to love—to Christ, who gives Himself that we might live.

*"Follow Christ!"* is God's divine command.

This brings us up sharply. It slices cleanly through the melee of conflicting concerns within the church. It calls us back to the supreme good in life. We do not have to debate the issues any longer. We need not be in the dark about our highest aim or greatest good.

It is to follow Christ.

Because I have dealt with this subject in such depth in the book *A Shepherd Looks at Psalm 23* (pages 75–80), there is no need to go over that ground here again. In that volume the matter of "following Christ" is approached from the very practical aspect of our personal, daily life with Christ, what it means in actual cost to *follow love* in an unloving world.

Here at the conclusion of this study, my desire is to reveal to the reader a little of what it means *to follow love* from God's viewpoint.

First and foremost, let it be said emphatically that

*to follow Christ,* as He so often invited men to do when He was here amongst us, is not to be bound into following rigid rules and regulations. It is not to be inhibited and constricted by certain inexorable instructions that must be followed religiously.

No! Ten thousand times no!

To be called by Christ, to follow Him into His love, is to be invited to enter the freedom of marvelous sonship with God Our Father. It means coming to enjoy the remarkable friendship of Christ our dearest One. It leads us into the exciting liberty of enjoying the constant comradeship of His Holy Spirit, our counselor, who will lead us aright.

*This is what it is to follow Christ ... to love God.*

In all of this sublime interaction between God and me, the enfolding love of Christ that surrounds my life and pervades my spirit leads me to loyalty, unity of purpose and overwhelming gratitude. *I love because He first loved me.*

Christ's desires become my desires.

His standards become my standards.

His work becomes my work in the world.

His will becomes my will—always!

This is not to be bound into grudging servitude. Just the opposite! It is to be set free to follow The Most High as a comrade on the high road of a noble, splendid life.

The consequences of such intimate companionship with Christ are enormous. No longer am I a mere man drifting in despair through the uncharted depths of life's stormy experiences. No longer am I tossed to and fro like flotsam by the adverse waves of my years here. No longer am I dismayed by the powerful tides of time that seem to run deep against me.

Why? Because He who is in me and with me is greater, far greater, than any elemental force at work in the world. It is the powerful life of Christ within who counteracts the down-drag of sin. It is the expulsive energy and force of His presence that puts to rout the enemy of my soul. It is the purifying influence of His character that counteracts the corrosion of my old self nature.

His love, His life, His light dispel the darkness, flooding my life with goodwill, hope, faith and love.

So in His calm assurance I find repose—*all is well!*

Beyond all of this there comes the acute awareness that because of this relationship with God, all things do actually work out for my eventual benefit and well-being. It matters not how painful the paroxysms of life may be or how crushing its circumstances, Christ is arranging them for my ultimate good.

Such strength and such confidence can come only to the person who has responded decisively to The Master's call, who has chosen deliberately to follow Him no matter how acute the cost, who has come to love The Lord with intense loyalty.

The Spirit of God puts it this way, "We know that all things work together for good to them that love God, to them who are the called according to his purpose" (Rom. 8:28).

This is not a matter of mere wishful thinking. It is more than just hoping it might happen. It is the profoundly moving reality of a life bound up in the strong purposes of my Father for me as His child. At every turn in the long trail of my years I can look back to see that His hand has been upon me for good. His presence has gone with me to protect from harm and to preserve in patience. Everywhere I see living, irrefutable evidence of His love, care and compassion that surround my steps. My ways have been ordered and arranged by His Gracious Spirit in incredible love.

It is difficult to describe in language the inner serenity, the exquisite contentment from enjoying the companionship of Christ in this way. There is such a deep, satisfying dimension of delight to it that the most winsome attractions of the world pale beside it. They seem so fickle, so feeble, so fleeting. They fade to nothing.

He becomes the enduring, wondrous One.

Finally, it is appropriate to point out that the man or woman who earnestly "follows love" by keeping company with Christ is the one whose prayers will be answered. Not only will their own personal walk with God be the supreme pleasure of life, but also the impact of that love relationship will reach to the ends of the earth. Enormous blessing and benefit will emanate from their communion with Christ to touch uncounted multitudes. The Spirit of The Most High who resides in such a life will move in and through it to touch ten thousand other hearts.

The reason for this is not always understood. It is because the soul in harmony with Christ, in unity with His Spirit, sensitive to His Father's wishes, will pray in accordance with His will. Such petitions and intercessions are bound to be honoured simply because they originate and consummate with God!

Out of this harmonious and loving interaction

between God and man, more great things are achieved upon the planet than this weary world has ever dreamed of. For the Christian who daily delights in the love of God, who literally revels in the company of Christ, prayer and praise and upwelling gratitude come as naturally as breathing air, drinking water or eating fruit. For in actual fact the very love of God, the life of Christ, the presence of His Spirit become the ever-present environment that energizes his total being. It is "in Him we live, and move, and have our being" (Acts 17:28).

Nor is this some exclusive experience reserved only for an elite group. It can be the joyous, personal testimony and quiet strength of anyone called of Christ. The choice is ours how we shall respond to His gracious, generous overtures of love. For those who do decide irrevocably to share life with Him there comes the remarkable assurance: *"I have become absolutely convinced that neither death nor life, neither messenger of Heaven nor monarch of earth, neither what happens today nor what may happen tomorrow, neither a power from on high nor a power from below, nor anything else in God's whole world has any power to separate us from the love of God in Jesus Christ our Lord!"* (Rom. 8:38-39, Phillips).

Amen and Amen!